Nina Bell is gaining a reputation for compelling family dramas that touch the core of big emotional issues. ~~Her books include *The Inheritance*~~ ('You never really know your family ~~until something~~...') ~~over'~~) and *Sisters-in-Law*, which taps ~~...~~ relationships woven or destroyed by ~~...~~ written six radio plays for BBC Radio ~~...~~ newspapers and magazines. She live~~s~~ ~~...~~ teenage children.

Praise for *The Inheritance*

'This month we're loving . . . *The Inheritance*, Nina Bell's dramatic family saga starring the warring Beaumont sisters' *InStyle*

'Heart-warming, beautifully written and thoroughly enjoyable' *The Sun*

'A hugely enjoyable family tale which is just right for a winter's night in front of the fire' *Cambridge Style*

'An intriguing tale' *Hot Stars*

'. . . the characters are well-rounded, the pace is brisk and the storyline conceals plenty of surprises' *Irish Examiner*

'Nina Bell's dramatic family saga is interwoven with a lovely sense of place and time . . . this is a book for anyone who relishes a good, satisfying read with plenty of drama and intrigue' *Kent and Sussex Today*

Praise for *Sisters-in-Law*

'Completely compulsive reading – this-is-a-no-sleep-until-you're-done novel' *Heat*

'Be prepared to put your life on hold while you devour this story about the three Fox sisters-in-law and one vixen' *Heat*

'If you like family-relationship driven books with a twist, then *Sisters-in-Law* may well be the book for you! I loved Nina Bell's writing style which kept me hooked . . . I just couldn't put it down' *Chicklitreviews.com*

'You won't be able to put this book down. Nina Bell tells the story of the three Fox sisters-in-law and one predatory divorcee. Perfect for cuddling up on the couch on those wild autumn nights' *Daily Record*

'Crammed with incident and interest, this is a page-turning tale of family dynamics and the middle classes in crisis' *Daily Mail*

Also by Nina Bell

The Inheritance
Sisters-in-Law

Lovers and Liars

NINA BELL

SPHERE

First published in Great Britain as a paperback original in 2010 by Sphere

A CIP catalogue record for this book
is available from the British Library.

ISBN 978-0-7515-4367-4

Typeset in Bembo by M Rules
Printed and bound in Great Britain by
Clays Ltd, St Ives plc

Papers used by Sphere are natural, renewable and
recyclable products sourced from well-managed forests and certified
in accordance with the rules of the Forest Stewardship Council.

Mixed Sources
Product group from well-managed
forests and other controlled sources
www.fsc.org Cert no. SGS-COC-004081
© 1996 Forest Stewardship Council

FSC

Sphere
An imprint of
Little, Brown Book Group
100 Victoria Embankment
London EC4Y 0DY

An Hachette Livre UK Company
www.hachettelivre.co.uk

www.littlebrown.co.uk

To Rosie Iron, Lucy Iron, Alecka Micklewright,
Dido Chubb and Leonora Sefi

Chapter 1

'I'm sure I can help,' said Sophie. 'Just let me find a pen.' Intent on answering the request at the other end of the line she forgot the rule written in invisible ink above the door of her father's study. It was a no-go area. Forbidden. Knock first and enter at your peril. Sophie felt like an overawed child, instead of a mother of three on her thirtieth birthday.

She pushed the door open with her shoulder, hand outstretched for the pen she knew she'd find on her father's desk.

There was a flash of storm grey wool and cream silk as fabric moved quickly, and two heads turned to face her.

'Sophie, what are you doing here?' The familiar mottled red crept up Bill Raven's face. 'I've told you to knock, you idiot girl. Can't you get anything right?'

Sophie backed away, taking in his breathlessness, Anthea's sleek expression, and the possessive way in which she placed a hand on Bill Raven's sleeve.

'That's all right, Bill, isn't it? After all, we had finished the Orchard Park accounts, hadn't we?' She directed a steely smile at Sophie. 'Sophie, darling, that dress is divine. You always scrub up so well. Doesn't she, Bill? She's such a credit to you.'

And with that Anthea gathered up a pile of papers and walked out, sliding Sophie a mocking glance. The air was heavy as she passed, thick with some spicy, fruity perfume, with undercurrents of something chemical, almost like insecticide. Anthea left a trail of smoke in her wake.

She was Bill Raven's accountant, the miracle worker who made the figures stack up at the end of the year, and Bill declared that, without her, he'd be a much poorer man. Indeed, he liked to add with a meaningful glance round the dinner table as he refilled his glass, they'd all be much poorer.

'Well?' he demanded of Sophie. He was still breathing heavily, she noticed. 'What do you want?'

'I wanted a pen. But it doesn't matter.' She tensed, wondering whether a stream of invective was about to rain down on her head.

'Fine,' he said. 'Here's one. No need to give it back. Do you want some paper as well?'

Sophie edged towards him to take the pen. 'That would be good,' she said, keeping an eye out for any sudden change of mood. 'If that's OK.'

'Of course.' He reached towards her, suddenly full of bonhomie and she could smell red wine on his breath. 'Anything my little chicken wants on her birthday, she shall have.'

She sighed quietly with relief. He was in a good mood. He was the father she loved, the one whose arms she had run into every day as a small child, full of excitement about her day, and who had lifted her up into the air, listening to her gabbled accounts with a smile on his face. That father had loved her more than anything, and told her so often. But there was another father behind the mask, one whose anger she feared.

She took the paper and thanked him quietly, hoping to escape without any further exchange so she could process what she'd seen.

'Oh, and Sophie,' he said as she was almost out the door. 'Anthea. She's having a bit of a tricky time at the moment with some boyfriend. I'm a bit of a shoulder to cry on, know what I mean?'

Sophie, her stomach crawling at the thought, did know exactly what he meant. She nodded.

'But don't mention anything to your mother, eh? She . . . er . . . thinks I spend too much time thinking about work and not enough time relaxing, and she rather blames Anthea for it. Ha ha.'

Sophie shrugged. 'Fine. It's no big deal.'

'And Soph?'

'Yes?'

'Your mum's a bit low at the moment. We all need to look after her. Not worry her with anything.'

Sophie got out before Bill Raven could check his face in a mirror and see the smudge of coral lipstick beside his mouth. Closing the door behind her, she stood trembling, gathering herself to go back outside to the party, to safety, to where her mother had created the perfect birthday lunch for Sophie's friends and family. Sophie's husband and daughters were waiting for her to blow out the thirty candles on her cake.

'Hello? Are you still there?' she said to the mobile phone. 'I'll take that number and ring you back.'

Sophie liked to help. She was always the first person anyone rang when they wanted something done.

But how to help now? Should her mother hear about what Anthea and Bill were up to, or would it be better to protect her from being hurt?

Sophie believed that sometimes you had to tell little white lies, especially to her father. He was the most important person in the family. He worked so hard. He looked after them all. He was wiser and cleverer, more sensible and more practical than the rest of them. And often, of course, very tired. So you had to understand. Don't upset Daddy. He's had a hard day.

Sophie did understand. She was the only one in her family who did, because her younger sister Jess was so pointlessly rebellious and her mother – well, as Dad always said, she was just hopeless.

But the bedrock that had been her family had just developed a fault line, and Sophie wasn't sure if this was the beginning of an earthquake or just a tiny crack in the earth that would vanish with the next fall of rain. Tell the truth or keep quiet? Protect her mother or support her father? Tell the truth or keep quiet? The options ticked back and forth, like a pendulum on a clock.

Chapter 2

Anthea Jones straightened her skirt with satisfaction as she left Bill's study. There was no way that Sophie Raven – no, she'd taken the name of her wet rag of a husband, hadn't she, so she was Sophie Mason now – was going to keep what she'd seen a secret. Whether she let it out slowly, with whispers of confidentiality to carefully chosen people, creating a series of small bangs like the early part of a firework display, or whether she went for the big rocket straight off, there was no way that spoilt Sophie had the self-control to keep her father's infidelity to herself. Apart from anything else, she had 'principles', and believed in honesty and doing the right thing and all that stuff.

Anthea hated Sophie almost more than she hated Bill's wife Paige. Sophie had everything that Anthea had never had in life. She'd been born beautiful, for example. Anthea could never resist poring over the photos of Sophie that were pasted up on the fridge, framed along the mantelpiece and hung on the downstairs lavatory wall in a big collage. Over the years, even amid the blondness of privately educated prep-school children, Sophie was always the blondest, with the bluest eyes and the widest smile. As she morphed into a teenager she stayed slim and her long hair blew about her face with unconscious grace.

People like Sophie belonged in magazines, not in real life, twisting her father round her little finger. Bill often called her a daddy's girl when he grew mawkish. 'She takes after her old man, she does,' he'd say over a drink at Anthea's flat (all she could afford, while Paige queened it in a five-bedroom mansion with three acres of garden and a swimming pool, and Sophie Mason, *fourteen* years younger, lived in a four-bedroom house in London courtesy of her father's and husband's money). Then he'd check the label on the wine bottle. 'Where'd you get this? It's not bad.'

Anthea was a freelance accountant using her second bedroom as an office, although she usually visited her clients on site. Occasionally, very special clients were allowed to drop in to go over important things in private. The boundaries blurred in a very useful way.

Bill was a very special client indeed, and a good-looking man with the fine bone structure he'd passed on to Sophie. If he'd put on a bit of weight over the years it suited him. It made him appear more powerful and he could afford suits that were well cut enough to hide any suggestion of a paunch. Sophie had inherited his Nordic blond hair, too, and blue eyes (Bill's grandmother had been half-Finnish, apparently). They also shared a rather delicate pale skin. The only thing that Sophie Mason couldn't do easily and naturally was tan, mused Anthea, looking at her own nut-brown limbs with a sense of superiority. Although she hated the tissue-paper texture just beginning to appear on her hands, and the freckly patches of sun damage that denoted age. But that was just detail. Men liked tanned skin and strong limbs, and thrice weekly sessions at the gym and tanning salon ensured both. Like Sophie, Bill didn't tan either, and now had rather a high colour because of all those days spent on building sites supervising the men and the weekends on the golf course or negotiating the tides of the Thames Estuary on his yacht – called, of course, the *Sophia R.*

But otherwise, where Bill was shrewd – even tough – Sophie was soft and idealistic. Bill earned money by being a hard-nosed businessman. Sophie was a photographer, working five or six days a month 'being creative' and did fun runs to raise money for Cancer Research. Anthea knew exactly what Sophie earned – you got to find out a lot about people's families when you did their accounts. Bill sometimes gave his daughters – especially Sophie – lavish presents, but seemed to take pleasure in telling Anthea how little they earned, although Sophie, of course, was 'very talented'. Anthea couldn't imagine how Sophie thought that taking photographs of rusted chairs in front of a window could ever earn you a living, but then rich men's daughters were like that.

Anthea didn't mind Jess so much, because not only did Jess have the sullen face of a rebellious schoolboy, and mouse-brown hair cut in a pudding basin, but she also kicked against everything. She caused more trouble in that family than anything else, and Anthea sometimes wondered if that was the role, the niche, that Jess had carved out for herself. After all, if you're born second and are not as clever, not as good-looking, not as loved, you've got to make yourself special somehow, haven't you? Anthea thought that Jess had, since adolescence, been taking revenge on Bill and Paige for always paying more attention to their elder and brighter child. Or perhaps people with perfect lives had to have a problem to focus on or they'd die of boredom. But she didn't have that much sympathy for Jess – there was no reason why anyone born into that family should have to feel quite so sorry for herself. Welcome to the world, Jess, thought Anthea. That's what it's like. There's always someone out there who will take what is yours.

As for Paige, she was just a typical middle-aged married woman who'd never done a day's work in her life. Well, she might have worked until Jess and Sophie came along and 'needed' her more so she could enjoy a life of leisure on Bill's hard-earned money, but that had been twenty-two years ago. Since then it had been school runs and coffee mornings, Pony Club, aerobics and Brownies, then watching matches and competitions followed by opening the garden for charity and re-doing the house . . . and now grandchildren. Paige was always driving up to London to take care of everything while Sophie had another baby, or to look after Bella, Lottie and Summer when she had a shoot. 'Poor Sophie works so hard,' Paige always cried. 'I like to do what I can to help.'

Paige was considered 'delightful' locally, with such a lovely garden, and Sophie 'so nice'. Bill was everybody's best friend, while Jess was 'rather a handful'. It all made Anthea want to stick her fingers down her throat, but she just smiled and kept her counsel. She despised their smug, spoilt ways from the bottom of her heart. One day . . .

This was the first time she'd actually been invited to Bill's house socially, although, of course, they had both murmured something about 'accounts' to steal a secret kiss in Bill's study. Every detail was a precious insight into how his marriage really worked. So far it all tied in with what he'd told her. As she walked back into the party and saw the huge bunches of scented flowers – hyacinth and narcissi from the 'cutting patch' – the champagne, the soft bluey-green paint shades and well-chosen watercolours on the walls of the drawing room, and someone kissing Sophie as they pressed yet another beautifully wrapped present into her hand, Anthea smiled again.

A bomb has been planted under your lives, she thought. And I don't know how long it will be before it goes off, but when it does there'll be nothing but wreckage left.

After five years as Bill Raven's accountant, I'm in an excellent position to make sure of that. Particularly with the Orchard Park business coming to fruition. And as for the other business, the small matter of Bill Raven's heart, well, let's just say that all that is going very nicely too. Anthea contemplated her beautifully manicured nails. Everything is as it should be. Timing is all.

Oh yes, Sophie. Timing is all.

Chapter 3

Sophie was on autopilot as she walked through the party, being congratulated by two old friends from art school, both now married with their own children, a couple of single friends she'd kept up with (often introducing them to 'spare' men in the hope of matchmaking), three or four families whose mothers she'd met at ante-natal classes and with whom she now did childcare swaps or school runs, people she'd been at school with or worked with and several old friends of her parents she'd known almost all her life . . . she was so lucky that everybody had come to wish her a happy birthday. She was grateful for it every day, and especially for Harry, his big square face pockmarked by teenage acne. The scars made him look more rugged and less desk-bound than his colleagues in the insurance industry, and his solid shoulders made him look like a typical rugby player. He made her feel safe and loved.

After the cake had been brought in and everyone had sung 'Happy Birthday' and Sophie had blown the candles out, Bill made a speech about his lovely daughter and how family and friends were the most important thing in anyone's life. Harry put an arm round her. 'Are you OK, Soph?' he whispered.

She nodded, not quite ready to confide in him. She needed to talk to someone, but not someone who would judge so quickly. Harry often criticised Bill's outbursts of rage, while Bill had never quite come to terms with the fact that his little princess had grown up and got married. It took all Sophie's efforts to get Harry to placate Bill, and not to challenge him.

'He shouldn't talk to you all like that,' Harry would say after one of Bill's rants. 'And I'm going to tell him so one of these days.'

Sophie would tell him that she didn't mind, it was just her father's way of speaking, he didn't mean it, he loved them all and he worked so hard, he was just worried . . . and, in a way, it showed he cared (Harry always exploded with exasperation at that point) and most of the time he was fine, wasn't he? No one's perfect. Her persuasion always ended in a plea: 'Please Harry, for me, just be nice to him. If you challenge him, it's Mum who'll take the brunt. He'll be fuming about it for days and might even forbid her to see us and I don't think I could work without Mum's help and . . .' Harry always reluctantly agreed that just this once, 'just because I love you'.

Sophie privately agreed that Bill's behaviour was sometimes on the outer edge of what was acceptable, and one day she was going to tell her father so, but now he was too busy, too worried, they must just get through this crisis with . . .

'Are you all right, Sophie?' Harry repeated, and she realised that her face was probably blank and that everyone suddenly seemed very far away.

She put an arm round his waist and felt his arm tighten around her shoulders, propping her up and giving her the strength to look up at him and tell him that everything was absolutely fine. 'Just a dizzy spell. I've probably had a glass of champagne more than I should.' She tried to smile.

'You need something to eat.' He sounded worried, but at least it got rid of him. Harry set off to find some food for her, returning with a chicken salad. She managed to eat two mouthfuls before hiding the plate behind a huge bunch of flowers. One of her mother's friends came over to tell her how lovely her frock looked. 'Is it vintage? It reminds me of the forties, in that pretty velvet.'

Sophie thanked her and continued to scan the crowd for someone to confide in, who would genuinely keep what she had seen a secret. She didn't want to throw a stone into a pool of gossip and watch the ripples slowly spread out until they swamped her mother in a wave of innuendo and rumour. And she didn't want someone who would automatically insist that she told Paige, because she had to be protected. That's what Bill always said. 'Don't tell your mother, she'll only worry.' Or, 'We'd better keep an eye on your mother; she's not all that strong/bright/competent/knowledgeable.'

She knew it would go round Kent like wildfire. Everyone loved Bill. Everybody respected Paige as his wife. He was a Mason, a member of the Rotary Club and every local-business cabal going, and often in the local paper as he opened charity extensions and sponsored festivals with smiling bonhomie. Bill Raven had personally raised more for charity than anyone else in the village, and had helped save the local primary school from closure.

If he didn't push himself so hard, for his family, his company and even his village, he probably wouldn't have these outbursts. Sophie knew he was particularly worried about the largest deal he'd ever done, Orchard Park. He said that if it went wrong he and Paige could lose everything.

She saw Bill come in to the room and work it, putting his arm around the shoulders of an elderly lady as he bent down to listen to her, slapping a business contact on the back and then, as Lottie, Sophie's three-year-old daughter, began tugging at her grandfather's trousers, excusing himself to lift her up on to his shoulders so she could see the whole room. Sophie saw several people smile as Lottie waved her fat little arms. 'Mummy!' she shrieked. 'Mummy's birthday.'

As Bill lowered Lottie to the ground Sophie spotted her sister. Jess was standing by the open French windows, puffing a cigarette out in the direction of the garden as a nod to their father's no-smoking rule, while still filling the drawing room around her with a noxious cloud of roll-your-own tobacco smoke. Sophie wouldn't normally take a problem to Jess, because she was so hopelessly irresponsible and could barely look after herself, let alone anyone else, but she was the only one who could possibly understand the light and shadow of the situation. She wouldn't need to explain it all to Jess, or defend anyone.

It was also essential to get Jess out into the garden because, since he'd given up, Bill hated smoking and forbade it in the house, which of course meant that Jess deliberately lit up to provoke him. Sophie didn't want a scene on her birthday.

'Jess,' hissed Sophie. 'We need to talk.'

Jess glared at her. 'Really? Or are you just trying to get me to smoke outside?'

'Never mind that.' Sophie seized her arm. 'Come here.'

As soon as they got out in to the parterre – the square of geometric box topiary, now dotted with daffodils, that her mother had so lovingly created – someone else came up and complimented Sophie on how lovely she was looking. Jess's shoulders hunched even higher and she took sharp, angry puffs on the tiny brown roll-up.

'Where can we talk?' Sophie looked left and right. There were people everywhere.

'In my bedroom?' suggested Jess, surprise replacing anger in her face.

'No, that means going back past Dad. We can't do that.'

'What about Sparrow Palace?'

Sophie was about to object when she saw Bill's blond head towering over the tops of everyone else, clearly looking for her. She could hear his baritone voice, full of good humour. 'Where's the most beautiful girl in the world? Anyone seen our birthday girl?' People murmured in response, heads turning to look for Sophie.

'Yes, quick. Now. Before he sees us.'

Jess knew exactly what she meant. Without a word both

12

women shot off in different directions, circled the garden and went down to the edge of the far lawns, which abutted onto the fields, meeting up again beside two huge blue pines, whose spreading skirts almost concealed a small brick path.

Their mother had planted the pines when they were six and eight. These had grown to almost thirty feet tall, hiding Sparrow Palace, named because their father had built 'a palace for his little sparrows'. They had almost forgotten it was there. Sophie smiled as she pushed the door open, smelling only a faint touch of damp in the square brick room. Their old scrubbed pine table, picked out of a skip, was still there, and two chairs. 'Dad knew what he was doing when he built this, didn't he? He made it out of things he found or got from jobs, and we did it every weekend with him? Do you remember? You were very good at bricklaying.'

'Vaguely,' said Jess. 'Have you brought me here for a trip down memory lane?'

'No, not really.' Sophie tried to dust the seat of one of the chairs with her hands. 'It's just that he was happy once. We were all happy once, weren't we? Or am I imagining it?'

Jess rolled her eyes. 'Speak for yourself. I thought it was all shite. And now they live *this* life.' She waved in the direction of the party; a muted roar and the occasional high laugh indicated that everyone was still having a good time. 'I think it's Mum that drives it all, with all her building work and charity functions. She didn't need to convert the stables last year. That must have cost a couple of hundred grand. Come on now, spit it out. Whatever's worrying you.'

'I like your trousers.' Once Sophie told Jess that would be it. She wouldn't be able to take the words back.

'No you don't. You wouldn't be seen dead in combats. Dad said I looked like a navvy. Whatever that is. Probably nothing flattering anyway. He said that just because I wasn't naturally as pretty as my sister, it didn't mean I had to look like a navvy. That I could be quite attractive if I made a bit of an effort.' She sat down without dusting the chair down, lighting another cigarette. 'So what's all this about?'

'It's Dad.'

'Yeah, well, you didn't have to drag me down here to tell me that. The man's psychotic. Why Mum sticks it I can't imagine. Although I think she's done her fair share of making him go mad.'

'He's not psychotic. Just a bit stressed sometimes. But I think – just *think*, mind you – that he's having an affair with Anthea.' Sophie bit her nails, a habit she'd trained herself out of. 'But I might be wrong.'

Jess stared at her. After a minute's silence she burst into laughter. She went on laughing until Sophie thought Jess might have finally gone completely mad. Perhaps it was a mistake to have confided in her. Maybe this was more than Jess could take.

'Jess, are you OK?'

Jess wiped her eyes. 'Honestly, I'd forgotten how funny you are. Anthea's a desperate woman, you can tell that just by looking at her. A real bunny boiler. There's no way Dad would have an affair with her.'

'She's considered a very attractive woman. And a good bit younger than Mum, don't you think?'

'But Dad would never go for all that make-up and those teeny-tiny skirts and tarty tops that Anthea wears, and that crinkled cleavage . . . yeuch. You don't seriously think Dad would consider it? At least Mum hasn't baked her skin into something resembling a tortoise's armpit.'

'Dad and Anthea seemed to be in each other's arms when I went into the study. They sprang apart and he had lipstick on his face. And he shouted at me.'

'He always shouts at me. Welcome to the club. It doesn't mean anything. What did he say?'

'After Anthea left the room he said that she'd been having boyfriend trouble and that he'd been trying to cheer her up, but that I shouldn't mention it to Mum.'

14

Jess sniggered again. 'Well, I expect that's what happened. It might have been a bit of a drunken grapple and I totally agree with you that Anthea's got the hots for him, sad cow, so she probably lunged at him and he was just trying to disentangle himself nicely. But you can't construct an entire affair just from that. Sophie, you always had a terrific imagination, that's why it was such fun playing here . . .' She indicated the brick walls and little fireplace of Sparrow Palace '. . .but you can't go turning this into some great affair.'

Perhaps Jess was right. 'Well, I—'

'If you really think he's having an affair, tell Mum. She'll leave him, they can get divorced and they'll both be much happier. Job done.'

'I don't think it's quite that simple.' Sophie began to shiver. It was a sunny late-March day, but it was still too early to be outside without a coat for any length of time. 'They have a nice life together. And he's always saying how family is the most important thing in the world. Lots of men have a middle-aged fling.'

Jess shrugged. 'Still, Mum should stand up for herself more.'

'She does stand up for herself. When she needs to.' Sophie was determined to be fair. 'But she can be very irritating, you know, when she goes on and on about something, and I think he gets very frustrated and tells her she's stupid. And I think it sticks, destroys her confidence. Although she does do some daft things.'

'Do you want me to tell her?'

'No! Promise you won't. Not until we've found out some more.'

'And how are we going to do that? Hire a private detective to follow them?' Jess was smiling again now.

'That would cost a lot.' Sophie was worried about money: Harry thought he might be made redundant as his company was being taken over. 'Anyway, it would be ridiculous and I wouldn't feel comfortable doing it. But we could come down a bit more often and keep our eyes open.'

'I'm surprised you haven't opened up Sparrow Palace for your girls,' said Jess.

Sophie was jolted by the sudden change of subject. But perhaps Jess was more upset than she made out, and wanted to talk about something else.

'Would you mind?' It was a private part of their past, representing a golden age. It belonged to her and Jess together. 'It'll be full of pink Barbie-doll outfits. And soft toys.'

'I don't mind,' said Jess, looking round. 'Children ought to play here. It was fun, wasn't it? Until you discovered boys and decided it was childish. I used to come here on my own or with friends from school, but it wasn't as good.'

'Sorry,' said Sophie, flushing. She did feel awful about how she'd treated Jess when they were teenagers, but Jess had always been in the way, wanting to get involved, dragging her back to childhood. Sophie had been trying to grow up as quickly as she could so she could get out of the increasingly toxic atmosphere at home. 'Jess, I really am sorry,' she said to the floor.

'It's OK,' her sister replied. 'I found boys myself only a few years later.'

And partying. And alcohol. And drugs. And rebellion. Two abortions. A caution from the police over the possession of marijuana. Expelled from school in A-level year. Crashing the car and writing it off, injuring a pedestrian. Never keeping a job for more than six months. Yes, we know. Jess had been a one-woman whirlwind throughout her teens and twenties. She had eventually managed a degree from art school and worked as a graphic designer, but no one was sure how long that would last.

'I've got a new man.' Jess suddenly switched back to their earlier conversation. 'And I'm not exposing him to Dad. So if you want to be a detective, you're on your own.'

'Tell me about him.'

'You know those guys you meet who say they'll call, and then don't . . . well, perhaps you don't.'

16

'Jess, every woman has had to deal with those guys. Of course I've been out with people who promise to call and haven't.'

'Well, Jake is the exact opposite. He rings me every day, no matter where he is. We've been going out for ninety-three days and we have spoken on every single one of them. Sometimes twice. And a text last thing at night, if we're not together, to say goodnight. We had our three-month anniversary the other night. He took me to an amazing little place he knows and—'

'You should have brought him today.'

Jess shook her head. 'He's just come out of a shitty relationship with some selfish cow who's taken him to the cleaners, and he got hurt really badly so we've agreed to take it slowly, but . . . yeah . . .' She smiled. 'One day. Maybe soon.'

Sophie realised that, with Jess occupied, it would have to be her who sorted out this latest crisis in her parents' lives. 'Well, I'm going to try to come down a bit more often, to keep an eye on things, so bring him down when you feel ready. It would be great.'

Jess smiled, her whole face softening. Sophie wanted to tell her how much she'd missed the old Jess, who used to be her best friend. But looking at Jess's face as the smile died away, settling back into hard downward frown lines between her eyebrows, she didn't quite dare.

'Yes, you keep an eye on things,' echoed Jess. 'You're good at that. But just bear in mind you think you can control everything, Sophie, but you can't really.'

But as she had tried to say it nicely, Sophie decided it would be best to ignore Jess's remarks in case she lost her temper. The pain and rage barely concealed in Jess's voice made her feel even more guilty than ever. She had to make it up to her sister somehow.

Chapter 4

Paige and Bill stood at the head of the sweeping gravel drive and waved goodbye to the last remnants of the party.

First Anthea swished out in her sports car, tooting farewell. Then Jess kicked her motorbike into action and, assuring her mother that she hadn't been drinking, roared off into Anthea's exhaust fumes. Finally Harry and Sophie piled their estate car high with potties, carrier bags, baskets, bottles of juice, toys and brightly coloured plastic objects that broke into tinny tunes when they were squashed into the boot. Having buckled the girls into their car seats, Harry pumped Bill's hand and kissed Paige goodbye. Sophie hung on to her mother until Paige was forced to disentangle herself.

'Thank you so much for a lovely birthday,' Sophie whispered. 'I had such a good time.'

Paige wasn't sure. There was something haunted about Sophie's eyes, but it might just have been tiredness. Paige didn't think that Sophie had slept through the night since her first child was born.

Sophie pecked her father on the cheek. 'Thanks Dad, it was great.'

He held her tightly then drew back, looking into her eyes. 'Don't forget what I told you.'

'What did you tell her?' asked Paige when Sophie had wriggled free and Harry had driven them all off.

'Nothing,' he said, turning back into the house. 'Just that she should take it a bit easier.'

'I wish she would, but she won't. She's stubborn. Like you.' The words slipped out before she could stop them.

'What do you mean, like me?'

'I just meant that you both work so hard,' she said wearily, hoping to avert an argument.

But Bill wasn't listening. He drifted back into the garden, humming to himself over the soprano of 'Pie Jesu', which was creeping out over the gardens from the drawing room. It was a beautiful evening, nearly six o'clock. The sun was turning the sky an iridescent pink as it disappeared over the fields.

Paige began to clear up. She was tired herself. It was difficult living on the knife-edge of Bill's irritation. Although that wasn't entirely fair. He was just over-worked. Anyone would get irritable with the responsibilities he had. And there were good times. Lots of them. Today, for example.

She wished he wasn't so angry, though. Not just angry at her, but at life. The government and its total lack of support for small businesses. The roads, always full of mothers in huge gas-guzzling cars driving just one child around. Automated telephone systems. American foreign policy. So much. She couldn't remember when it had started because now it seemed always to have been there. She was sure he couldn't have been angry when they met, so perhaps it was her fault after all? That's what he said, over and over again. Her fault. She knew it often wasn't and sometimes said so. But it wore you down, over the years. She tried to think back, to remember how it all began.

In the seventies her brother Rob had been working on a building site during the university vacation and had introduced her to one of the brickies: tall, lanky Bill Raven, with his shock of blond hair and easy, open expression. Kids today didn't seem to work on building sites, did they? She wondered why not. Probably something to do with Elfin Safety, as Bill liked to call it, usually purple with rage at the very word 'safety'.

In those days Bill had had the likeable, energetic air of someone who intended to get somewhere in life. Despite his lack of formal education (he'd left a secondary modern school with five O levels), he'd gone down well with her family. They were relieved to see the back of her previous boyfriend, who'd had a moustache, long hair and an Afghan coat that smelt of dead sheep in the rain. Bill was very capable, able to fix taps and cut down trees in the garden. She'd been at university herself, reading history, but had dropped out when she'd got pregnant with Sophie. Bill insisted on their getting married.

He was determined to start his own building business. After a few years of him working double shifts and her working part-time as a doctor's receptionist, and them both doing up the houses they lived in and selling them on at a profit, plus some investment from her father and a bit more from a partner, Brian Harris, Raven Restore & Build Ltd was born. Building and renovating houses was profitable but precarious, and they nearly went bankrupt at the beginning of the eighties and again in the nineties.

Bill decided to diversify and started Raven Decorating, then Raven Tiles, which he said never made any money at all. Then there was Raven Investments, which was 'just a vehicle', whatever that meant. One or other of the four Raven companies was always on the verge of collapse, and he'd already put two companies – Raven & Harris Ltd and RH Decorating – into voluntary liquidation.

Running it all on his own was clearly a strain for Bill. Perhaps the anger had started when Brian Harris had retired. Bill often came home muttering that 'I don't know how long we can hang on to The Rowans'. Once or twice she asked him how bad the situation really was, and how much money they actually had.

He had snapped, 'Don't be such a fool, it's far, far too complicated to say "this is how much money we've got". You clearly don't understand the first thing about business or you would never ask such idiotic questions.'

When she replied that she only wanted to know so that she could budget better, he shouted that he didn't want her to 'budget better' – he waggled his fingers in the air to indicate quotation marks – he just wanted her to stop spending his money on fucking unnecessary things.

'What unnecessary things?' she had asked, determined not to let him walk over her.

He had stared at her as if she was quite mad. 'The fact that you have to ask says everything, doesn't it?' he snarled, seizing a bottle of wine out of the fridge and pouring himself a glass before storming off.

Paige did occasionally point out that wine cost money, and perhaps they could cut down. He replied, furiously, that he hoped she wasn't trying to take away the only pleasure he enjoyed after a hard day's work. 'Anyone as stressed as I am needs a drink.'

Or perhaps the anger had started after her father died.

Bill enjoyed the public show of his success – the gradual conversion of the sweet but small Rowan Cottage (an Edwardian gardener's cottage) into The Rowans, adding a kitchen, lavish master bedroom and guest suites, plus a study, and then buying a couple of adjacent fields, adding stables and a swimming pool, followed by a three-car garage with a studio flat above. Bill belonged to the Rotary Club, golf club and tennis club: he said it was important to keep up local contacts. He could do more business on the golf course than in the office. He accepted that having a well-dressed wife was part of being a successful man, but scrutinised what Paige spent on clothes. Entertaining was fine, provided it was with 'important' or 'useful' people. He was so bad-tempered about wasting money on food and drink for people who were 'just friends' that she had stopped trying to do it. And he had never once taken Paige out to dinner in a restaurant on their own. Even Sophie's party had been an opportunity for him to show off to business contacts.

Above all, Bill liked showing off to Paige's family. She now realised that he'd felt inferior when he'd first met them, because her father was solicitor and they lived in a leafy, middle-class suburb near Guildford. Or perhaps it was her parents' fault – maybe they'd *made* him feel inferior. Whatever it was, Bill stopped talking about being on the verge of bankruptcy when Rob and her parents were around. They were always asked over to admire the new extension or the new (second-hand but swanky) car he'd bought, or to listen to details of the new houses he was about to build.

So when her father died, eighteen months after her mother, he left all his money to Rob 'because he needed it more.' Paige thought Bill was going to have a heart attack.

'That fucking bastard, why should I subsidise your fucking failure of a fucking brother . . .'

'He felt you were such a success that I didn't need any money.'

Bill rounded on her. 'And why the fuck did you let him think that? You were boasting, weren't you? Making your fucking brother feel even more of a fucking failure.'

'I don't think it was just me, I think that because we have so much more than he does, we—'

'So it's all my fucking fault now, is it? You'd like to blame me for your father not loving you enough to leave you anything.'

'He's left me the contents of the house.' Paige did, deep down, wonder if her father hadn't loved her as much as her brother. She could see the logic in giving so much to Rob, because he was out of work, with a wife and two small children, but it still hurt.

'Great. And how much is that worth? We got the valuer from Bonhams in and what did he say? Tell me what he said. No, I'll tell you. One thousand eight hundred pounds for every fucking stick of worthless furniture and shoddy painting. Your parents behaved like Lord and Lady Muck, but they weren't so grand after all, were they? With crap like that in their home, there was no reason to look down on me—'

'They didn't,' interrupted Paige. 'They were very fond of you.'

'I don't think so. They cut us out of their will.'

'He left me the shares in Raven Restore & Build. From his original investment.'

'I don't care about the fucking shares. They're worthless. The company is about to go under, you fool, but you can't see it.'

Bill insisted that he didn't want second-rate furniture in his house, although there were several chairs that Paige loved, and two or three pictures. He also forbade her to give any of it to Rob – 'The bastard's taken enough from me' – but she managed to smuggle some things to her brother, and others she stored in the loft. She persuaded Bill to let her hang one picture over the fireplace in the new extension because they didn't have anything else they could put on that wall. The rest she sold for nine hundred pounds. The company was going through a particularly rocky time so she handed it over, wishing it had been more.

From then on, every time Bill had a bad debt or couldn't find financing for a project he blamed her father. 'If you'd had your rightful inheritance, we wouldn't be in this situation,' he said.

Paige occasionally retorted that they would have spent it twenty times over at that rate but was told, with a red-eyed glare and a sigh, that you had to speculate to accumulate. 'Sometimes you terrify me,' he said. 'You're so stupid. I hope that neither of the girls has inherited your lack of brains.'

It was exhausting having to defend herself so it was often easier to avoid confrontation. She looked out of the window during his tirades and concentrated on the swath of daffodils she'd planted under the trees, or the yew and box that she'd grown from tiny cuttings into a series of dark green balls that could have graced a stately home.

Everyone admired Paige's garden. It was where she could

shut out Bill's anger and know that there was something she'd achieved all by herself. Planning it lulled her to sleep at night and seeing each flower unfurl with the lengthening days gave her a sense of peace – and of achievement – that made all the difficult times worthwhile. 'I think everybody enjoyed themselves, don't you?' she suggested to Bill.

'Mmm,' he said, not really concentrating and picking up one of the Sunday papers.

She made them some cheese on toast and they ate it reading papers and watching television, finishing up the dregs of the party wine. That was what being married was about, she thought. The quietly companionable evenings.

Bill grunted.

'What?'

'This story here.' He folded the newspaper over several times, so that just a section of the page was visible.

She felt the usual creeping chill as she read the piece. It was about a man who had accelerated his car over his wife as she had been weeding the front drive, and who was now on trial for murder.

'Ridiculous, isn't it? They haven't said anything about what she did to cause him to behave like that.'

She handed the paper back. 'I think this is just the prosecution case. The case for the defence hasn't started.'

He chuckled as he shook the paper out again and turned the page. 'Anyway,' he said jovially, 'You'd better not weed our drive when I'm going in and out. I don't want to find myself on trial for murder.' It was his favourite joke. He'd pick out a story about a man killing his wife or girlfriend and show it to her, tapping his finger on the newspaper, explaining how the woman involved was to blame. '*Crime passionel*: of course he couldn't let his girl run off with someone else. Can't blame him.' Or, 'It doesn't count when you're so drunk you don't know what you're doing.' Or even, 'You can see it was an accident. It could happen to anyone.'

A few years ago she'd thought of leaving him, but she knew his company was always on a tightrope. She didn't think her marriage was any worse than most of their friends', and she had promised 'in sickness and in health', hadn't she? Stress was a kind of sickness.

Soon he would be through this latest crisis – the Orchard Park business – and then if he continued to blow up from time to time she would try to get him to see a doctor. They'd been happy once, and they could be happy again if only he took it a little easier. But now was not the time to challenge him.

Chapter 5

Harry and Sophie argued on the way home, while the girls slept in a row, their tousled heads nodding on to grubby T-shirts, exhausted after a day of running round the garden and being fed chocolate biscuits by doting guests.

Harry wanted to leave his job as an insurance broker and start up on his own. 'I think there's still a market for niche insurance products: cancer patients find it difficult to get holiday insurance, for example, and teenagers are all tarred with the same brush and have huge car-insurance premiums.'

Sophie was too terrified even to listen to the detail of what he was saying. 'That's what went wrong with my father. And my parents' marriage. That's why he's always in such a filthy temper and is so vile to everyone. People think that working for yourself is going to be easier than answering to a boss and having to keep regular hours, but it isn't, it's ten times harder.'

'I am not that naive,' said Harry, braking as the traffic ahead of them slowed to a crawl. 'I am not trying to get away from a boss or regular hours. I'd work through the night if it is was my own company.'

'That's exactly what I mean. We've got three young children. Do you think I want them to grow up feeling about you the way Jess and I feel about Dad? He's not a bad man, not at all – in fact, he's a great person – but he spent our childhood exhausted and worried – working through the night, as you put it – and that occasionally made him very unpleasant to live with.'

'I'm not your father.' Harry's hands tightened on the steering wheel. 'And I find it very offensive that you should even think to compare us.'

Sophie backed off. 'I wasn't comparing you. And even if I was, what's wrong with that? He does his best. I was just pointing out the hazards. Oh Harry, please. I've lived with this all my life. My father mortgaging our home over and over again to buy land or keep the company going, and hearing my parents argue late at night when they thought I wasn't listening: Daddy used to say that we'd lose our home any moment, and I really thought we would . . .'

A cold, churning feeling – a kind of vertigo – gripped Sophie's insides. She remembered overhearing this for the first time, eavesdropping on an argument between Paige and Bill. She'd been twelve, and it was during the property crash of the nineties.

'We'll have to sell up,' shouted Bill. 'Sell everything. God knows where we'll live. The girls will have to leave St Margaret's and go to that crap school in the village. Where they'll get their heads shoved down the WC for being posh. And you bought that stupid lamp. How can you waste money like that? When we're on the bread line?'

She couldn't hear her mother's reply.

'You stupid fucking woman,' her father shouted. 'I work all the hours God gives me and what do you do?'

'The children might hear . . .' Someone closed the door and Sophie couldn't hear any more. She'd been terrified. Where would they live? And what about her friends? Would she really be attacked for being posh?

The door opened briefly and her mother emerged. 'We'll have to sell everything,' Bill shouted after her. 'Or the bailiffs will take it all.'

Did that include her pony? And what about the dogs? She

whimpered and clutched her pillow. Would they have to sleep on a park bench, like the vagrants she'd seen on the local news? She had curled up in her nightie, invisible at the top of the stairs, with her safe, secure little world collapsing around her ears. She remembered raising her hands and making a picture frame with her fingers as she saw her mother pass on the stairs below her and go into the kitchen, mentally concentrated on turning the scene into a photograph, distancing it from reality and making it a series of shapes and shadows, not something that was happening to her. She had just been given a camera and, through it, had begun to find a way of making sense of the world.

She hadn't told Jess about the arguments. It was the first time she'd kept a secret from her, but she had always been told that she had to look after her little sister. When they were older, about sixteen and fourteen, she'd once been so exasperated by Jess that she'd told her that Daddy was tired and worried about paying for their school fees and that if his company didn't succeed they'd lose the house.

Jess had laughed. 'So what?' she'd said. 'I hate school. And I hate the house.' And she'd stomped out, slamming the door.

Sophie wished she could be like that. But she wasn't. She did everything she could to make it all better. She'd heard the mothers talking about scholarships at a coffee morning. 'They'll always hang onto their Oxbridge potential,' one mother had said.

So Sophie decided that she would make sure she was top of the class, because then she wouldn't have to leave school if her father lost everything. She worked to be popular, too, in case she really did have to leave. She wanted people to like her enough to go on knowing her even if she had to move. If she worked enough, smiled enough, volunteered enough, and was polite enough . . . well, she could control the chaos that threatened to engulf her. It was up to her. Jess was too young, her mother was too busy and her father was too tired. When

Sophie got a sixth form scholarship she was thrilled to know that she would be staying at school with her friends no matter what happened.

And Harry having a good job had been so wonderful. Harry would never ask for their house to be mortgaged against a business. He had saved her from all that. But now he was talking about . . . she felt almost too sick and dizzy to think.

'What about starting your own company in a few years time?' she suggested, trying to keep the panic out of her voice. 'When the economy's recovered for a bit longer, or when the girls are older, but—'

'What if I get made redundant?'

'Harry, please! Don't go volunteering for redundancy just to get the chance to start up on your own. We've got a big mortgage and you know I can't work much because the girls are so little. Look, even if we wait until Summer starts school, and that's only a few years, even that would be easier. I could work more, and . . . and Dad might invest then too. If the Orchard Park thing is successful. He really might.'

'I'm not sure I want anything from your father.'

'Don't be ridiculous. He'd do it as an investment, and you can't be too fussy about who invests in your company, can you? I mean, money's money.' Sophie thought for a moment. 'Well, obviously you mustn't benefit from money made out of drugs or blood diamonds or guns . . .'

Harry smiled. 'I'll try to avoid investment from drug-runners or gangsters.'

Sophie managed a wobbly smile in return. She knew that Harry deserved to follow his dream. But not yet. Not until she, Sophie, was at least in a position to keep the family ticking over. She didn't want them to throw themselves over the precipice of insecurity. It wasn't necessary. Harry had a good job.

'Please, Harry, please. You know what I'm saying makes sense. If you wait until Summer starts school I'll work more and talk to Dad about investing properly in you.'

Harry sighed. 'I can see what you're saying. OK, not for the time being. By the way, I saw you disappear with Jess. You were gone for quite a long time. Did you have a good talk?'

Sophie tensed. She wasn't sure that she could quite trust Harry – even her dearest Harry – with this latest conundrum. Anyway, Jess might be right, and perhaps Dad wasn't having an affair with Anthea. She'd feel pretty silly if she told people, and it all turned out to be completely wrong, wouldn't she?

Her veins ran cold again. A careless word could destroy her mother's whole life, particularly now, with her father so laden with debt because of Orchard Park. Paige might lose her beloved garden, the home she'd lavished so much love and care on, maybe even her friends or her standing in the community and, presumably, her husband, the man who'd stood beside her for over thirty years. She would be devastated, and she'd had enough to contend with over the years. And if Bill was accused of having an affair he would be very, very angry.

No, thought Sophie. The price of getting it wrong was too high. If she was to protect her mother she would have to learn to keep her mouth shut.

'Earth to Sophie,' joked Harry. 'Hello?'

She jerked out of her reverie. 'Sorry. I was just thinking about Jess. It was nice to talk to her properly again. I feel we've slipped out of touch. What with having the girls and . . . I'm sure that if we had her round more, then she wouldn't feel so isolated, and maybe it would help.'

Harry's smile was resigned as he edged forward in the busy London traffic. 'Fine. I'm happy with that.'

'In fact, she suggested that we all go down to The Rowans a bit more often, just to keep an eye on Mum and Dad.'

'Why? They're not exactly in their dotage yet, you know.'

'Perhaps she just wants to go home,' improvised Sophie, wondering if she should tell Harry about Bill and Anthea after all. 'And she needs me there.'

Harry looked as if he was about to say something, but she

could see that he bit it back. 'OK. We can go down more often if you like.'

'Thank you.' Sophie put her head against his arm. 'You are so lovely to me. I don't deserve you.'

Harry smiled down at her. 'Silly thing. And Sophie?'

'Yes?' She suddenly felt frightened. Whatever it was that he was going to say, she didn't want to hear it. It would either be more about setting up on his own, or some criticism of her father. Harry was her saviour, her knight on a white charger, the man who had scooped her up and given her something solid to hold on to. Harry and the girls were like an insulating layer between her and her father, and Jess didn't have that. Sophie knew she owed her.

They would all go down to The Rowans more often. It was Sophie's responsibility to help them all. Just as long as Harry kept his job. She looked up at him anxiously.

'Never mind,' he said, squeezing her shoulder. 'Is there anything to watch tonight?'

'No, nothing.' Sophie knew that wasn't what he'd intended to ask.

But keep it all calm and nice, and the monsters would go away. That was her philosophy.

They spent the rest of the evening curled up on the sofa, watching Sunday night comedy and a documentary on the Second World War, Sophie with her toes tucked under the warmth of Harry's solid body and occasionally picking a segment of orange off his plate. Being with Harry, Sophie often thought, had all the good points of being on your own – that you could do what you liked and didn't have to tiptoe round anyone else's feelings – but also had the advantage that there was someone to share everything with. He grinned down at her as she filched yet another segment of the orange he'd spent five minutes peeling, and she kissed his cheek as a thank-you. He never got cross with her, whatever she did or didn't do.

Chapter 6

Jess, on the other hand, knew all about Bill's anger. He'd told her lots of times, with an open wine bottle on the kitchen table and a half-empty glass beside it, the smoke from his cigarette curling up from the ashtray. There would be classical music playing in the background – she could never hear Elgar's *Enigma Variations* without thinking of her father smoking – and the kitchen door would be open. Paige would be gardening, on her hands and knees at the other end of the garden, and Sophie would be off having a good time.

Jess, gunning her motorbike through the South London traffic, a light drizzle sprinkling water on the road, remembered it all so clearly. She pushed up close behind a slow car, infuriated by someone who was silly enough to do twenty-eight miles per hour in a thirty zone, then nipped past it, just dodging an oncoming lorry. The car hooted. As she went round the next corner too fast she felt her wheels begin to skid under her on the oily road.

She regained her balance, sharpened by the jolt of adrenalin, and reached her basement flat in Peckham in record time, throwing her leather jacket down on the sofa and shaking her hair out of her helmet. She looked at her watch. Only half an hour until Jake arrived.

She spent the time tidying up, though usually she was almost proud of the mess, and pulling together a salad dressing. Jake was a journalist on the business pages of a daily newspaper. Although she'd only been seeing him for ninety-three days, she could feel a connection between them. They finished each other's sentences and laughed at the same things. They often sat up late into the night, talking urgently about the world, about life . . . even about themselves. Jess knew that she wanted to spend her life with Jake. You knew, didn't you, when it was right?

If Jake was with her she wouldn't care how much her father shouted at her. If she and Jake had children, everything would be all right. Her father's words, spoken so often throughout her childhood still echoed in her head.

'A man needs a son,' Bill would say to her ever since she could remember. 'A son. It's a very basic human need to pass on your work to someone who bears your name.'

'I bear your name,' Jess always replied. 'I'd never change it if I got married. And I want to be an architect. Then I could come and work with you.'

He'd look at her as if she'd said something very profound and murmur, 'Sweet. You're very sweet, little Jessica.' Or sometimes he'd narrow his eyes, and she knew the temper was about to change. 'Who fucking asked you?' or 'You stupid girl, what do you know about building?' Or he'd completely ignore what she'd said.

'We never had a name for you when you were born,' he'd say over and over again. 'We were so sure you'd be a boy. We were going to call you Tom.' This name had changed over the years: it had been Philip, then John. If she reminded him of this he'd ask whether she was able to remember that time in her life as well as he did, seeing as how she had been only a few weeks old and he had been twenty-seven.

Or he would say: 'Your mother couldn't have any more children. She had pre-eclampsia, and nearly died having you.' Or: 'Do you know how much your school fees cost? You're bleeding me dry, you two are.'

Guilt seeped through Jess at the memories, but she closed her ears to the old refrain. She was here, now, away from all that. She had a man in her life. They might have children. A grandson would do, wouldn't it, and Sophie only had daughters. Jess thought she might be able to make it up to her father in the end, that she could be the one to make him happy. And once he was happy they could all breathe again.

The doorbell rang and Jake stood in the doorway, tall and lean. He had a narrow, vulpine face and dark hair, one shiny lock constantly flopping over his eyes and repeatedly being brushed back with his hand. He had a deep sculptural dimple in his chin.

She kissed him and drew him in. 'I have had the most awful day,' she said. 'My sister's thirtieth. My mad father, frothing at the mouth at us all while being unbelievably unctuous to anyone he thinks is important. My sad mother, who just accepts everything he says and dances round him making sure he's king of his own particular castle. Everyone smiling, pretending we're the perfect family . . .'

She poured two glasses of wine and handed him one, carrying on talking so that she could look at him. He sprawled so confidently on her sofa, comfortable in his own skin and looking at her as if she was beautiful.

'What do you mean mad?' he asked, amused. He undid a button on her cardigan and straightened her collar. 'There, that looks better. And look, a present.' He brought out a small parcel.

Jess unwrapped it with a cry of glee. It was a pair of dangly turquoise earrings.

'I've always told you you'd look good with earrings,' said Jake with a smile. 'Now all you need to do is get rid of all those studs.'

She felt her ears. 'I like having them.' She set the earrings down carefully.

Jake laughed. 'Time to grow up, Miss Jessica. Gypsy boys

have studs. Proper women wear earrings.' He took all five studs out and inserted the earrings. 'Now you look like a good girl.' He got up and threw the studs in the bin.

'One of those was a diamond.'

He grinned. 'In that case, you'll have to empty out the bin when I've gone. But don't let me see you wearing it again, unless it's part of a pair. Anyway, what were you saying about your father?'

'Oh, he's got the worst temper you'd imagine. Anything sets him off – the Labour party, the Tories, traffic laws, people painting their front doors Farrow & Ball blue, but mainly it's about the business. He's got a building company and a decorating company, both of which are always on the verge of collapse, and he takes it out on us. My mother used to get out of it by spending all her time in the garden, and my elder sister Sophie was always invited to stay with friends or went on school trips so it was pretty much me who had to deal with him at weekends . . .' Jess was surprised to feel a break in her voice and swallowed it down. This wasn't supposed to be a sob story. This was independent Jess showing how well she could cope. Being funny and interesting about her eccentric family.

'He used to tell me everything,' she continued, blinking away a tear. 'All about how the company was going down the tubes, and how he wished I'd been a boy (another lump in her throat here), and how some company had let him down and he'd have to write off a bad debt. Then he'd get angrier and angrier.'

Jake looked concerned. 'That sounds pretty unfair.' He hesitated, as if he was about to say something but had changed his mind. 'But you're pretty feisty – didn't you ever tell him where to get off?'

Jess nodded. 'Sure did. I'm the only one of the family who ever does. One summer holidays, when I was about fifteen, Mum was away looking after Gramps, who died of cancer not long afterwards, and Sophie was away somewhere, so I was alone with him for three days. When he came home from work in the evening, I prepared a simple meal or defrosted food Mum had left in the freezer.

'He used to open a bottle of wine and offered me a glass. I wanted to be friendly, so I took a few sips, though it didn't taste very nice. He started to go on about the publicity over the house price slump. This was 1995, and I remember him showing me a copy of *The Times* and shouting at me: "Bloody journos. They write headlines like 'bad publicity hits house prices'. Look at it. *The Times*, no less. Today's date. 7 July 1995. 'Bad fucking publicity hits fucking house prices.' Well, of course it fucking does. Nobody's going to go ahead with buying a fucking house after they've read this, are they? Answer me. You. Don't just sit there nodding, drinking my wine. Answer me."'

Jess never knew if it was the unexpected warmth of the wine that gave her the courage or whether all the bottled-up years of her childhood had suddenly exploded inside her, but she got up from the table.

'Just shut up,' she'd shouted. 'I'm sick of your self-pitying rants. So house prices are low. They go up and down, Dad, they always have. So what? Why is it my problem?'

'Because,' his voice was low and menacing, 'you're the daughter of a house-builder, and this cosy little home you take so utterly for granted is in hock to the bank, and if those houses don't sell for enough money you, my dear daughter, and your selfish mother and sister – who, by the way, also take absolutely no notice of house prices and why they affect them – will be out on the street.'

'You always say that, but it never happens.' She'd locked herself in her bedroom with the music turned up very loud. Bill banged on the door repeatedly, shouting at her, but eventually went downstairs and turned on the classical music again.

When Paige returned she went upstairs to Jess's room. 'Jess, darling, Daddy says you've been rude to him, and—'

'I told him what he needed to hear, and if you had any spine you would too. Why do you let him go on like this? He never stops complaining. And he talks to you – and to the rest of us – as if we were idiot servant girls who can't be trusted to get anything right.'

Paige sighed. 'He's just worried. House prices keep falling, but no one thinks we're at the bottom of the market yet. He had to buy the land at the top, and if it goes on we could lose everything.' Her face was pale and strained, and, for a moment, Jess felt guilty. But then she remembered the way her father blamed her, Jess, for everything. Why couldn't her mother defend her, for once, not Bill? So she turned her back. 'Just go away. I'm sick of the pair of you.'

Jess was back in the dark, confused days of teenagerdom, and became aware that Jake was looking at her. She'd stopped talking. She wasn't quite sure where she'd left the narrative and drifted off into memories. 'Jess?' He sounded worried.

'I never really got on with any of them after that,' she said, taking another sip of wine. 'I wasn't prepared to put up with anything my parents did or said. It seemed that if house prices were going up my father stood to lose a lot of money because he had to pay so much for the land or the properties for renovation. If it went down, he lost even more. Nothing ever seemed to change. My mother used to bang on about working hard for exams and my father bellowed about my having the wrong sort of friends. But so what? Their life wasn't so great, was it?'

She didn't add that she had also discovered that they rarely noticed if she took wine or cigarettes from the house, or the occasional twenty-pound note from the fat roll of cash her father kept in his desk drawer. More fool them. Occasionally she took a bit too much and there was a monumental row – and he started to lock his study door – but there'd been so many arguments over the years, what was one more? The expulsion meant she didn't get the A-level results for architecture, of course, which was a good way of telling her father that she no longer wanted to work for him.

'What about your sister?' asked Jake thoughtfully.

'Sophie danced through it all, looking pretty and sweet, doing well at exams and pleading with me to "be nice" before taking off with yet another well-heeled boyfriend, leaving me alone in a house with a father who swore at least a hundred times a day.'

'Poor little Jess.' He smiled that slow, tender smile that took her breath away.

'I don't feel sorry for myself.' She didn't want to sound like a victim. 'Lots of people have worse childhoods. Lots. We had nice things. We were lucky. But Mum never stood up for me against Dad. Everything was always about him, or about Sophie. They had one of those baby books for her, you know, with photographs and the date she got her first tooth, and said her first word. For me? Zilch. I'm in photographs with her, never on my own.' She laughed, to show that she thought it was funny.

Jake laughed with her.

'So.' Strong Jess was back. 'I got expelled two months before my A levels and sat my exams at the local comp, then left home at seventeen, because I had to get away from it. I lived in a squat. My father tried to drag me back but Ian, the man who ran the squat, slammed the door in his face and everyone left it at that. Mum and Dad were clearly glad to get rid of me.'

And, eleven years later, nothing seemed to have changed. The resentment surged up in her throat like bile. Bill shouting at Paige. Paige taking the abuse with a bowed head, hardly ever sticking up for herself.

'It infuriates me that my mother doesn't see how badly she's treated. Any sensible woman would have left him years ago.

'Anyway,' she concluded. 'Today Sophie walked in on him snogging his accountant in his study. She thinks he's having an affair with her.'

'She's probably right.'

'So what do we do about it? Do we tell or not? Wouldn't this be the last push she needs to get her life together?'

'Not.' One of the things that was so attractive about Jake was his sureness. 'If she wants to know she'll find out for herself.'

This had not occurred to Jess. 'I think she's too scared. If she leaves him, she'll have nothing.'

'She'll have a divorce settlement.'

'I don't think they've got much money. Well, there's the house, of course, but it would have to be split down the middle, and . . .'

Jake looked around at her kitchen, with its single line of white-painted units, black-stained pine floor and French windows out on to a small terrace. 'He gave you this flat. He can't be short of a bob or two.'

'Oh, I think that was an unexpectedly good year, mostly they scrape by.'

'Scrape by?' queried Jake. 'I'm not sure that having ponies and a swimming pool is a good definition of "scraping by".'

Jess shrugged. 'Dad's always worried. The company is always about to go under, apparently.'

'Is it a limited company?'

Jess thought for a moment. 'Yes. Raven Restore & Build Ltd.'

'Look them up at Companies House. They have to file accounts by law, so you can see what the profits are and what the directors get.'

Jess almost felt she had been handed the key to Pandora's Box. No one had ever suggested checking out her father's allegations. 'What, anyone can do it? Wouldn't it cost a lot?'

'Anyone can do it. Just go online. It's a pound for a report. We can do it now if you like.' Jake swung forward, his narrow face alight. 'I often do it when I'm writing about a company. There isn't much information, but what there is can be very illuminating.'

Jess was surprised by how nervous she felt as she logged on. As if her father might come in at any moment and roar at her for poking her nose into his business.

'You click on "WebCHeck",' said Jake when she called up Companies House. 'And type in the company name, then click on that.'

It took a few seconds.

'Do you have a credit card?' asked Jake.

'Can anyone find out who's accessed their company data?' asked Jess nervously, still afraid of her father finding out.

He shook his head. 'It's public information.'

'You do it,' said Jess, her mouth dry with nerves. If there was some kind of trace, she didn't want her father knowing. 'I'll pay.'

'Any trace would be to your computer, not the credit card, but he'll never know. Don't worry. I think I can afford a pound.' Jake tapped in his credit card details and pulled up the company accounts. 'Hmm.'

'What?'

'Your father trousered about a quarter of a million pounds last year, between him and your mother, who seems to own forty-nine per cent of the shares.'

'I think she inherited them from her father, who helped Dad set up the company.'

'She probably had some anyway. It's tax efficient for owners of small businesses to give shares to their families. As a half-owner of a company yielding dividends of quarter of a million a year, I don't think she needs to worry about the divorce settlement. It would be generous. And the courts always award more to women.' He grimaced. 'As I know to my cost. We can look at the previous year's accounts if you like.'

Her heart beating faster, Jess nodded. 'It was probably an exceptionally good year for some reason.'

'Let's see.' After a few minutes he looked up. 'The year before was pretty good, too. Two hundred grand. Shall we go on?'

'One more. If he really is well off, why is he so angry with us all the time? Why does he keep shouting at us all? And why does my mother put up with it?'

Jake stopped. 'Has it occurred to you that, in some way, this kind of life suits her? That for some psychological reason she's *chosen* this kind of pain?'

'She can't have done. Look, I know all that stuff about women sticking with violent men for years, or going back to them because they promise they won't do it again. But he's not physically violent and he certainly doesn't ever promise not to do it again. He doesn't even see that there's a problem.' Jake called up another profitable year for Raven Restore & Build.

'I think Orchard Park could wipe the company out, though,' Jess continued. 'My father bought an orchard and got planning permission for four cottages and a block of six flats. He had to spend about two years fighting the neighbours, because he really needed to build fourteen flats to get his money back, and now he can only build six because they all protested so much. Now the cost of materials has gone up and up because there's been such a delay since they planned the project, and house prices are static.'

Jake raised an eyebrow. 'I don't think they are. Unless you've got some very peculiar local variations down here.'

'Oh who cares, they go up and down and Dad seems to lose out whichever way.'

Jake was laughing by now. 'I don't think so, Jessie darling. I really don't. You may not realise it, but you are the daughter of a pretty wealthy man.'

Jess was disconcerted. Her father as a victim of circumstance was tattooed into her brain. 'Well I don't see why he'd pretend to be broke if he wasn't.'

'Lots of people pretend. Lots of people lie.'

Jess knew that Jake's ex-wife had lied and manipulated to make sure that she was awarded a larger share of their house than she deserved. It was one of the reasons, he said, why they had to think carefully before they got too involved. He didn't want to get hurt again, and he didn't want to hurt Jess. She drew her feet up on to the sofa, her chin on her knees, and tried to regain her earlier bravery. 'Maybe he's only just started doing well.'

'We can have a look: the online records go back to the mid-nineties.'

'No point. Dad's a survivor. I'm sure he's not really going to lose everything.' She had to force the words out. She didn't want to know what was really behind his anger. Because she knew. It didn't matter how well his company was doing or not doing. His real problem was that he didn't have a son to pass it on to. Her stomach spasmed in rage and fear.

'Jess,' said Jake gently. 'Your dad isn't going bust. And your mother can live her own life. She's a grown woman.' He touched her face, and Jess let herself be drawn into the warmth of his arms.

'What about you?' she asked. 'What are your parents like?'

Jake rarely mentioned his parents, although they seem to have been conventional enough. They had both died when he was in his early thirties, of cancer and heart disease. Poor Jake. More heartbreak. She looked up at his dark eyes and willed him to talk about his childhood.

'My parents.' He rolled his eyes. 'Enough said. Now, let's go to bed.'

But before she turned her attention fully to him she phoned Sophie and told her what they'd found out. 'Dad's rich, apparently. We can tell Mum he's having an affair and she can afford to leave him.'

'I don't think it's that simple.' Sophie's voice was anguished. 'Please, Jess, let's find out more before we absolutely destroy everything she believes in. He does love her, you know, and does his best to look after her, even though he gets it wrong sometimes. And she depends on him for everything, so we can't tear that apart for something as minor as—'

'As an affair?' Jess allowed cynicism to drip into her voice. Sophie was like a fifties housewife sometimes.

The following day Jess carefully tipped out the bin and rummaged through some stinky tea bags and old food remains, eventually finding her diamond stud.

Chapter 7

The sight of Bill and Anthea in each other's arms obsessed Sophie, although she was aware that she should instead be focusing on taking her portfolio around various advertising agencies and art directors, or listening to Bella and Lottie learning to read or concentrating on a hundred and one other things that were much more urgent. And she still didn't want to confide her worries about her parents in Harry. Harry was so straight and honest, and she didn't trust him to see the complexities of the situation.

So she confided in Caroline, the stylist she worked with most regularly. A publishing company, Life Style, had asked them to do a book about seaside homes together, to be called *Shore Style*. Sophie and Caroline met in a coffee shop in Holborn, just outside Life Style's headquarters, to discuss it before they went in for the main meeting.

'It's the copyright I'm concerned about,' said Sophie. 'We ask people – friends, usually – if we can photograph their homes, and sometimes that's quite a hassle for them. If I don't keep the copyright to those pictures, they could find their bedrooms or kitchens or whatever turning up in any old context and some of them really hate that. I can't keep control of where the pictures go unless I keep copyright.'

'I know it's difficult,' said Caroline, breaking up a piece of muffin and nibbling it. 'But the publishers make money selling the pictures on.'

'So would I. They pay us little enough as it is. And at least I know where they're going, and can let anyone who does care about that sort of thing veto it. I do hate not having control.'

Caroline laughed. 'In life? Or just in photography?'

Sophie conceded the point with a wry smile. 'The thing I'm really worried about at the moment is my mother and father.' She mapped out the dilemma to Caroline.

'Who are you closer to?' asked Caroline. 'Your father or your mother?'

Sophie thought about it. 'My father, I suppose, although he can be quite difficult. I've always felt that I had to look after my mother and that can be irritating. It makes me not want to tell her things that might worry her.' She sighed. 'Aren't families impossible?'

'And you haven't told Harry?' Caroline and her partner Nigel often came to supper, so they knew Harry well.

Sophie knew she looked guilty. 'He's so black-and-white about everything. So decent. He'll just insist we do the right thing and that's not necessarily the best thing in this situation. And he doesn't like Dad, so he's not always fair to him.'

'So Sophie the control freak hangs on by keeping it a secret?'

Sophie wondered if this was a criticism, but Caroline's voice was friendly, almost as if she was joking. She looked at her watch. 'The meeting starts in ten minutes – we'd better pay and go.'

They sat through a two-hour meeting with Mary, the book's editor, discussing what the titles of the different chapters should be, conferring over the proposed layout, looking at snapshots of possible houses and working out what they still needed. 'A lot of these houses have white or cream interiors,' commented Sophie. 'With quite a lot of blue. I know those are the main colours beside the sea, but I do think we need to show at least

45

one house that's a bit different to get the balance of the whole book right.'

'I've got a friend who lives near Ramsgate, whose house is a riot of zingy colours, really quite spectacular,' said Caroline. 'I'll ask her.'

Mary pulled out some cuttings of houses she'd seen in magazines. 'I thought this one could work if we can get hold of them.'

Getting agreement to photograph the houses was complicated, because some people would only do it as a personal favour, on the strict understanding that their names and locations would never be published, while others wanted their homes photographed to publicise their business. Two others wanted location fees.

'We can't afford more than one location fee,' said Mary. 'Let's have this one, it's the best, and let the other house go.' Sophie knew that books on interiors never sold as many copies as cookery books or even gardening books, and that if they were ever to get off the ground they had to sell in the US and at least five or six other countries, but it was still frustrating to do everything on such a tight budget.

They agreed on a time frame for the work and that they'd need another meeting. Sophie lost the copyright battle, but managed to negotiate a clause that said certain house owners could veto pictures of their homes being sold on.

Caroline and Sophie signed their contracts, Sophie as usual noting that it was quite a lot of work for less money than she'd have expected if she was working for magazines, and far, far less than she'd have got for advertising. But advertising was thin on the ground now, and at least this was work, as well as a good showcase for her work. Wasn't it? Sophie suppressed another flutter of anxiety. She couldn't work any harder while the girls were small. Could she? And now there was this business with her parents. Fear churned inside her and her chest tightened.

Caroline and Sophie stepped out into the sharp spring sunshine and walked to the Tube station together.

Caroline kissed Sophie goodbye. 'Tell Harry,' she urged. 'See what he thinks.'

Sophie decided to test the waters by raising the subject as they were getting ready for bed. Harry was brushing his teeth.

'I was talking to Caroline today,' she said. 'And she's got a dilemma. She knows about . . . an . . . um . . . friend of hers who's being unfaithful and she doesn't know whether to tell the other partner. What do you think? Would you want to know if I was unfaithful?'

Harry's shoulders squared and stiffened. Then he speeded up his brushing, spat out the toothpaste and swung round to her. 'What are you trying to tell me, Soph?'

Sophie realised he'd misinterpreted her words. 'Oh not us, absolutely not. Really not. Just . . . um . . . some friends of Caroline's.'

He looked suspicious. 'And why are you getting involved?'

'Well, I . . . Of course I'm not. Not really. And as for it being anything to do with us . . .' – she tried to laugh – '. . . I mean, can you imagine me adding a lover to my to-do list? It's far too long as it is, I'd never be able to fit having an affair in between the school run, the shopping and doing the digital development of my pix.'

He studied her very carefully. 'Sophie, I do know you. Are you trying to rescue someone again? Because they might not want or even need rescuing. And, as you've just pointed out, you don't have space in your life for any more responsibilities.'

'No, of course not. What do you mean "rescue"?'

'You've got the girls and me, your career, your family and your friends to think about. You really don't need to spend time worrying about some friend of Caroline's. You'll be wading in, sending her leaflets and recommendations of thera-pists and bottles of Rescue Remedy, and spending hours on the phone talking to Caroline about her . . . and then you'll get cross and feel hurt when she doesn't take your advice after all your hard work. I've seen it all before.'

Sophie was annoyed. The conversation was not going the way she'd expected it to. 'Of course I'm not going to expend all that effort on a friend-of-a-friend. It's just *theoretically* what would you think if I was having an affair? Would you want to know or not?'

Harry ducked back into the shower room, put his toothbrush back, washed his face and tidied the towel away.

'Yes,' he said when he returned, 'and no.' He grinned down at her. 'Not much help, am I? And anyway, I know you: you won't be able to resist helping this "friend", will you?'

Sophie threw a pillow at him, laughing.

Chapter 8

Paige was busy over the following months. Sophie, Harry and the girls came down to stay in the Stable Cottage every few weeks. Bill emerged from his study to play with Bella, Lottie and Summer, giving them rides on his shoulders and telling them stories about the wicked witch who lived in the forest, after which the three children raced around the garden and played in Sparrow Palace.

Jess kept her new boyfriend away from them all but occasionally came down to The Rowans on her own when he was busy, constantly fingering her mobile phone, a smile playing over her face as she received his texts.

'Not at the dinner table, young lady,' roared Bill. 'Give me that.' He took the phone from her and dropped it into his water glass. 'There. That sorts that out. I can't bear rudeness.'

'You bastard.' Jess got up, slammed the door and left on her bike, while Paige and Sophie tried to pretend nothing was wrong. Sophie kicked Harry and signalled with her eyes. Do not make a fuss. Not in front of the girls.

But Jess was back three weeks later. 'Jake gave me a new mobile. An even better one.' She showed Paige. 'Can I bring him down?'

Paige was delighted. 'Of course, darling. We would love to meet him. What does he do?' Paige opened her diary. 'Would three weeks from now be OK?'

Jess folded her arms. 'Jake's a journalist. A business journalist. Three weeks would be fine but you'd better prime Dad not to be vile to him. You know what he's like about the press.'

'I'm sure he'll be fine,' said Paige, sure of no such thing.

Sophie looked up from spooning gunge into Summer's mouth. 'You should be more assertive, Mum. You can't let him get away with the way he talks to you. You have to stand up for yourself. Not nastily, or anything. You're empowering his bullying with the way you behave. Here, read this.' She handed Paige her magazine.

'It's not bullying, he just gets tired and short-tempered.' Paige read the piece after they'd gone. She had read lots like it before, and had even tried to put some of the advice into practice. Maybe this one would work, though: it explained that you should never get into shouting matches, but that you should repeat your message, clearly and calmly, until the other party understood that you were not going to be bullied.

When Bill crashed into the house on Wednesday evening Paige came downstairs as calmly as she could, knowing that he couldn't hear her heartbeat speeding up or see the way her mind seemed to have shattered like glass. 'How are you, darling?' she said in her sweetest tones. 'Have you had a nice day?'

'I've had a fucking awful day, but that's not what's worrying me. What the fuck have you done to the borders in the front of the house? Or have we been burgled by plant thieves?'

Paige was taken aback. He never noticed anything in the garden. 'I've been clearing them,' she said. 'I always do at the end of the season.'

'Well, clearing them is one thing, but stripping them out completely is another. How are you going to replace those plants? By spending all my money, I suppose?'

'They're annuals in that bed, and I grow them all from seed. It doesn't cost much.' Paige kept herself calm. Repeat your message, she told herself. Repeat. 'I always clear the borders in autumn. Every gardener does, unless they've got shrubs or—'

'I don't want to hear a lot of gobbledygook. I go by the evidence of my own eyes. When I left this morning those borders looked fine. Now you've spent all fucking day – so you'll be too tired even to speak this evening, let alone fucking cook – pulling every sodding plant out. It looks like a desert out there. It's destroying the value of the house. Suppose we had to put it on the market now, with the front looking like that?'

Paige, now fighting on the dual front of gardening and cooking, and terrified that this argument was leading to him telling her that Orchard Park had failed and that they had to sell the house, nevertheless stuck to her message.

'I always clear the borders in autumn,' she said again. 'It's what gardeners do. And I've cooked a meal tonight, of course. I always do that too.'

'Always do that too,' Bill mimicked. 'Just because you've always done something, it doesn't mean it's right. Sometimes I worry about you. You don't have the faintest idea why you do things; you just do them, like clearing those beds, because you've always done them. Haven't you heard that "the unexamined life is not worth living"?'

She wondered how she could respond. Maintain the message? Or grapple with the new argument? 'I don't need to examine my life to know what to do with my borders,' she said, allowing herself to get drawn in.

'No, you wouldn't, would you?' He pulled a bottle of wine out of the fridge and uncorked it with a sigh. 'I despair of you, I really do.'

'We did say we wouldn't drink during the week.'

He glared at her. 'Did we? I don't think I did. And when all I get when I cross the threshold after a hard day is an argument about flowers and borders, then I need a drink. Anyone would.'

Paige didn't want to point out that he'd started the argument. She looked at the wine bottle. It had a light frosting of condensation. She imagined the cool liquid sliding down her throat, and the warmth as it hit, blurring the edges of their

51

argument and lifting her tiredness. She longed for a drink too, but how could she ask Bill to cut down if she didn't?

He waved the bottle at her. 'Want one?'

She hovered. He'd already poured himself a glass. Her not having one wasn't going to make any difference.

Just one. That's all. Just one, to smooth the jagged edges.

Bill laughed as she took her first sip. 'You've got absolutely no willpower, have you?'

She ignored him. The wine gave her the courage to ask: 'How's Orchard Park? Is there any news?'

He glared at her. 'There's no fucking news. And it's none of your fucking business. So get off my back. I don't need nag, nag, nag every evening when I get home. Is that clear?'

Bill took his wine in to his study and slammed the door.

That hadn't gone too badly. Not when you thought about it. Sometimes he went on and on. By being assertive, she had got him to change the subject and to stop fairly quickly. It was a start. That's what you had to be, quiet and dignified, and he would respect that. Ultimately.

Perhaps she should make more of an effort to understand what he did, and thereby to understand him. The question was how. If only she could talk to Anthea, who, apart from Jenny, Bill's assistant, was probably the only person who really understood Raven Restore & Build and its various satellite companies. But she was frightened of Anthea, of her smartness. She was always so carefully coordinated and fashionable: if sloppy boots, short skirts and huge hoop earrings were in, Anthea wore them, but without ever looking anything less than completely professional. Paige had to be careful about buying clothes that were too trendy, because hers had to last.

The phone rang. It was her friend Rose, who was organising a dinner party to welcome a new neighbour, a widower called George Boxer who had just retired and bought Glebe House, on the edge of the village, and who was a source of much speculation.

'He wants help with the garden, so I thought of you. I've told him that you know everything. And he's re-doing the house, too.'

Paige tapped softly on Bill's door. 'Can we go to Rose and Andrew's? Next Thursday?'

'Midweek?' he asked. 'Are you quite mad? I can't go to dinner parties in the middle of the week.'

'It's for the new man at Glebe House. He's completely re-doing the house and garden. Rose thought we might be able to advise him.'

Bill's expression changed. 'Well, why didn't you say so before? You never tell me anything. We'd better go then, hadn't we? Before anyone else's company gets there. He'll need to be warned if he's to avoid some of the cowboys in the construction industry these days.'

Chapter 9

Anthea was concerned. It had been over six months since Sophie's party and nothing had happened. Sophie and Harry came down to The Rowans with the three little girls, and even Jess skulked around from time to time. Neither girl treated Anthea any differently from how they'd always done. Which was to say that they pretty much ignored her. Anthea burned with indignation. She could see their eyes sliding over her, and the way their body language excluded her: the tiniest shift of shoulder to block her light, the way they spoke across her, or answering her questions briefly with a hard look in their eyes and never asking her any of their own.

Well, their time would come. But fate needed another little nudge. Somehow Anthea had to get at Paige directly. Anthea was determined not to lose again. She had always been the one who got left. Always.

Her father had left when she was five, leaving her mother weeping and defeated. Little Anthea was handed round a series of babysitters and relatives while her mother tried to earn enough money to keep them. Sometimes she was the last child to be picked up at the school gates, and often her mother was always too tired, or depressed, to have any time to listen to Anthea's news. Anthea also sensed that the babysitters and relatives were only either looking after her for the money or because 'they felt they ought to'. Sometimes she sat in front of the television with her mother, just to spend time with her, discussing the fate of various characters in *Coronation Street*, but even these conversations were accompanied by sighs and her mother's oft-stated theory that 'all men are bastards, you'll see'.

Anthea had no idea whether her father had ever tried to see her, but when she was eight her mother informed her that 'Daddy has a new little girl now, he won't need you'. When Anthea was twenty-two her mother died of pancreatic cancer, doubtless nudged along by the ever-open bottle of wine on the kitchen table. Her father came to the funeral, no longer the strong, laughing hero of her memories but a plump, contented man, preening himself in a blazer. They tried to find something to talk about but the conversation faltered into a series of polite exchanges about Anthea's degree in accountancy and her father's second family, about whom she wished to hear nothing at all. Any remnants of affection between them had been buried along with her mother. Anthea resolved to be tougher about relationships in future, and to treat other women as the enemy they undoubtedly were. Even if she was dumped – and she so often was – she was determined never to play the victim, or to worry about what other women might be feeling. All is fair in love and war. Which brought her back to Paige and Bill. She had to move things on a bit.

Fate delivered its nudge about ten days later. Anthea took a trip up to London to go to the theatre with an old friend from school and, on the way back, saw Paige waiting at the other end of the platform at Victoria.

'Paige!' cried Anthea, click-clacking along the platform and kissing her on both cheeks.

'Oh, hello Anthea.' She thought Paige looked nervous, as well as surprised.

'What fun seeing you here. Are you going back to Martyr's Forstal?'

Paige said that she was. The train drew in and Anthea found

a foursome with a table, which she commandeered by spreading her coat and handbag over the spare seats. 'How lovely to have a chance to chat,' she said to Paige before she could run away.

But in fact Paige seemed equally glad to see her. 'Yes, isn't it?'

The smell of chips and takeaway spread through the carriage and Anthea's nose wrinkled. 'I've always loved that jacket,' she said as Paige took off her own coat and spread it over the seat beside her. 'It suits you so well.'

'Thank you.' Paige didn't seem to notice the emphasis on the word 'always'. That jacket needed pensioning off. Perhaps Paige really was as thick as Bill always said she was. 'I wish my wife would take a bit more interest in fashion,' he'd said to Anthea, eyeing her cropped cardigan and the shreds of lace camisole it revealed. He'd sighed. 'Paige's tastes are very conventional, I'm afraid. She buys clothes that won't date or wear out. Not like you.'

'I'm afraid I buy clothes that I hope won't date,' said Paige to Anthea, over the grubby train table, confirming everything Bill had said. 'Maybe if Orchard Park comes up trumps I can have a complete makeover.'

Not if I have anything to do with it, thought Anthea, while smiling non-commitally.

'So how *is* Orchard Park?' ventured Paige. 'Have you heard any news?'

Anthea arranged a sombre expression on her face. 'Well,' she took a deep breath. 'You know that although some people are saying the market is up, those headlines are just headlines. Underneath, there are huge variations.'

Paige nodded. 'Yes, Bill always says that.'

'Bill is a very wise man.' Anthea watched Paige from under her lashes. 'He's just so good at his job. There's almost nothing he doesn't know about building or decorating. And he's so nice with it. Everyone in the office is in love with him.'

56

'Are they?' Paige looked startled.

'Oh, there's no need for you to be worried about it. I mean, he comes home on time every evening, doesn't he? And spends his weekends on the golf course or on the boat. It's not as if you have great unexplained tracts of time that he hasn't accounted for.'

Paige's brow furrowed. Come on, Paige, come on, Anthea thought. Where do you think he is between five and seven-thirty most weekdays? Still in the office? Anthea turned away to check her reflection in the train window as the lights of Herne Hill rattled past.

'Well, he works very hard,' said Paige, twisting her wedding ring nervously. 'Especially at the moment. With Orchard Park being the biggest risk of his career.'

Hmm. Paige was clearly so obsessed with Orchard Park that she wasn't focusing on what else Bill might be up to.

'Well, it is very risky, of course,' said Anthea, deciding she should downgrade the hazards of the project to give Paige the opportunity to worry about something else. 'But I don't think you should think about it too much, because Bill is so very, very good at what he does. And, although it's the first project he's undertaken without partners to spread the risk, he's made sure that he only pays full whack for the land once the properties are sold. He's got an over-arching agreement with the farmer who sold it to him, so that the farmer got an initial basic price, with more to come at the end.'

Paige looked puzzled. She clearly had no idea what an over-arching agreement was. You'd have thought that after thirty years of marriage to a builder she'd have found out a bit about what he did. 'Oh good,' said Paige hesitantly. 'But what about the rise in the cost of materials? And labour?'

Anthea knew she had to play this carefully. Bill did not like his business being discussed, and would be furious if she said anything to Paige that might result in another request for redecorating the drawing room. And Bill had often told her how manipulative Paige was: that she seemed nice as pie when you first met her, but that anything you said could be taken down and used in evidence against you. She didn't want to say anything that might create problems for Bill.

'Well, costs are an issue, of course. But I think we'll get away with it. I don't think he'll make anything like the money he'd hoped to make if the market had been going his way, but I really do think there is a good chance that he'll break even at least. He might even make a small profit.'

'But he's extended the mortgage on The Rowans, so he'll need to pay that off.'

Anthea did not permit her expression to change, even as something cold and heavy dropped into the pit of her stomach. This was news to her. If indeed he *had* done so. He'd have told her, wouldn't he? His accountant? 'Oh well,' she said, 'for someone like Bill mortgages come and go. Don't worry about it. Really, it's not the sort of thing that should be keeping you awake at night.'

Paige smiled. 'That's very kind of you to say so. I'm so glad we bumped into each other tonight. It's nice to see beyond the business persona and Bill thinks so highly of you.' She laughed. 'I think of you as his business wife. I read an article about that recently, the relationships between men and women at work where they almost become like an old married couple but without the sex.' Paige blushed, which Anthea thought charmingly idiotic of her.

'Well, we're not quite like that,' she said, trying not to laugh out loud. 'But I like to think that Bill values my ideas, and that I'm more than just a number-cruncher as far as he's concerned.'

'Oh you are, I'm sure,' said Paige warmly. 'Look, it's been so nice talking, why don't you come to lunch on Sunday? We've got Jess's new boyfriend coming, and to be honest I need to dilute Bill with someone he won't growl at. Or Jess will never bring him down again.'

'That would be lovely.' Anthea was coming to the conclusion

that Sophie was too loyal – or too wrapped up in her own family – to tell Paige what her father was up to, or even to gossip to anyone else, but Jess was a one-woman roadside bomb. All Anthea needed to do was to set her off.

'Oh, and there's a new single man in the village too,' said Paige. 'George Boxer. He's recently bought Glebe House and it needs total renovation, so Bill has been talking to him about what needs doing. We met him at dinner the other day. I'm sure we could invite him, because Bill does like to show prospective clients what we've done with The Rowans.'

'He does, I know,' Anthea agreed. 'He's very proud of the house.'

'It's not that I'm setting you up with him, of course,' added Paige. 'But I always think it's nice for single people to meet each other. There aren't so many of them round here.'

'No, there aren't,' Anthea replied, thinking that quite soon Paige would find this out for herself.

'Bill doesn't get on very well with Jess,' admitted Paige. 'So Jess has never brought any boyfriends home before. That's why I think a big party is best, don't you? So that he can't roar at this Jake person?'

'You're so right,' murmured Anthea. 'And it would be lovely to meet a new, single man.'

As Paige droned on about George Boxer being rich, but a self-made man – as if she and Bill were descended from the aristocracy – and how he was a widower, but one of those men who seemed to be in dire need of a new wife, Anthea ran a mental audit over this claim that Bill had remortgaged The Rowans to fund Orchard Park.

Was that where he'd got the money from? Anthea didn't like the idea that Bill might be keeping secrets from her too.

Chapter 10

Arriving at The Rowans for the lunch party to meet Jake, Sophie unpacked the car with one hand and jiggled Summer on her hip with the other. Thank heaven for Stable Cottage. It wasn't big, consisting of two small square bedrooms and a single kitchen-living room, with very little in the way of storage or cupboards, but at least it meant that they were spared the breakfast-time spats between Paige and Bill.

'Do you suppose I'll be able to dodge the trip to the pub?' asked Harry, hauling a suitcase out of the boot and hefting it on to their double bed. 'Your father holds court at the end of the bar, pontificating about everything under the sun. I think I've had overload over the last few months. If that's OK with you.'

Sophie was disconcerted. Harry always seemed to enjoy the trip to the pub. 'Well, if I help Mum in the kitchen perhaps you could say you need to keep an eye on the girls. But apparently, if people complain a lot you should deal with them by agreeing as much as you can. It's called the Disarming Technique. I read about it in a newspaper recently.'

Harry's face crinkled into a smile. 'Tell me more.'

'You mustn't dismiss his complaint or suggest it's trivial. Like Jess does. You should never try to cheer a grumbler up, and the worst thing is to suggest that he should just get over it. It risks the complainer upping the ante and getting even more angry.'

'So I have to suppress what I think and feel?' asked Harry.

'Well, no, I think they said you could express your own feelings, but you should convey respect. It does sound a bit difficult but it's worth a try, don't you think?'

Harry snorted. 'I always convey respect. After a few hours with your father, I feel as if I'm disappearing up his backside. And Soph . . . could we have some time alone together, do you think? Would your mother babysit if we went out tonight?'

'Well . . .' Sophie giggled, but felt even more uneasy. Harry getting her alone was going to mean Harry petitioning to set up his own business. And she didn't think she could deal with it. Sorting out her parents had to come first. And Jess, because she wasn't sure about this boyfriend. So far he'd seemed worryingly unavailable at weekends, and Jess had a habit of picking men who let her down. Then, once everyone was happy, maybe she, Sophie, could . . . She didn't understand, sometimes, why she felt so afraid. Perhaps because it was all down to her. To keep the family together. 'Everywhere will be booked up,' she said. 'Down here, there's not much choice.'

'Just the pub would be fine.'

Sophie wrinkled her nose. 'Oh no, not the pub. It's so noisy you can't hear yourself think. And I can't bear the lighting, it's so strong overhead. And, Harry, I'm so tired. Summer has been up three times a night recently and . . .'

Sophie maintained that she should do all the nights because Harry had to go to work, but, in return, there was an unspoken agreement that if she said she was tired she would be believed.

On Sunday morning Harry took the girls out to play in the garden while Bill hunkered down in his study. Paige and Sophie peeled potatoes, rolled out pastry and chopped carrots. The kitchen filled with the smell of roast lamb, garlic and rosemary.

'How's Dad?'

'Much the same,' said Paige. 'You know.'

'Did that article I gave you help?'

'Oh yes,' Paige smiled at her daughter. 'I think it did. A bit. But until Orchard Park's all sold I don't want to stir anything up. I thought perhaps I could suggest he goes for counselling. Or tries anti-depressants. All that stress, over such a long period of time, it really can't be good for him. It could be depression, don't you think? I know he's really trying to do the best he can for us all.'

'Mum . . .' Sophie could hardly bear to hold on to her secret any longer. Maybe Jess was right. Her mother, surely, ought to know that Sophie thought she'd seen Anthea and her father wrapped round each other. Even if there had been an innocent explanation.

'I've invited Anthea for lunch, by the way,' said Paige before Sophie could continue, 'and this new man, George Boxer. I'm match-making. So I think we'll need more potatoes than that. Sorry, what did you want to say?'

'Nothing.' Sophie's heart sank. She couldn't tell her mother now.

'Is Harry around for a heart-starter?' Bill appeared in the doorway.

'Oh darling, don't go to the pub,' pleaded Paige. 'People will be arriving in a minute.'

Bill glared at her. 'I don't know why you always invite so many fucking people round. It's a Sunday, a day of rest, don't you know, and you've got us all running round laying tables and peeling potatoes.'

'We agreed that we wanted Jess to bring her new boyfriend, I discussed it with you. And it's only for a few hours and . . .'

'Dad, I understand that you need a rest on Sunday and it must be irritating not to be able to go to the pub,' chirped Sophie, bent on her new strategy.

'Who asked you?'

'I just wanted to say that I understand how you feel. You're right to—'

'Anyway, Sophie and I are doing all the work. We're not

asking you to lay any tables,' interrupted Paige, undoing Sophie's efforts.

'Don't be such a fucking martyr,' said Bill. 'I can't bear martyrdom. And Sophie, you're going to turn out like your mother if you're not careful. A head full of trivia and no idea about anything.'

'That's not . . .' Sophie flashed, before remembering that the Disarming Technique meant that she had to find something to agree with. 'You're right, martyrdom isn't very pleasant.'

His eyebrows shot up. 'What are you after young lady? Don't tell me I don't know when I'm being soft-soaped. Is that husband of yours after a start-up loan again?'

'No!' shrieked Sophie. 'He hasn't asked you for money, has he?'

'Over and over again. Everybody asks me for money. And I'm fed up with it. You know where to find me if you need me.' And the back door slammed.

'The pub,' said Paige. 'I did so hope he wouldn't. Jess has never brought a boyfriend home before. Roast potatoes are never nice if they're kept hanging around.'

'I can't believe that Harry has gone behind my back,' whispered Sophie, fear squeezing the breath out of her lungs. 'He promised not to.'

'Perhaps your father is exaggerating,' suggested Paige, placing a hand on Sophie's back. 'Or making it up?'

Sophie was shaking with worry and rage. 'Even Dad couldn't have invented that. How would he know about it unless Harry had mentioned it? And we've agreed. Now is not the time for Harry to be starting up on his own.'

'Oh look, they've arrived.' Paige took her apron off at the sound of the gravel crunching on the drive. 'Have we more or less finished?'

Sophie swallowed back tears. How could Harry go behind her back to her father? Of all people? When he had promised?

Jess flung open the front door and called out, sounding happy. 'We're here!'

Paige went out to kiss her and Sophie could hear the sound of introductions.

'Sophie.' Jess burst into the room hugged her sister.

'You look great,' said Sophie, hugging her back. Jess had bright blue dangly earrings, was wearing lipstick and eye shadow, and even a turquoise cardigan instead of her usual muddy combat colours and pale face.

'Meet Jake,' said Jess, her face alight with pleasure.

Sophie, still trembling with rage at Harry's betrayal, raised her eyes to Jake's dark ones, taking in his intense narrow face and the way the air around him crackled with energy.

Jake took her hand. 'I've heard so much about you.'

'Yes. I've heard about you too.' Sophie heard her voice from a long way away, sounding happy and different.

Because her insides had been scooped out in a sudden jolt of recognition. This man is looking at me, she thought. He sees me. Nobody has looked at me like that for so long. Sophie swallowed and turned away. 'Let me get you a drink.'

I remember that feeling, she thought. From way back when. When I used to be a person, not just Bella's mum or Harry's wife. It was fun. I'd forgotten about fun.

But Jake belongs to Jess. And I have three darling daughters who are more precious to me than life itself, and who love their daddy.

So that, of course, is that. The world returned to its usual size and shape with a puff of relief. But Sophie felt more alive as she brushed past Harry, who came in as she left the room. She couldn't trust herself to look him in the eye. He had lied to her.

Chapter 11

Sophie enjoyed talking and laughing as they gathered in the drawing room before lunch. The awful Anthea appeared, clogged in eye-make-up. Sophie spent the minimum of time talking to her, merely making sure that she was introduced to George Boxer, who looked like a rugby ball in a tank top. The log-burning stove her father had recently installed pumped out heat on an industrial scale. As her cheeks became more and more flushed, Sophie resolved that she would never let a small amount of irritation about Harry's behaviour deceive her into thinking she found another man attractive. Because that's all it is, she told herself, pressing her face to the cool mirror in the downstairs lavatory. You're furious with Harry, so you meet Jake and suddenly you remember what it was like to be single. She would like to photograph him, though, because the bones of his face were fine and sharp, with strong, definite eyebrows, and when he smiled his mouth curled in the most unexpected way. As if he were the Cheshire cat in Alice in Wonderland and might vanish completely, leaving only his smile behind.

She rootled around in her bag for an old lipstick, because it was time she started taking more care of her appearance. She'd let herself get into the habit of a bare face and unstyled hair. She ran cold water over her wrists as she resolved to treat this situation with Harry, and the business of him asking her father for a loan, quite calmly.

'Mummy? Mummy, where are you?' She could hear Lottie and Bella rattling on the door so she opened it, her arms wide, to take them both in a long hug. 'I'm here. I didn't go anywhere.'

Bill came back from the pub in time for the roast potatoes to be saved, but insisted on pouring everyone another drink.

'The potatoes won't be so nice if we wait any longer,' pleaded Paige.

'It's Sunday,' boomed Bill. 'We don't have to clock-watch. George, mate, it's good to see you here. What's your poison? What, mineral water? We can't have that. I've got a particularly good claret here.'

George allowed himself to be tempted by Bill's latest Wine Society claret, and Bill moved on to Jake, clapping him on the back and asking if he was talking about 'bloody journalists'. 'Not *the* Jake Wild, are you? The one on the business pages of the . . . what is it now? It seems my younger daughter has some taste after all.' Jake agreed with him that the press often got things wrong, and laughed at Bill's jokes. Jess gazed at him adoringly.

Paige sat them all down, with Anthea between Bill and George Boxer, a bull terrier of a man, short, broad and almost completely bald. Sophie managed a few standard exchanges with him about moving to Martyr's Forstal. ('Audrey, my dear wife, would have loved it,' he said, bringing her name into the conversation at every opportunity.)

Bill grumbled that the potatoes were overdone. 'I suppose I'll have to tell the cook that if you leave them in too long they get wrinkled.' He winked at Anthea. 'I buy her a new cookery book every Christmas, but she never learns.'

Sophie hoped her mother wasn't going to retaliate. Jess needed Bill to stay in a good mood, so that he'd go on being nice to Jake. She looked at Paige and saw her bite back a response. Sophie thought she could feel Jake's eyes on her whenever she got up to help her mother or to sort out one of the children, who were tucked away watching a DVD in the television room.

At one point Harry and Jess both got up together to take plates out. Sophie met Jake's eyes.

'So do you . . .?'

'So are you . . .?'

They stopped and Jake smiled, his whole face creasing up. 'You first,' he said.

Sophie felt happy again, with the exhilaration of being on a boat as it suddenly tips and tacks into wind. 'I was only going to ask where you lived,' she said.

'I have a flat in the Barbican. What about you?'

'Clapham. Not very interesting at all.'

'So what do you do?'

Sophie pulled herself together. 'Oh, I'm a photographer. Still life and portrait mainly, not fashion.'

'How interesting.' He sounded as if he meant it. 'What sort of clients do you have?'

By the time she'd finished explaining that she balanced her work between 'editorial' – say, pages of Christmas presents or photographs of a featured home – and lucrative advertising shoots for almost anybody ('I've got a shoot for a soup company on Thursday, they've been big in packet soups for ages, but now they want people to think of themselves as wholesome and fresh so I've got to come up with images that tick every possible box: contemporary garden, vintage farm, comforting, exciting – in fact, every contradiction you could think of.') she realised that he was a good questioner. But then he was a jour-nalist; he would be.

'Mmm,' he said of the soups. 'I'm doing a piece on compa-nies that revitalise their image without losing their core customers. Maybe I should interview their marketing manager. Do you know who I should contact?'

'The PR, I should think, but I don't know who that would be. The Head Office is in Birmingham and the marketing director is called Derek Lawson.'

Harry, carrying a large apple crumble, sat down beside her again. She avoided his questioning look and pushed the crumble round her plate. She was still furious with him for asking her father for money.

At the other end of the table she could see Anthea sparkling at George Boxer, which would certainly solve some problems. Maybe Paige wasn't as innocent as she seemed. Perhaps she knew, on some unconscious level, that a single Anthea was a threat to her. Although George was not in the least bit sexy.

Or perhaps her mother was a kind person who wanted other people to be happy. Sophie got up. 'I think I can hear one of the girls crying.'

But she went outside, where the grasses and dahlias so lovingly planted by her mother created a tapestry of russet, red and gold with the holly berries and rosehips that tangled through the hedges. The autumn air cooled her face.

'What's wrong?' asked Harry, laying a hand on her shoulder, just as she began to decide how she would photograph the colours, with a rich red dahlia in the foreground.

She jumped. 'Oh, it's you.'

'Who else would it be?'

'Harry, you asked my father for a loan to set up your company. He told me about it.'

'I haven't.' Harry, her solid, truthful, loving Harry folded his arms and lied.

'Well, he can scarcely have invented it, can he?'

'Sophie. Your father is an alcoholic. He will invent anything he damn well likes. Anything that gives him an excuse to go out to the pub or to open another bottle.'

'No, he's not!' Sophie thought this was so ridiculous that it barely registered with her. 'He never touches spirits. And he works, he's very good at what he does, so he doesn't drink during the day! You know what Jess found out on the Companies House website. He's really doing very well. That's hardly likely to be the case if he's an alcoholic, is it? I know he does have a bit too much at weekends, but who doesn't?'

'Very few people drink as much as he does. I've been watching him. Two or three pints in the pub. A bottle of wine, maybe two, over lunch. The pub again in the evening. Maybe another bottle or so with dinner. Every day.'

'Just at the weekend. He's stressed. But he doesn't drink during the week. Which is most of the time.' She took a deep breath. 'You're changing the subject. You don't want to admit that you asked him for a loan. After we'd promised that you wouldn't set up on your own at least until Summer was at school and I could work more.'

'I did mention my plans,' admitted Harry. 'But that was before you and I agreed to wait. It was before your birthday.'

'So neither of you has mentioned it since?'

Harry looked at the ground.

'I see,' said Sophie.

'No, you don't. I haven't asked him for a loan. He has promised one, the way he promises things when he's three pints in. He keeps saying, "Let me know when you want a helping hand, my boy, only too glad to get in on the ground floor."'

'You must have said something. For him to go on offering it. Don't try to tell me you've turned him down.'

Harry didn't reply.

'No. You didn't.'

'I have to say something on these interminable pub visits you insist we go on together. I can't just listen to him banging on with his philosophy of the world, you know. I have to speak. But I didn't *ask* him for a loan. I just told him about my ideas. You wanted me to spend time with him. To bond with him.'

'So it's my fault, is it?' Sophie hugged her arms to herself, the chill autumn air biting into her bones. 'And if he brings it up so often, why haven't you told me about it?'

'Because you won't discuss anything about my future plans at all.'

'That's not true. And it's not fair to say that it is. We've talked about all this over and over again. And you never said anything about Dad. Anyway, why has *he* only mentioned it now if it's something he discussed with you ages ago?'

'Probably because you were putting him under pressure not to drink, I imagine,' said Harry.

'I wasn't putting him under pressure. I was agreeing with him, and trying the Disarming Technique.'

'He doesn't want to be disarmed,' said Harry. 'He wants to drink.'

'That's ridiculous. You're trying to distract me by accusing him. That's what he does in arguments. He twists your words and makes attacks instead of replying properly. You're being like him.'

'Be very careful, Sophie, before you compare me with your father. Be very careful.'

With an effort, Sophie reined herself in. 'He drinks too much. I accept that. But that's just because he's so stressed. And he's in control of his life. He knows what he's doing.'

'Sophie.' Harry placed a hand on her arm. 'Believe me. I didn't ask him for a loan.'

She would have to accept it. She had no choice. But his words didn't quite stretch to cover the whole truth, and nothing but the truth.

'All I ask,' she said in a low voice, 'is that you don't go round telling people that my father's an alcoholic. He's got a reputation round here, and that's part of why he's so successful in business. He's respected for what he does. We in the family know he drinks a bit too much some times, but no one else does. You could bring the whole thing crashing down if you blacken his name.'

'You must have a very low opinion of me,' said Harry, dropping his hand and going indoors.

Chapter 12

Anthea was fascinated by her second glimpse into Bill's home life. She'd heard so much about his loveless marriage and his stupid, vain and greedy wife, and the way he had to do everything for her. They hadn't slept together for years. There was no intimacy at all. He was staying with her out of duty because she would never be able to manage on her own. They'd originally married because she'd got pregnant. He often wondered if she'd done it on purpose to trap him. Now she looked at him just as an open cheque book. 'Sometimes I feel my name should be Wallet, not Bill,' he joked.

Poor Bill. Although Anthea knew that men were, at the very least, somewhat economical with the truth when it came to whether they slept with their wives or not. She'd once had an affair with a married man who had got his wife pregnant during the time he and Anthea were seeing each other. When she queried it he'd explained that he'd had to have regular sex (Anthea had been away at a conference) otherwise he might have finished up getting prostate cancer: 'It's not good for it to stay up there, you know, it causes a funny kind of cell division. Everyone knows prostate cancer is caused by women who won't give their men enough sex.'

'I think not,' Anthea had replied crisply, before telling him that he would have to find his future cancer prevention elsewhere. So she wasn't a complete idiot about married men and their lies.

But Bill was different and, more important, he was at a good time to get away. The children had grown up and there was still time for Paige to make a life of her own, if only she was prepared to make the effort. Anthea, who looked at life through spreadsheets, projections and calculations of weighted averages, could see that a woman of fifty had, in theory, fifteen more years in the workplace. A woman of sixty had very few earning options, especially if she hadn't worked for a long time. Any divorce, then, would be accompanied by a serious division of capital and pension. So if Paige was to get off her butt and stop relying on Bill she'd better do it soon.

Sophie's birthday party had been very much what Anthea had expected, stuffed with local dignitaries and the wealthy, pervaded by an atmosphere of comfort and privilege. Anthea couldn't help thinking of the council flat in which she and her mother had lived after their father left, with its concrete stairways, graffiti and smell of urine. And the noise of the television on one side and the regular screams, shouts and crashing of a couple arguing on the other. Sometimes Anthea had been woken up by the noise and had thought she was back in their old home, with her father and her mother throwing things at each other.

Anthea had fought to get away from there, but it was frustrating that the last hurdle, a home and family of her own with a secure long-term future, had always been out of reach because of married women clinging on to husbands they no longer really loved or wanted.

This smaller lunch party offered a different window on to Bill's life. She watched carefully for small signs of intimacy but found none. Paige seemed calm – almost cold – when he complained about the roast potatoes. At one point she got flustered when Bill pointed out that she'd brought the wrong wine up from the cellar. 'I don't know,' he said, cheerfully winking at Anthea. 'I have to do everything round here.'

After being snubbed by Sophie, who barely even said hello to Anthea before turning her back, Anthea concentrated on her 'date'.

George Boxer. Oh, the condescension of it. Married women always assumed that single women were desperate for anything with a willy. This George Boxer had to be one of the least attractive men Anthea had met in a long time. How could Paige honestly think that she was so desperate that she'd stoop to going out with a man who was short, fat and balding. With huge horn-rimmed glasses.

Anthea sighed and braced herself to be polite to him. 'I'm an accountant,' she replied, when he asked what she did.

'Oh, really? I admire you. My wife – Audrey – was a book-keeper. We did discuss whether she should go all the way and become a chartered accountant but, as you know, it's an enormous amount of work – like doing another degree, really – and the children were small . . .' He smiled sadly. 'To be honest, I don't think she ever had the confidence that she could be that clever. I wish I'd encouraged her more now. Where did you start out?'

As Anthea gave an account of her career path, she thought, Oh dear, here's a man who can only talk about his dead or departed wife. But at least he was someone who knew the difference between a book-keeper and a chartered accountant, and who respected what she'd achieved. He also knew several of the companies she'd worked for, one of which had been involved in the sale of his company. 'Did you ever work with old Michelson? He was a number-cruncher to beat all number-crunchers. And I use that as a term of endearment: I don't think we'd ever have got what we did without him.'

As everyone was getting up and taking plates in, or going out to the garden, Jake joined their group, pulling up an empty chair. He held out his hand to each of them in turn and apologised for not getting the chance to talk to them properly before lunch. George deferred to Anthea. 'After you.'

'I'm Bill's accountant.'

Jake laughed. 'You look far too glamorous to be a boring accountant. Doesn't she, babe?' He addressed this to Jess who, coming up behind him, took his arm possessively.

'I want to show you Sparrow Palace,' she said, ignoring Anthea. She dragged him away.

Rude little brat, though Anthea, flushing as she met George's eye.

'Lovers,' he said with another smile. 'They're in a world of their own at that stage, aren't they? Meanwhile, back to what we were saying, I wondered what you thought about the way the government's handling this latest tax crisis . . .'

He was rescuing her from the snub, Anthea realised, and she rallied, trying to remember what the Chancellor had proposed and why it would be such a disaster. Why should she let that little bitch get to her?

Chapter 13

Paige, heaving a sigh of relief as the front door closed behind Bill on Monday morning, was pleased with how the lunch party had gone. Jake had been a surprise. A bit older than she'd expected. Around forty, she reckoned, so about twelve years older than Jess. A quick intelligence, she decided, and bags of charm. He'd deferred to Bill and George, flattered Anthea, made Sophie sparkle, praised Paige's garden, admired Bella and Lottie's dolls and talked to Harry about business. Jess had sparkled possessively, hanging on Jake's arm.

Paige edged a small slice off the remains of the apple crumble and, nibbling it, cleared away the breakfast plates. Bill had left the newspaper neatly quartered, leaving one particular story face up as if for special attention. It was an account of a woman who had been stabbed to death by her husband for having an affair. Paige read it, then opened the paper up again and put it on the sideboard for Bill's return.

The phone rang. It was George Boxer, thanking her for lunch.

'Oh, it was a pleasure.'

'And I thought your garden was terrific.'

'Thank you.'

He cleared his throat. 'I wondered . . . if you might have a look at mine. Give me some pointers. If you don't mind.'

He'd mentioned this at lunch, but Paige had assumed he was just being kind. 'Oh, well, of course, I'd love to. Whenever. Just say when you're free.'

George was free that week. He suggested she pop round 'during the day because it's too dark in the evening. We could have a spot of lunch.'

Paige didn't mention it to Bill. It was easier not to. She didn't know if Raven Restore & Build was putting in a bid to do the work on Glebe House, but in any case it would be better if she weren't involved.

On Friday morning she walked down the lane to Glebe House and George opened the door. Every time she saw him her fantasies of getting him together with Anthea faded. Unless you liked men who were wider than they were high, he could not be considered attractive. But he seemed kind, he was well-off and several of Paige's divorced friends just wanted to be married again. To anyone, more or less.

But George couldn't stop talking about his wife.

'My wife would have loved this garden,' he said, showing Paige round the overgrown mass of dark shrubs and conifers that were the legacy of Glebe House's previous owner, an elderly lady. 'Audrey always wanted to live in the country, but until I sold my company we couldn't do it. It'd have meant us living apart during the week and neither of us could have stood that.'

'I'm so sorry,' said Paige. 'So sorry that she died. It seems such a waste.'

'Yes.' George put his hands on his hips and contemplated a tangle of brambles and bindweed. 'A waste . . . It's difficult to put your heart into a new place and make it home without someone there beside you.'

Paige wondered why, in that case, he had moved. 'The garden,' she said. 'I think you need to start with clearing it. So that you can see the view behind. The orchards and fields must be stunning at certain times of year. I don't suppose old Mrs Parsons meant the trees and shrubs to grow so high when she put them in.'

'You can see the view from the upstairs windows,' said George. 'I'll show you.'

He led her through the house – a flat-fronted early Gothic gem with arched windows and a castellated ridge to its roof – past faded wallpapers and dusty windows to one of the bedrooms. Paige rubbed a patch in the grimy glass and saw the apple trees, some still dotted with a few crimson apples, undulating in serried rows towards the distance. 'The views are important,' she said, 'for the house and the garden. They'll make it worth living here.'

'What will make it worth living here,' George replied, 'is finding someone to share it with me.'

He was in such pain. Paige put a hand on his arm. 'You will find someone, I'm sure. Once you get to know people.'

He shook his head. 'Audrey did all that. I don't know how to start. And I certainly couldn't give a party on my own. Funny, isn't it? I can run a company, but I can't give a party.'

'You could join things. Like NADFAS.'

He looked doubtful.

'The National Association of Decorative and Fine Arts Societies. They have very good lectures, and lots of women.'

'Right. I'll do that.' He took out a little leather pad and made a note. 'Windows, views, NADFAS,' he wrote down. 'Right. I'll show you the rest of the house and then let's get some lunch.'

He whisked Paige off in his red sports car to the Fishing Smack, a gastropub on the edge of the marshes. 'Everyone talks about this place,' she said in delight. 'But we've never been.'

'Oh I'd have thought you and Bill would know all the best places around here.'

'Well . . .' She didn't want to say that they never ate out. She didn't want George to know that Bill didn't do as well as everyone thought he did. It might deter him from engaging Raven to do his renovation, and with Orchard Park not selling

77

as fast as everyone had hoped the company needed the extra work.

It was exciting, choosing what she wanted to eat, and tasting each separate, exquisite flavour. George ordered her a glass of very good wine, but declined any for himself. 'I'm driving.' She felt guilty.

'Oh, I should have driven.'

'Nonsense. I just don't drink at lunchtimes. I don't like feeling sleepy in the afternoon.'

He told her about his wife's illness and death, and how quick it had been. 'We only had four months after her diagnosis. Only four months to say goodbye after a lifetime together.'

Paige asked about his children. He had a son and a daughter, in their thirties, both happily married. One grandchild, a baby boy. He'd bought Glebe House for him, really, because his daughter needed somewhere in the country to take her family at weekends. In return, Paige told George about Harry and Sophie, and the dear little girls, and how concerned she was about Jess.

'I liked Jake,' she said. 'but something worried me about him. But I'm not a good judge of character, at least that's what Bill always says.'

'I found it very difficult to judge my daughter's boyfriends. I don't think any of us are good about it.'

Paige had longed to have this conversation with Bill, but he'd dismissed her fears, telling her how stupid she was.

'Becky brought some terrible men home before she met Tim,' said George gently. 'They've got to make their own mistakes, these young of ours.'

'But Jess has made so many,' fretted Paige. 'And I feel it's my fault in some way, that I ought to help her, that we've – I've – let her down . . .'

'I'm sure you haven't.' George put his hand over hers, comforting her. 'I'm sure you've been the best mother you could be, in the circumstances.'

'Paige? Paige, is it really you?'

Paige looked up. To see Anthea standing over them, looking astonished. And behind Anthea stood Bill, his colour mottled and red. Although he seemed to be smiling cordially, she knew that look in his eyes. It was sheer, murderous rage.

Chapter 14

Jake dropped Jess at her flat after Sunday lunch.

'Got an early start tomorrow. What are your plans this week?'

Jess was excited. 'Wine labels. For an Italian wine. It's my big chance, the first time I've actually been allowed to develop a label myself. If they like it, it'll mean my getting stuff to actually design, rather than just tidying up everyone else's work. I'm thinking of going big on a classical theme. What are your plans?'

His face went blank. 'I don't know. I'll call you.' There was a flatness to his voice that spelt trouble.

She let herself in, feeling sick to her heart. It was her family that had put Jake off. Or rather her father. His rambling philosophies. His swearing. The way he despised everything to do with the media. She knew she shouldn't have taken Jake down to meet them.

Over the next few days she managed to convince herself that she was imagining it all. That Jake was busy, that he was tied up or out of town on a story. She clicked on to her email every few minutes, and checked her mobile obsessively.

She tried to concentrate on work, re-running different fonts and typefaces across classical columns, then seeing if a bust would work, then trying out a statue of a Roman goddess. The goddess looked good, she thought. And why hadn't Jake called? He always called every day.

By the time he phoned on Wednesday morning Jess was convinced that, for some reason, it was over. That he no longer loved her. 'I've got some tickets for tonight,' he said, as if it was quite normal for them not to speak for three whole days. 'A friend can't use them, so we can have them. And there's a VIP invitation for the party afterwards.'

'What time does the show start? I can't really get away much before seven.'

'Oh, I think that might be a bit late. But don't worry. I can ask someone else.'

'No, no. I'd love to come. I can't stay too late at the party afterwards, though, because I'll need to get in early to finish off these labels.'

In the end the party was an extravaganza of champagne and famous faces, and it went on until two in the morning. Every time she and Jake tried to get away he bumped into someone else he knew, introducing her as his girlfriend. 'Have you met Jess?' he said to one smiling face after another, his arm around her.

'They're all so nice,' she whispered.

'They like you. They wonder where I've been hiding you.'

It was true. Jake and Jess had spent their time in his flat or hers, shutting out the world, reluctant to share each other with anyone else. This must be a new phase in their relationship, she thought, a less intense, more natural, more settled one, where they shared each other's lives and took each other just a little bit for granted.

Jake pulled her towards him. 'We need to go. It's two o'clock, and you've got to be up early.'

Jess drained her glass of champagne. 'Who's that? That girl looking at you over there?'

A tall, thin girl with a black lace camisole and a blunt Louise Brooks bob was staring at them.

'Nobody,' said Jake. 'We need to go. Get your coat.'

They tumbled out of the Roundhouse and almost immediately into a taxi. Jake was good at things like that – taxis always seemed to appear out of nowhere and glide to a halt beside him.

'She looked as if she knew you. That rather creepy woman with the purple fingernails and the short skirt.'

'That's Camilla. My ex-sister in law. She hates me. The ex told them all lies about me. That's how she managed to get so much money off me, by telling lies. I'm public enemy number one.' He turned her face to his, and kissed her thoroughly, unbuttoning her black satin shirt and pinching one nipple gently between his fingers. As electricity shot through her Jess saw the eyes of the taxi driver in rear-view mirror and tried to pull her shirt closed, but Jake's hand was too strong for her.

'Wait,' she whispered.

He withdrew his hand and she buttoned up her shirt, embarrassed.

When she lay beneath him on her bed at home she drew him towards her, but he laid a finger across her lips.

'You made me wait. Now I'm going to make you wait.' He ran his fingers down across her collarbone and wove a pattern slowly from one nipple to another and, with infinite slowness, tracing the finger down towards her belly button, then back up again, then lower the next time. 'If you move a muscle, I'll go back to the beginning and start again,' he whispered. 'You must do exactly what I say. Nothing more, nothing less.'

By the time, damp and gasping, he had finally entered her, and they cried out together, it was half past three and her alarm was set to go off at six.

Two and a half hours' sleep did not improve the wine labels. Tina, her boss, slapped them down on her desk. 'Jess. I don't expect brilliance, not from you anyway, but now that you have been here nearly six months I do expect some level of competence. Did you actually spend any time on these designs or were you too interested in phoning and texting your boyfriend to give them any attention at all?'

Jess was frightened. This was her first proper job, she couldn't blow it now. She stayed at the office that evening, working until ten. Her eyes felt dry and her head ached. She mainlined cola and her heart began to race. She cancelled a drink with two girlfriends and collapsed into her bed at midnight, throbbing with exhaustion, checking her messages desperately for one from Jake.

It came at four o'clock in the morning. Her phone burbled beside her and she grabbed it, terrified of an emergency. 'Hello?'

'I just wanted to say goodnight,' said Jake.

'It's almost morning. Don't you ever sleep?'

He laughed.

'Will I see you tonight?'

'Sure,' he said. 'How did today go?'

'Badly. Tina didn't like the wine labels. But I've got today to sort it out.'

'Don't let her bully you. You have to stand up to the boss class, it's what they respect. You're being walked over. You could get another job.'

When the alarm went at seven-thirty Jess put out a hand and turned it off. Just five seconds more.

In the end she arrived at work half an hour late and Tina didn't like the revised designs. 'This work is just sloppy, Jess.'

Jess burned with fury. She almost told Tina to stuff her job, but knew that her father would be furious and would go on and on about what a failure she was. And the designs she'd worked so hard over looked childish, even to her eyes. 'Uh . . . I thought . . .'

'No, I don't think you did think, did you?' Tina sighed. 'We can't present these to the client.'

'I'll re-do them.' But how? She'd tried so hard the first time. She didn't really understand what Tina wanted.

'No, there's no time. Cathy will have to make the best of

them. Cathy!' Tina flung the designs on to the next desk to Jess's.

'Yes?' Cathy, who looked like a younger version of Tina – blonde hair in a boyish cut, severe glasses and dressed in black from head to toe – began thumbing through them.

'See if you can rescue that lot, will you? In fact, come into my office and we'll go through it all together.' Tina sighed again. 'I don't know what art schools think they're turning out these days. I suppose even Chelsea's having to dumb down – they're terrified of failing anyone in case they lose their funding. It's not your fault, it's the system. It's just not rigorous enough any more.'

Jess, sick to the bone, wondered if Tina was right. 'Can I sit in on your meeting?' She forced the words out. 'It would be helpful to know where I've gone wrong. So I don't make the same mistakes again.'

Tina rolled her eyes. 'We won't have time to stop and explain things. Make yourself useful instead: take over the artworking for the Special Mints account from Cathy.'

Artworking was preparing the work to go to the printers, making sure that the photograph was of a high enough resolution and that all the words were in the right place. And all the pictures were on the right pages, and that she'd replaced the dummy copy with what the client really wanted to say. Doing someone else's artworking was humiliating, even if she was a junior designer.

'Oh, and I've got some artworking too. You can get on with that when you've finished Cathy's,' added Tina as the door closed on her.

Jess had always known she was worth nothing. She was not as pretty as Sophie, who had claimed all the prizes, all through their lives. She had clawed her way to art school, always believing that she was going to fail but eventually buoyed up by her tutors' faith in her. Now, however hard she listened or tried, she couldn't understand what Tina wanted of her.

It was obvious she was no good in the world of work. Jess was terrified. If she lost this job, who would employ her? She would have to go back to waitressing again. Unless she and Jake were a couple. They could have babies. A son, who would have the Raven name – because she and Jake were too unconventional to marry – and then her father would be happy.

Jake picked her up from work that evening. 'So. Did they love the wine labels?'

Jess shook her head, her eyes filling with tears she was determined he would not see.

But he twisted her face towards him and kissed them off her cheeks. 'My poor little Jessie. Tell you what: tomorrow we go shopping. My treat.'

'But you don't have any money,' sniffed Jess. 'Cassie took it all. I'm not like her.'

'I can afford to treat you. Just this once.' He put the car into drive. 'We will give you a makeover.'

'What sort of a makeover?'

'We're going to make you look like a woman. That gamine figure of yours would look great in a frock.'

'Frock!' shrieked Jess. 'Who wears *frocks* these days? I haven't worn one since Mum stopped dressing us both in smocked numbers when I was about four. Anyway, you haven't got enough money to spend it on me.'

He looked at her tenderly. 'Most women wouldn't think about that. They'd want someone to spend money on them.'

'I'm not most women.'

'No,' he said. 'That's what's so delicious about you.'

'Well, you're not buying me a dress.'

He grinned. 'Oh yes I am. And eyeliner, I think. The ex used to go to a great make-up artist. I'll book you in there.'

Jess slid down in her seat. 'I am not, repeat not, wearing eyeliner. That's the sort of thing Sophie would make me do.'

'Your sister's got taste. You would look like Audrey Hepburn with eyeliner and a black satin dress.'

'Audrey Hepburn was dark. I'm light mouse, in case you hadn't noticed.'

'Well, my darling light mouse, we can always change that.' His eyes slid towards hers in amusement. 'Perhaps a trip to the salon as well. Hmm?'

'Don't you dare, Jake Wild. Don't you dare. That's all I have to say.'

'Is that a challenge, Jessica Raven? Is that a challenge? Because if so, you have one thing to learn about me.'

'What's that?'

'I never give up. And your dear father has brought you up as his non-existent son for far too long. I am going to turn you into the girl you always were.'

'I suppose you're going to say that that's because I'm worth it,' she tried to joke.

'You will be,' he said. 'By the time I've finished with you.'

Finished with you. The words echoed in Jess's head.

Chapter 15

Sophie wondered why she felt like dancing. It was like waking up after a long sleep, to find that the old Sophie, the one she'd buried in wifedom and motherhood, was still there.

'You're in a good mood,' said Harry, closing the door on Lottie and Bella after reading them a story.

'Am I?' Sophie had been singing Summer to sleep in her little box room. 'I was just wondering what we ought to do for a holiday this year. Do you think Jess and Jake might like to join us in a villa in Tuscany?'

Harry laughed as they went downstairs to their basement kitchen to make supper. 'A newly in love couple share a holiday with three screaming tinies? They'd have to be saints. And I think a Tuscany villa might be a bit over our budget this year.'

'Were you thinking a fortnight at The Rowans instead? I don't mind, I always like going home and it would be cheap.' Sophie pulled a salad out of the fridge and began to wash it.

'If your mother wouldn't mind babysitting for a couple of days, maybe you and I could nip across the Channel and have a break in France?' suggested Harry, setting out plates and knives on the table

'That's a good idea. Maybe Jess and Jake would like to join us on that instead? A foursome.'

Harry was about to reply, when the door above them

opened. 'Mummy!' shouted Bella. 'I've got to have a bear costume for tomorrow at school.'

It took Sophie a couple of hours to rustle up a bear costume out of an old fake-fur gilet and a furry cushion left over from a shoot. 'There!' said Sophie, exhausted. 'She'll be the best bear in the class.'

'It's always a competition for you, isn't it?' asked Harry.

'Is that meant to be a criticism?'

'No, not at all. But you can't be everything to everyone, you'll drive yourself mad. You've barely eaten your supper because you're so determined that Bella will be the best bear. You'll be exhausted tomorrow.

'I had a huge lunch,' Sophie lied. 'I wasn't hungry. Anyway, it's only natural, wanting the best for your children.'

'I've always wondered what drove you,' said Harry, switching on the news. 'You never stop. But sometimes I think it's all about your father. He's always told you women were useless and you're running yourself ragged to prove him wrong.'

Sophie twitched at the implied criticism, but decided to ignore his remarks for three reasons. First, she was always stopping. She felt guilty about every extra moment she spent lying in the bath or listening to the car radio when she should have been doing something with the girls, tidying the house or seeing an art director about more work. She knew she never quite tried hard enough. Never. Secondly, she thought Harry was perhaps a bit too laid back. And thirdly, well, anyway the whole thing was ridiculous. Of course every mother wanted her daughter to be the best bear in class. Harry didn't like her father and that was all there was to it.

That night, though, she dreamt she was running and running, away from shadowy figures who were accusing her of something. She stayed just ahead of their hands, which clutched at her like the tendrils of some malevolent weed, ready to pull her down. Finally she managed to lift herself up and fly through the air, away from the slippery tips of the greedy, evil fingers that brushed against her toes and made her freeze. They almost got her but with a magnificent effort she flew above them, straining every muscle. Then she felt one of the hands clamp on to her shoulder and she woke up screaming.

'Sophie! Sophie!' It was Harry shaking her awake.

'Sorry. It was a bad dream.' She was still cold with terror.

He drew her to him. 'What was it about?'

'Nothing important. Nothing. Just running. I'm fine now.'

The following day she found that getting the girls off to school, playgroup and the childminder with all the right clothes and things in their satchels was as physically demanding as two hours in the gym, but once she had finally, reluctantly, shut the childminder's front door on a sobbing Summer she went home and poured herself a strong black coffee. With her assistant, a photography student called Bruno, she packed the car: three cameras, the laptop, lights, plus a small bag of gardening props – a traditional metal watering can, some Victorian garden tools and half a dozen old terracotta pots. Although Caroline, who was styling the shoot, brought most of the props, there would always be something extra she needed to make that final difference.

It took a while to get the shoot going. Various marketing managers, brand managers and directors all had to be introduced, and the concept discussed yet again. Then three of them – all brand managers for different divisions of Souper Soup – withdrew to a row of chairs at the side of the cavernous studio and spent the rest of the day slumped over their BlackBerries, discussing their hangovers. Sophie had already heard quite enough about hangovers from Bruno and wished they would all shut up and go away. She preferred to work on her own, without having people who knew nothing about photographs peering at the image on her laptop and occasionally saying things like 'The new Souper Soup brand is contemporary. Edgy. But we don't want anything too modern. The Souper Soup customer won't like it.' Occasionally they criticised the picture.

'What's that crappy old watering can doing there?'

Sophie asked Bruno to remove the watering can and looked at the scene again. It seemed flatter without it.

The door opened at half past twelve and Jake walked in with a girl in a black suit. Sophie's heart dropped a thousand feet into a chasm that had suddenly opened up at her feet.

'Hi, I'm Fenella. The PR for Souper Soup. We've got a journalist who's tracking the way we're turning the brand around. Derek Lawson said he should get some background colour, if Sophie's happy for him to be on the shoot.'

Sophie tried not to blush. 'It's fine,' she said to her camera lens, hiding her face in examining the composition of soup, a bunch of carrots and a trowel sitting on the white background. Derek Lawson's word was law at Souper Soup.

But it was impossible to concentrate. 'I think we'll break for lunch now,' she said half an hour later.

'Perhaps you could talk me through what you're doing?' suggested Jake. 'Then I could be out of your hair in an hour or so.'

Bruno came back from the sandwich shop with a pile of sandwiches, salads, fruit juices and fizzy waters, but the three brand managers and Fenella went off to find a pub, leaving Sophie, Caroline, Bruno and Jake.

Caroline picked at a salad and frowned at the props. 'Those flowers are looking a bit dead, Bruno, I think we ought to find a florist and see if we can get some more.'

Bruno finished his sandwich and sighed. 'We'll be back soon.'

'So,' Jake pulled out a notebook as they perched on two chairs at a small table. 'Why did Souper Soup choose you to photograph their new brand?'

Sophie hated talking about her work. 'I suppose they liked my portfolio.'

He tried to get her to explain what she was doing, but all she could say was that she thought it was about creating an illusion, making something look antique or traditional when it wasn't.

'Like making yourself look happy when you aren't?' said Jake, closing his notebook.

Sophie met his gaze warily, but once their eyes locked she felt that he was a friend. Someone she could trust. She didn't have to worry about anything because he was Jess's boyfriend. 'I . . . am happy. Or I was happy. I don't know. I was just angry on Sunday because . . .' She stopped. 'I don't want to talk about it.'

'You can talk to me.'

He was right. She knew she could talk to him. That he would listen but not judge, and not be angry with her the way Harry or her father was.

'I don't need to talk.'

'Yes, you do.' He waited.

Sophie tried to change the subject. 'How's Jess?'

'Working hard. They treat her badly at that place. But she's OK.'

'She's very vulnerable. Dad's always been vile to her.'

'I know,' he said gently. 'I'll look after her. Make sure she doesn't get into any more trouble.'

Sophie was relieved. 'Dad's always tried to turn her into the son he never had, then has been furious when it didn't work. As it couldn't. Poor Jess.'

'Yes, I thought something of the kind had happened. I liked your Dad, though, he seemed like one of the good guys.'

Sophie grimaced. 'I think he probably is. Underneath the grouchiness. But I should think everyone is grouchy sometimes.'

Jake smiled at her, and the smile curled all the way under his cheekbones again.

'Do you and Jess want to come over some time?' offered Sophie.

He inclined his head. 'That would be great. So, now that we're friends, are you going to tell me why you were upset on Sunday?'

'Yes,' said Sophie. 'But it was just a . . . well, Harry was being like my father when he's in one of his moods, trying to turn everything I said around, making it all my fault, not telling me the full story, telling me he hadn't done something when he had. Dealing with my father is like trying to fight fog. You can't see clearly, and nothing's ever exactly what he claims it is. You can never accuse him of lying because he twists things, but that's what it is.'

'Some men are like that. Some women like it that way.'

'Well I don't. I get enough of it all from my father,' she said bitterly. 'I love Dad to bits, and I've never bought Jess's view that he's bad, but I've always promised myself that I'd never fall for anyone like him. I'm not a doormat like my mother.'

'Perhaps, deep down, she likes being a doormat.'

Sophie had always suspected something of the kind. She looked Jake directly in the eye. 'The thing is, I was so sure that Harry was completely unlike him. But then Dad didn't used to be like he is now. He was lovely when we were little; it's happened over the years because it's really tough managing a business on your own. And now Harry wants to do exactly the same. That's really why I was angry. I don't want history to repeat itself.'

'I see,' said Jake.

Sophie wrenched herself away, gathering up the uneaten remains of the sandwiches. 'I must get back to work. And this evening I'll call Jess to fix up a date for you both to come over.'

'I'll look forward to it.'

Sophie bundled the sandwich remains into the bin and walked over to where Caroline and Bruno had begun to arrange soup packets and tomatoes against the white background again.

Jake followed her. 'See you soon, then.' She could feel the warmth of his breath by her ear. He grasped her arm and she could feel the strength of his hand, and the sandpaper texture of his skin against hers as he kissed her on each cheek. She could feel the roughness of his skin brushing against hers.

'Oh Jake,' she said. 'I've only talked about this to Jess. No one else.' She didn't count Caroline, because she was nothing to do with her family. 'I haven't even told Harry,' she added. 'So . . .'

'I'm flattered,' he said. 'It will be our secret. And thank you.' He spoke the last few words loudly enough for Bruno and Caroline to hear. 'That was fascinating. Here's my card if you think of anything else. Call me any time.'

And before she could say anything else he left the studio, colliding with the three brand managers and Derek Lawson.

'When's the article out?' shouted one of them.

'Soon,' called Jake. 'I'll let Fenella know.'

'He was rather attractive,' said Caroline.

'Do you think so?' replied Sophie. 'I hadn't noticed. But he'll certainly cheer up family gatherings in the future. He's good with my father, which Harry isn't.'

For the rest of the afternoon, because they were in the presence of Derek Lawson, the three brand managers tried to look as if they were contributing.

'We need to reflect the traditional values of Souper Soup,' said one. 'I think we need something antique in the mix.'

'What about the old-fashioned watering can?' asked another brightly. The watering can was brought out again.

In the end it was difficult to make a packet of soup look contemporary, traditional, edgy (but not too modern), classy but good value, luxurious but not too expensive, ground-breaking and appealing to the young without alienating its core older market. Sophie thought, as she prepared to leave the studio at half past eight that evening, she might have got as close as anyone could. She was so lucky, she reflected, as she packed up her equipment, that her work was so absorbing.

She was so lucky, she reminded herself again, as she phoned Harry to say that she'd be late and to check that the girls were

93

fine. She was lucky, lucky, lucky. A nice house, a great life. Three beautiful daughters. All well and happy. A husband she loved.

But, after hesitating several times, she picked up the business card and slipped it into her bag.

Chapter 16

Anthea enjoyed her lunch at the Fishing Smack. Especially when they tripped over Paige Raven lunching with George Boxer. That had been such a stroke of good fortune.

She was a little concerned at how furious Bill was. As she buckled herself into the passenger seat of his car she flashed him a glance out of the corner of her eye. He was angrier than she had ever known him. That indicated that he was fonder of Paige than he'd led her to believe. Unless it was just pride.

'I'd no idea that you and Paige knew George Boxer so well,' she said lightly. 'Presumably you knew his wife? It's so sad, isn't it? Did he move down here to be close to you two?'

Bill grunted. 'Never met the bloke till the other day.'

'Well I think you're wonderful. To be so relaxed about Paige comforting him.'

'She's a slut,' he said, going dangerously fast round a corner. 'She was a slut when I married her and she hasn't changed.'

That was a shock. Paige always seemed so well brought up.

'Oh, well . . .' Anthea hoped they would survive this car journey, as Bill accelerated down a short straight stretch of lane. 'Maybe she's just bored. You know, people like her, whose children have grown up and who don't have to work, often don't have enough to do.' She gripped the car door as Bill swung round the next corner too fast and the back of the car slewed round and almost hit a hedge.

'Anthea, you should be careful about how friendly you get with that bitch. I know she seemed nice when she invited you to lunch, but she was obviously pretending because she's getting suspicious about us. She wants to lull you into a false sense of security so you'll let something slip.'

That was also Anthea's intention. She nodded.

'Anthea, you and I will be together one day, but we can't move too soon. The bitch will get some fancy lawyer and take the lot, so you and I will be left with virtually nothing except what we both earn. And I'll be making hefty maintenance payments, unless we're very clever.'

Anthea was entranced. Bill had referred to the future only in the vaguest way before, but now he was speaking of it as if it were all settled. Except for Paige's greed, of course. That sort of a woman always thought she was entitled to everything. She could see his point. They needed to stay on top of the timing. And it was probably time to explain that to Bill:

'If you were thinking of divorcing her, financially, the sooner the better, while she can still earn.'

Bill turned into the office parking space a little too sharply but came safely, if suddenly, to a stop. Anthea heaved a sigh of relief.

'Hmm,' he said, switching the ignition and carefully clearing the car of a few invisible specks of dirt and a ticket for a car park. 'Good point. Very good point.'

Back at the office they received the news that an offer on 4 Orchard Park had just fallen through. There were four semi-detached cottages on the development and three had been under offer. Now there were only two. Bill swore under his breath. 'That's my fucking profit for the year down the pan. Jesus, how much more can go wrong today?'

'It's not necessarily a bad thing,' said Anthea, wondering why people who were really quite rich always worried about money so much. 'As I told another client, who's divorcing his wife, you don't want to be making too much profit if your marriage is in trouble.'

She saw the cogs in his brain begin to move. Bill sat down behind his desk and contemplated her. 'Tell me more.'

'Well, obviously it's not relevant to you and Paige just yet, of course not . . .'

'But if it was?'

'Well, it's just that it's better for you to divorce in a bad year rather than a good one. In fact, you need two or three bad years ideally.'

'I think we could manage that. The way things are going.' He thought for a moment. 'I can tell you, I'm not giving half of my hard-earned money away to some lazy cow who's done nothing to earn it. It's in all the papers these days, women getting huge payouts from men. It's not fair and it's not right.'

'It certainly isn't,' agreed Anthea. 'But, as I said to my other client, there are ways and ways . . . of making sure that years aren't good. If you haven't got any pesky shareholders or partners to ask difficult questions, that is.' She leant forward. 'A man with a small business, a one-man band, is in the best possible situation as far as divorce is concerned.'

'I'd better be,' Bill drummed his hand on the desk. 'I can tell you, I'd rather knock her off and bury her under someone's patio then let her have a penny.'

Anthea, momentarily chilled, reminded herself that this was the sort of joke people often made. She allowed a herself a small laugh in deference to it. 'You won't need to. With an employee everything is done by PAYE, so it's easier to see how much money there is and where it comes from. And to work out if any has been stashed away. And when it comes to the very rich, forensic accountants get employed. But with someone like you, well, who's to say what you own and where you put your money?'

She saw the shutters come down behind his eyes. He was thinking.

'Would you like a drink at my place after work? You've had a nasty shock, and if you want a friend to talk it through with . . .' She placed a hand on his arm. 'Paige has behaved appallingly. You don't deserve it. Everything you've done has been for that family, and Paige has no idea how hard you've worked.'

Bill lifted her hand to his lips and kissed it. 'Bless you. I don't know where I'd be without you. And a drink later would be very nice. I've got to be on site this afternoon, but I'll see you about six?'

Anthea picked up some files and left the offices of Raven Build & Restore, laughing to herself. How could Paige have been so stupid? To lunch with her lover publicly? But she hoped this little episode wouldn't propel Bill into trying to mend their marriage out of jealousy.

The Bill that arrived at her flat that evening didn't seem like a man who wanted to mend his marriage. Over the afternoon, his anger had clearly built up. 'She's a fucking bitch,' he said over and over again. 'A fucking bitch who's taking me for a ride.'

'You're so right,' soothed Anthea, pouring him a drink. 'You shouldn't be treated like this. Paige is being disloyal. What will everyone think?'

'They'll think she's a fucking bitch,' repeated Bill. 'All the people around here are my friends. They respect me. She's just a parasite.'

And on it went. Over and over again.

'By the way,' added Anthea, when she had heard enough anti-Paige ranting to make her feel confident enough to ask the question. 'Paige seems to think you've remortgaged The Rowans to fund Orchard Park.'

He laughed. 'She's so stupid. I always tell her I've remort-gaged. It keeps her on her toes. Stops her wasting money.'

Anthea's eyes met his. She wasn't quite sure if he was telling the truth, and lying to your wife might be necessary to stop her spending money but lying to your accountant was . . . well, that seemed an awful lot worse. Dishonest, really. Her certitude that he was right wavered for a second, and then she remembered that Paige herself was unlikely to bother much about honesty once she faced the divorce courts. People like her showed their true colours when they were faced with losing some of what they took for granted.

'On the other hand,' she suggested, gently edging her scheme along, 'if you are . . . er . . . contemplating any major changes in your life, it's not such a bad idea. To free up capital.'

He studied her carefully. 'If the bitch was to leave me for her lover, what would happen to The Rowans?'

'Either Paige or you could remain in it as the marital home, with some financial agreement that effectively bought the other out. Or perhaps, as the wife, she might be awarded The Rowans outright. Plus maintenance. Wives often get hotshot lawyers who screw men into the ground. You'd finish up in a flat somewhere giving her half your income every year.'

She saw his face darken. 'That will never happen,' he said. 'I'll make sure of that. Whatever I have to do.'

'Well, if your bank statements showed you couldn't afford to buy Paige out or give her the house outright it would have to be sold and, after the mortgage was paid off, what remains would be divided between you as part of the settlement.'

'Oh, I couldn't possibly buy her out. With the business the way it is it would be quite unaffordable. I'd be bankrupted.'

'As your accountant,' said Anthea with a smile, 'I would have to agree with you.'

'So if I haven't got a mortgage on The Rowans now, I could still take one out?'

'You might need to. With Orchard Park going the way it is. You'll need more capital to plough into the business. Just to keep it going. Paige would have to engage some very clever forensic accountants to find out where the money had gone.'

'She wouldn't know what a forensic accountant was if it bit her on the ankle.'

'Well, they don't bite, but they are very expensive,' said Anthea. 'Non-earning women often don't have access to much cash when they're actually going through the divorce – and you need to be quite careful that they don't, by the way. You give them just enough to keep everything ticking over and so they don't apply for any emergency injunctions. But not enough to have them paying someone hundreds of pounds an hour to look for bank accounts that may not exist.'

Bill looked at her very thoughtfully. 'You are a clever girl, Anthea. If only I'd been married to someone as bright as you, then I wouldn't be in this situation . . .'

But Paige wasn't as bright as Anthea. She was too busy thinking about her garden.

Big mistake, Paige, thought Anthea, smiling again as Bill kissed her goodbye and got into his car. 'I'm ready to face her,' he said. 'She needn't think she can get away with this.'

'She can't,' agreed Anthea. 'You're so right.'

Mind you, Paige, she thought as she cleansed her face of make-up before bed, I might be saving your life. Saving you from being buried under the paving.

Just joking.

Anthea switched off the light. She was going to work very hard to find out everything Bill needed to know about getting rid of Paige without paying her too much money. She should have what was fair after a long marriage, of course.

But women shouldn't think that marrying a rich man was the passport to a life of leisure.

Chapter 17

Paige, letting herself into The Rowans with a shaking hand, reflected that the few minutes that passed in the Fishing Smack when Bill and Anthea hovered over the table would have appeared entirely cordial to anyone watching. Bill had slapped George on the back. 'I hope you're looking after my wife,' he'd joked. And Anthea thanked Paige for a delicious lunch on Sunday and complimented her on her sweater. 'Is it new?'

Paige's heart was beating in double time. Someone had once told her that if you lived for a long time in an earthquake zone and had regularly experienced earth tremors, then you could sense the juddering of a major earthquake a few seconds before newcomers realised anything was wrong. She could feel everything cracking apart under her feet, but no one else seemed to have noticed. 'Oh, this old thing,' she said gaily of her sweater. 'I've had it for ages.'

'That's always what we women say when they've bought something new, isn't it?' laughed Anthea. 'But never mind, it suits you.'

Paige could barely finish her creamy rhubarb fool after Anthea and Bill left.

'Are you all right?' asked George. 'Will that be embarrassing for you? Having lunch with me?'

'No, of course not. Everything's fine.' She kept an eye out of the window, and saw Bill's sports car drive off. 'But I need to get back. I've got . . . a plumber coming. To fix the . . . er . . . shower.' She looked at her watch. 'This has been lovely. Thank you.'

She almost expected Bill to be waiting for her when she got home, but the house was silent and empty. She rehearsed what she was going to say. She would just tell him the truth, calmly. She almost rang him to get it over with, but she knew it irritated him to be called at work. She reminded herself that he had never been violent towards her. In fact, he often spoke disparagingly of 'wife beaters' when reading out stories from the newspapers to her. But violence was in the air between them like a summer heat haze at the dawn of an August day. You didn't know how hot it might get later on.

Paige tidied the house. The sun went down at around six, and wind rustled through the bushes in the garden, whispering that Bill would be home soon, and that he would be very, very angry. At six-thirty, she started to prepare the supper, dropping and breaking a china dish. She swept it up with shaking hands. Tried to concentrate on the newspaper. The words made no sense. At seven-thirty he still wasn't home.

Nothing unusual there. He was often late back. She toured the house to see if there was anything out of place, anything that could fuel his fury further. Perhaps she'd better put some washing through in case there was a shirt he needed or he'd run out of socks.

The washing took an hour and five minutes to go through its cycle and Bill still wasn't home when she began to hang the damp clothes in the utility room. She told herself that she had done nothing wrong, that it had only been a lunch with a neighbour. But she knew that look in his eyes. She'd had thirty years of interpreting his expressions.

At nine o'clock she opened the newspaper again and saw the news item Bill had been reading on page five, the one about the woman who had been stabbed by her husband with one of her own kitchen knives, and her heart turned cold. Should she put the knife block, with its smart, sharp Global knives, away somewhere?

Don't be ridiculous. But when he wasn't back by quarter to ten she put the knife block in a cupboard. Perhaps she should go to bed. Or phone him. She took the knife block out and put it back where it usually sat, on the granite work surface beside the kettle.

At a quarter past ten she heard the whir of the gates at the end of the drive and the crunch of a car on the gravel. In a panic, she put the knife block back into the cupboard again. Bill seemed to spend ages fiddling about in the garage, and by the time he walked into the kitchen she could scarcely breathe.

'Would you like some supper or have you eaten already?' she asked, trying not to sound frightened.

'You whore. You sleazy, lying, disloyal little whore.' He lumbered into the kitchen like an angry bear.

'It was only lunch. We didn't do anything, I promise.' Her voice came out in a squeak.

'I saw that man holding hands with you. As if he had done so many times before. Perhaps he even bought that house here to be close to you. Do not ask me to doubt the evidence of my own eyes. And in a pub so close to home, where all our friends go – how could you be such a slut?'

Paige took a deep breath. 'You were with Anthea. Surely friends would wonder about that too.'

'How dare you mention Anthea. She's my accountant. Of course I have lunch with her. I'm so fucking busy that I have to work over lunch, and I had to ask Anthea to work over lunch too. It's only fair that I take her out.' He poured himself a drink. 'You think you can get out of this by blaming Anthea. Well, you can't. I want to hear it all, now. The whole story.'

'George rang me up to say thank you for lunch, and he asked me for my advice on the garden. I said I'd be glad to, so he suggested I come over and see it. Then he took me out to lunch to say thank you. That's all it was. One meeting. Entirely innocent. He put his hand on mine, very briefly, to comfort me for worrying about Jess.'

'If it was so entirely innocent,' roared Bill, 'then why the fuck didn't you tell me about it first?'

This was difficult to answer. 'I . . . er . . . forgot. Because it was nothing.'

'Because it was nothing,' he imitated her squeaky voice. 'Because it was fucking nothing? Going to the Fishing Smack, the smartest pub for miles around, is nothing for you, is it? Well in that case I'd like to know who you've been going there with, because it isn't something I can afford often, I can tell you.'

'I've never been there before. And I didn't know we were going there then.'

'Really? How convenient. He just happened to take you?'

Paige swallowed. 'Yes. I've never had an affair and I never would.'

'Anyone seeing you and George in that pub would find that very hard to believe. Married women do not usually have lunch with men on their own. In new clothes they'd bought specially for the occasion. How do you think I felt? In front of Anthea?'

'I didn't buy new clothes especially for the occasion. I've had that sweater for months.'

'Really? In that case, why haven't I seen it?'

'You have, but you probably never noticed it.'

'So it's all my fault, is it? I don't take enough notice of my wife, so that justifies her catting around with every man in the neighbourhood?'

'It wasn't every man, it was only George.'

'So you admit it? You were catting around with George Boxer.'

'No! That's not what I meant. I meant—'

He turned away. 'Spare me the lies. Just spare me. If you've got a shred of decency you'll never speak to that man again.'

'I won't,' said Paige, trembling. 'I promise.'

'You'd better. Because if I find you've so much as been saying "Hello, what a nice day", you are out of here. Out on your arse without a penny. You needn't think you can claim this house, you know, it's in my name and paid for with my hard-earned money. If you go you take nothing with you. You can't claim maintenance because the children are grown up. Lover boy will have to look after you and I don't know how keen he'll be when he finds out that you have nothing and earn nothing. That you do nothing. Except spend, spend, spend.'

Paige didn't reply. She was too frightened.

'Is there any fucking supper? I've been working my arse off all day, the least you can do, between trysts with your lovers, is make some supper.'

'It's here,' she said. 'Lasagne. And salad. And an apple.'

Bill looked round the kitchen. 'Where's the knife block?' He could be surprisingly observant at times.

She jumped. 'I . . . er . . . don't know. I was dusting. W-w-wiping down the surfaces. I must have put it somewhere. To get it out of the way.'

He walked round the kitchen table towards her and wrenched open the cupboard door. She shrank back. 'Ah,' he said. 'Here. A knife block, put in a cupboard. This is some pretence, I suppose, that you have a violent husband. "My lord, after he found me having lunch with my lover, I was so frightened I had to hide the knives away." You're planning on saying that in the divorce court? Yes?' He picked a knife out of the block and held it up to her face, just below her right eye. 'Tell me that that's what you were planning.'

She could smell the wine on his breath and see his red eyes close to hers. If she said she wasn't planning anything like that at all would he be even angrier? Or should she agree with him to keep him calm, the way she often did?

'I know you've never been violent,' she whispered. 'You've never hurt me.'

He laid the knife against her cheek. 'A knife doesn't hurt when it goes in, apparently. It just slips into the skin. The pain comes when you pull it out again. That's what someone told me once. Then it goes on hurting, more and more. Sometimes you can feel a knife wound forty years later.'

Paige held her breath.

'But perhaps you like it rough. Perhaps that's what you find attractive about Mr George Boxer? Is it? Do you want to be hurt?'

'No.'

It was the right reply. He threw the knife down on the floor. She bent down to pick up the knife and almost thought, for a moment, that he was going to kick her, so she straightened up as quickly as she could. Pretending that she had to wash the knife after it had been on the floor gave her the opportunity to hang on to it for a little longer but eventually, under his scornful gaze, she returned it to the knife block and put the whole thing back where it belonged.

'I'll be sleeping in the spare room tonight,' he said, taking the plate of lasagne into the study. 'I don't want to be near you when you've had sex with another man.'

'I haven't,' she said. 'I really haven't.'

'And Paige, I think we'd better keep this sordid little affair between us. I don't think you want the whole village gossiping about what you get up to. Assuming, that is, that they don't know what a slag you are already.'

'Nobody knows anything,' said Paige, wishing, later, that she'd had the strength to add 'there's nothing to know'.

'Good,' said Bill. 'Let's keep it that way. And we don't want the girls to hear that their mother's been whoring around, do we?'

'I haven't,' she whispered. But she made up the bed in the spare room for him, and when she went back to their own room and got into bed she hitched a chair under the door, hoping he wouldn't try to get in.

Chapter 18

Sophie was happy. She felt like her old self, who she had been before she became a mother. The lightness in her head and the way food seemed suddenly so unappetising, her sudden desire to dance when music came on the radio . . . well, it was all about the children growing up, not being babies any more. And Sophie remembering who she was and what life was like. She was alive again. She began to burn with creativity and to see photographs everywhere, in the diamonds scattered across the pavement when a car window was broken, in the shaft of sunlight across the graffitied fence, in an old shop hoarding with its peeling posters and flaking paint.

Every day Harry went out to work early and returned late, unless Sophie herself was working and asked him to pick the girls up. They took it in turns to cook: Harry was an easy, relaxed cook, with stir fries his speciality, and they ate supper together watching the television. He no longer mentioned setting up on his own. He was dear old Harry. Reliable. Nice. Helpful. Friendly. Not like Bill in any way. Sophie always felt she didn't have to try too hard when he was around. She could relax.

It flashed into her mind that she didn't want to relax. She might fall apart.

She phoned her mother twice a week. Paige seemed twittery

and Sophie repressed a sigh of impatience. If only Paige would open her eyes to what Bill was up to, then she wouldn't have to do it for her. 'How's Dad?' she asked.

'Oh, um, er . . . working hard, you know.'

'Is he drinking?'

'Well, a bit. No more than usual.'

They wound their way through various issues in the garden, and in Martyr's Forstal, and what Bella, Lottie and Summer had done that week. 'I liked Jake,' said Sophie.

'Yes, I thought he was nice too,' replied Paige.

At the end of the conversation Sophie worried that she didn't have a very close relationship with her mother. 'It's sort of hard to get through to her,' she complained to Harry over supper.

'Maybe she's trying to protect you from whatever's going on in her life.'

'There isn't much going on in her life, that's the point,' Sophie snapped back. A few minutes later she felt guilty. 'Do you really think Dad might have a problem with alcohol?' It was the closest she could get to saying sorry about arguing with him about her father.

Harry chewed as he thought about it. 'I think it's possible.' His wary admission, a retreat from an outright statement of fact, was his way of saying sorry. They looked at each other with tenderness. 'You could check it out, perhaps,' Harry added. 'Or would you like me to?'

Sophie shook her head. 'No, you're busy.' Later that evening, she looked up Alcoholics Anonymous on the internet and wondered if perhaps Harry was right, and, if so, whether she could persuade Bill to stop drinking. If anyone could it would be her. Or perhaps the family should get together and tackle her father jointly. Her hand hovered over the phone. She called Jess.

Jess's voice was thick with sobbing.

'Jess! What's up?'

Jess blew her nose. 'It's Jake, I haven't heard from him for ten days. He always calls twice a day.'

'Perhaps he's busy.'

'There's no way you can be so busy that you can't text. And we . . . had a row.'

'I'll be straight over.' Sophie put down the phone. 'Harry, you can babysit the girls, can't you? I'm worried about Jess and I think I'll drive over there to check she's OK.'

'All the way from Clapham to Peckham? This evening?' Harry looked at her long and hard, as if he thought she was concealing something from him.

She dropped her eyes. 'Please, Harry. She's my sister. She's distraught. Jake hasn't called and she's usually so take it or leave it about men.'

'Ah,' said Harry. 'Of course. Fine. Off you go. I don't mind. As long as you do really think it's worth it.'

Sophie drove to Jess's flat and banged on the door, peering through the letterbox when it wasn't answered. There were lights on and Sophie could hear Jess's favourite Cuban music playing.

She knocked as hard as she could and rang the bell again, then pressed her face to the window, shading her eyes with her hands against the glass. 'Jess! Jess! I know you're there.'

Perhaps Jess was drunk. Maybe Jake was on the phone and it had all just been a scare. 'Jess! It's Sophie. Let me in.' She tried to get her hand through the letterbox to slip the catch but it wasn't possible. She phoned Jess's mobile and her land line, then rang the doorbell again.

Suddenly the door opened and Jess stood there in pyjamas, her hair a tangle of honey, blonde and toffee tones. 'Sorry.'

'You weren't answering. I was worried. And have you gone blonde?'

Jess seemed crumpled, as if she'd just fallen out of bed. 'Come in.'

'How are you?' asked Sophie, casting her eyes round the flat for empty bottles and glasses. There was a strong smell of cigarette smoke and incense, but it was otherwise tidy. Jess had a restrained but bohemian style. Like Paige, she could find an old bucket in a junk shop, fill it with flowers and make it look as desirable as a designer vase. 'Now tell me. Start at the beginning.'

Jess collapsed into a surprisingly small heap on the sofa. 'He bought me clothes. We had a makeover weekend – that's what he called it. He threw away my combats and three of my pairs of jeans, and . . .' – she blew her nose again – '. . . booked me in at a hairdresser: that's where the blonde has come from.'

'It really suits you,' said Sophie. 'Or it would if it was brushed. Go on.'

'Then we went to a make-up artist and he took me to a department store with a personal shopper.' She stopped, her eyes far away. 'I guess Dad was right, men don't like girls who dress like navvies.'

'No, Jake fell for you while you were dressed like a, er . . . well, the way you dressed. He must have liked it.'

'He bought me these shoes.' Jess handed them over.

'Wow, Jess, some girls would kill for these.'

'I wouldn't. I don't like heels. They hurt.'

'Well, they might hurt a bit, but *il faut souffrir pour être belle*.'

'What?'

'One must suffer to be beautiful. These shoes must make your legs look endless.'

'I told Jake I couldn't wear them and he just walked off. Without saying when he'd see me again or anything. That was ten days ago.'

'OK. Now did he actually "just walk off" or did he say something?'

Jess sniffed. 'He said he had to go and would call me soon. But his eyes were all dead, you know, how people's eyes go.'

'It still doesn't sound too bad to me. It is a bit long to be out of touch, but he may have an explanation. A family crisis or something.'

'He doesn't get on with his family.' Jess blew her nose. 'Could you call him? I just want to find out if I've done something wrong.'

'Well no, I don't think I could do that, it would be . . . but . . . how's the job?'

'Coffee? The job's fine. Or do you want a drink?'

'Jess, are you drinking too much?'

'Why are you worrying about drink?'

'Harry thought that maybe the reason why the Orchard Park project isn't doing as well as it ought to be is because Dad's on autopilot and not thinking properly. Because he's drinking too much. So I went on to the AA website and . . .'

'I think Britain must be getting like California. There you get called an addict if you have more than teaspoonful of sherry. Sophie, I don't drink any more than any other single woman of my age. Is this your latest thing? That we're all alkies? Just because Harry doesn't like Dad? And you won't stop campaigning until we've all gone into rehab?'

Sophie couldn't help smiling. Jess knew her so well. 'I'd like that coffee.'

Jess made them both coffee while Sophie edged round the room to see if there were bottles anywhere, surreptitiously moving Jess's huge ottoman cushions and feeling discreetly under a large fake-fur throw on the sofa. She couldn't see or feel anything unusual. But she did wonder whether it might be her mother, rather than her father, who had the drink problem. Perhaps Paige was a secret drinker. It would explain why she was so ineffective at handling Bill. Or Jess. Maybe that was why she screwed up her life all the time.

When Sophie opened Jess's fridge, under the pretext that she needed a drop more milk, there was a half-empty bottle of white wine in the door. Sophie supposed that was a good sign. Didn't alcoholics drink everything in sight?

Jess sat on the sofa, cross-legged and crushed, rolling herself a cigarette. She looked like a ten-year-old boy. 'So what shall I do about Jake?'

'Jess, this is so unlike you. You've always been a love 'em and leave 'em girl.'

Jess sniffed. 'I love Jake. That's the difference. I didn't love any of the others. We used to see or speak to each other every day. Until the high heels came into it.'

'Jess, the shoes are not what it's all about. Believe me. And ten days is still not too long.'

'Maybe. Maybe not.' Jess lit up and drew the smoke in. 'Have you heard from the parents?'

'I spoke to Mum yesterday evening. There's no particular news. She sounded a bit tired. Look, are you sure things are all right at work?'

'Actually, it's fucked. I'm so tired, I can't stop thinking about Jake and the people I work for are bullying me. Jake says I should stand up for myself more.'

'Jess, this is probably why you're in such a state. You've always bugged out when the going got tough. You went. You walked out. You gave up. Now you've finally got a proper job and you're just discovering that this is what it's like. Maybe you're not being bullied, this is just real life, it being about time you found out about it. And maybe this is just a hiccup in your relationship with Jake that you've just got to sit out. Be a little more patient, Jess. Nothing happens easily.'

'That's easy for you to say. You've never had to try at anything.'

'I have tried. I try every single day of my life. Jess, there are no easy options you know.'

'It's so frustrating,' said Sophie to Harry later that night. 'She wants me to call Jake and to make it all better. Like a big sister should. She doesn't understand that life can be hard and you've got to stick it out.'

'Is that what you think? That life is hard and you have to stick it out?' Harry's look was careful, searching, concerned.

'No, darling, of course not our life.' Sophie suddenly saw an abyss open between them. 'But I do think it's odd that Jake hasn't called, don't you?'

'Sometimes men don't. Maybe it all got too intense too quickly. Jess should sort herself out at work, and if Jake's coming back he'll come back.'

'Yes, that's what I thought,' said Sophie gratefully as the abyss shimmered and disappeared.

Chapter 19

Bill's flash of temper evaporated over night.

He seemed to have forgotten all about George Boxer, the Fishing Smack and his allegation that Paige had been unfaithful. For the next few weeks he behaved normally, going about the kitchen whistling and offering to make cups of tea. He had also returned to their bed after a night. Paige always went to bed at about eleven, while Bill usually fell asleep in front of the television after supper. He would start awake at about midnight, then go into his study for a few hours, coming to their bed at around two or three in the morning, turning the light on, undressing noisily and slamming drawers. When Paige woke to find his great bulk standing over the bed beside her she was too frightened to go back to sleep at first.

But eventually she did, and she managed to persuade herself that his behaviour was completely normal, because if she didn't she'd never get any sleep. She woke at any tiny sound, lying staring into the darkness for at least an hour, wondering whether he had forgiven her or what he was planning to do. Eventually she decided that he was probably rather sorry that he'd overreacted as he had, and that he was too embarrassed to make a proper apology.

Yes, that must be it. She slept a little better but still woke up at the slightest sound. There was no one she could talk to about it all. She didn't want to confide in Sophie or Jess because a parent should never ask their child, even a grown-up child, to take sides. And anyway, they might think she had done wrong in having lunch with George Boxer behind Bill's back. Jess would certainly think she'd been a fool. Well, she was a fool, she knew that now. How she could ever have thought that Bill would have been happy for her to go out to lunch with George, of course it would embarrass him, any man would have felt the same . . . the same old arguments wound themselves round and round in her head, tying themselves in tighter and tighter knots.

Perhaps she should suggest they went for counselling. But that would open the whole thing up again.

All the couples in the area were friends of them both. Paige would never have dreamed of criticising Bill to them, except in the most general terms when all of the other wives were grumbling about their husbands. Indeed, from what other women said, Bill was by no means the worst. But she couldn't let him down by confiding the full details of that terrible day to anyone, and besides, it might damage the business. Bill had often said that a builder lived and died on his reputation. That what she did and how she behaved could influence whether they got a job or not.

So when Rose, who had originally introduced them to George Boxer, dropped in with some gardening magazines, Paige thanked her and offered her coffee, but didn't intend to confide in her.

'I saw George the other day,' ventured Rose. 'I gather you had lunch together.'

'Oh, just briefly.' Paige's heart beat faster. 'He asked me about the garden and took me to the Fishing Smack for a quick snack to say thank you. Funnily enough, we bumped into Bill and Anthea who were having a working lunch. But I haven't seen George since.'

'Bill treats his staff very well if he gives them working lunches at the Fishing Smack.'

'Oh he does,' agreed Paige. 'They all think the world of him. It's a very happy company.'

A silence settled over the table.

Rose broke it. 'Paige, I know it's none of my business, but are you all right? We haven't seen you for ages.'

'Oh I've just been busy. I pop up to London to help Sophie out whenever I can, and November is quite hectic in the garden.' She wondered if it would be all right to ask Rose what she thought she should do. In confidence, of course.

Rose looked surprised. 'Is it? You must be a perfectionist, because I hardly ever go outside between now and about March.'

'Rose, if I tell you something, could you absolutely promise not to mention it to anyone? Even to Andrew? I do need to talk it through with someone and I don't want it going round the whole village – it wouldn't be fair on Bill.'

'I promise. It stays between us.'

Paige explained about the lunch with George and the implication that Bill had drawn from it.

Rose frowned. 'But what about him lunching with Anthea?'

'Oh, that was business.'

Rose didn't say anything.

'It was business.' Paige repeated, studying Rose's face with a sinking heart. 'Wasn't it?'

'I don't know. But the Fishing Smack is an expensive place for a working lunch. Look, Paige, I don't want to upset you unnecessarily but it strikes me that Bill is being a bit of a bully over this.'

'Oh no, he's just upset, you see, he gets very frustrated with me because . . .'

'And do you get frustrated with him?'

'I try to understand what he needs,' admitted Paige. 'But it's very difficult being married sometimes. Don't you think?'

'Yes, I do. But I don't think you did anything wrong.'

'Don't you? Bill is worried that it will put George off engaging Raven Build & Restore for his house.'

'I don't see why it should. Raven has a very good reputation.'

'Well, we'll see,' said Paige firmly. 'Bill always says I should keep out of the business, and he's right. Don't you think?'

'I think you should see someone. Because you do seem very, very anxious. I know a very good therapist.'

'Oh, I don't need therapy,' said Paige. 'That's not going to make any difference to the facts of the matter. All we need is for the Orchard Park project to be finished and sold on. That's what's upsetting Bill really, I know that. He's a workaholic, but . . .' She looked out of the kitchen window and saw her beloved garden stretching out. 'I wouldn't have all this if he wasn't. I do know I'm really very lucky.'

'Paige,' said Rose. 'Here's the number of a therapist. You should go. It helps to sort your thoughts out.'

Paige had no intention of going to see someone who would probably tell her how unsupportive she was of Bill. Who would ask her how long she spent in the garden as opposed to how much time she spent fostering the marriage. Who might suggest that she and Bill rekindle their passion for each other by having 'date nights'. Who would be full of bright, breezy suggestions that Paige had already considered or tried, and which hadn't worked.

Or someone who would open up the pain, loneliness and darkness in Paige's heart and expose her for what she really was. Unloveable.

No, no one would want to pay good money to be given a whole load of unpleasant insights into how terrible they really were. Paige was managing fine as she was. She looked around her kitchen and was soothed by how warm and comforting it all looked. Everyone said that Paige's kitchen was the nicest in the village.

'I'll see if I can persuade Bill that it's a good idea,' she said, tucking the card away. 'Once the Orchard Park business is sorted and he has a bit more time.'

If Bill was happy then Paige would be happy. It was as simple as that.

Chapter 20

Sophie twisted Jake's card under her fingers. It was in the pocket of her jacket, and she fingered it as if it were a talisman that could protect her from harm. And Jess. If they still had a relationship. What was he up to? Maybe he just wasn't that into her, as the saying went. If so, the sooner Jess knew the sooner she could get on with her life. Or maybe there'd been a misunderstanding between them, in which case wouldn't it be good if Sophie could sort it out?

After all, Jess herself had asked her to call him. Not that she could ring him and ask him directly, of course, but what if she were to ask him to do a bit more investigation about her father's finances? Money shouldn't matter, but it did, and if her parents could afford to divorce it would be so much easier for her to release the information about what she'd seen between him and Anthea.

She couldn't discuss any of this with Harry because he'd only accuse her of trying to rescue people again. Sometimes she thought Harry was rather selfish. Of course you had to try help people you loved. You couldn't just stand by and watch them suffer, especially if you could see what they needed to do to sort themselves out.

It took three goes before she managed to dial the whole number. Jake answered immediately.

'Oh, er, hello, it's . . . er . . . Sophie.'

'Sophie.' His voice was warm and welcoming, like a caress. 'What can I do for you?'

She explained, stammering, that she still wasn't sure what to do about her father, her mother and Anthea, but thought that if she knew more about the financial situation it might be easier to know which direction to go in.

'Sure,' he said easily. 'It's difficult to find out about smaller companies but I'll have a nose around. I'll take you out to lunch, shall I?'

Sophie said that she couldn't impose, she really couldn't . . .

'It's on expenses,' he said with a smile in his voice, 'so not imposing on me in any way. What about Thursday? I've got a booking at The Ivy and my guest has just cancelled. If you can make it then you'd be doing me a favour.'

Sophie said that she could.

So on Thursday morning she spent ages trying to decide between a simple black jacket and trousers, for an elegant, understated look, or a pencil skirt with a cashmere cardigan, casually tied and draped with long beads. She eventually settled on the cashmere, because it reflected the colour of her eyes. When she got to the restaurant, Jake rose from his seat to kiss her on both cheeks. He was whippet-thin, she noted, but with strength in his shoulders and upper arms. Everything about him was taut, as if he might spring into action at any time.

'Glass of champagne?'

'Oh, I . . . well, I suppose . . .' She gave in. If you were a working mother of three small children, being bought champagne in an achingly cool restaurant by an extremely attractive man was just too good to turn down. She smiled at him as the glasses were placed in front of them.

'*Salud!*' He touched the rim of his glass to hers, and laid a piece of paper in front of her.

She picked up the paper. 'What does this mean?'

'You know how you can find out your credit rating? Well,

there are also similar services for companies. So if you're researching a business or planning to employ them you can find out if they generally pay their bills on time or are nearing bankruptcy. Your father's company has a good credit rating. And I also asked a few contacts in the construction industry. Your Dad's got a very good reputation. He finishes on time, on budget. Knows his stuff, that's the word.'

'So probably not about to go under?'

'Probably not about to go under.' He lifted his glass to her again and smiled.

'And Dad has probably been lying to us when he said it would?'

Jake shrugged. 'I don't know why he says what he says. He may be someone who feels insecure, or perhaps he doesn't want to tell your mother that everything's going well in case she spends too much.'

'But that's . . . well, not really fair.' Sophie felt a twinge of unease. Her father was strong. And he was right, and he loved them all. Those facts had always underpinned her childhood and, although she knew he had his faults, she didn't think he was a liar. She didn't want to think he would lie to *her*, even if he found himself occasionally having to lie to Paige or Jess for their own good.

'Hey.' She felt Jake's thumb on her cheek, wiping a tear that she hadn't known was there.

She shook her head and blinked another tear away. 'I'm fine.'

'Sure you are.' He leant back, studying her. 'It's not easy to find out that your father isn't quite what you thought, but at least the news is good.'

'Well, he probably wasn't lying when he said he was going under when we were children. It probably was really tough then, and maybe he got into the habit of treating everything as a crisis. People do, you know. Brains get set into patterns. I read about it somewhere.'

'Sure,' he said again, smiling down at her then touching her

121

arm lightly. 'Don't take the troubles of the world on your shoulders. You're not responsible for your father. Or your mother.'

'That's what Harry says.'

'How is Harry?'

'Fine.' Sophie remembered the real reason for this lunch. 'How about Jess? Are you . . .'

His face shadowed over. 'I don't know what to do about Jess. I wanted to help her, you know, she's always felt like the ugly sister, because you're so beautiful . . .' His eyes acknowledged this, and Sophie blushed and tried to murmur something, but he waved it away.

'You are. And that's been tough for Jess, which is why she deliberately dressed like a boy. At least that's what I thought. I wanted to set free the lovely woman underneath all that, but maybe I frightened her or took it too fast, and she got really angry. So I thought it was better to pull back a bit.'

'Typical Jess,' said Sophie. 'Never have I known anyone who so personified the statement "her own worst enemy". She feels bad because things don't work out, then you try to help her so she sulks or snarls. I've been trying to help her all her life, and she throws it in my face. I think she's doing the same at work – it's the first time she's had a really decent job and I suspect she's sulking and scowling at everyone and taking all criticism personally. She'll never learn.'

'You and I are very alike, I think,' said Jake.

Sophie was warmed by the thought. 'But Jess is a lovely, lovely person underneath all that,' she said, leaning towards Jake. 'She is so kind and brave . . . and talented. Really, really talented, *much* more than I am, but she sees life as a battle and she always tries to get the first blow in. That's not the way to get on. People don't like it if you jump down their throat the minute they open their mouths.'

'You do yourself down. I've seen some of your photographs. On your website. They're terrific.'

Sophie was pleased that he'd bothered to check out her website. The waiter placed a frondy salad in front her. Sophie began to eat, but she couldn't taste anything. It might as well have been cardboard for all she cared as she and Jake compared notes on Jess and how she could get the most out of life.

'So will you get back in touch with Jess?' asked Sophie anxiously, hoping she hadn't put Jake off even more.

'Yeah,' he said. 'I thought maybe she didn't want to see any more of me, but now I've talked to you I can see that might all be a front.'

'Oh, I'm sure it is.' Sophie was pleased that she'd managed to straighten that out.

'Also . . .' For the first time he seemed uneasy. 'I had a really bad break-up and I'm just very careful not to go through all that again. And not to put anyone else through it. So even if I . . .' He raised his hands in the air. 'You know, really *like* someone, I've got this thing ticking away at the back of my mind saying . . . be careful . . . be careful. Maybe that's silly.'

'I'm sure it's not. It's quite normal, and very sensible.'

They smiled at each other.

At ten past three Jake looked at his watch. 'I'd no idea that was the time.'

'I've got to pick up the girls. But thank you for a lovely lunch.'

'Thank *you*,' he said. 'For getting in touch. I really wanted to know what you thought, but didn't want Jess to feel that I was going behind her back. So I probably won't mention this lunch, if that's OK by you?'

'Of course not. We won't say anything, either of us,' agreed Sophie, kissing him and hoping that everything was now sorted between him and Jess. He was the most promising boyfriend she had ever found, and it would be great if he stayed in the family.

Jess, oh Jess, she thought, exasperated at her sister, as she caught a bus home. If only you were a little bit nicer to the world, the world would be nicer to you. And as for Dad, well, maybe he wasn't exactly lying. Just being Dad. It was understandable, when you thought about it.

Chapter 21

Jess told her company that she had flu and spent several days in bed, checking the caller ID every time the phone rang, then not answering it. She would open a bottle of wine at lunchtime and finish it by three o'clock. Then she would open another at six.

She was too humiliated to tell anyone she'd been dumped. Jess knew she wasn't good enough. That's why she always dumped before she could be dumped. She didn't even let Sophie know that.

Sophie was very intuitive, though, she always had been. But, oh, Jess felt the weight of her condescension. There she was, with her perfect little life, dropping in on her sister to see if she was all right. Expecting gratitude, no doubt.

Well Jess wasn't very grateful. She went back to work the following week and sat with her arms folded, glaring at her desk while everyone else was engrossed in their computers. She was no good. Of course she was no good. Her father had always pointed out that she 'wasn't academic'. That there was no point in her going to university. That people like her were just as good as those who were clever, and there was no point in pretending to be something she wasn't. No Point. No Point. The refrain drummed through her brain, making it impossible to concentrate.

'Where's the brief for the Donald Hotels project?' Tina demanded.

Jess couldn't prevent a blush from creeping up her neck. 'I haven't got it.'

'Yes, you have, I put it on your desk yesterday. Don't tell me you've lost it already. Can't you do anything right?'

Jess searched her desk three times and eventually found it underneath a newspaper. Briefly looking through it to see a list of words that 'stood for' Donald Hotels – Trust, Comfort, Luxury, Exclusiveness, Difference, Service – she could swear it hadn't been there before, but that would mean that someone had slid them under the newspaper while she'd been in the loo. She looked round the room, but everyone was bent over their desks.

'Here they are.' She knocked timidly on Tina's door.

Tina rolled her eyes. 'I knew you had them. I suppose it's too much to ask whether you've gone through them yet?'

'I . . . I'll take them home with me this evening and go through them overnight.'

Tina sighed. 'No, give them to Cathy, for God's sake. I know how you like to keep your evenings for your other plans.'

Jess was about to turn away, to ring a friend so they could go out and get drunk, when she saw a flash of her mother cowering in front of her father. She'd always sworn she'd be different. She took a deep breath. 'Actually, I do have other plans. As of now. I'm sick of being treated like dirt.'

Tina raised her head, her mouth in an o of astonishment.

Jess gathered her courage. She suddenly knew that if she went on letting herself be bullied, one day she would kill herself. 'I do try hard, and all you do is humiliate me.' She forced herself on. She was fighting for her life. 'I'm leaving in three minutes, and if you don't pay my salary until the end of the month, which, by the way, is only three days away, I'll sue you for constructive dismissal.' Jess had no idea whether she could but it sounded right. She walked out into the open-plan area and gathered up her possessions.

'Bye everyone,' she shouted as she left. 'Have a good life.' She put her head back in. 'And Cathy, you're being bullied and being turned into a bully. You need a reality check.'

That felt good. She was very shaky, but proud of herself.

Next, Paige. She would tell her mother about her father's money. And about Anthea. Then she would think about what to do next. Maybe she would emigrate, get away from the lot of them. Rent her flat out and live off the rent. Secrecy was corrosive.

Paige seemed distracted when she rang her. 'Your father's not in a very good mood.'

'Oh really? Why not?'

Paige burbled something about Orchard Park and a sale falling through. Jess was sick of it. The pretence that they had a happy family. Her family had put Jake off her. It was after that visit that he turned cold. Well, not immediately after, but in the weeks that followed. They hadn't spoken for two weeks now.

Still fuelled with adrenalin, Jess got on to her motorbike and rode down to The Rowans, arriving in the middle of the afternoon.

'Darling!'

'I've left my job.'

'Oh no.' Paige sank down on a chair. 'I'd hoped you were happy. Or maybe . . . what about Jake? Are you . . . maybe you're . . .' Her expression was anxious. Paige did not want to hear anything unpleasant.

Jess crossed her arms. 'Jake's dumped me. At least I assume he has. And Dad's cheating on you with Anthea. Sophie saw them in a clinch at her birthday party. He said he was comforting her about some boyfriend. And he's really quite rich. Jake looked his company up at Companies House when we were still together. So that's you sorted out. I've taken a grip of my life: I'm going to rent out my flat, go abroad and stop feeling sorry for myself, and you should too.'

Paige looked bewildered. 'Rent out your flat?'

'Mum, can't you hear me? Dad is having an affair with

Anthea and he's really quite nicely off – you can divorce him. He treats you like shit. Just like my company was treating me like shit. I left them, you can leave him.'

Paige shook her head. 'The company may be OK, but he puts all his money back into it. And Orchard Park could bring everything down on our heads . . .'

'Stop blaming Orchard Park for everything. Get your head together.'

'There's nothing wrong with my head.'

Jess spent the next hour trying to persuade Paige that she should leave Bill or, at the very least, lay down some rules about how she was treated.

Paige seemed to think that she could deal with it once Orchard Park was through. Jess tried not to scream at her. 'Orchard Park has nothing to do with it.'

'You've got to be realistic,' retorted Paige. 'If Orchard Park fails, your father and I will have nothing.'

'That is not true. And if you weren't so determined to keep everything exactly the way it's always been, you'd realise that. Why don't you at least go to marriage guidance counselling? Wouldn't that help?'

'Yes, but your father doesn't have time. Not with the Orchard Park project, plus his other work.'

'Well, why don't you go to counselling on your own, to sort out how you feel?'

'Yes, but I know how I feel.' For someone who was so tentative about offering her own opinion, Paige could be surprisingly stubborn. 'My only problem is your father, and I'm worried about him because he's so stressed.'

'And drunk, don't forget. I can't remember when I saw him without a glass in his hand. Hasn't it occurred to you that he could be an alcoholic?'

'He does drink a bit too much,' Paige conceded. 'But that's because of the stress. I don't think he could run the company if he was really an alcoholic.'

'Aren't you concerned about what he's up to with Anthea?'

'We've discussed it. He says that his relationship with Anthea is purely business.'

'And you believe him?'

For one moment Jess saw hesitation in Paige's face, but then the mask was back in place. 'I have to believe him,' she said. 'He's my husband. Once I stop believing him, then . . . Look, Jess, I just don't have a choice.'

'You do. Everyone does.'

But Paige seemed incapable of allowing the idea of change anywhere near her.

'I'm beginning to think Dad's right,' shouted Jess, infuriated. 'I think you are stupid. Or mad. You live under this appalling strain, being raged at night and day, but you don't seem to think there's anything unusual about it.'

'There isn't,' said Paige. 'And he's not always in a bad mood, only—'

'Only at the end of the day after he's opened a bottle of wine.'

After nearly an hour of talking, with Paige countering every suggestion, Jess threw her hands up in the air. 'Mum, tell me: what did Dad say about me to Jake? We were fine until we came down here.'

Paige buried her face in her hands. 'I am so, so sorry. I don't know what he did. I wanted it all to be nice for you. I'm sorry. I'm sorry.'

Paige's habit of over-apologising irritated Jess. 'Mum!' She thumped her hand on the table. 'It wasn't your fault and you don't have to apologise for him. You would drive any sane person completely mad. Wake up and smell the coffee! Dad is not happy. Neither are you. And the successful completion of Orchard Park is *not* a magic wand that can be waved over the whole situation to make it go away.'

Paige kept her face in her hands and didn't reply.

'Stop being such a victim! You have choices. Use them. Or

you'll ruin what's left of your life because you just won't face up to reality.'

Paige cautiously raised her head and Jess saw the fear in her face. 'I could say the same to you,' she whispered as she got up and pushed her chair aside.

Jess stood back. 'I'm nothing like you. That's why I've rebelled against it all.' She followed her mother to the sink and shouted in her ear. 'I didn't want to be like you. And I'm not.'

Paige's hands were shaking so badly she could barely fill the kettle. 'I have to wait until Orchard Park is sorted. I don't have a choice. Really, I have no choice. None at all. Your father and I are fine for the moment.'

Jess was about to walk out in fury. She looked at Paige, hunched over the sink. She had started to bully her mother just as her father did.

'OK,' she said, trying to keep her voice steady and to quell the frustration. 'Mum, I'm sorry. I shouldn't have spoken to you like that. I shouldn't have shouted. Look, I'll do a deal with you. I'll sort myself out – counselling, re-training, whatever – if you go for help yourself. What help you choose is up to you. Marriage guidance, counselling, group therapy . . . just anything . . . just try.'

'I've tried,' said Paige wearily. 'But there's nothing I can do until your father is less stressed.'

'I mean it, Mum. It's a deal.' She picked up her motorcycle helmet and opened the kitchen door. 'I'm not coming home for a bit. I don't like what it does to me. But I'll be back for Christmas as long as you promise me you'll have been for help.'

'It's a bit busy between now and then,' said Paige. 'I probably won't have time. But I'll go in the New Year.'

'Tough.' Jess walked out the door. 'If you want me home, you'll get help by Christmas. And if you haven't, I will make other plans.'

But as she swung her leg over her bike she knew it was hopeless. Her mother was never going to change. Everybody was right. For some reason she needed her life to be like this. But why? Instead of staying at The Rowans, apparently immobilised by her fear of change, she had rights, legal rights. Why didn't she use them?

Chapter 22

Jess's allegations about Bill and Anthea were like the scratching of a cat at a bedroom door. They niggled and were hard to ignore. But Paige knew that now wasn't the time to challenge him.

Bill arrived back in a good mood and took a bottle of wine off to his study after supper. Three times Paige opened her mouth to tell Bill about Jess, but then shut it again. Should she wait until Jess had decided what she wanted to do? She didn't want to spoil Bill's relative cheerfulness by telling him any sooner than she had to, and Jess hadn't given her permission to tell him either. She was always careful to protect the girls from his rages.

'What did you do today?' he asked.

'A bit of gardening, and I took some books back to the library.'

An hour later Bill strode out of his study and leant against the kitchen cupboard, arms folded, feet planted firmly on the floor, as if defending his territory. 'I gather,' he said, his voice low with menace, 'that you've been complaining about me around the village.'

'I haven't.' Paige's heart leapt.

'Liar.' His eyes were dark with fury. 'You have been moaning about me to Rose.'

'I didn't . . . she said she wouldn't . . .' Paige was frightened.

'She has clearly told the whole village that you think I'm having an affair with Anthea. Have you any idea how awkward you've made life for me? Have you the slightest inkling of how your mad, destructive lies will ruin my business?'

'I haven't been saying that. And I don't see how it could ruin your business. People hire you for . . .'

'No, you don't see, because you are quite, quite mad and very stupid to boot. But I see. I have to see for both of us. And what I see is you bad-mouthing me and my colleagues to your friends, and even to our own children, while carrying on behind my back with George Boxer.'

'Not that again. I told you, we didn't do anything.'

'You *also* told me you hadn't talked about me to Rose, when you clearly have. You said you'd just done a bit of gardening today. And you haven't mentioned Jess giving up her job and coming down here. So how can you expect me to believe a word you say? These people are my friends, you know. They're loyal to me. Everyone feels sorry for me, having a wife who can't cope with the simplest thing. They know that everything we have is down to me.'

Paige withdrew within herself, deciding not to answer.

'Jess agrees with me, by the way. She thinks you're mad too. She said so.'

Paige swallowed and looked at the floor.

'Didn't she?' shouted Bill. 'Look at me, not at your boots! Jess has just phoned me and said that she came down here to tell us she'd given up her job. And you didn't even mention it to me. But she did say she thinks you need treatment.'

'I'm sorry. I was going to tell you. When you were less busy.'

'Oh, so it's my fault now, is it? We're playing the old blame game again, are we?'

Paige felt trapped, and looked out of the window. It was dark, so she couldn't see the garden. She concentrated on a vase of flowers she'd arranged, a mix of teasel and rosehips, with a few green leaves. The golden spikes of the teasel threw shadows on the wall.

'You're not even listening to me,' accused Bill.

'I am. But I haven't complained about you. And I haven't had an affair.'

'So why has my phone been ringing off the hook for the last hour with people telling me things "they think I ought to know"?' He wiggled his fingers to indicate quotation marks.

'Which people? I didn't hear a phone.'

'That's because . . .' He spoke slowly, as if she was a very small child. 'I have a mobile. Which I often keep on vibrate. That means, my little pea head, that I can feel a call coming in but I don't disturb anyone with its ringing. It's a modern invention. Only about fifteen years old, so perhaps you haven't heard about it yet.'

'I do know how mobile phones work.' Paige was determined not to let Jess down, not to say that it was she who had made the allegations about the affair.

But Bill had a way of seeing inside her brain. 'Jess seems to have picked something up from Sophie, who saw me comforting Anthea in the study during her party. I told Sophie at the time that Anthea was very upset about her father being ill, and that putting a friendly arm round her was the least I could do.'

Something flickered at the back of Paige's mind. She was sure that wasn't what Jess had said. 'I didn't know Anthea's father had been ill.'

'No, well, you don't make much effort to get to know her, do you?'

'I invited her for lunch.'

'Once in five years,' he sneered.

'Jess did suggest we go for marriage guidance counselling,' suggested Paige, terrified that this might make him even more angry.

Bill looked at her as if measuring up his response. 'Well,' he said eventually. 'If that would make you see sense, then I'm all

134

for it. I'm at my wits end trying to understand what it is you need.'

Paige considered saying that all she needed was for him to stop shouting, but decided that perhaps she should quit now she'd got an agreement out of him.

'Fix it up,' he said, picking up his glass and going to the study. 'It's not as if things could get any worse.'

She wondered who she could ask about counselling, but she didn't dare try. Rose had promised not to disclose their conversation, yet had clearly told everyone in just a matter of hours and the story must have been distorted like some terrible Chinese whisper. She couldn't go to Rose's therapist, or anywhere near Rose. It would have to be the internet. Or the telephone directory.

There was no one and nothing else she could trust.

Chapter 23

Sophie dreamed about Jake. She felt his hand on her arm, his breath on her neck, and smelt the clean cedarwood smell of him. She dreamed he told her that he loved Jess, but then he turned into her father, angry about something, then into Harry, shaking her awake. 'Sophie, you were shouting. Are you all right?'

'Just a bad dream.'

He stroked her hair. She wished he'd stop. It set her teeth on edge. She wriggled away from him. 'I'm fine now. I'll just check on the girls.' Too restless to get back into bed, she checked her mobile and saw a missed call from Jess.

'Hi, it's Soph.'

'Thanks for getting back.' She heard Jess pull on a cigarette. 'I've jacked in my job.'

'Oh Jess, no.'

'Yes, Sophie, yes. I'm sorry if that upsets you. I was being bullied.'

'Jobs are like that, Jess, you have to work hard enough to get beyond that. To get promoted.'

'So you can bully someone else in turn? Very nice. And I don't see you having to go into an office every day and be given menial tasks, and never being allowed any responsibility.'

Sophie didn't want to point out that, although she worked

for herself, she too had to deal with unreasonable demands and difficult clients. Jess always believed that Sophie's life was smooth and easy, then got angry if Sophie suggested otherwise. And anything that might imply that Sophie had more talent or was cleverer was definitely out. She had to tread so carefully round Jess's inferiority complex.

'Anyway, I'm back to waitressing. At least it's a dignified way of earning money.'

'That's great.' Sophie couldn't see why it was any more dignified than anything else. 'And . . . er . . . what about Jake?'

'He texted me to say that he was very busy, but that he'd be in touch soon.'

'That's good. Isn't it?'

'I think so. I texted back that I was wearing the high heels every day. He said he couldn't wait to see me in them. But he hasn't said when. Anyway, I've told Mum everything. Walking out on my job. About you seeing Anthea with Dad.'

'No! Jess! Jess, we agreed . . .'

'Don't worry, I might as well have not bothered. It's like talking to someone lying at the bottom of a swimming pool. They can just about see you're there, but that's about it. She won't hear a word against him, and is determined that nothing can even be thought about until Orchard Park is finished. Her view is that Anthea is his accountant and that's that. And Dad drinks a bit too much, but isn't an alcoholic, it's stress.'

Sophie sighed. 'I don't think Dad's an alcoholic either, but he's pretty close to it. What is she thinking of? I'd never put up with treatment like that from Harry. I think it's as much her fault as his, you know, for letting him get away with it for so many years. Or maybe she really is going to wait until Orchard Park's fully sold and then go from there. It would make sense.'

'You're beginning to sound like her.'

'Well, you've got to be practical. Money shouldn't matter, but it does.'

'I'd rather be destitute than live like she does. That's why I packed in the job. It wasn't worth it, to be made to feel useless all the time.'

'Jess, you have no idea what destitute means.'

'And you have no idea what it's like to feel useless.' Jess slammed the phone down. Sophie thought of calling her back, but there was no point. Jess would always expect someone else to look after her, to pick up the pieces. She didn't worry about money or stick to jobs because she knew that Sophie would lend her fifty pounds when she needed it, or would pick her up from the roadside when her bike broke down. That was the youngest for you: no sense of responsibility, just perpetual whingeing about Sophie being given all the breaks. Sophie tossed and turned, furious with Jess for screwing up her life yet again. The next thing she knew was Lottie trying to prise her eyes open. It was six o'clock in the morning. 'Mummy, I want some breakfast.'

Chapter 24

It took Paige three weeks to find the courage to go to a counsellor. She made three appointments, then cancelled them when she couldn't face mentioning it to Bill again. But Sophie, Harry and the girls had agreed to come home for Christmas and Jess, in the two phone calls she'd made home, had said, 'Any movement on our deal, Mum? I need to know because they're asking about who's around for Christmas shifts at work.'

The thought of Jess working as a waitress on Christmas Day, then going back to a lonely flat, tore at Paige's heart. Jess was certainly stubborn enough to carry out her threat. She considered lying to her, but decided she wouldn't be able to carry it off. Jess was a fierce little questioner, and was quite likely to trip her up with queries about the colour of the therapist's walls or what Bill had said. And if there was any chance of getting Bill to swear and shout less she had to take it. Although the counsellor might be on Bill's side and say it was all her fault. Well, if it was she'd find out how to change. It couldn't be that difficult, could it?

'This is a whole lot of rubbish, you know,' said Bill as they knocked on the door. 'An excuse for women to get together and say that men treat them badly. That's what therapy means.' Paige swallowed nervously as they were welcomed into a bland, badly lit room.

'My name is Ruth,' said the counsellor. 'Do sit down.'

Three chairs had been set in a triangle. All had wooden legs and arms and olive green stretch covers. They were the sort of chairs you only ever saw in second-hand shops or care homes, thought Paige, perching on the edge of one and hoping that nothing she said would make Bill furious later. She looked around at the cream walls; a poster of the Lake District had been pinned up on one of them. The carpet was the kind that minimised stains. Perhaps the room had been chosen so as not to be noticed in any way. Not to make anyone feel uneasy or inferior. There was a coffee table between the three chairs, with a box of tissues on it. Paige wondered if she was expected to cry. That carpet would make anyone weep.

Concentrate, Paige. She'd already missed Ruth's introductory speech on how counselling worked. Bill stretched back in his chair, a hand on each knee and a smile playing around his mouth. He looked relaxed and confident. He looked like a nice man, who intended to do his best.

'I'll just ask you a few basic questions,' said Ruth, running down a checklist about health, medication and alcohol consumption. 'How much do you drink?'

Bill grinned. 'Oh, if you go by the headlines you see in the papers we're both middle-class alcoholics. We open a bottle of wine over supper most evenings, don't we darling?'

'Um. Yes, but—'

'But, seriously, it's all under control. I know when to drink and when not to drink. I've got a lot of responsibilities at work and am often on sites where safety is an issue. You don't get drunk on the job in my world.'

'Paige?' Ruth's pencil was poised.

'Well, I do know I'm supposed to stick to about fourteen units a week, but I'm afraid it's usually a bit more than that . . .'

Bill laughed. 'You like a tipple, don't you? Bit of an alkie, my wife is. No, darling, I'm joking. *Jo-king.*' He nodded towards her. 'She does the driving after parties, you see, so we have to keep her on the straight and narrow. Ha ha.'

'Any other addictions?'

'No,' they said together.

'And your sex life?' Ruth looked at them steadily.

'Um . . .' Paige looked at Bill.

'I don't think my wife would want us to talk about that. And I'd like to respect her privacy, if that's all right by you.'

'Paige?'

'Fine. Everything's fine.' She tried to see if Bill thought that was the right answer.

'I'd like to hear a bit about yourselves, how you met, what originally attracted you to each other, that sort of thing. Just one rule, by the way: I ask you not to talk about each other in the third person. I know I'm here, and you feel you're talking to me, but I'd like you to address each other. Say "you" rather than "she", for example.' She looked enquiringly from one to the other.

Bill looked at Paige. 'You start, darling.' He turned to Ruth. 'I want my wife to understand that I only have her best interests at heart.'

Paige supposed he did. 'Well, when I met Bill he was . . . well, different from anyone I'd met before . . .' She glanced at Bill. Would he be angry at being described as different? 'I mean you,' she emphasised. '*You* could do things. You were confident.' This was excruciating. 'Um. Full of ideas. Er, exciting, I suppose. Tall and blond.' She flicked him a quick glance. 'Very strong, I thought. And . . . er . . . different. I remember when you built that playhouse for the girls. Sparrow Palace. It was magical. You made them feel involved. And you taught them so much while you were doing it.'

'It sounds as if you've been a good father, Bill,' said Ruth. 'And what about you? What attracted you to Paige?' Her pen was poised over her notebook.

'I wanted to look after her,' said Bill, his voice suddenly husky. Paige glanced at him quickly, under her lashes, to see if he was joking again, but he seemed quite serious. 'She's a bit

141

hopeless, always was, and I thought, well, I thought I could help her.'

Ruth seemed not to notice that Bill was talking about her in the third person. 'And Paige, how do you feel about that?'

'Well, I am pretty hopeless really. I suppose. I mean, I've never really had much of a career, I was a secretary for a bit, then a receptionist, but that was ages ago. And I don't understand Bill's business, which I think he – I mean . . .' She flicked a glance towards Bill. 'I mean *you* probably find rather irritating. I bother him – you – about trivial things when you're trying to work. And we're always running out of things like, um, washing up liquid because, um, I make lists and then leave them behind. Well, not always running out of everything, I think I get most things in, but there always seems to be something not quite right.'

Ruth asked a few more questions, mainly about Sophie and Jess, which Bill diverted to Paige, and then asked them what they wanted from these sessions.

'Ask her,' said Bill, but without rancour. 'She's the one who wanted to come.' He winked at Ruth.

Paige missed Ruth's response because she looked at the carpet again, following the trace of its golden brown leaves against a chocolate brown background. 'I feel we shout at each other too much,' she managed, not daring to suggest that it was Bill doing most of the shouting. 'I'd like us to argue less.'

'Bill, how do you feel about that?'

'Fine by me. I find it very stressful to get home in the evening to an argument, so I'm absolutely with my wife there.' He smiled at Ruth. 'To be honest, I'm quite worried about her, which is why I agreed to come. I think she might be suffering from depression. Or perhaps it's the menopause. I'm just a simple man, these things are beyond my ken. But I'm worried.'

Paige looked at him quickly. He was always telling her she didn't think things through, but had never mentioned depression before.

'How do you feel about that, Paige?'

'Um, I don't think I'm depressed. Not really. In fact, I thought maybe Bill . . . but . . .'

'Not really?'

'I'm just worried about a project of Bill's which is one of the reasons why he's working so hard. If it all goes wrong, we might lose our home and that upsets me because it's where the children grew up and we've both put a lot of work into it. We're both too old to start again, so what would become of us?'

Ruth invited them to tell her about the financial situation.

'It's far too complicated to explain,' said Bill.

'Bill has four companies,' said Paige. 'And one of them is developing a piece of land just outside our village. Bill doesn't have any other investors to spread the risk of it all, so he's mortgaged our house to raise the money.'

Ruth turned to Bill. 'All this sounds like very hard work for you, Bill.'

'That's what I have been trying to get across to the wife for years. But she constantly disturbs me about little things, such as which plumber we should call in.'

'That's because you said you didn't want me making decisions on my own,' flashed Paige. 'I don't *want* to bother you and I *try* to wait until the evening, but if you can only talk to the plumber at nine-thirty and there's water pouring out of the tank, then that's when I have to call you about it.'

'Hardly pouring. It was a tiny drip. You could have used a bit of initiative. Like putting a bucket under it.' Out of the corner of her eye she saw Bill shrug and smile at Ruth, as if to say 'Now you see what I have to contend with'.

Ruth looked down at her notes. 'I think, if you both agree, that we should address the issue of depression first. Paige, you've obviously been a very good mother. I get the sense that you're trying hard to get it right for everyone, but that you feel you're not managing that. That's a very lonely and frightening place to be. So I think you and I, perhaps, could have a few sessions about that, then we can get together again with Bill. How does that sound?'

Paige heard the words 'lonely' and 'frightened'. They flickered like tiny candles on a dark, wet night. Then she saw Bill look at his watch.

'Fine, fine,' he said. 'I'm pretty busy at the moment, so if she can sort herself out on her own, so much the better.'

'Paige?'

Paige dropped her head so that neither of them would see the tears welling up. Crying irritated Bill more than anything else. But she nodded, and by the time Ruth had finished shuffling papers and saying something sympathetic to Bill, Paige had control of herself again.

'Well,' said Bill cheerfully as Paige drove them home. 'Counselling is money for old rope. All she did was ask us how we felt. Still, I'd call her assessment pretty conclusive. You are bonkers. Officially in need of treatment.'

Chapter 25

Jess, waitressing in the Dizzy Donkey, asked the seventeenth customer of the day how spicy they would like their order. Her feet ached, sending pain up through her legs, and she thought she would never get the smell of the deep fat fryer out of her hair. It even permeated her sleep.

But at least she did sleep. She was too tired not to. And the staff were expected to eat at the beginning of each shift, so she stopped picking and ate two proper meals a day. The others consisted of Bryn and Elle, both gap year students, a Swedish girl called Kristen, Mel, a cheery Australian in her thirties who was working her way round the world, a very tall and silent man called Dan who, according to Mel, 'had been to Eton or some very posh school, then was an investment banker and had a nervous breakdown', and a trio of duty managers, Sal, Rick and Paul. Sal was the only one of the three that she respected. Paul was always putting money from the tip box into the till and not, as far she could see, ever replacing it, and Rick was having an affair with Kristen, which meant that she took extra long breaks and arrived late on her shifts. Dan was an efficient waiter and always seemed to be there, but he almost never spoke, except in a soft, low voice, using the minimum of words. He had long hair that curled down below his shoulders and a goatee beard. Jess tried to draw him out in conversation but soon gave up, which left only Mel as a friend.

On the quieter shifts they exchanged some personal details. 'So what are you going to do after this?' Mel asked

'After? I've only just got here.' Jess didn't want to look at the years ahead of her. She was working double shifts as often as she could to save up money, which had the extra advantage of preventing her from attending the stream of engagement parties, house warmings and celebrations of promotion that all her friends seemed to be enjoying. She hadn't seen Jake for three and a half weeks.

'Come travelling with me,' suggested Mel. 'You can leave all your problems behind.'

It crossed Jess's mind, fleetingly, that her problems were quite capable of smuggling themselves into her backpack and coming with her. She could see herself travelling the world with a collection of angry monkeys chattering on her shoulder. But she looked up and saw a familiar frame cross the window.

Jake. He walked into the Dizzy Donkey with a woman and a man. It looked like business. Jess turned away, feeling hollow, as he sat down at table six. One of hers.

'Mel! Could you do my table six?'

'Sorry mate, I'm off duty and I've got a dentist's appointment. I can't be late.'

The only other waiter on duty was Dan. 'Dan,' she hissed. 'Can you take my table six?'

'OK.' He flicked his notebook out of his apron pocket and stood over the table, silent and patient, while they sorted out a confusing mix of decaffeinated skimmed-milk lattes, a wine and mineral water spritzer and Jake's black coffee, very strong. She remembered him knocking back an espresso every morning.

Mel took off her apron and hung it up with a grin. 'So you're going to tell me that when you asked for a job here you didn't know he came in here?'

'He?' hedged Jess.

'The dark guy on the left with no tie. The one who looks like Lucas from *Spooks*.'

'Oh him. Yes, well. We did have a thing for a bit.' Jess could hear her own heartbeat, pounding in her ears. 'But I'd forgotten he came here.' That was a lie. She and Jake had had their first coffee in this restaurant. Jake's office was round the corner. When she'd been job hunting her feet had taken her past every restaurant and coffee bar she and Jake had been to, and she'd seen a notice in this window. 'It was a coincidence.'

'Yeah, right.' But Mel patted her on the shoulder. 'What happened?'

'We were together for nearly eight months. Two hundred and thirty-three days, to be exact.' She tried to smile. 'It was great. He was probably the most normal boyfriend I'd ever had, more like the sort of person my sister always went out with before she got married. Good job. Nice manners. Great flat. Calls when he says he's going to. Just out of a very tough relationship so still hurting, but very aware of how that could affect us. Great to talk to. Bought me flowers. Discussions about the future.' She thought of adding 'good in bed' but that was private. Between her and Jake. 'Then *bam*,' she continued, 'I took him home to meet my family and it was as if a light had gone out. He must have looked at my mother – who has to be the most irritating woman alive – or my bully of a father and thought, I don't want that. Then he didn't call for a bit, then he was back, and then we had a fabulous weekend that ended in a huge row over a pair of shoes, and *bam*, he was gone. He sent a text two days ago, saying he'd like to get together soon, but nothing definite. And now he walks in here.'

'Weird,' said Mel.

Jess nodded, trying not to let her eyes fill with tears. 'I do know that he's been so hurt by Cassie – that's his ex-wife – that he finds it very hard to trust women and to get close.'

'You're well out of it,' said Mel, touching her on the shoulder again. 'My number-one tip for spotting a bastard is someone who pulls your strings about how badly his last girl treated him. If he keeps telling you how betrayed he's been, and how that's preventing him from committing to you, watch out.'

'Because he's been so damaged by her?'

Mel grinned. 'Nope. Because he's lying.'

Jess shook her head. 'I don't think Jake is lying. All his friends said they were so glad we were together after the way she'd jerked him around. She was a first-class bitch, apparently.'

'Well, trust your own instincts. You're the expert on you. Don't listen to me or anyone else. And don't change yourself for anyone. You're great. If he can't see that, he's a fool.' She looked at her watch. 'Late again. Shit.'

She left. Jess spent the next hour trying not to look at table six. Waitresses were often invisible. Jake was always very focused on what he was doing and the conversation was intense.

But after an hour he slapped his notebook shut, disentangled his long legs from the table and got up, looking around. 'Jess! What are you doing here?'

'Waitressing.' Her heart had moved up to her throat now and was ticking furiously.

'What happened to graphic design?' He looked down at her, as if he really cared.

'I walked out. I was being bullied.'

He nodded slowly. 'Good for you.' His gaze travelled lazily up and down. 'You look great. Except for the shoes.' He gave that funny, quirky, sympathetic smile, she'd missed so much.

She felt as if she had stepped over a cliff. The ground beneath her had fallen away, taking the restaurant with it. All she could see were a pair of dark eyes and the message in them. 'I'll be wearing them tomorrow,' she whispered. 'The shoes, I mean.'

He smiled and touched her cheek. 'I'll be in. I've missed you so much, Jess.'

'But why didn't you call?'

He smiled sadly. 'I could see that I was taking it all too fast, that you weren't ready, that you didn't want to make the kind of changes people need to make when they're serious about each other. I wanted to give you some space.'

Jess swallowed. 'I don't need space. I just need you.'

'Good.' He kissed her on the lips, lingering just long enough for her to taste the coffee he had drunk. 'I'll be in tomorrow.'

'I'll be wearing the shoes.'

Jake came in the following afternoon alone, for coffee. This time, Jess didn't feel she had to get Dan to take his order. 'Hi Jess,' he said. 'An espresso.' He smiled up at her, and then down at the shoes.

Wearing high heels all day hurt. But it was worth it. Jake picked her up from the restaurant when she finished her shift.

'Anywhere I don't have to stand.' She took one shoe off, massaging her foot.

'A long, hot bath then. For two. I'm going to spoil you. I shall kiss every little pain away.'

Chapter 26

Paige was very nervous about the idea of one-to-one counselling, but she knew that if she didn't follow up Bill would
be unable to resist telling the girls. She could see him now,
slapping the table with mirth. 'Your mother demanded that
we go to a counselling session. And guess what? The counsellor decided the problems were all on her side. We were
asked a whole load of questions, and the upshot was that
your mum was pronounced completely potty.' The girls
would look at her and ask her what she'd done about it.
Especially Jess.

'You won't tell the girls I'm seeing a counsellor, will you?'
she asked Bill at breakfast.

'Course not,' he said, squeezing her shoulder sympathetically.
'It's up to you what you say, but I think you're right. Secrecy is
the best policy.'

Paige nodded. It was worse than a cervical smear or mam-
mogram, she told herself, driving into town. Or going for a
blood test. She knocked on the door and forced herself to
smile. Ruth let her in and offered her a glass of water.

'Going back to our last session, I picked up a little uneasiness
over the sexual side of your relationship,' said Ruth.

Paige had hoped she wasn't going to talk about this. 'Well,
um, it's been . . . well, difficult. I was very ill after the birth of

each of our daughters, and I think that's really affected Bill. I don't think he's ever quite recovered from it.'

'And how old are your daughters?'

'Twenty-eight and thirty.'

Ruth's eyebrows went up. 'That's quite a long time ago. Can you tell me what happened?'

Paige explained that she'd had pre-eclampsia when she was pregnant with Sophie, and had to have a caesarean two months early, 'when they told me it would be very dangerous for me to have another baby. Something to do with my blood – I can't remember the exact reason, but anyway it was highly likely to happen again. The consultant suggested that either Bill or I be sterilised, but Bill wasn't keen. He thought it was too perma-nent, and that we would regret it if there were medical advances in a few years time.'

Ruth nodded.

'But it made me very nervous about sex for a bit. Bill thought I shouldn't take the pill because it made me put on weight, and he knew how unhappy that made me, but he got very impatient with all my fussing over condoms and caps and things.' Paige stopped, trying to remember those days. They seemed so far away. 'One night we both got very drunk and did it without any contraception. And that was Jess. The compli-cations for the whole of that pregnancy were horrendous. I nearly died, and so did she. She was born at twenty-six weeks, even more premature than Sophie, and . . . Bill was obviously disappointed that she wasn't a boy, and . . . oh . . . this is all very trivial compared to what lots of people go through, don't you think?'

'Well, there was obviously a lot of tension and anxiety around her birth,' said Ruth carefully. 'And perhaps some of those issues still need to be resolved.'

'I think it has affected us. It's always Jess causing the problem in the family. She winds him up and he can't help getting angry with her. I know I ought to be sorting them both out but I'm hopeless at it. It's my fault, I know, but I can't see how to. Everything I do and say seems to make it worse. But I do try.'

'I see,' said Ruth. 'Going back to the evening when she was conceived: when you say you were both very drunk, how drunk was that?'

'Oh, I don't know. It was far too long ago. I remember Bill cooked me a special meal because we'd been getting on rather badly and having a lot of arguments, and he's a really good cook when he tries. And he did try – he lit candles and played soft music . . . and bought champagne, which I love, although he thinks it's over-rated. In fact, he says he can't stand the stuff.'

'So you may have drunk more than he did?'

Paige blushed. 'I'm sure I did. I had the most terrible hangover the following day. I can remember it now. I know I do drink too much sometimes. Do you think I've got a problem?'

Ruth ignored her question. 'I'm just surprised that he was able to make love if he was so drunk.'

'I don't think he drank as much as I did,' admitted Paige, ashamed. 'I've always felt bad about that, getting so out of it that I forgot about contraception. It's one of the signs of alcoholism, isn't it, when you take terrible risks, like driving a car when you know you can barely walk?'

'Paige, I don't think you're an alcoholic. Your husband was not as drunk as you were, he bought and then poured you your favourite drink and then, while he was sober enough to be able to make love, did so without taking precautions, knowing that a pregnancy might kill you. Is that correct?'

'Oh, that sounds a bit . . . well, clinical. He just forgot. And he always said it was a woman's right to take responsibility for her own body, so it was up to me.'

'Although he was frequently irritated when you insisted on using contraception?'

Paige looked at the floor. 'It was my fault. I didn't handle it properly. But he was also sorry; he kept saying that he shouldn't have trusted me to remember something that important. He

152

was wonderful throughout the pregnancy, very caring and protective, and told everyone how much danger I was in.'

'In what sense?'

'Well, I remember him saying that I couldn't go out in the evening because I mustn't have any additional strain. There was one doctor who told me not to worry too much. Bill insisted on making sure I didn't see him again because he didn't want someone who wasn't taking my condition seriously anywhere near me. It was all rather embarrassing, as you can imagine.'

'It must have been terrifying.'

Paige tried to laugh. 'Yes, I had to do a will and everything. We discussed how I would want Sophie brought up and I wrote little letters for her to open on her birthdays. I had nightmares about it for years afterwards, I was so sure I was going to die. So was Bill, and everybody else. It was like in a silent movie, as if I was strapped to some awful conveyor belt inching me towards a giant saw that would cut me to ribbons. Nobody liked to talk about next year's holidays in front of me.'

'Did you consider an abortion? As it was so dangerous to continue with the pregnancy?'

'Oh no, I couldn't do that. That was the whole point when I got pregnant with Sophie. Neither of us believed in abortion so we got married.'

Ruth probed further. 'And after that? What happened to sex and intimacy?'

'For years Bill went on protecting me. It was as if we could never quite let go, because he was so worried it might happen again, and he would go through phases of saying he didn't think it was worth us taking the risk. He did admit that he'd an affair during the pregnancy.' Paige looked at the floor, because she had hoped she would never have to tell anyone about this. 'He really felt bad about it, but a man can't be expected to do without sex completely, can he? And the affair was just that, just sex. He said that she was just a silly little bitch out for whatever she could get, and he was very honest about it. He told me everything . . .'

Paige took a deep breath as it all came tumbling out. Things she hadn't thought about for years. 'That's why I'm not too worried about everyone suggesting he might be having an affair with his accountant, Anthea, because he's always been so keen on honesty. And he's looked after me so carefully – he was very careful about my not having late nights, or doing too much voluntary work at the girls' school. When someone offered me a part-time job he was horrified. It even took me ages to get him to agree that I could join the village book group, and in the end he only gave in because they got books out of the library and it ended before ten.'

'What did your health have to do with getting books out of the library?'

'Oh, we couldn't afford books. We're not as rich as people think, and there certainly isn't any spare for books.'

'Does he buy books?'

'He doesn't read much. He gets magazines about yachting and golf.'

'And your magazines are?'

'Well, women don't really need magazines these days, do they? With the way the Sunday papers have such great free supplements. I can get recipes off the internet, and Bill always gives me a new cookbook for Christmas. So it's not a problem.'

'Paige, I think you may find this thought rather surprising, but everything you say indicates you're a victim of domestic abuse.'

'Oh no,' replied Paige. 'He has a bit of a bad temper, but he's never hit me or anything. In thirty years, remember. That truly isn't where our problems lie. If people need help in our village he's the first to offer, and he ran the local fun run for children in poverty in Africa and . . . everyone says he's wonderful. He does so much for me. And for everyone else.'

'Domestic abuse isn't always about hitting women. It's about controlling, insulting, disrespecting and belittling them.'

Paige shook her head. 'You make me sound like some poor,

154

sad little victim who can't stand up for herself. But I do, I argue with him – too often if anything. In many ways it's very much my fault that we're not getting on all that well at the moment.'

'That's a definitive symptom of abuse. Victims always blame themselves.'

Paige didn't think Ruth was right. 'My daughter Sophie, who's always reading articles about psychology, says that if one person in a partnership changes it's often all that's needed to change the whole dynamic. All I need to do is learn how to handle him properly and then he'll react to me better.'

'Paige,' said Ruth. 'Abusers don't change whatever you do. They feel completely justified in their actions and their lives are best when they're getting their own way all the time. They don't need to see anyone else's point of view. They don't see why they should.' She hesitated, looking at Paige carefully, as if not sure whether to say any more.

'Having seen you together and heard what you've said, I think I should warn you to be quite careful. If you confront him or if you leave, you must always think about your own safety. That's when an abusive man can become highly retalia-tory.'

Paige wasn't quite sure what she meant.

Seeing her puzzled look, Ruth added: 'Paige, you've been frightened quite often enough over the course of your mar-riage, so I'm reluctant to say anything that will add to that fear. But you are a very able woman, you've brought up a family and obviously have a lovely home, and you clearly look after Bill just as much as he looks after you. You're not mad – not at all – and you are intelligent enough to decide how you want to live your life. But if that means leaving Bill you need to plan care-fully. He could be dangerous.'

Chapter 27

Sophie longed to know whether Jess and Jake had got back together, but Jess was very non-committal about her life.

Sophie had texted Jake to thank him for lunch and had got a text back: 'It was great. Let me know if you're ever in the area, and we can do it again.' Not that she would. But she did want to know if Jake had taken her advice, and whether Jess had seen sense and stopped being what Bill always called bolshie.

It seemed that she had. 'We're coming down to The Rowans for Christmas,' said Jess, one evening on the phone. 'We'll arrive on Christmas Eve for supper, then back up to London on Boxing Day. Forty-eight hours with The Beast should be quite enough.'

'We? And don't call Daddy The Beast, he doesn't deserve it.' Jake's research into Bill's business activities, and his conclusion that Bill wasn't being wholly honest with them all about his wealth, lodged in Sophie like a piece of broken glass. If she thought about it the jagged edges hurt. But in the family script she always defended him, and if she gave that up he would be on his own. There must be some explanation for his behaviour with Anthea. And for why he felt the need to pretend he was so broke. Or maybe Jake had got it all wrong, and the website he'd consulted was out of date.

She tuned back in to her sister. 'Me'n Jake,' said Jess with satisfaction. 'We're back together again. Not absolutely the way it was, but relationships change, don't they? He doesn't get on with his family so I invited him to join us. Mum's thrilled.'

'Oh good.' Sophie almost wanted to tell Jess about her part in it, but suppressed the desire to blurt it all out.

'He was giving me some space. He thought I wasn't ready to change, and he says that when you're in a committed relationship both of you have to change.'

'Harry and I haven't.'

'Well, maybe . . .' Jess broke off, but Sophie knew what she meant. Maybe she and Harry should have changed. Maybe what they had was friendship, not love. It was something that worried Sophie from time to time.

It made her feel cross with Jess. So she was suddenly the expert on relationships, was she? She and Jake wouldn't even be back together if Sophie hadn't got involved, and now Jess was criticising her and Harry. 'Are you sure Jake's ready for something as full-on as a family Christmas?' She pointed out that he'd recently emerged from a very destructive relationship and might not be ready to commit and—

'I'm not asking for commitment,' said Jess. 'I'm cool about all that.'

Harry, clearing away the remains of supper, couldn't understand why Sophie was so angry when she put down the phone. 'Jess is twenty-eight. She knows the score. If she wants to invite Jake down she's entitled to.'

'I just think she's blowing it by inviting him down for a family Christmas too soon. He's had a tough time with his ex-wife, and their relationship is still quite fragile.'

'How do you know?' asked Harry.

Sophie pulled open the dishwasher and began loading it, to hide her face. 'When he . . . er . . . came to see me on the Souper Soups shoot he mentioned it, I can't remember why . . .'

157

'What do you mean, came to see you on the Souper Soups shoot? You never told me.'

'Didn't I?' Sophie had forgotten that keeping secrets was difficult. 'Well, I don't tell you *everything*, any more than you tell me everything.' As she spoke she realised that she could have phrased it better.

Harry crossed his arms, looking hurt and puzzled. 'But . . .'

'I mean,' amended Sophie, 'I don't tell you every detail of my day any more than you tell me every detail of yours.'

Harry was a sporting man and for him the ball was either in or out, the horse won or lost or you were on his team or were the opposition. Sophie had always found it difficult to persuade him that in the light and shade of emotional matters you had to think of photo-finishes and disputed goals, of judgement rather than facts. 'Well, I'd tell you if Jake or Jess turned up at my office,' he said.

He probably would. Sophie sighed. 'Never mind, it's not important,' she told a sticky plate. She straightened up, more confident of herself. 'The important thing is whether Jess is going to blow yet another of her chances in life by being Jess, and when it all ends we'll have to pick up the pieces.'

'We don't have to. It's not compulsory.'

Sophie was irritated. Of course they had to. She loved Jess and intended to be there for her. Sometimes Harry was so unsupportive. But, on the other hand, Christmas would be more fun with Jake. So far, he seemed good with Bill, which meant an easier Christmas all round. It was worth buying that black satin dress she'd seen recently, figure-hugging with a sweetheart neckline and a surprisingly low back. Her blonde hair would look striking against the black. Or should she wear it up?

'What other things don't you tell me?' asked Harry.

'Oh Harry, do we have to do this now? Of course I tell you everything important. But Jake coming to the shoot for his article was just one of those things that I forgot about as soon as I got home. And speaking of forgetting things, I've got to check my Christmas to-do list.' She didn't dare look Harry in the face, because he would know she was fibbing. Sophie whipped a long list out of her handbag and began ticking things off: presents for the girls' teachers, for the girls, for friends, the food she was contributing to The Rowans. Presents for Jess. And Jake. What could she get Jake? What did you get a man you hardly knew?

Chapter 28

Bella, Lottie and Summer thought Christmas at The Rowans was magical. Every other year they all trudged off to Harry's parents, who lived in a bungalow in Morden. Harry's mother had china animals on every surface and a fat, smelly spaniel. Bella, Lottie and Summer adored these, but loved running around the large, rambling garden at The Rowans more. And Bella was just old enough to remember that Bill dressed up as Father Christmas, coming up the drive with his sack full of presents and roaring 'Ho-ho-ho, who's been a good girl?' at his shrieking granddaughters. 'Will Father Christmas come up the drive?' asked Lottie.

'Of course,' promised Paige. 'Because you've all been very good girls.'

Sophie had to admit that Paige had decorated The Rowans beautifully, with swags of greenery from the garden draped over the mantelpiece and twisted over the banisters. She'd lit white church candles everywhere, placed bowls of white forced hyacinths on tables and a log fire blazed in every fireplace. Outside, white fairy lights wound through the yew domes that stood sentinel on either side of the front door. A handmade wreath of holly and fir cones from the woods hung on the doorknocker.

At six o'clock on Christmas Eve Jess and Jake burst through

the kitchen door, laughing and weighed down with presents, Jess scooping Lottie, then Summer, into her arms and Jake swinging Bella up into the air to her delighted shrieks. Everyone kissed everyone – Sophie saw that even Jess and Bill embraced with something approaching father-and-daughter affection. Jess went upstairs with Sophie to play favourite auntie and persuade the girls that Father Christmas would arrive more quickly if they went to sleep. By the time they came downstairs again, Bill had poured his best vintage claret for Harry and Jake.

'Do you want any help, Mum?' asked Sophie, and was given a plate of smoked salmon canapés to take out to the men.

'She's looking like the fairy on top of the Christmas tree,' said Bill, putting his arm around Sophie. 'Don't you think she's a smasher, Jake?'

Jake, smiling down at her, agreed that she was. Sophie felt safe with her father's strong arm around her, hearing his big jovial laugh booming out. It was what coming home was all about. He squeezed her shoulder again and reluctantly released her to Harry.

Paige called them all into the dining room, and soon there was a happy hubbub round the table, with Bill and Jake alternately holding everyone's attention, occasionally punctuated by a shout from Jess or Harry's low, considered statements. Jake was wittier, but Bill commanded deference. Sophie watched them, content to see her family so happy and Jess's face flush with wine and love.

Her mother had been right to dismiss Jess's claims about Anthea, thought Sophie. Paige seemed to have chosen keeping the family together over any fuss about adultery. And as for Bill's protestations of poverty . . . well, parents often withheld information from their children if they thought it was best for them. Didn't they?

'Do we always tell our children absolutely the whole truth?' she asked Harry later, as they undressed in The Rowan's large and comfortable spare room, with plump floral cushions everywhere. She turned her back to him, so that he could unzip her dress.

Harry kissed her shoulder as he peeled the black satin away from her skin. 'Well, not about Father Christmas. Or the Tooth Fairy. What's brought this on, anyway?'

'Just puzzling over why Dad always makes out he's so broke, that's all.'

Harry kissed her other shoulder. 'That's easy. It gives him control. No one can argue when he says no to something.'

Sophie didn't think Harry was being quite fair, but he had a point about the Tooth Fairy and Father Christmas, and perhaps pretending to be broke was like that. She turned round and embraced him, revelling in his solidity.

The following morning the girls were up at five to open their stockings and breakfast on chocolate ('Harry, *really*, you should have taken the chocolate money away from them'). They raced around on a sugar high, demanding to see Father Christmas, until Jess and Jake appeared from Stable Cottage. 'He'll come at ten o'clock,' promised Jess. 'Look, when the little hand is on ten and the big hand on twelve.'

'It's ten o'clock,' cried Bella half an hour later. 'The little hand is on ten, look.'

But Bill was in his study. Sophie tried to calm the girls down, in case they broke the chairs jumping up and down on them to see out of the window, waiting for Father Christmas's arrival.

'When is he going to come?' asked Bella as ten past ten crept by. 'I've been a good girl, haven't I?'

'You've been a very good girl,' soothed Sophie. 'You've all been very good girls and Father Christmas will be here soon.' She exchanged glances over their heads with Harry, who offered to give them rides on his knee while they were waiting.

'He's in his study,' whispered Jess. 'There's no sign of his cos-tume.'

Sophie looked at Paige. Between them they'd tried to think of every possible way of keeping Bill happy that Christmas, from making sure that he had his favourite freshly squeezed orange juice at breakfast to checking that his Father Christmas outfit still fitted. Together they'd reminded him how young the little girls were and asked him what time he'd like to give them their presents. 'So we can make sure they're not waiting too long. You know what little children are like.'

'You're so good with them,' Paige added.

'Yes, Dad,' said Sophie. 'They adore you and Father Christmas is the big thing for them at that age. Last year, Bella talked about Father Christmas coming up the drive for weeks afterwards.' Bill, who'd been very cheerful for days, had assured them that he would be ready at ten, if they could get the girls lined up at the hall window. 'And don't be late,' he added. 'I don't want it to go off half-cock.'

Now the girls were whining and fidgeting, and Harry was looking at his watch. Sophie and Harry had been up since five, trying to find ways of distracting Lottie and Bella. Even Summer had caught something of the Christmas fever. Paige went upstairs, asking Sophie to make sure that the children were out of the way while she smuggled the Father Christmas outfit and the sack of presents into Bill's study. She tapped softly on the door. 'I thought it might save a little time if I brought these down,' Sophie heard her say. 'The little ones are so excited and they're waiting for you.'

'He waved me away,' she whispered to Sophie. 'But I'm sure he'll be out soon.' At ten-thirty Bella began to cry. 'Father Christmas thinks I've been naughty,' she sobbed. 'I didn't mean to be.' Lottie and Summer burst into tears as well.

'No,' said Harry, bending down to hug his daughters. 'Father Christmas is probably stuck in traffic. On Christmas Day the skies are full of reindeer jams.'

'Don't be silly Daddy. Only Father Christmas has got reindeer.' Bella stopped crying long enough to give him an incredulous look, one perfect tear drying on her cheek, before she redoubled her sobbing. Sophie heard Paige sigh and saw her march back towards Bill's study. Sophie pulled her mother back. 'Mum, don't challenge him. You know what he's like. If you go on at him he'll never come out.'

'It's all right, Sophie. Let me do this.'

Sophie had never heard her mother so determined. It was quite a shock. She was used to thinking of Paige as someone who would go along with whatever was easiest. Sometimes she'd barely felt she had a mother, because Paige had been so self-effacing. It didn't feel right, Paige taking the initiative. 'No Mum, really . . .' She tried to call her mother back but Paige knocked on the door again and Sophie drew back, ready to step in if her mother goaded her father too far.

'For God's sake, what is it now?' Sophie could hear Bill's voice. 'Can't you see I'm busy?'

'No,' said Paige. 'I can see that you are being manipulative. You cannot possibly have any work to do on Christmas Day, and even if you did you could do it after the girls have had their presents. I saw you do this with Sophie and Jess – you were loving and affectionate until they were old enough to be manipulated, and then you played mind games with them until they didn't know the difference between love and guilt. I will not let you do it all over again to our grandchildren. Bella thinks that Father Christmas isn't coming because she's been naughty, and that it's all her fault. If you don't get out there and behave like a decent human being I will leave you. That's all.'

Sophie shrank back, but saw the shadow of her father getting up from his desk. 'I don't think you quite know what you're saying,' he said in a low voice. 'I have urgent work to do and I will not, repeat will not, play Father Christmas until I have finished. You cannot expect the household to run to your controlling timetable, and neither can you expect your selfish desires to be fulfilled to the letter on every occasion. It's time you learned a lesson, and I will make sure that you do.'

Sophie ran to find Harry, Jess and Jake all pretending to be horses in the hall, bouncing Bella, Lottie and Summer on their shoulders and racing each other. They stopped and lowered the girls down. 'I think Dad's going to kill Mum,' whispered Sophie.

Harry, Jake and Jess stared at her.

'That was a figure of speech. But they're really angry at each other.'

'Shall I see if I can sort it out?' asked Jake. 'Sometimes a stranger can get through better than a member of the family.' Sophie heard Paige rush upstairs and wondered if she should follow to comfort her, but she had quite enough to do stopping the children screaming and crying. Why Paige should think Christmas Day was a suitable time for a showdown, Sophie couldn't imagine. They all knew what Bill was like, and Paige must have realised that nothing would inflame him more than an ultimatum.

Ten minutes later Jake emerged. 'Father Christmas en route,' he whispered.

'Mum,' shouted Sophie up the stairs. 'Father Christmas.'

The cry was taken up by the three children.

'Ho-ho-ho,' came the roar from the end of the drive and a white bearded figure with a sack over his back strode towards them.

'You're amazing,' whispered Sophie to Jake.

He winked at her. 'Your father hadn't realised how upset the girls were, and your mother just went blasting in with all sorts of over-the-top threats about divorce. But he was very understanding about it, because he knows how hard she's worked to make this a good Christmas, and thinks she got hysterical because she's over-tired. He's going to give Bella a special extra present – a fiver, I think – and tell her that she really has been a good girl.'

Sophie thought about it. 'I suppose he's right. No one actually told him they were upset because we were all so busy trying not to upset *him*. I know he's difficult but Mum does handle it badly because she tiptoes round him and caters to his every need, then suddenly blows up into a huge explosion. I don't suppose he ever knows quite where he is with her.' She sighed. 'Maybe Harry's right, he's an alcoholic and when he's not drunk he's a lovely person but when he is he's a fiend.'

Jake smiled down at her. 'You're looking very beautiful.'

Sophie moved back an inch. 'Oh, well, thank you. And Jake . . .' She hesitated. 'It's all going well with Jess now, isn't it?'

'Of course.' He continued to smile. 'I feel such a shit about not phoning her for a month. Jess was giving off "stay away" vibes over those bloody shoes I'd bought her and I thought I'd taken it all too far, too fast. I wanted to give her a magical weekend, with treatments and beautiful presents . . . but she seemed quite angry about it all, you know what she's like. So I backed off, thinking she'd get in touch when she was ready.' His eyes softened. 'But talking to you made me realise how wrong I was. Thank you. Thank you so much.'

Sophie nodded. 'I was worried. I don't want anyone to mess her around.'

Jake put a hand on her arm. 'Sophie, please believe me. Jess is my number one priority. If ever this happens again will you contact me? As a friend?'

'Of course.' Jake had that quality of making you feel more alive. Sophie could see that even Paige felt it, and that she brightened every time he spoke to her. Jess no longer looked like a Boy Scout but reminded Sophie of a heroine in an arty French film, with killer heels, Hepburn-esque eyeliner and a lacy camisole hinting at the suggestion of a cleavage.

Sophie's every nerve end fizzled. Just looking at Jake was like walking through an icy shower. She shivered with exhilaration. A light flirtation was fine. It made being home just slightly more fun. She shot a look at Harry but he hadn't noticed, too occupied in helping Summer play with her new toys. 'Where's Granny?' asked Bella, running back to them, followed by Bill in his Father Christmas outfit. 'Granny didn't see Father Christmas.'

'I think your mother is in one of her sulks,' murmured

Father Christmas through his beard. 'Perhaps someone should go up and find out how she is.'

Sophie wished that everyone, including Paige, would remember that Christmas was about children.

Chapter 29

Paige was trembling, struggling not to cry as she hurried upstairs. If you confront him, Ruth had said, plan it carefully to ensure your own safety, but she wasn't sure what that meant. She hadn't meant to do anything on Christmas Day, but seeing the tears on Bella's cheeks and remembering Jess at her age, she couldn't help it. There'd been one Christmas Eve, after she'd begged Bill to spend a bit of time with Jess on her own, because he either played with the girls together or favoured Sophie. So he had agreed to take Jess for a walk to the playground in the village, but had gone to the pub while Jess played on the swings. He'd then come home without her, leaving her alone in the playground aged five. Paige, thinking they'd been out for a long time, had noticed Bill in his study as she passed. 'Where's Jess?'

'How should I know? She's your responsibility.' He genuinely seemed to have forgotten that she had been with him.

Paige drove down the lane to the playground, white with terror. Every dark bush she drove past was hunched with menace. Jess could be under any of them, frightened – even injured or dead. A small child on her own in an open playground was an easy target. Paige's hands were shaking on the wheel. She wanted to run down the road screaming for help but forced herself to start with where Jess had last been seen.

The playground. She found Jess hunched up on a swing, shivering, with tears on her cheeks. 'I'm frightened, Mummy,' she sobbed. 'And cold. Daddy left me. I didn't know what to do.'

Paige had been furious with Bill, but he maintained that if she didn't like the way he looked after Jess then he wouldn't bother helping her out in future. Oh, and you'd better not tell anyone. Social Services might take her away, along with Sophie. 'They'd ask whether a competent mother would have left it until evening before she asked herself where her five-year-old child was.' That had been the end of Bill and Jess having 'quality time' together.

She looked round her bedroom. What might he do now? What could she do to defend herself? She sank down on the bed, hearing the cries of 'Father Christmas!' from a long way away. She didn't want anyone to see her with red eyes, and she only had these few minutes, while she knew Bill was occupied, to work out what to do.

He kept her passport locked up in the study, but she usually had her driving licence in her bag. She had some jewellery, although how you would go about turning it into money she had no idea. But the pearls and the diamond brooch, both of which came from her mother, were allegedly valuable. She wore the pearls all the time, but you couldn't wear a diamond brooch very often. And she had two credit cards. With fumbling hands she took one out of her purse, deciding that she would keep it, along with her driving licence and the diamond brooch, in her old gardening coat that always hung beside the back door. And a spare set of keys to her car, so that if ever she had to run she could just grab her coat. It would be good if she could also put away a little cash, but Bill insisted on seeing all receipts and went through them carefully. It would be difficult to smuggle even a few pounds out. After lunch she would find an empty bottle of wine – there would be no shortage of those – and she would leave it under the bed, where Bill would never look, in case she ever needed a weapon. There was very little else she could do.

But now she had a turkey to serve and the whole family were waiting for her. Paige splashed cold water on her eyes, re-did her make-up and went downstairs.

She would have to wait, to see what revenge Bill decided to mete out. Unless she left him first. She didn't even dare to think about that option.

She served the turkey without looking at him, but once everyone was seated, wearing paper hats and pulling crackers, she got up to fetch another batch of gravy from the kitchen. Bill took her hand as she passed. 'Are you all right, darling?' he asked. 'Everything looks delicious.'

She was aware of everyone's eyes on her. 'I'm fine. Just going to get some more gravy.'

'Come back soon,' said Bill, squeezing her hand so hard that she almost cried out. 'We all want Christmas to be nice, don't we?'

As she sat down he raised a glass. 'It's a great pleasure for your mother and me to have all our family round the table at Christmas. So I'd like you all to raise your glasses to the cook, who's done us such a marvellous lunch.'

As Paige looked around the table, she took in each beloved face. Sophie, a fairy princess with her blonde hair and black satin dress, flushed and vivacious. Dear, stolid Harry with Summer falling asleep on his lap. Jake's quick, dark face turned from Jess to Sophie and back again. And there was her darling Jess, her glass raised and her curled hair bubbling out in a halo over her head, her eyes bright, looking like a person in her own right at last rather than a pale echo of Sophie, and then the two girls, Bella and Lottie, almost identically blonde, their blue eyes round with wonder. Her family, all together. It was what she longed for. If she left it would tear them apart, because she knew that, deep down, Sophie would take Bill's side, and that Jess would reject them both.

She met Bill's eyes over his raised glass and knew that he wouldn't do anything while they were all here. And whatever he did do, eventually, it would be something that she couldn't fight with a credit card in a gardening coat or a wine bottle hidden under a bed.

Chapter 30

Bill was in a good temper after Christmas, even offering to make a bonfire of the Christmas tree. He picked up the paper. 'Oh, look at this. A new report based on the latest murder statistics.' He laughed. 'All you women terrified of walking along a lonely lane on a dark night are clearly mad. If you are going to get killed, it'll be your nearest and dearest doing it. Here, read this.' He laid the paper down on the table and jabbed his finger at the headline as he read it out.

'"Every three days a woman is murdered by her partner." *Partner*,' he sneered. 'I can't stand that word. As if a man and a woman were like business partners. They should be getting married. No wonder the silly sluts are getting killed.'

'Well, most of them get caught, don't they?' Paige replied. 'After all, the husband is always the primary suspect, isn't he?'

'Oh don't worry, the courts understand when a man has been provoked beyond reason. They get very light sentences, these domestic murderers. And it's a better deal for them than divorce because they don't get half their assets ripped off.'

'Would you like a coffee?' Paige decided to change the subject.

Bill took the mug of coffee without acknowledgement. 'Well, that was a good Christmas. I'm glad to see that Jess has found herself a sensible man at last. He's a good bloke, that Jake.'

'I thought Sophie and Harry seemed a bit strained, though.'

Bill's grin flickered with malice. 'Our Soph has had it all a bit too much her own way throughout her life, and now she's stuck with that bore of a husband. She's jealous of Jess. I saw her looking at Jake, like a cat waiting outside a mouse hole.'

'I thought you liked Harry.'

'Oh, he's fine for a trip to the pub, but he's brain-dead. Sophie runs him like a train: he's scarcely capable of independent thought. He goes on and on about his plans to start his own company, but it's all pie-in-the-sky. He'll never make anything of himself. But Jake's got a good head on his shoulders. He knows the price of fish.'

Paige thought Bill might even have forgotten about his promise to teach her a lesson.

'Might' was the word. She had known him take his revenge slowly in the past, and it made her jumpy.

'Seen this?' He handed her a page from the local newspaper. It was about a man who told everyone that his wife had left him but, twenty years later, had been found to have buried her at the end of his garden.

She read it. 'Do we know them?'

'Know who?' He sounded irritated.

'I just wondered why you were showing me this.' Paige was determined to be brave. 'As we don't know the people involved.'

He took the paper back, looked at it, then handed it back to her. 'You fool,' he said. 'I was showing you the piece underneath, the one about planning permission being granted for a block of flats on the London Road. I was thinking of buying that land, but decided it wouldn't get permission.' He sighed. 'I don't think that Ruth woman is doing you any good at all,' he added. 'Ever since you've been seeing her you've been behaving erratically. Jumping out of your skin half the time, bursting into tears and taking offence at everything I say. She's making you paranoid. That's the trouble with these people, they have to keep you coming back to ensure an income so they create problems for you to have. I don't blame her . . .' He folded the newspaper and banged it down on the table. 'She runs a business and so do I. That's why I can see through these tactics. They're set up to catch women like you, who have no idea of commercial realities.'

Paige froze. Her sessions with Ruth were a lifeline. She was the only person who didn't think she was mad. 'I do feel better,' she said. 'I think she's very good.'

'What?'

'I said, I thought she was very good.'

'What?' He flicked through to the sports pages and read for a few minutes while Paige hovered. Then he put the paper down. 'You don't know what makes a good therapist,' he said quite reasonably. 'But I've done a bit of a background check on her. She's divorced and lives alone, and I think, deep down, she probably finds a couple who have been together all their adult lives, and who are clearly, in spite of our current difficulties, devoted to each other . . .' – he held both hands out towards her, again, as if to embrace her – '. . . very threatening. Don't you think? Some of these therapists are very unhappy people themselves, they get into the whole thing because they have so many unresolved problems.'

Paige's heart reached out to the word 'devoted'. Her parents had been devoted to each other, and they had also argued a lot. 'Well . . .'

'I've been talking to Rose and Andrew,' continued Bill. 'I thought you wouldn't mind because I know you've confided in Rose. They had a sticky patch themselves a few years ago and went to a very good guy, so I've got his number, if that's OK. I thought perhaps we should go to him together again, then you could stop seeing Ruth.'

'Perhaps I should see her one more time, just to sign off?' hedged Paige.

Bill looked at her long and hard, as if thinking it through. 'No, actually, if you don't mind I'd rather you just gave her a

174

call. I think we should be absolutely sure that whoever we see is really going to help, and you just got that woman off the internet. Michael . . .' – he picked a card out of his pocket – '. . . Percy is someone who has been recommended by someone we know and trust. OK?' He smiled at her. 'I'm only trying to do what's best for *you*, Munchkin.' Munchkin was his old pet name for her, which he hadn't used for years.

Paige nodded and put her hand out for the card. 'Do you want me to make the appointment?'

So Bill and Paige ended up in another anonymous room, this time with prints of seascapes on the wall and blue-and-white checked curtains – unlined, Paige noted – in front of Michael Percy. He shook their hands and settled down to ask the same set of questions. Bill was confident and answered them with practised ease. Paige was wary.

'What worries me,' said Bill halfway through the session as he leant towards Michael, 'is that I've always placed a high value on honesty in our marriage – haven't I, darling – even when telling the truth hasn't placed me in the best light. But recently I've become aware that my wife is concealing things from me, perhaps even telling me lies.'

They looked at Paige. She decided that she had to make a stand. 'Bill drinks,' she said. 'And I'm afraid of him when he's drunk. That's when I feel I have to lie.'

Bill caught Michael's eye and smiled. 'Sweetheart, that's ridiculous. We both drink. Often when we share a bottle of wine, you sometimes have a glass more than me, don't you? If it's a wine you like and I don't?'

Paige nodded reluctantly.

'Do I have a bottle of vodka when I wake up in the morning? Am I ever so drunk that I can't stand? Do I get so hung over that I can't get to work? Do you ever find any empty bottles hidden away?' He appealed to Michael. 'Like a lot of women, she doesn't really think things through. Darling, answer me. Do I do any of these things?'

'No, but you drink every day,' whispered Paige, concentrating on the floor. 'And you regularly consume more units than the health guidelines.'

'Health guidelines.' He smiled at Michael again, holding his hands out as if to surrender. 'Who follows those? I've never met anyone who stuck to them, not even you, my darling. And even when I do drink, have I ever threatened you? With a weapon? With my fists? With anything?'

Paige swallowed. 'You picked up one of the kitchen knives once . . .'

'Picked up a knife?' He looked bewildered. 'Was this knife put away where it ought to be, or was it out of place in some way? Because that's the only reason I would have picked it up, to put it away. Go on, tell us. Be honest, wife of mine, I beg you. Tell Michael everything he needs to know and perhaps he can help us out.'

Paige wished she wasn't so thirsty. 'The knife block wasn't in the right place,' she said, her tongue sticking to the roof of her mouth. 'I'd put it away in a cupboard, well, by accident, but when you got it out you didn't just move it, you picked out one of the knives and . . . you were holding one of the knives when you were talking to me. And you were angry.'

Bill ran his hands through his hair, his face rumpled in concern. 'Paige, you are imagining things. And that is why I am so worried about you.'

By the time the hour had ended Paige knew that Michael Percy saw her as a deluded, jealous, nagging, neurotic fool and Bill as a caring, but despairing, loyal husband. Perhaps he was.

As Michael and Bill leant towards each other to agree on meeting at the same time next week, shaking hands, mirroring each other's stance, Michael asked about Bill's boat. 'It was good to see you the other day, Bill, we all thought you'd given up on the *Sophia R.*'

Bill nodded. 'Well, I've been very busy lately and, of course, I haven't wanted to leave the wife on her own too much while she's so depressed, but I hope . . .' He turned to Paige. 'Maybe we could go out together one weekend, just you and me, darling? Michael did suggest that we find more things we can do together.'

Paige was terrified of boats. And of being out in the open sea with a husband who had vowed to teach her a lesson. Not to mention a therapist who clearly knew Bill from the sailing club. She muttered something and rushed down the steps.

'That was a bit rude, darling,' said Bill, on the way home. 'Rushing off without saying goodbye. But at least Michael has seen how nervy you are at the moment.'

'I thought you said he was recommended by Rose and Andrew?' she made herself ask. 'Not that he was a friend from the sailing club.'

'He was recommended by Rose and Andrew. Until we got there, I didn't realise he was the same Michael that I knew at the sailing club. But that doesn't matter. These people are completely professional and he'll never say anything to anyone.'

Chapter 31

Anthea was very busy after New Year, but was slightly concerned that Bill had suggested that they back-pedal their relationship for a bit.

'Trust me, sweetheart,' he said, kissing her. 'It's just a question of waiting a little longer. Strategy. That's what we need to focus on. Strategy.'

Anthea did trust him. Of course. But she was hungry for news of how Bill and Paige's relationship was faring, and had to rely on gossip.

Their strategy meant that she was spending more and more time on Raven affairs, in the Raven office, listening to Jenny, Bill's PA, fuming about Paige. Jenny was spitting with fury because Raven Restore & Build had not won the contract to restore George Boxer's house. 'We lost the contract at Glebe House because of that fuss over Paige and the lunch,' said Jenny. 'Bill's been very good about it, but he said George more or less told him that Paige's behaviour had been inappropriate and it would be too embarrassing to engage Raven. Bill's not blaming her at all, just saying what an unfortunate misunderstanding it's all been. But it will mean no bonus this year.'

Anthea murmured something.

'It's all very well for Paige,' muttered Jenny, 'she doesn't have to worry about things like mortgages and whether she can afford a new car. Bill does all the worrying for her. I would slap that woman's face, I really would, if she ever came anywhere near the office. But of course she can't be bothered, can she?' Jenny rifled furiously through a filing cabinet. 'I hear that Paige and George were actually kissing. In the pub at lunchtime, of all places. How tacky can you get?'

'Well,' said Anthea, 'I was there. They weren't actually kissing, they were holding hands.' Much as she disliked Paige she wasn't going to lie about what she'd seen.

Jenny shrugged. 'It's not much better, is it? Just being there is bad enough. Bill's such a nice man, and whether or not Paige was actually having an affair with George Boxer, not many men would have liked to come across their wives holding hands with another man in the most expensive gastropub in Kent. And it lost us the contract.'

Anthea found that if she asked Jenny to sign a document in the middle of an anti-Paige tirade, she checked it much less carefully than she usually did. 'Jenny, we need a witness for this document. But it has to be completely confidential. Bill could lose a lot of money if the wrong people heard about it.'

Jenny looked cautious. She always needed reassurance that what they were doing was tax avoidance, not tax evasion.

'It's nothing to do with the Inland Revenue,' Anthea assured her. 'Bill needs to safeguard the company in case the downturn gets any worse.'

Jenny's colour rose. 'I'll sign anything you like. Anything.'

Anthea had a quiet word with Bill about the bonus, and he found a way of making sure that Jenny got something extra. In spite of losing the Glebe House contract, he said. 'It wasn't your fault, Jenny, why should you suffer for the mistakes I make in my private life?' Jenny spent so long telling Anthea what a lovely man Bill was that Anthea rather wished she hadn't bothered.

★

On a train journey to London Anthea spotted Rose, whom she knew by sight. She didn't think Rose knew her, but raised her magazine to hide her face as Rose walked past.

'Rose!' she heard the woman in the seat behind her cry.

Rose's reply was indistinct, but the women were clearly old friends and both heading in to London. 'Do you mind if I sit here?' Anthea heard the rustle of Rose removing her coat, and her light, fluting voice as she settled herself down.

A few words emerged from the rumble of talk behind her, including 'Bill and Paige Raven.'

'Those two,' said the other woman, whose name seemed to be Clare. The rest of her words disappeared into a mumble. Anthea adjusted her head to hear better, pretending to doze with her face against the edge of the seat and the grimy train window, her magazine shielding her eyes.

'I don't think she'll ever leave him,' said Rose.

'He might. Isn't he having an affair with his accountant at the moment?'

Anthea's heart flip-flopped.

'It looks like it.' Rose's voice was casual. 'But it's like that interior designer girl he was supposed to be seeing a few years back. He takes it to the limit, then goes back to Paige. I don't know why she puts up with it.'

Anthea felt like popping her head over the seat and asking them why they thought Bill should put up with Paige. He funded her leisurely lifestyle, made sure she had everything she wanted and this was how she thanked him: by complaining about him to the neighbours.

'It's the house, I think. They've both poured so much of themselves into it,' said Clare authoritatively. 'As far as I can gather it's like those couples who mend their bad patches by having another baby. Bill's unfaithful, Paige finds out, they build another extension.'

Anthea was busy calculating the timing of the Stables Cottage conversion. It had just been completed when she and

Bill had first extended an afternoon accountancy session into an evening drink. Bill had never said anything about any interior designers. The talons of uncertainty dug sharply into Anthea's guts. She thought she might have to race for the loo, but she didn't want to miss a moment of the conversation.

'Well,' Rose yawned. 'I don't see how much further they could extend. They've done the garage and games room, master bedroom and en suite, the kitchen–family room, the tennis court and the swimming pool, Stables Cottage . . . by your calculations that should account for something between four and seven affairs.'

'I think they did some of it all at once. Maybe four affairs?' Clare sounded as if she was thoroughly enjoying the conversation. 'In my mother's time, those sort of women used to demand fur coats, apparently, as compensation for their husband's infidelities.'

Rose laughed. 'Or diamonds, I seem to remember.'

'And what of Paige? Has she had any affairs, do you think? What about this George Boxer?'

'I find that rumour very odd,' said Rose. 'He's completely obsessed with his dead wife. I keep throwing single women at him, but all he does is talk about Audrey.'

'Quite a few people think Paige is a bit odd, though. You know, warm and welcoming one minute, standoffish the next. You never quite know where you are with her.'

'Yet Bill is such a straightforward bloke,' Clare continued. 'He's always got a smile and good word for everyone. Always willing to help. I don't know how we'd ever have had the church hall renovated if it hadn't been for him . . . So do you think perhaps this time it's game, set and match to the accountant? That they might really split this time, now that the extensions are all finished?'

'You can never tell what goes on in a marriage unless you get in to bed between them at night and sit under their breakfast table in the morning,' said Rose. 'But I would say not. I think

Paige is too frightened of change. And it's usually the woman who leaves, isn't it?'

Anthea, furious and terrified, did not agree. But she hadn't heard about any of the other affairs before – although, to be fair, she had never asked. When the train reached Victoria she let Rose and Clare get out first, leaving it until the last minute before she picked up her own coat and bag.

She was concerned at reports of Bill's efforts to patch up his marriage. She had heard one or two people saying he'd been asking around for the names of good counsellors. 'How's the counselling going?' she had asked him one day, fishing for information but trying to keep the anxiety out of her voice.

He squeezed her shoulder and winked. 'It's a load of crap.' He lowered his voice to a whisper. 'I think about you while I'm there. I think about how good our life will be together once we've got all this bullshit out of the way.'

So that was all right, then. Wasn't it? Nobody, in all that gossip, had ever talked about the most important thing. Did Bill love Paige? Did Paige love Bill? Anthea thought not. Not the way she loved him. It was as simple as that. Love was what mattered, not house extensions.

'Bill?' she asked as he left the room. 'Were there others? Before me, I mean?'

He sat down again, looking serious, and took her hand. 'Things have been difficult between me and Paige for a long, long time, and at times I have found comfort elsewhere. I have to be honest with you about that. I'm not proud of it. I had three affairs over thirty miserable years of marriage, but there has never been anybody like you.' He turned over the palm of her hand and kissed it. 'Never.'

Chapter 32

Sophie was getting angrier with Jess every day, but wasn't quite sure why. It was irritating hearing her talking about 'us' and 'we', slipping Jake's name into every conversation while she wasted time waitressing and clearly wasn't getting on with finding herself a decent job. She talked about Jake taking her shopping, and how he took an interest in everything she wore. Sophie wished Jess would realise that life was a serious business and had to be treated seriously once you got into your late twenties. And then she looked at Harry, at Bella, Lottie and Summer, and sighed, then threw herself into her own work.

'Harry, don't.' She slapped his hand away from a plate of strawberries. 'I've been commissioned to illustrate an article on summer fruit for a newspaper supplement and it's been quite hard enough to find decent-looking strawberries at the end of February.'

'I thought you could get strawberries any time. And why are you so irritable these days?'

Sophie peered at the image on her laptop and moved a cream jug. 'I'm not. I'm just worried about Jess. She's pinning all her hopes on Jake and I don't think she should. She should find a proper job, not all this waitressing. And there's Mum, who I think must be having a breakdown. And, well . . .' She sat back, deciding she was so cross with everyone that she might as well confide in Harry. If he forbade her to go home again . . . well, so what?

'I think Dad's having an affair with Anthea. And I'm also worried whether, as you say, he's an alcoholic. So, as you see, plenty to be irritable about.'

Harry didn't reply at first, but he put a hand on her shoulder. As if she was a team-mate, she thought as she resisted the temptation to fling it off. 'I'm sorry,' he said. 'Do you want to talk about it?'

'Nothing to talk about.'

'I think your mum and dad can sort it out between them, you know.'

'But Mum's so hopeless and Dad's such a bully.' Sophie surprised herself with the analysis. She'd never actually said it before.

But Harry picked it up immediately. 'Yes, he is a bully. But he bullies you too, and Jess.'

'He bullies Jess. Not me. I'm the golden girl, haven't you noticed?'

'It's a form of bullying, what he does with you two.'

But once again Sophie couldn't bear to have Harry criticise her father. It would only lead to trouble later on. 'Anyway,' she said. 'It's fine. I'm fine.' She wanted him to go away. Jake was easier to talk to about all this – they had had several private conversations when Jess and Harry were out of earshot. He would lean forward and listen intently, and Sophie would feel his eyes on her face and feel alive again. But Harry . . .

She moved the cream jug three centimetres to the left again, and squeezed the camera trigger. 'Harry, I need to get on with this shoot. I've got to email the pictures to the magazine by this evening, latest.'

Her mobile phone rang. It was Bill, inviting Sophie to have lunch with him in three days' time. 'I'll come up to you. We need to go somewhere cheap.'

Sophie found it quite difficult to concentrate on strawberries after that. The things Jake had told her, about her father's business being better than he said, still niggled, along with the Anthea affair. She had noticed a couple of things that her father had said over Christmas that didn't quite add up. And, for the first time, she'd studied her mother's face and noticed how pale and strained it was.

Bill arrived late. He looked older and scruffier than he had at Christmas. The shock of blond hair suddenly seemed white, and much thinner. Bill had let it get too long and, blown about in the wind across Clapham Common, he looked dishevelled. Half the collar of his coat was tucked inwards, as if he'd shrugged it on in a hurry.

'Sophie. Darling.' He kissed her, emanating the comforting fatherly smell of sandalwood soap. 'Let's order some wine.'

'I'm not drinking during the week.'

'Not pregnant again, I hope?' He laughed as his eye flickered down to her stomach.

'No, Daddy, of course not. It's just that . . .' But he had waved down a waiter and ordered a bottle.

'This is nice,' he said when it arrived. 'It's so good to see you.'

Sophie tensed up. 'Good to see you too, Daddy,' she parroted, wondering what it was all about.

'I realised I haven't been the best of fathers—'

'Daddy, you've been lovely, it's just that I think you . . .'

He waved his hand to silence her. 'I haven't been the best of fathers. And I feel very guilty about this. But I have your best interests at heart.'

'Of course you do, but—'

'I've had to sell Orchard Park,' he interrupted. 'The whole estate. Before it was finished. As a half-finished project. My debts were too high and I could have gone bankrupt if the creditors had pushed me. I've had to take a fraction of what the project's worth, but at least it covers the debt. It's a foreign company, based in Bucharest, and they'll carry on using us as the builders, so that's something. At least people will keep their jobs, but I had put everything into it and I'm getting less out than I put in.'

'Bucharest? Daddy, I'm so sorry . . .' Sophie was shaken. What about that credit rating Jake had shown her, the one that said the company paid its bills on time? She put a hand on his sleeve. 'This is awful. And you worked so hard.'

He shook his head. 'Not enough. In the end, I wasn't good enough.' She could see tears in his eyes. 'Sophie, I've been a fool, an utter, utter fool. I've screwed it all up. All of it.'

'Dad, not everything. You've still got us, and Mum and The Rowans, and the rest of your business . . .'

'Your mother's leaving me. You heard her at Christmas. She hasn't changed her mind. She's says she's had enough. That she needs to move on, whatever that means. We've been going to counselling and doing our best to save the marriage, but I can see that her heart's not in it. She wants out, Sophie, and she wants to take everything I have left.'

Sophie felt sick. She had thought she'd seen this coming. She'd thought it might even be a good thing. But it wasn't. This was everything coming apart at once. 'Is this about Anthea?'

'Anthea?' He looked puzzled. 'Whatever has it got to do with Anthea?'

'Well, you know, Daddy, when I saw you . . .'

He rolled his eyes. 'I did explain that, but you seem to have told Jess who, exaggerating wildly as usual, told your mother something and, of course, that hasn't helped at all. I don't think it's really at the heart of it all, though, because what your mother got up to with George Boxer was very, very hurtful and damaged our marriage beyond belief.'

'Daddy, are you absolutely sure that she had an affair with George? She said she didn't.'

Bill looked sad. 'One thing that has really worried me about all this is discovering the way your mother lies. I don't know if she's always lied, or whether it's part of this new . . . I don't know . . . depression or psychosis, or maybe it is the menopause after all. But time and again I've caught her out, either in a direct lie or I find out that she's just not telling me things.' He sighed. 'All I know is that, whatever went on between her and George, I feel it as a betrayal in my heart.'

'Yes, of course, Daddy, I can imagine that . . . but you are very bad-tempered sometimes and I know it's about the worry, but if you could perhaps do something about that, maybe try anti-depressants or something – anger management, maybe – I'm sure Mum would stay. She loves you and she's never wanted to leave you. She's always said so.'

'Sophie, we – that is, your mother and I – have been to a number of experts over the past few months and one thing that has been made absolutely clear to me is that it is your mother who has the problems. I have been trying to look after her all her life, and now I'm having to face up to the fact that I've failed. Not one therapist has suggested that what I've done and how I've behaved has been anything other than exemplary. I have behaved completely honourably throughout.'

'I'm sure you've done everything you can, Dad, but the shouting is quite difficult to—'

'Sophie.' Steel crept into his voice. 'I don't like the shouting any more than you do, but it's the only way to get her, and the rest of you sometimes, to listen. If I ask her to do something in an ordinary voice she takes absolutely no notice. You've seen her, sitting in a dream, not replying when I've been desperate to get some point across, haven't you? Or justifying herself when she's done something completely idiotic or even danger-ous.'

'Yes, but I think she's . . .'

'Sophie, when someone shouts it's because they're not being heard. They are forced to shout. There is no point in blaming them. It's the people who don't listen who need to change. It's like blaming the smoke alarm for going off when there's a fire.'

'Yes, but . . .'

'Sophie, are you taking your mother's side in this? I need to know, because men often get treated very unfairly in divorces. I would be very sorry for us to be estranged, but if you're going to insist on it you'd better let me know now. I might as well have all the blows at once.' His eyes brimmed with tears.

She placed a hand on his forearm. 'No Dad, of course not. I am totally, totally, in sympathy with you. And with Mum too, of course. I wouldn't dream of taking sides.'

'That's good.' He squeezed her hand. 'That's my darling girl. And be careful when you're listening to her. Don't get too taken in. Remember that she's in a very bad way, and isn't seeing things straight. That's why she's had to have extra counselling. Although, to be honest . . .' He put his head in his hands. 'I think some of it has made everything worse. I have no idea what to do for the best. Will you help me, Sophie? Keep an eye on Mum and let me know if you're really worried about her?'

Sophie squeezed her father's hand back. 'Of course, I will. And Dad, think about your health. I do think you drink a bit too much and . . .'

He looked at her sharply. 'What do you mean?'

'If you were drinking too much,' said Sophie. 'That could be why the business has gone downhill, and it would make . . .'

'Let me make one thing clear. When you go to psychotherapists, marriage guidance counsellors, psychologists . . . whatever they're called, they ask you how much you drink. So I have discussed it. And it has been made quite clear to me that not one of these experts we've been seeing, with all their years of training, is in any way concerned about my drinking or any other aspect of my behaviour. They are worried about your mother. In fact, they are *very* worried about your mother, but they do not in any way think that I have a problem. Of any sort. Is that clear?'

'Good,' whispered Sophie. 'Yes, absolutely. That's what I thought, but Harry said . . .'

'If you don't believe me about any of this you can go and see them yourself. With my permission.'

'I believe you.'

'And that sorry excuse for a husband you've got, Sophie, really, doesn't he ever get on your nerves? He must be the most spineless man I've ever met. Thank goodness Jess has better sense. I like Jake.' He finished his glass and signalled for the bill. 'Well, we'd better go.' He got out his wallet and chuckled. 'Who would have thought it, eh? Little wildcat Jess getting the better man!'

'Jake is not the better man,' said Sophie, feeling sick as her world tilted again.

'Really?' Her father laughed again. 'Mind you, I think Jess has taken on a bit more than she's bargained for. He's licked her into shape all right. She's never looked so good in all her life. All those blonde curls and some proper make-up for a change. She's certainly not the ugly sister any longer.'

'I'm not entirely sure that their relationship is going to last,' said Sophie, desperately.

'And why would you think that, my little petal?' Bill tilted her chin up so that he could look into her eyes. 'After him yourself, are you?'

Sophie knew how to handle her father when he got like this. 'Silly Daddy,' she said, twisting out of his grasp. 'Now promise me you'll look after yourself. You'll eat properly, won't you?'

He pinched her cheek affectionately. 'You must come down and look after me if I don't. Tell Jess about your mother and me, will you?'

'You don't want to tell her yourself?'

'It's too painful for me,' he said, looking serious again as he picked up his coat. 'You know how Jess is. She'll blame me for everything, and I couldn't take that just now. I can only do my best, Sophie, I can't be superman. I'm sorry. I know I've failed you all. I've let you down.'

'No you haven't Daddy, of course you haven't.'

Sophie rang Paige as soon as lunch was over. 'Mum, I've heard the news. I'm so sorry.'

'What news?'

'That you're leaving Dad. That you've been going to counselling, and that he's sold Orchard Park but lost all his money, and that . . .' Sophie found herself crying down the line. 'Mum, I'm sorry, I should have done more. What can I do . . .'

'Sophie, I don't understand. What are you trying to say?'

'That I know,' screamed Sophie. 'I know *everything*. Stop trying to protect me. I'm not a baby. I know that Dad's had to sell the Orchard Park business in its entirety without getting all the money back, and you're leaving him, and . . . Mum, please, just be straight with me about this. Just for once. I almost feel I haven't *got* a mother, you're so . . . I'm sorry, I'll call you back.'

Sophie sobbed all the way home, hurrying along the narrow terraced streets, dodging pedestrians and stepping angrily out in front of cars. If anyone wanted to mug her, she thought, as she strode past the mouth of a dark alleyway, now would be the time. She was ready to fight back. She marched to the local park, usually a haunt of feral youths, and sat down on a graffitied bench, gulping back the tears. She would have to tell Jess before she went home. She dialled her mobile.

'Jess's phone,' said Jake. 'Hello Sophie.'

Chapter 33

At The Rowans Paige replaced the phone in its handset, and sat slowly down on a rush-backed kitchen chair. She let the darkness drop slowly down on the house, folding itself into shadows like a blanket, and she heard the click and whir of the central heating coming on. The phone rang twice. Normally she would have jumped to get it, but she sat listening to all the familiar rustlings of the birds outside settling themselves for the night, and the distant barking of a dog. Rain tittle-tattled against the window. Occasionally her heart sped up as a car drove along the lane outside, its wheels rumbling in the wet road, slowing down for the corner, but then she'd hear it accelerate again as it passed the house. At one point she got up and put on the gardening coat, feeling in the pockets for the car keys, the credit card, the brooch and a few pounds that she had hidden away.

This was it. He always took his revenge disproportionately. And he always took it. She was a fool to think he had forgotten. Their next session with Michael Percy was that evening, but he had told Sophie that she, Paige, was leaving. He didn't do anything without careful planning, so what was he expecting her to do? Refuse to go to the session? Or was she expected to go and accuse him of forcing her out? Or was he going to accuse her of leaving him? Which move in the game? And what about Sophie? She sounded so unhappy. Paige wanted to comfort her.

She had often wanted to comfort Sophie and Jess, but Bill had prevented her, especially after Jess was born. 'Let her cry, you mustn't spoil her.' The memory was like a spear through her heart. If she showed either girl too much love when he was around he always found a way of punishing her or them. Paige had learned to give quietly, and to get Sophie to ask Bill directly if she wanted something. Bill liked to be the one who handed out treats. It was why he occasionally bought the girls lavish presents. She had appeased him each time, hoping that it wouldn't happen again, that if only she knew how to handle him he wouldn't make these demands. Now she knew that a chasm lay between her and her daughters, and that at some level she was almost afraid of them too – of Sophie's bossiness and Jess's resentment.

She heard the crunch of gravel and the automatic light in the drive came on.

Bill didn't seem surprised to find her sitting alone in the dark. 'Oh, hello. I phoned you. You didn't answer.' He flicked the kitchen light on and she blinked.

'I spoke to Sophie.'

'What did she say?'

'You know what she said.'

'That I'd had to sell Orchard Park and that you were leaving me.' He put his briefcase on the table. 'Well, it's true, isn't it? You told me you were leaving me at Christmas. We haven't exactly got anywhere with these ridiculous sessions, have we? What will you do now?'

'What do you mean?'

'What do you mean?' mimicked Bill. 'What do you mean? I mean, where are you going to go? This is my house, you can't stay here. Or if you do, you stay here under my rules.'

'It's our house,' she said. 'The house of our marriage. It would be divided between us. By the court.' She swallowed. She wasn't sure whether it would be.

'You can forget about getting anything from me in court. You're the one who wants to leave, and leave you will. Without a penny. I've lost all my money, so you can't take anything. There's nothing to take.'

Paige was suddenly guilty that she hadn't thought more about his business. 'I'm so sorry to hear about Orchard Park. So very sorry. Did you really have to sell it?'

'Of course I fucking had to sell it,' he roared at her. 'Are you suggesting that you know my business better than I do?'

Paige moved towards the door, just one step. 'No, no, I think you're very good at your business. I'm just sorry that you had to take a risk and that it didn't come off.'

'It didn't fucking come off because you were distracting me with all this talk of counsellors and leaving me. You can't expect anyone to run a business with that kind of stuff going on in the background. It was your fault, you know that. But you don't care.' He slid the largest of the kitchen knives out of the block and examined it. 'It was the one time I needed a bit of fucking support from you, but all you do is nag, nag, nag and then drag me to bleeding therapy sessions. I haven't been able to concentrate.'

'I'm sorry,' repeated Paige. 'I hadn't realised it was so serious. You always say you're on the verge of bankruptcy and I'd got used to it.'

'Christ, you're thick.' He touched the tip of the knife with his finger, as if assessing its sharpness. 'Even a ten-year-old might have realised that building six flats and four houses was a rather bigger project than I'd ever undertaken before. Anyway, money all gone so time for wife to go too. That's what women always do when men are down, isn't it? When the money goes they go too. Fucking leeches.'

'If it would help, I would stay.'

He looked up. 'I'll tell you what would really help. You sticking your head in the gas oven. I could collect on the insurance then. No? Not quite unselfish enough? I didn't think so.

Pity. It's all me, me, me with you, isn't it? There was a piece in the paper about a chap who did just that. He – quite justifiably – used to give his wife the odd walloping when she burnt the dinner. She then committed suicide and he trousered a quarter of a million. Her family tried to fight it, presumably because they wanted the money, but she'd never filed a complaint of domestic violence so there was no evidence. British law, my dear Paige, requires evidence.' He laughed and raised the knife as if it were a dart, closing one eye and lining it up with her face. 'What do you think I've insured you for?' The steel of the blade gleamed under the downlighters over the sink.

Paige dared not answer, and tried to inch a little closer to the door.

'Speak up, speak up. I'd like to hear how much you think you're worth. Eh?'

'I don't suppose I'm worth all that much,' muttered Paige.

'Too right. But I'm a generous man, so I've insured you for three hundred thousand. You can't say fairer than that, can you? I'm a man who values women. You're lucky to have me.'

Paige had inched a little closer to the back door when he shouted 'Aren't you? And fucking get away from that door.'

She screamed as he threw the knife. It landed neatly in the centre of the scrubbed pine kitchen table with a soft thud, vibrating slightly with its tip stuck in the wood. Paige ran towards her car. She managed to unlock the car and pull the door open, then got in and slammed it shut as Bill appeared at the back door of the house. The automatic gates opened as if in slow motion and he took easy strides towards them. He could easily push them closed if he tried.

She revved the car up and accelerated through the gates as soon as the gap was wide enough, hearing the scrape of wood against the car door. In the rear-view mirror she saw him standing four square, legs astride and arms folded, a man seeing an intruding child off his property, as the gates opened to their maximum width.

The road was icy and the car slithered around the corner, its back end swinging towards the hedge as she pushed down on the accelerator pedal. It won't do any good to have an accident, she told herself. Breathe. Bill always said that women were terrible drivers. He would laugh if she only got as far as the junction.

She drove out towards the motorway, looking for a service station and stopping at the first one that advertised beds for the night. At least she would be able to sleep. She would be able to lock the door and sleep, and no one could get at her. The thought shimmered like a mirage in the desert. Sleep. Just one night without waking up to find him there snoring. Or to be woken by him crashing furiously about the bedroom, looking for something. She could do anything, cope with anything, if she could just have one night's sleep.

She proffered the credit card.

A young Polish girl with tired eyes ran it through her computer. 'Sorry,' she said. 'Card no good. You have other?'

Chapter 34

'Sophie, Sophie, is that you? Try to take deep breaths, darling. Are you hurt? Tell me where you are and I'll come and get you.'

Being called darling by Jake was like dose of smelling salts. Sophie swallowed abruptly. 'I've just had lunch with my father,' she gasped. 'And my mother's chucking him out. Leaving him. Whatever. I wanted to tell Jess before she heard it from anyone else and . . .'

'Where are you?' asked Jake. 'Do you need me to come round? Or would you like to come to us this evening?'

'I'm just outside our front door,' said Sophie, leaning against the wall. 'I'm just waiting until I look decent enough for the girls – I don't want to frighten them. And Harry'll be back tonight, but yes, could you come round? I can't leave the girls without a babysitter and I would like to talk to Jess, face to face. Decide what we can do to help.' She sniffed.

'We'll be round as soon as Jess finishes her shift,' said Jake. 'It'll be around seven this evening, is that OK?'

Sophie agreed, then remembered that she hadn't asked why he had Jess's mobile phone with him. Jess had probably left it behind, that would be typical of her. She managed to get into the house to clean up her face before the girls discovered her, then said goodbye to Patrizia, the Italian student who sometimes babysat for her. 'No Patrizia, I'm fine, really, I promise.'

Then she rang Harry and told him.

'Oh,' he said. 'It's about time. I thought your mother was going to go on being bullied for ever.'

'Harry! That's not fair. Mum is just as difficult to Dad as he is to her. You know how infuriating she is, she doesn't think things through. If she'd stood up for herself a bit better in the early years we might not ever have got to this point. Dad is absolutely shattered, he looks terrible and she sounds quite calm. And I don't know what it'll do to their lifestyle. Dad loves The Rowans to bits, and I've no idea what's going to happen over that.'

'So no more treats from Daddy, then? I presume those cheques he used to press into your hand almost every time we saw him, for a new dress or even a holiday, will have to stop?'

'Harry, how can you think about things like that at a time like this? Life's not just about money, you know.' Sophie always felt guilty about being the recipient of her father's sporadic generosity, because Jess needed it more and he rarely gave her anything.

'I only meant that we will have to cut down if you're getting less. We'll have to decide what we can do without.'

'This is not about us, Harry, it's about Dad. And Mum. Jess and Jake are coming this evening so we can talk about it all then.'

'I'm working late on this latest merger. Do you need me? I'm happy to fit in with whatever.'

'No, that's fine.' She knew that Harry would probably say very little, that she and Jess would chatter like machine-guns, that Jake would interpose carefully thought-out points and ask them questions about what they felt, and occasionally Harry would grin lazily and suggest something unhelpful about everybody minding their own business. He was also clearly on her mother's side, and Sophie didn't want anyone to take sides. Her father was not perfect, not at all, but he was often only tired and worried, although he did drink a bit too much, and she was determined to be fair to both of them. Demonising Dad was too easy.

As she put the phone down she decided that men like Harry just didn't do emotions. They counted money and were part of the team, and if they were in the canoe club all their best friends were in the canoe club, and when they left the canoe club they never saw any of them again. As for discussing their feelings rather than England's chances in the World Cup or whether the rugby coach was giving new talent enough chance when he chose the line-up for the Six Nations, well, Harry and his friend would rather take off all their clothes and run naked around a rugby pitch.

In fact, they'd *much* rather take off all their clothes and run naked round a rugby pitch than talk about what they felt.

Chapter 35

Paige proffered the debit card from their joint account with a trembling hand.

The tired Polish girl ran it through and shook her head. 'No good.'

Bill had closed all their accounts. Paige fumbled about in her pocket and brought out the diamond brooch. 'I just need to spend one night here. Can I pay with this?'

A weary shake of the head. 'I get the manager.'

'No, no, don't do that.' Paige had visions of an angry night manager. She couldn't argue with anyone, not now. She backed out of the motel. She would have to sleep in the car.

But it was uncomfortable. She tried lying curled up on the back seat, but kept jerking awake in fright. Then she thought that she could lower the front seat back as far as possible and sleep on her back.

She was woken by a torch shining in her face and a police ID slapped against the window. She shook her head and rolled down the window. 'I'm sorry?'

'You can't sleep here. It's a private car park. The manager has complained.'

'Oh, I'm sorry,' repeated Paige, feeling tears rising up in her throat. 'I . . . er . . . haven't got any money, and I've . . . er . . . had an argument with my husband.'

199

'Do you need us to come back to your home with you? To ensure your safety?'

Paige shook her head furiously. She wouldn't dare go back there, certainly not with two police officers. Bill would be furious after they'd gone.

One was a man – older, she thought, even in his fifties – and the other was a broad-faced blonde in her thirties. Their thick navy stab vests bulked them out, making them look strong and big, bulwarks of safety. They had short-sleeved white shirts on underneath. In February.

'I don't know what to do,' she said. 'He keeps telling me that every three days a man kills his wife. Here in Britain.'

'Was he perhaps just commenting on the news?' asked the woman officer. 'Making conversation?'

Paige shook her head. 'He only talks about the news if there's a woman killed on it. He never wants to talk about anything else. I try discussing politics with him, or the weather, or the economy, but he just ignores me.' She closed her eyes in exhaustion. They wouldn't believe her. She had never before told anyone about the cuttings Bill left her from the papers. But she was too frightened to lie, and these were two strangers she would never see again.

The officer slid into the driving seat. 'Tell me about it.'

So Paige told her. About Ruth and her diagnosis. About the marriage guidance counsellor who sailed with Bill. That they were still going to marriage guidance counselling when Bill had told their daughters that they were splitting up. 'The first I knew of it was when my elder daughter called me to tell me. Of course, I didn't let her know that, but . . .' About her three granddaughters. 'I don't want him to start manipulating them. Making them feel they're not worth anything. Like he did to my younger daughter. And he's cancelled all the bank accounts so I can't go anywhere or do anything.'

'You have two choices. We can take you home, so that he knows that we have heard your side of the story, and that if he does try anything we will be on to him. Or we can take you to a refuge. Then in the morning you can go to a solicitor or to the Citizens Advice Bureau.'

'Oh no,' said Paige. 'People like me don't go to refuges.'

The constable raised an eyebrow.

'Not because of . . .' Paige wondered if she was sounding like a snob, '. . . aren't they for women with children?'

'All kinds of women go there. With or without children. From every level of society. Do you have access to a computer?'

'There's one in my husband's study.'

The police officer hesitated, her blonde hair bobbing as she scribbled in her notebook, then tore out the sheet. 'Here,' she said. 'Refuge and Women's Aid. Two websites that might help. But perhaps it would be better to go to your local library to access them.'

Paige gave in. She could not imagine going to a refuge. 'No, it's fine,' she muttered as she stuffed the paper into her pocket without looking at it. 'If you take me home he can't do anything to me, can he?'

'Has he ever hit you?'

Paige shook her head. 'He threw a knife at the kitchen table tonight. But not at me.'

'Then he's done nothing illegal and we can't do anything. But he will know that we are aware.'

Paige nodded.

'I'll come with you in your car. If you're fine to drive,' said the WPC. 'My colleague can follow us.'

Paige almost expected Bill to have disabled the automatic gates, but they opened smoothly at the touch of her remote control button. The Rowans looked peaceful and prosperous, with lights burning on the porch and glimmering through the curtains of the downstairs windows. Paige noted that she needed to prune the topiary on either side of the front door before spring came. The woman officer rang the doorbell.

It was opened by Bill. He was rumpled, confused, affable.

'Darling! I wondered where you'd gone. I do hope she hasn't been drinking and driving, officers.'

'May we come in?'

'Of course, of course. Would you like a cup of tea? Come through to the kitchen, just through here. Are you all right, darling? You look a bit windswept. I was just beginning to worry, but I thought you'd have popped into Rose's for a drink.' He turned to the police officers. 'I expect my wife's told you we had words tonight. I'm afraid I had a very bad bit of news about my business and arrived home in a very down mood. I blame myself, she wasn't aware of how bad things had got, and I think she just flipped, didn't you darling? I have to tell you . . .' He bent towards the police officers in a confiding way. 'At one point she had a knife in her hand and I thought she was going to throw it at me. But it hit the kitchen table. There's a huge gash – look, there, you can see it?' He chuckled as he ran his hands over the mark. 'And if you've got an address of a refuge for battered husbands, perhaps I'd better take it. What do you say, wifie? Temper tantrum over or do I have to live in fear of my life?'

Paige just stared at him. She'd caught sight of herself in the hall mirror as she passed, her lank hair straggly and her face pale and not made up. Her eyes were red. She looked strained. Mad, even. Bill, in contrast, looked like a cuddly bear or everybody's favourite uncle as he made tea, chatting to the police officers ('One sugar or two, Officer? You must need a lot of energy for your job. I'm afraid I have to stick to artificial sweeteners now that age has given me what you might call a bow window.') and asking them about a senior police officer who sailed, and another who played golf ('Jerry's a character. If he's half as good a detective as he is a golfer, it's not surprising that you chaps do such a good job round here.'). They sipped their mugs of tea and the kitchen glowed in the light of the lamps, with Bella, Lottie and Summer's drawings tacked onto the fridge and family photographs on the walls.

'Mrs Raven has made the allegation that you threw the knife at her,' said the female officer. 'And she says you have also made threatening remarks to her.'

'Allegations?' asked Bill, looking from one to the other. 'I'm afraid I don't understand. What threatening remarks could I possibly have made? I'm so sorry, but my wife has been under treatment for depression for some months. However, she's never accused me of anything before. Does this mean she's getting worse? Do you think I should call a doctor?' He ran his hand through his hair. 'This is terrible,' he murmured.

Paige could see doubt in the eyes of both police officers. 'Thank you,' she said hastily. 'I'll be fine now. Thank you so much for bringing me back.' She wanted them out of her kitchen, to take their uniforms and radios, with their reminders of death and danger, away from the blue-and-white plates on her blue-painted dresser, away from the cleverly 'found' tin pendant lights hanging in a row over the kitchen table. If only they would go, life could slip back into its normal routine. Bill looked exhausted and repentant, a man deeply concerned about his wife and remorseful of any misunderstanding.

Perhaps this was what they'd needed. A reality check. A shock. A chance for them to pull together, to come through this together. To help each other. She heard Bill's protestations from far away as he begged the police officers to advise him on how best to help her ('I can't bear to think of my wife feeling frightened, although she's always been nervy. Remember me to Jerry, won't you?').

'I'll pop in tomorrow to see if you're all right,' said the WPC to Paige.

'That's so kind of you,' said Bill, 'but we would hate to waste police time.' He opened the front door for them.

'It's no problem.'

The other officer asked Bill about security, burglars and the Neighbourhood Watch, and Bill went out on to the drive to show where the security systems were.

The woman officer turned to Paige. She spoke in a low voice. 'I'm sure you're all right, but you may need help. One way or the other. Don't forget those websites.'

What did 'one way or the other' mean? Paige scrunched up the piece of paper in her pocket, making it very small. She was being silly. Paige had never known, or even heard of a friend of a friend who had ever died at the hands of her partner, and she and Bill knew hundreds of people. They had dinner parties, painted their homes in historic paint colours and tried to send their children to good schools. They might argue, they might divorce, they might even throw things at each other or break things. But they didn't kill each other.

Bill closed the door behind them and turned to Paige, glaring at her as he bared his teeth in a smile. 'Now fuck off to bed, you bitch,' he said. 'In the spare room. Then tomorrow we'll talk.'

But the following day she woke up late after a restless night to find that he had gone and she had been locked in the house, the deadlocks on the front and back doors double-locked. Her keys had gone from the pocket of her gardening coat – she was sure she'd left them there, but perhaps she hadn't – and the spare set of keys, the ones that always hung beside the front door, had also gone. All the windows had security locks. They were careful to ensure that windows were always secured properly because almost everyone they knew had been burgled at some point, but surely one window might have been forgotten?

It was all a coincidence, it must have been. He had locked her in a few times before, always accidentally, because he'd taken the spare keys after leaving his own at the office. If it coincided with her losing her own keys herself – once they'd turned up in the footwell of the car – she climbed in and out of a downstairs window. Once Bill had driven back from work, furious with her for losing her keys, to give her the spare set.

She should phone him. Or the office. She couldn't phone

204

the police, not to say that she'd lost her keys. She lifted the telephone. It was dead. Perhaps it had been unplugged. She ferreted around under the table, pulling the jack in and out of the socket. Nothing. She had her mobile, but it was a pay-as-you-go, so if she phoned him, and he wasn't prepared to come and let her out (he had once refused, because he said he was too busy and too far away, and that she would just have to wait), she would risk using up her last few pence of credit. She would have to think very carefully about who she phoned, and what she would say, because if this was all coincidence – and it probably was – and if it was she who had lost her keys and not he who had locked her in, then everybody really would think she was mad.

The window locks were all operated by a single allen key, kept on the key holder in Bill's study, the door of which was always kept locked. Paige tried each window in turn but was only able to open the dormer window in the attic. It gave on to a smooth slope of red-tiled roof, and then a drop of two stories on to a terrace of York stone paving dotted with Paige's treasured collection of terracotta pots and urns, the wintry stalks of the remaining plants poking up towards her.

Paige thought that it might be easier to throw herself out of her attic window and end it all. The spikes of *Agrostis nebulosa 'Fibre optics'* waved up at her, and the terrace shimmered in a hypnotic welcome. *You can forget everything if you just lie on me. Come closer.* For a moment, she put her head right out of the window and it seemed as if jumping, tumbling through the air into oblivion was the only logical way to go. The only way.

You really are mad, said a small voice, and she forced herself to draw back, away from the temptation. She could imagine spinning over and over. And over. Then nothing.

But she might not die, not from that height. There must be another way. Paige felt her way almost blindly down the narrow, winding stairs again, trembling at how close she had come to giving up.

Think, Paige, think. She couldn't phone Sophie or Jess because she didn't want to involve them in anything against their father and, if they weren't in, leaving a message would use up the remaining credit on her mobile. She thumbed desperately through the telephone directory, looking up Charities and then Counselling, but almost all the telephone numbers were landlines and would charge. There was just one freefone number, for parents to talk to other parents, plus the police hate crimes and race crimes hotlines. Did Bill hate her? Perhaps. Had he committed a crime by losing his keys the day after his company had sold its major asset? No. She certainly couldn't dial 999 simply because she was locked in.

She continued to search for a free phone line. Under 'Domestic' she only found 'cleaning' and not 'abuse' (between Doll's Houses and Door Manufacturers). Nor was there anything for 'Divorce' between 'Diving Schools' and 'DIY Stores', and no sign of 'Refuges' between 'Refrigeration Equipment' and 'Refurbishment Commercial Premises'. Nothing about 'Violence' between 'Videoconferencing' and 'Voice Coaches'. She couldn't even afford to call the Samaritans. She closed the telephone directory, and went to the pocket of her gardening coat, for the piece of paper with the names of the two websites on it. At first she thought it had gone – perhaps Bill had found it – but eventually she pulled out the tiny scrunched-up ball. www.womensaid.org.uk and www.refuge.org.uk. But she had no computer. She checked the telephone directory but neither was in it. Think, Paige, think. She took a deep breath and rang Sophie.

She got the answering machine, a long message that gave Bella, Lottie and Summer's names and both Sophie's and Harry's mobile numbers, repeating them as the precious credit ticked away. 'Soph, call me,' said Paige. The line went dead. She hadn't said who she was, or left a number, although Sophie would probably recognise her voice. If she was out all day it would be too late anyway.

She could break into the study to get the window keys, but there was no guarantee that Bill had left them there. And he would be furious. And she might be able to break a window and climb out, although the panes of glass were quite small and it might be more difficult than it sounded. Certainly the windows on the newer part of the house, which were all double-glazed – although entirely traditional to look at – could not be broken, not by her anyway. But the kitchen windows, part of the original house, were a possibility. But what about burglary, repairs and Bill's rage?

She began to clear away the stuff that had accumulated around the window: the cookery books and the blue-and-white Cornishware storage jars – which she rarely moved as she liked looking at them rather than using them – and found a small silver object she'd never noticed before. It looked like something electronic. Paige put it on the table, and was just about to pick up a kitchen chair and try to find a way of throwing it through the kitchen window to clear a big enough space to climb through, when her mobile rang. Paige seized it.

'Mum?' It was Sophie, sounding as if she had a cold.

Paige explained that she had been so silly, she'd lost her keys and Bill had accidentally taken the spares and . . .

'You need a locksmith,' said Sophie. 'He can presumably change the locks from outside.' Her voice sounded dead.

'I haven't got any money,' admitted Paige, mortified.

'I'll pay. On my credit card, over the phone.'

'Soph, darling, don't mention this to Dad yet.' Paige knew it was important to sound normal and upbeat. 'He'll need to be in a good mood about it.'

There was a silence. 'OK. But Mum, give Dad a break, OK? He's just lost Orchard Park and he's really down. I know what he's like about money, so I won't say anything, and don't worry about paying me back soon, but please be nice to him.'

'I know,' said Paige. 'Don't worry. I know.'

Two hours later, with the locks changed, the locksmith came

in to the kitchen to ask her to sign for the work, and to give her three new sets of keys. Paige signed.

'Recording our conversation, are you?' he asked cheerily.

Paige looked at him. 'No, why?'

He pointed to the silver device. 'The voice-activated recorder. We sell them in the shop. For journalists and dictation and the like. Top of the range, that one is.' He checked her signature and folded up his clipboard. 'Mind you, we call it spyware. People checking up on each other, or their nannies. There's no trust these days, is there?'

'Oh, I don't think it can be working. It must have been left by my daughter's boyfriend when he came for Christmas. He's a journalist.'

'Nah,' said the locksmith, picking it up. 'It's recording now. Listen. It does a lot of hours, this one, but it wouldn't last all that time.' He pressed the buttons and Paige heard her own words: 'It must have been left by my daughter's boyfriend when he came for Christmas.'

He laughed. 'Maybe your old man's keeping an eye on you. Not that he'd leave it in full view if he was. He'd hide it in a corner somewhere you probably wouldn't look. I tell you,' – he hefted his bag on to his shoulder and turned to go – 'all that spyware stuff is dead profitable. We couldn't do without it now. This model's our best seller, but we also have gadgets that record telephone conversations and keystrokes on the computer, so you can check if your kids are looking up unsuitable sites on the web, know what I mean? He probably bought that from us. See ya later.'

Paige went upstairs, took out two suitcases and packed as many of Bill's possessions as she could find. She put the suitcases in the porch, with a note to say she was filing for divorce and that they should speak via a solicitor. This, she knew, was an act of great bravado as she couldn't see how she could afford a solicitor, but it was all she could think of. She closed shutters and checked the window locks again. Bill had made the house very hard to get into. Very hard to get out of. And now he would be on the outside.

She went round the house looking for things she could sell for cash, that day. She knew the antique shop owners, and she knew what they liked, but prices were low.

And when she had the cash — two hundred and fifty-seven pounds from a dinner set, a silver teapot, a large urn, an oil painting of flowers and had left another two pictures with an auction room — she bought thirty pounds' worth of phone vouchers and called first Rose and then Jess.

'Tell me, Rose, completely honestly, because I really don't mind what the answer is. Did you ever tell anyone about our conversation about Anthea?'

'Of course not,' said Rose immediately. 'Not even Andrew. It was between us.'

'And,' said Paige, clutching the mobile tightly. 'Would you be very kind and tell me honestly if you really think Bill's having an affair with her.'

Rose paused. 'I don't really know,' she said carefully. 'But I've seen them in restaurants, and I saw him coming out of her flat quite late at night once, when I was driving past. And other people say . . .'

'So I'm not going mad?' asked Paige.

'Of course you're not.' Rose sounded surprised. 'Why would you think that? But we all thought you . . . well, nothing.'

'Please tell me. All I want is the truth. I don't mind how painful it is.'

'Well, everyone thought you . . . you sort of tolerated his affairs. That it was just part of your relationship. I'm not judging, I know some people are fine about that sort of thing and it's what works for you that matters, isn't it?'

'Affairs?' whispered Paige.

'I'm *so* sorry,' cried Rose. 'I should never have said that. I just thought, well, I'm sorry, but they were so obvious, we couldn't see how you couldn't know.'

'I've often been suspicious about various women, like that interior designer who worked on his last project, but he told me I was paranoid. Stupid. Ridiculous to think anything of the sort. And . . . just one more thing.'

'Yes?' Rose sounded wary.

'Did you or Andrew ever recommend a marriage guidance counsellor to him called Michael Percy, one you'd been to?'

'Us? A marriage guidance counsellor?' Rose gave a peal of laughter. 'I can see you're confusing Andrew with a man who would go anywhere near a counsellor of any kind. He calls them all "trick cyclists". He got furious when I went to see that therapist. No, our marriage isn't perfect, far from it, but I can confirm that I've never heard of Michael Percy and I'd be surprised if Andrew had either.'

'I can see that I am very stupid,' said Paige. 'Bill always says so.'

'Nonsense,' replied Rose politely.

Paige thanked her and rang off.

Then she dialled Jess. 'Jess, when you came down here to tell me you'd given up your job, and that Dad was having an affair with Anthea, did you ever ring Dad about it on his mobile?'

Jess snorted. 'You must be joking. I never ring Dad. I sometimes have to speak to him when he answers the home phone, but I don't even have his mobile number. Sophie says you've chucked him out, by the way. She seems to be rather upset about it, but I think it's brilliant.' Her voice had the lazy, invulnerable quality of someone who was happy in love.

Paige hoped it would stay that way. Jess didn't need any problems now.

'Let me know if you need any help, Mum. Jake and I could come down.'

'That's sweet of you, darling, but we can manage.' She put the phone down.

'So many lies. So many cruel lies,' she whispered to the twilight. 'But why?

Paige sat, hardly aware of the tears trickling down her face, of the snot she wiped away with her hand, until she heard the whirr of the main gates opening and the sound of his tyres on the gravel. Then she sniffed back her tears and curled up under the kitchen table, her hands over her ears as he shouted through the letterbox and kicked the front door. She heard the thud of a brick bouncing off the double glazing and Bill cursing. Then his feet striding round the house. He pushed open the letterbox of the kitchen door.

'You fucking bitch. I know you're there. Open the fucking door.'

She was too frozen to move.

'Paige,' he whispered, like a malevolent ghost. 'I know you're there. If you open the door and let me in, I'll give you a divorce. I'll pay you maintenance and you can have half the house.' He waited. 'But if you don't,' his whisper grew slower and softer, 'if you don't open this door *now*, I'll make sure that you never have a *penny*. You'll never see the girls. No one will want to know you once I've finished with you. You won't have a friend in the world. They'll all know how badly you've treated me.'

The habit of obeying him was so strong that Paige started to unravel and crawl towards the door, her heartbeat thumping against her skull. But think of the lies, she repeated to herself, think of the lies. If he killed you on the doorstep, beside your note, it would be a crime of passion. She would be considered to have brought it on herself. As he'd repeatedly said to her, he'd only get a few years and he wouldn't have half his assets stripped by divorce. He was going to trick her into opening the door, and then he would kill her. She stopped, frozen, on her hands and knees. She could hear his breathing.

'You've chosen,' he croaked. 'You can't blame me. You chose. It's all your fault. Everything that happens to you now is all your own fucking fault.' There was a pause. She thought he might be standing up.

'You bitch,' he suddenly shouted through the letterbox, making her jump.

And then she heard him get into the car and drive away, and the soft click of the gates closing.

She was pleased he had chosen a gravel sweep around the house. 'You can always hear someone creeping around over gravel,' he'd said. 'It's the best anti-burglar precaution there is.' So she knew he had gone.

But it was still over an hour before she dared come out from under the kitchen table.

Chapter 36

Bill arrived at Anthea's flat at ten past eight. She was surprised to see him.

'She's thrown me out. Once she'd heard all the money was gone, she packed my cases and stuck them on the doorstep. Didn't even have the guts to talk to me directly.'

'That's awful,' said Anthea, appalled but delighted. 'Come in, come in. Is there more in the car?' She took a case from him.

Bill sank down on the sofa and ran his hands through his hair. He looked exhausted. 'I can't believe it,' he said. 'That's my fucking house, paid for with my money, and she's changed the locks while I was at work, earning more fucking money for her to squander on tapestry cushions and fucking duck egg blue paint.'

'It does seem extraordinary.' Anthea was surprised. She hadn't expected Paige to cave in like this. Oh well, it just showed you. Take the money away and some wives couldn't take it. 'Would you like a drink?'

He smiled at her. 'Love one. Just what I need. We'd better leave the rest of the stuff in the car. I don't think I can be seen to be moving in with you. It might give . . . the courts . . . the wrong idea.' He took the wine from her and drank it down. 'Thanks.' He put a hand out towards her. 'And thanks for being here, and just letting me turn up. I do appreciate it, you know.'

'Of course you can just turn up.' She held his hand tightly and sat down beside him, her mind wild with possibilities.

'I never imagined she'd do something like that,' he said, leaning back on her sofa and looking at her sideways over his glass. 'I just can't believe it. She's going to take everything I've got, isn't she? I mean, if she's prepared to lock me out the house, she's not going to stop at anything.'

Anthea smiled. However greedy and needy Paige was, she was just a housewife, and Anthea was an accountant. 'She can't beat us if we're together.' She got up and began to knead his shoulders. 'She won't take everything. I promise.'

Bill drew her towards him. 'Anthea, I've never told you this, because I've never felt free to do so. But now that I am no longer a married man, I want to say that . . . I love you.'

She kissed him, and felt his hand trace down the lace of her bra and in towards her nipple. She liked that he had held back saying that he loved her because of Paige, even though things were so bad between them. It made her feel less . . .

But Bill's hand made her forget what she wanted to feel less of.

The following morning Bill left for the office early. 'You're due in today, aren't you?'

Anthea nodded. 'Around ten.'

'I'll be on site by then. I'll see you this evening.'

Jenny was fizzing with it all.

'Anthea? Anthea? Have you heard? Because Bill's had to sell the Orchard Park project before it was complete and he's lost so much money, Paige has walked out. She's upped and left him. Or rather, she changed the locks while he was at work and threw all his stuff out the window.'

'Are you sure?' Anthea had not reckoned that Paige was the kind of woman who threw packed suitcases out of windows.

She wasn't fiery enough. Too insipid and polite, Anthea thought. And Jenny was always so busy finishing everyone else's sentences that she quite often got things wrong.

'Bill obviously hasn't slept; he's in a terrible state. The poor man. It's the one time he really needed a bit of support, and what does she do? Go off to her lover.'

'Has she?'

'Well, I expect she'll move him in to Bill's bed, don't you think? Now that the coast is clear.'

'He's got a very nice house of his own,' said Anthea, thinking that it would be an awful lot more convenient if Paige did go off with George Boxer. But that would really be a fairytale ending, and somehow Anthea didn't see it happening. Wealthy widowers didn't marry loony divorcees. They were usually wise enough to steer clear of women like Paige. 'And Bill says—' she tried to continue, but Jenny cut across her.

'Anyway, poor Bill is moving into one of the unsold flats at Orchard Park. He's renting it from this Lithuanian company that bought the whole project. What do you think of that? To work all your life then finish up in a rented flat while your wife lives alone with five bedrooms and three receptions? Not to mention that enormous garden.'

As this was precisely the strategy Anthea herself had suggested, she made no comment. 'I think there are four reception rooms at The Rowans,' she said after a short mental calculation. 'Maybe five if you count Bill's study. And the company isn't Lithuanian, it's—'

'I really don't know how some women live with themselves. Bill is such a lovely, lovely person, and Paige is just a parasite.'

Anthea realised that she and Bill still needed to be extremely careful about not letting Jenny know about their relationship, and gave Jenny a long, considered look.

'Sorry,' said Jenny, misinterpreting it. 'I know you must feel loyal to Paige because you know her better. But I just think she's been very, very shitty about this whole thing. I mean, everyone understands that marriages end, but there has to be some fairness about it all. Martin agrees with me. I called him the minute Bill went to the site and he's as shocked as I am.'

Jenny shared every minute of her life with her husband Martin, a football-playing plasterer. 'Anyway,' Jenny bowled along, 'I can't believe that she's prepared to throw away everything they've built up together just because she's found some other guy she thinks might be interested in her. When I married Martin,' Jenny put a hand on her chest, 'I took a vow. A *vow*. For richer, for *poorer*. Forsaking all others. Paige is letting us down, letting all women down. This is the sort of behaviour that makes men think less of women.'

Anthea wondered whether she should point out that earlier on in the conversation Jenny had said that everyone understood that marriages had to end, but suspected she wouldn't get to the end of the sentence. She started up her computer instead.

'Oh Anthea, I don't want to upset you in any way,' Jenny dropped her voice. 'But I thought you ought to have a right of reply. Did you know there have been whispers about you and Bill?'

Anthea's eyebrows shot up. She'd thought they'd been so careful. 'I think they're probably just Paige putting rumours about to justify her own behaviour,' she murmured. 'You mustn't worry about them. And we do often have to work out of what would strictly be seen as work hours. You see, Bill is so worried about the company at the moment, and he—'

'Bill is thinking of trying to persuade Paige to come to mediation,' interrupted Jenny, as if passing on a great secret, 'in the hope that she will see some sense, at least about how they divide up the money, but at the moment she refuses even to *speak* to him. I do hope she's not going to drag him into some long, expensive court case.' A furrow appeared between her brows. 'I don't think the company could take it. I mean, I know Bill will be paying personally, but he's pretty broke, isn't he?'

Anthea tried to word her reply carefully because you never knew what Jenny would take away from a conversation. 'Well,' she said. 'As you know, even without the Orchard Park project, Raven's turnover is holding up nicely. But there are a few bad debts coming up so I wouldn't like to say. But nothing for you to worry about yet,' she added as she saw Jenny's face go blotchy with alarm. 'Bill has a fantastic reputation and he'll always get work, even if Raven Restore & Build goes bankrupt.'

'Bankrupt!' shrieked Jenny. 'I didn't know things were that bad.'

'Jenny, they're not. Not yet. It's only the remotest possibility. If things go . . .'

'I had no idea that things were so bad. No idea at all, no wonder Bill's in such a state.'

Anthea tried to get a grip of the conversation as she didn't want Jenny going round saying that Raven Restore & Build was going under. 'Jenny,' she said. 'Try not to worry. Bill says . . .'

'Oh, I'm not worried about myself,' said Jenny. 'Just about Bill. It's such a shame for him, going bankrupt.'

'Jenny!' barked Anthea. 'Bill is not going bankrupt. I only said 'if the *company* did go bankrupt he'd go on working. But it's highly . . .'

Jenny opened her mouth.

'Let me *finish*,' growled Anthea. 'It's highly unlikely that there will be any question of bankruptcy.'

'Oh I know, I know,' said Jenny, reaching for the phone and clearly not listening.

'Jenny, listen to me, please. Do *not* tell anyone that he is going bankrupt. Do you understand?'

Jenny's eyes filled with tears. 'You don't have to snap. I can keep a secret.'

Anthea tried to concentrate because there was a lot of work to do with the end of the financial year only six weeks away and the company returns up to the end of April due to be filed.

But she couldn't help dreaming. Maybe, at last, her time had come. If they got the divorce going as quickly as possible she and Bill could be together openly. Provided that happened soon enough . . . She was only in her early forties, perhaps there was a chance, still, of . . .

But you couldn't think like that. Dreams only led to disappointment. Other women got their dreams. Pretty, privileged, pampered women like Paige and Sophie. Life had always been hard for Anthea. She pulled out a file and bent over her computer.

Chapter 37

Paige went to the library the following morning, after arranging for the phone line to be mended. Then she hurried to the library. She couldn't afford book fines. And she still had the scrunched-up piece of paper with the two websites on it. She wasn't sure that she wanted to find out any more, but she needed to know what to do now. She paid her fee and sat down to log on.

She almost logged off immediately. She could see case histories about women being beaten and references to domestic violence. All Bill had ever done, and only since losing the Orchard Park project, was to kick the front door and throw a knife at a table. That did not constitute violence in her book. She was being silly. But then she saw, in the top right corner, advice on covering your tracks online. For women whose husbands monitored what websites they looked up. She thought of the locksmith mentioning a device for recording keystrokes, and then of the voice-activated recorder, sitting behind her Cornishware jars. How long had it been there? No wonder Bill always seemed to know everything she'd said to anyone.

Taking a breath she clicked on 'recognising abuse'. There was a checklist. Are you afraid of your partner? Yes. Has he cut you off from your family and friends? Friends?, she thought. She didn't think she had any friends. They were all his friends, that's what he always said. That was her fault, she was no good at making friends. They hadn't seen her brother Rob for years – after the will, Bill had refused to see 'the man who has stolen our money'. But there was Jess and Sophie.

She moved on. Is he jealous and possessive? She tried not to think about the George Boxer incident. Bill had been worried about Orchard Park; he hadn't been thinking straight. Any man would be jealous if he thought his wife was holding hands with a strange man in the best restaurant around. The next was, Does he humiliate or insult you? Reluctantly, Paige put a mental tick against this one, although she knew some of it was her fault. Does he say you are useless and couldn't cope without him? She almost smiled. She had absolutely no idea how she was going to cope without him. He would undoubtedly be proved absolutely right. Has he threatened to hurt you or people close to you? No, thought Paige. He hasn't. The newspaper stories, the ones he always showed her and that now jumped out at her unbidden every day like an evil whisper straight from the page: honeymoon bride stabbed by husband, woman pricked with HIV needle by husband, woman strangled, woman buried in the garden, woman shot . . . So many women. So many terrible deaths. But they weren't, strictly speaking, threats to her. Were they?

Does he constantly criticise you? Does he have sudden changes of mood that affect the whole household? Well, all men do. Surely? Perhaps these websites were a little over-the-top. But it was a tick to both. Is he charming one minute and abusive the next? Does he control your money? Once again she was surprised to hear that such behaviour could be considered unusual. Perhaps she should ask Rose about it, whether Andrew was the same. There were another ten questions, such as 'do you change your behaviour to avoid triggering an attack?' And 'are you unsure of your own judgement?' She was so unsure of her own judgement that the only two she could definitely say no to were 'does he threaten to kill your pets?' and 'does he threaten to kidnap or get custody of the children?' It was so long since they'd had children whose custody was an issue that she couldn't remember.

She had a brief smile at the paragraph defining sexual abuse. One thing Bill had never done was tie her up or suggest threesomes or anything like that. The suggestion that 'he should not criticise your performance' seemed to her to be a counsel of perfection. He'd said she was boring in bed, but she was, she knew that. He'd often told her about a woman he'd slept with who could ripple her internal muscles to give a man greater pleasure but no amount of Pilates seemed to give Paige the ability to replicate the effect. It was part of the reason why she hadn't pursued the issue of infidelity very hard, because if other women could give him what he needed, well, why not? She wasn't very highly sexed, she knew that, and, with the worry over contraception and Bill's insistence that it was a violation to ask a man to have a vasectomy, it was an area of their marriage that she knew she had failed at.

On the whole, if you believed the websites, she had been abused. But wasn't this all part of making us a nation of victims? That was one of the things Bill often railed at. Counsellors and compensation claims and everything being turned into a syndrome. 'Life's tough,' he'd say, pouring himself another drink. 'Bad things happen. Get over it.' She spotted that there was a free helpline and wrote the number down, putting it in her purse. Not that she intended to get locked in again.

She felt a sense of failure. Although the words on the website stressed that anyone, of any age or in any financial situation, could suffer from domestic abuse, the pictures were all of younger women, many of them from different cultures. Middle-aged middle-class women clearly ought to be able to look after themselves. It underlined how stupid she'd been. How stupid she was. If you lived a privileged life, if you'd been given every possible advantage at birth, you should be able to avoid this sort of thing.

Paige could see the librarians looking at her, and realised she was crying. She quickly blew her nose and left, before she let the side down – as her mother used to call it – any further.

She got home to six messages on her answering machine. 'I'm so sorry,' Bill said. 'This has all been a terrible misunderstanding. We need to talk. I promise I'll change. I know I've been . . . a bit hard on you recently. It's just because . . .' there was a break as his voice choked up. 'Just because I've been so stressed about Orchard Park, and I've been worried you were growing away from me. I'll keep on going to the sessions with Michael, even if you don't. I want to help. Call me.'

Paige's heart jumped out of her chest. He sounded so down. She grubbed around in her bag to find her phone as his second message played.

'I'll go to AA too,' he said. 'I think it's the drink. You're right, I do drink too much and I don't like what it does to me.' There was another sob. 'Paige, you must help me. Please. If what we had together, all those years, our two lovely girls, if any of it meant anything at all . . .' The message ended.

Paige hovered indecisively. Of course it meant something. She couldn't bear to think of him so low. The third message came on. 'Paige? Paige, are you there? George Boxer is a loser. You may think he represents an escape from a mundane, boring life, but that man is no good for you. He'll let you down. I'm saying this because I care, and I don't want to see you hurt.'

Paige was genuinely puzzled by this message. She had always assumed that Bill had been using the George Boxer incident as an excuse to get angry, and as a way of diverting attention from Anthea. But it sounded as if he really believed that they were having an affair. Her instinct was to phone Bill immediately, to make it all clear and to reassure him that she still cared for him, but she made herself listen to the last few messages. One was from Sophie. She sounded cross. 'Mum, where are you? Dad's been on the line. He says you're not speaking to him. Mum, that's *not* fair. You at least owe him a proper conversation.

Between two human beings. Because that's what he is. He's not perfect, but he's not a demon either. Call me.'

Then Jess. 'Mum, hope you're fine. And don't listen to Dad saying he's sorry, he's never been sorry in his life.' She sounded happy. Paige wanted her to stay that way.

Then there was another message from Bill again. 'Munchkin, this is all quite unnecessary, call me. I quite understand if you want us to be apart for a while, and, of course, if it's what you want I'll give you a divorce, but at least let's talk. Michael is worried about you too, and says we can fit in a session any time.'

Should she ring him? Or not? Perhaps he was ready to change. No, those websites weren't for women like her. Not for women who lived in houses who painted their front doors with paints called Pigeon, Elephant's Breath or Farrow's Cream, and who had a four-by-four in a drive fringed by the huge white mop heads of hydrangea *arborescens Annabelle*, underplanted with frothy lime green alchemilla mollis.

But now she was tired, hopelessly bone-achingly tired. She unplugged the phone and switched off her mobile, carefully checked all the windows and doors again, and stumbled upstairs to bed.

Chapter 38

These days Jess always woke up with a sense of excitement, the way she'd felt about Christmas when she was very, very young and before her father had managed to spoil it all, the way he spoiled everything. She opened her eyes to see Jake lying asleep, his long, perfect body sprawled across the sheets. She marvelled quietly at the length of his dark lashes, at the lustrous quality of the black hair flopping over his face, over the shadows around the fine lines of his chin. Even asleep he looked strong, all bone, sinew and muscle, like a greyhound or a racehorse. She slid out of bed and made two cups of tea, his exactly how he liked it, strong and sweet. 'All that sugar,' she'd said to him. 'You'll get fat when you're older.'

'No I won't,' he'd replied with the supreme confidence that made her feel so safe. He slid his hand out and pinched a sliver of flesh on her abdomen. 'But you,' he said with his wicked grin. 'You'll have to watch it, Girls always do.'

She had worried about that for a few moments, but she knew she wasn't fat. All her life she'd had trouble keeping weight on, and she had always envied Sophie her curves.

He opened his eyes with a smile and took the tea from her, propping himself up in bed.

'I can't get over Mum actually finally telling Dad it's over,' she said, drawing her knees up as she sipped her tea. 'And I still

don't understand why Sophie's so wrecked about it. He's a bastard, an utter bastard, and I hope Mum now gets the chance to
live her own life.'

Sophie had burst into tears several times the evening before,
and Jess was beginning to feel her sympathy wearing thin.
You'd have thought someone had died. Jake had been great and
had put an arm round her, giving her his handkerchief. Harry,
when he returned at ten o'clock, had given his wife a rueful
grin and had commented that 'you look as if we'd lost the
World Cup on a penalty shoot-out'.

'No I don't,' said Sophie crossly, but she'd stopped snivelling.

Harry had wolfed down the remains of supper and then did
the washing up while the other three continued to dissect Bill
and Paige's relationship. Jess shook her head at the memory.
'Really, Mum should have left him years ago.'

'Don't be too hard on him,' said Jake. 'Give him a break.'

'He never gave me a break,' replied Jess, twisting her hair
around her finger, something she often did when she talked
about her father. 'So why should I?'

'Because you don't know the facts. You don't really know
what went on between them – not everything, anyway – and
how far your mother was complicit in making you the bad
apple of the family. It's like co-dependents and alcoholics. Some
women need – or think they need – to be treated badly. They
equate it with love. Her father was probably like that too. I'm
not excusing Bill's behaviour, but I'm sure he's a decent man
underneath it all. He's just a bit bad-tempered, that's all.' He
had grinned sideways at her. 'And I like him, even if you don't.
Have I got a clean shirt?'

'Somewhere.' Jess hopped out of bed and pulled out the
ironing board. Jake had to be in work by nine, whereas her
shifts rarely started until ten or eleven, so her mornings now
started with getting Jake off to work, because he was chaotic
about his clothes. Somehow he always managed to emerge
looking relaxed and immaculate, but she had no idea how he

did it because she spent her time pulling stray socks out from under the bed and finding dirty shirts strewn across the floor. He claimed not to be able to understand the controls of the washing machine – said with a huge wink – and when she tried to explain them he always had to dash off.

That was men for you. She quite enjoyed grumbling about it to Mel, because it made her feel part of a couple.

Jake checked himself in the mirror. Grey suit, white shirt open at the collar. 'I think you're more upset than you make out about your parents splitting,' he said over his shoulder.

Jess buttered his toast. 'No I'm not.'

He kissed the back of her neck as he took the toast, which he usually ate as he walked to the Tube station. 'Yes you are. I know you better than you know yourself.'

Jess thought this might possibly be true, but had no intention of admitting it.

'Anyway,' he said, his mouth full of toast. 'It makes you think, doesn't it?'

'Think?' Jess washed up the plate and knife and put them on the drainer.

'Yup, about us. Whether we should move in together. Go the opposite direction from your parents, as it were.'

Jess froze. She had thought about it, but hadn't wanted to frighten him away by mentioning it. But he spent most of his time at her flat now, and his possessions snaked their way over her sofa and chairs, and concealed themselves under her furniture.

'It doesn't seem worth paying two mortgages, does it? I could rent my place out and we could split the costs of living here. What do you think? Life would be cheaper for us both and you could do fewer shifts at the restaurant.'

Jess turned round from the sink and flung her arms round his neck.

'That's a yes, then, is it?' he asked, grinning down at her as he whirled her around the kitchen, one arm locked around her waist and the other holding the toast in the air, safely out of the way. 'What about tonight? Moving everything in and cleaning the place up for rental, starting now?'

'Oh, yes . . . except I was meeting the girls tonight, and I've missed the last three Thursdays . . .' She saw his face. 'But this is more important. I'll cancel.'

'Good girl. No point hanging around. If we move fast we might get a tenant in by next month.'

'Jake . . .' she hesitated, but she had to know.

'Yes?' He held her chin up in his hands, looking into her eyes. 'For you, anything.'

'Really, really anything?'

He nodded.

'I'd like to know what went wrong between you and Cassie. I know you hate talking about her, but . . .'

She thought something dark crossed his face, but he kissed the tip of her nose. 'Of course. You deserve to know. You have a right to know. But . . .' He took her chin in his hand again, tipping it up towards his face. 'I haven't told you before because I don't come out of it looking very good either. It wasn't all Cassie, darling, I made mistakes too. I'm . . . ashamed of my part in it all, and I don't want it to put you off.'

'You won't,' she said, sure of herself. 'You couldn't.' He kissed her, once, twice, on the lips, then on her forehead and pulled the door to behind him with his foot as he left.

Jess couldn't wait to ring round and tell everyone that Jake was moving in with her. Two of the girls were married and two single.

She got 'Go for it, girl. Don't worry about us, we can have a drink any time' from three of them.

And one 'Isn't this a bit sudden? Are you sure?'

'It's not at all sudden,' she said. 'We've gone very slowly, actually, because Jake had such a bad experience with Cassie. We've been together for eight and a half months.'

Harry answered the phone at Sophie's house. 'Oh hi Jess,

morning. How have you been since we last saw you . . . let me see . . . nine hours ago?'

'Jake and I are moving in together,' she said for the fifth time that morning. It still sounded good.

'Congratulations. I'm very pleased for you both.' His voice was warm. 'Soph will be delighted. I'll just get her.'

But Sophie's enthusiasm was muted, and she still sounded depressed. 'Good, good,' she said vaguely. 'But get it sorted legally, won't you? That he pays his share and everything?'

'Why wouldn't he?' demanded Jess. 'He's the most generous man I've ever met. He's always buying me presents. And why can't you just be happy for me for once?'

'Because you don't always think things through.'

'Sophie! That is the most patronising thing anyone can say to . . . well, anyone. It's what Dad always says to and about Mum, and I think it's actually, well, it's as offensive as you can get. It's like saying, "Here's wise old me and silly little you, and silly little you is going to make an utter mess of your life unless wise old me conveys all the wise old things I think". Which aren't necessarily wise at all. It's insulting and belittling, and . . .'

'Well there's no need to get so upset about it,' said Sophie. 'Someone's got to say it.'

'No, they haven't. If nobody ever said "you don't think things through" to anybody ever again, the world would be a much better place.' She rang off without saying goodbye. Sophie always had to have the last word, but she wasn't going to, not this time.

Chapter 39

Sophie was enjoying photographing *Shore Style*. She, Caroline and Bruno had travelled round the English coast on intermittent day trips, discovering a long, low weatherboarded shack on the sands near Whitstable, a converted pub overlooking a promenade on the South Coast, an old fisherman's cottage on the shingle in East Anglia, and now they were heading for two days in Devon, photographing a wooden Edwardian lodge tucked into the side of a cliff.

It was like a garden shed with three bedrooms, a kitchen and a bathroom with an old claw-footed bath and a stained Ascot heater. Huge glass windows overlooked a private cove, to the sound of waves slapping against the cliffs. Sophie took a deep breath of clean, salty air as the wind whipped around her ears. 'You could come to a place like this and leave everything behind,' she said. 'Irritating husbands, screaming children and badly behaved parents.'

'It's the perfect love nest,' commented Caroline, pulling blue fifties Devon china out of a cupboard and plumping up faded floral cushions. 'The hut that time forgot.'

An image of being here alone with Jake flashed into Sophie's head and she quickly banished it. She could never do that to Harry, or to Jess.

But if you were somewhere completely away from your real

life, where the wind and the waves could drown out the clamour of your conscience . . . well, would that count?

Yes, it would. She focused on the greys and blues of the sea and sand, lining up an old G-plan sofa in front of the window, throwing a colourful hand-crocheted rug over it, and then, at lunchtime, getting a lucky chance picture of a seagull swooping down on a sandwich that Bruno had put down for one moment. 'Great shot,' she murmured.

Her mobile peeped. She'd texted Jake to say congratulations on moving in together (did you congratulate people? She wasn't sure, but she wanted to be welcoming), and this was his answer. 'Looking forward to being part of the family.'

She texted the picture of the seagull to him. He thought they might be able to use it in the paper. She texted back that the publishers owned the copyright, but that it might be available when the book was published. He replied, telling her to get in touch then.

'Are you having an affair with someone?' asked Caroline.

'Don't be ridiculous. It's all about Jess. Jake's moving in with her. He's lovely, but I'm not sure he's right for *her*. I can't put my finger on why not, though.'

Sophie slipped her phone back into her pocket with a smile, and tried to decide how to photograph the little lean-to kitchen in a way that made it look more seaside and less mud hut.

She trailed home late, to find all three girls crying and Harry up to his elbows in toys.

'Harry! This place looks as if a bomb's hit it.'

He got off his hands and knees and came to kiss her. 'We had a tidying-up game, but it went wrong,' he said over the screams. All three girls wrapped themselves round her legs, almost pulling her over.

'I can see that.' She brushed him away, and staggered upstairs with Summer in her arms and Lottie and Bella clinging to her, whimpering, and finally managed to quiet them down while

Harry tidied everything away. An hour later they were opening a bottle of wine. Sophie boiled up some pasta while Harry made a salad dressing.

'Sorry about that,' said Harry cheerfully. 'I thought that if I based tidying up on cricket they'd find it more interesting. But they got a bit confused and frustrated . . .'

'I bet they did. Harry, they're girls. And they're only five, three and eighteen months. I'm thirty and I still don't understand cricket.'

'That's because you haven't grown up with it. I don't see why girls shouldn't enjoy cricket just as much as boys. The secret is to introduce it when they're young.'

Sophie rolled her eyes. Harry was one of those men born to have a son, but they'd discussed it and agreed that they couldn't cope with a fourth child. 'Don't go making one of them into the boy you never had, like Dad did with Jess, will you?' she said sharply.

He laughed. 'No, but I'm going to introduce all three of them to every sport I enjoy and see what takes. Bella's got excellent hand-eye coordination – I'd bet anything that she's definitely going to be playing *something*, and Lottie has an awareness of where a ball's going to be, which is very good for her age. Summer likes clapping everyone, which is always useful.'

'I wish you'd think about what they want to do rather than inflicting what you want on them.' Sophie sighed and forked in some pasta. 'I still can't get hold of Mum, and neither can Dad. He's really worried about her. I'm wondering if I ought to go down. She chucked him out over a week ago and no one's heard from her since. I even rang Rose and a couple of other of their friends. Zilch. And Rose said she's tried going round there but no one opens the gates.'

'It is a bit of a fortress, what with that great wall and those smart, remote-controlled gates,' mused Harry. 'Do you think your dad's knocked her off and buried her in the foundations of Orchard Park?'

Sophie was even more irritated. 'Of course not! But I am worried that Mum's done something silly or that she's having a complete breakdown. I don't think she could survive without Dad. He's always done everything for her, and . . .'

'Whenever we've been down there it always seems to be your mother doing everything for your father.'

'Oh that's just domestic stuff. No, I mean the larger things in life, dealing with forms and officialdom, paying your car tax . . . and, most importantly, getting a job. She'll need to work: divorce slashes middle-class households in half financially. Dad thinks she's unstable, probably suicidal. He's genuinely worried about her. And he's unbelievably hurt about thirty years of marriage ending with suitcases outside a locked front door, and I don't blame him. Anyone would find that hard to take.'

Harry got out two plates, forks and spoons, and they sat down. 'I think you should stay out of it, Sophie. I think it'll upset you too much – it already is – and they need to handle it on their own.'

'What, just stand by while my mother commits suicide? Harry, doesn't it ever occur to you that sometimes people need a bit of support in this world? Not everyone can be a healthy, sturdy rugby player you know.'

'Do you really think she would?' Harry ignored Sophie's last remark. 'She seems pretty sensible to me.'

'Sensible!' shrieked Sophie. 'One thing that my mother is *not* is sensible. All our lives, Dad has been asking us to watch out for her. And Jess is no help, she's so bewitched by Jake that she hasn't got room in her head for another thought. I wish she'd look for a proper job and stop all this pointless waitressing, but she's putting everything on hold because of him. It's such a mistake.'

'Sophie, you've got the girls to look after. Your mother and Jess . . . they're adults. They can look after themselves.'

'In other words, you don't want me to go bombing down to

The Rowans, leaving you in charge of three screaming children. It's all about you, isn't it?'

Harry didn't answer. Eventually he said that he wanted to catch *Match of the Day*, unless there was anything she wanted to watch.

Sophie, still feeling bruised – and rather guilty at being so vile – said that there wasn't, and he could have the remote control to himself.

'Sure?' He squeezed her shoulders. 'Soph, if you do want to go down to The Rowans and check on your Mum I can look after the girls in the evening. We can get Patrizia to pick them up after school.'

'I could take Summer. She hasn't got school to miss, and it might be nice for her to have some time alone with me,' said Sophie, conceding the argument without actually saying sorry.

'And it would save on childcare,' said Harry, who often concentrated on the financial side to the detriment of everything else. He buried himself in *Match of the Day*. She did wish he cared a bit more about them all and a bit less about sport, but that was men for you, wasn't it?

She also wished he was easier to talk to about it, like Jake, who knew more than she did about therapy and alcoholism, and seemed to be keen to go into everyone's motives and what it was in their pasts that meant they behaved like they did. 'I think your mother's co-dependent,' Jake had said, the evening they had all got together. 'Someone who equates love with pain, and who needs people to need them. Co-dependents have control problems and they worry about the silliest things.'

This seemed an accurate description of Paige, who could be quite hysterical if something wasn't exactly as their father had said he wanted it.

'The trouble is,' Jake had added, 'is that co-dependency, like alcoholism, is a progressive problem. It just gets worse. Co-dependents don't trust themselves, they don't trust their feelings

233

or other people. At the end of the road – well, there's getting withdrawn and isolated, hopelessness, addiction, even suicide.'

'You seem to know a lot about it,' said Jess adoringly.

'I did an article on some addiction centres,' said Jake, 'and I thought the most interesting part was the people around the addicts, the way they needed the addicts and alcoholics to go on being chemically dependent or the co-dependents themselves had to think about what they were going to do in life.'

'Dad drinks too much, so it makes sense that Mum would be co-dependent,' said Sophie.

'Well,' Jake looked serious, 'if that's the case, she may well have been undermining his efforts to drink less. For a co-dependent there's nothing more frightening than change.'

That was Mum in a nutshell, thought Sophie. Determined to maintain the status quo, insistent that she had no choices. And now, suddenly, she'd been seized by some demon and was turning her life completely upside down rather than going about it in a sensible and balanced fashion.

She phoned Jess and got Jake.

'Why do you always answer Jess's mobile?'

Jake laughed. 'Because she always leaves it everywhere and I spend my life chasing after her with it. I've tried to explain that just owning a mobile isn't enough, you have to switch it on and have it with you for it to work. Anyway, here she is.'

Jess, rather surprisingly, insisted that she could take the bike down and find out what was going on, and that there was no need for Sophie to bother.

Sophie wasn't quite sure why this irritated her so much, but it was, she supposed, easier for Jess if she didn't have shifts – which she never seemed to these days – than it was for her, with her layers of childcare to organise.

But it was just as well because she had a shoot the following day – summer accessories, all on a rose theme, which was challenging in February when there was so little natural light. The

234

house she was shooting in had lovely large Georgian windows out of which you could see only a chillingly white sky, leafless trees and bare shrubs. All the roses were so obviously florists' roses, there were no blowsy garden roses to be had.

Chapter 40

Jess let the rush hour subside and arrived outside The Rowans at twelve-thirty. She could barely see the house over the high, forbidding wall that her father had had built after their nearest neighbours had been burgled for the third time. You used to be able to see the house from the lane, but now she could only see the attic windows poking out over the top.

She pressed the buzzer at the main gates. There was no answer. Never mind, she could walk round and dodge in through the fields and garden at the back, which were only protected by a low fence. She dragged the bike into the field and hid it behind a hedge, then slithered and scrambled round through puddles of mud and rough pasture to the back of the garden, eventually crawling under some barbed wire and then walked up through the garden itself to ring the doorbell.

'Mum,' she shouted through the letterbox, trying to get some mud off her motorbike leathers. 'It's Jess. Just me, I'm on my own.'

There was a dense quality to the silence she could hear. No radio. No rustling. No eager sound of feet. 'Mum!' She sat down on the doorstep, leaning her back against the door, to assess the situation.

There was a chain round the main gates. On the inside. And no sign of her mother's car. Walking round the house, she peered in windows. Everything was deserted. She phoned Sophie. 'I think Mum must have moved out. There's no sign of her.'

'Perhaps she's just out shopping,' said Sophie. 'Bella, *don't* be such a silly girl! Sorry, what did you say?'

Jess rang off and sank down against the door again, wondering whether she should ring the police or, even worse, her father. She heard a rustling from the side of the house and saw Paige emerging from behind a bush.

'Mum!'

'Oh, hello darling, how lovely to see you.'

Jess thought her mother might have finally gone mad, as Bill had always feared. Her hair looked unbrushed and she wasn't wearing make-up. She had always – always – worn a little light foundation and lipstick. 'Your father likes it,' she'd always said. 'He gets cross if I look tired.'

Now she was bare-faced. 'Come in and have some coffee,' she said lightly.

'What's with the chains around the gate? And where's your car?'

Paige mumbled something about burglars, and a new place to park. Jess walked into the familiar kitchen, her senses alert for changes. 'Are you saying that you park your car five hundred yards down the road, outside the village hall, then walk here and come in round the back? Because of burglars? Mum, I do think you've finally lost it.'

Paige put the coffee on the table and sat down. 'Jess, I've had a lifetime of your father telling me I'm mad, and him telling you two that I'm mad. So I have just come back from my therapist, Ruth. She *doesn't* think I'm mad, and . . .' She took a deep breath. '. . . I . . . I . . . don't believe I am either. But I am frightened. Your father doesn't have the keys to the house, but he does have the remote control to the gates and he could drive in here and wait for me. And then I'd be locked in with him.'

'And do what?'

Paige shrugged. 'Shout at me. Threaten me.' She paused. 'Hurt me.'

'He's not that bad, surely. You know, "sticks and stones will break my bones but words will never hurt me". That old rhyme. I mean, he's not physically violent.'

Paige shook her head. 'Maybe. I don't know. Do you remember the time he accidentally spilled the boiling pasta water over my feet and I had to go to hospital? He said it was because he was so bad at cooking and it was my fault for having asked him to do it.'

'That *was* an accident, though, wasn't it?' Jess frowned, her heart furiously ticking away in her chest. The memory hurt. She remembered her mother screaming like a wounded animal, and her father calling the ambulance.

Another memory surfaced from that evening. Bill saying to Paige in an undertone, 'Now I hope you've learned your lesson. You should never have asked me to cook that pasta.' Then the ambulance men arriving and her father distraught as Paige was taken away on a stretcher. It had been several weeks before she could walk comfortably, and she still had a tight, shiny scar on one foot.

'Whether that particular occasion was an accident or not, he's . . . he always frightens me. And he's begun to make threats of violence, with a . . .' Jess could hear the pain in her mother's voice. '. . . well, he's threatened me with a knife twice now. I can't carry on living with it. He used to hide things, so I thought I was going mad – several times my keys, or something else important, haven't been where I know I left them. I think he might be dangerous. He's furious that I've broken the rules, you see, the rules that say he's completely in charge of everything I do and say, and he can't tolerate that.'

'But I thought you're quite absent-minded, anyway, aren't you?' Jess was, bemused, wondering how much of this had come from the therapist. She still couldn't quite believe it. Didn't therapists make their money by getting people to invent things? 'Are you sure he's been hiding things rather than you've been losing them?'

'I can't be sure of anything. That's what makes it so difficult. But your father isn't an absent-minded man himself, is he?'

Jess shook her head. 'No, he's meticulous about detail and where everything should be.' She grimaced. 'To a fault. He remembers everything.'

'So,' said Paige, 'if he accidentally leaves his keys behind, so has to take the spares, and my keys go missing at the same time and he double locks the doors so I can't get out, and this happens, say, four or five times, do you think that's a coincidence?'

Jess knew she could end this now. She could tell her mother that losing keys was something everyone did, that accidentally locking someone into a house was just that – an accident. That even her father might take three sets of keys without realising it. She could see in her mother's eyes the doubt and fear, and knew she could smooth it over, could bring back the safe, secure order of things by saying, 'Dad would never do that. Forget it.'

Or she could trust her own judgement. 'Go for it, Mum,' she said, after a short pause. 'You should have done this long ago.'

'I thought it was better to keep the family together. And I was afraid.'

'OK. But he belittled and undermined me, too. Don't you care about that? I've spent my life in a house where I was always told I wasn't good enough, wasn't as pretty or as clever as Sophie, where everything that went wrong was my fault . . .' The resentment surged up like bile.

'I'm sorry, Jess.' Paige hid her face in her hands. 'I really am. I thought you would be all right. I thought we couldn't survive on our own and I believed him when he said I was stupid. Jess, promise me, don't make the same mistakes in your relationships. Ever.'

Jess raised her eyebrows. 'Mum, if there is one thing I can

assure you, it is that if there was the slightest sign of a man behaving like Dad I'd be out of there. That's what's so fantastic about Jake – he laughs, he's loving, he's just so positive. Whereas Dad complains all the time. And Jake's . . . well, I know it's sounds silly and old-fashioned, but he's romantic. He buys me flowers. Funny little presents just because he's thinking of me. Little last-minute surprises. He picks me up from work or if I see friends . . . well, anyway. Just not like Dad.'

'Good.'

Jess picked up the voice-activated recorder, which was still lying on the kitchen table. 'Oh, Jake's got one of these.'

'Is that his?' Paige sounded hopeful.

'No, different brand. Anyway, we'd know about it if Jake lost his: he'd be frantic. He uses it for every interview. Why have you got one?'

Paige took a deep breath. 'Your father has been recording everything I say. I found this when he locked me in, after . . . after an argument when he threw a knife at me. Well, he aimed it at me but then threw it at the table. And he told the police I'd thrown the knife at him, and—'

'Hang on, hang on.' Jess couldn't quite take it all in.

Paige explained. About emotional abuse, and the websites she'd visited and the books she was reading, and how Ruth had been the first person in a long time not to tell her she was mad.

Jess opened her mouth to tell her mother that, of course, she was a bit . . . well, mad, but so were lots of people, but then closed it again. 'Oh, a label,' she said, instead. 'Abusive relationship. I love labels. And diagnoses. Which, presumably, means cures.'

'I don't think I've got quite that far,' admitted Paige. 'He wants to talk, but I'm afraid that as soon as he starts up I'll crumble again. And I'm terrified of him coming round here, but I know he's got to, because of his things.'

'Have someone here. Not us, we're wallpaper as far as he's concerned, at least I am, but if you've got friends round he'll be nice as pie in front of them.'

'Oh, I couldn't. It would be letting him down. I couldn't let people know I was afraid of him, they'd think he was a wife-beater or something and that might be bad for the business.'

'Which means you're still kowtowing to him and his moods. Try to start remembering that his business is his affair.' She fiddled with the voice-activated recorder, running it back to the beginning and pressing play. Paige's voice, arranging a doctor's appointment, emerged, followed by a cautious conversation with Rose.

'He always seemed to know what I'd said, and he told me that it was because everyone was his friend and would tell him if I was being disloyal. Now I've found out he was recording me, at least when I was in the kitchen. I haven't found anything anywhere else in the house.'

Jess played through a number of unremarkable domestic conversations until she came to the evening when Bill had thrown the knife at the table. 'Switch it off, Jess, it wasn't meant for anyone to hear. It should never have been recorded in the first place.' Paige reached out to take the recorder back.

Jess switched off the machine and put it in a drawer. 'This is evidence, Mum. We're keeping this. He meant it to spy on you, and in a glorious example of birds coming home to roost we've got it as evidence against him. Bet he never thought of that.'

'Apparently men like him don't think they're doing anything wrong. They think that if only everyone else behaved properly they wouldn't have to shout and swear and threaten. They think everything's our fault.'

'Yeah, well. So what else have you done? Have you got a lawyer?'

'It's a bit difficult, because if I get half the house, and I should do, I wouldn't qualify for legal aid. That would be fine if your father and I could work out something fair between us, but he says not. He says that he won't give me a penny.'

'Well, he'll have to. You've run his house and looked after

him while he built up his business. You're entitled to a share of what you've created together, whether he likes it or not.'

'Yes,' said Paige. 'But if he fights it, it will cost thousands. I can't afford it.'

'You can't afford *not* to fight. And he's got a successful company, he's a well-off man. Think about those company reports Jake downloaded.'

'He's had to sell Orchard Park before it was finished, so I think things are pretty bad at the moment.'

'He always says that. But first, let's get Andrew and Rose lined up.'

Jess rang Rose, and Rose agreed that she and Andrew would be only too happy to help.

Then Jess rang her father. 'Dad, if you want to pick up stuff these are the following times and dates. Andrew and Rose will be there to ensure fair play.'

Bill said he couldn't possibly make any of the times.

'Oh well,' said Jess. 'What a shame. But never mind, you'll get all your stuff in the end, after the final divvying up in court, and if you need anything urgently before then you can buy it.' She put the phone down and grinned at Paige.

'Oh Jess, your father is very busy, perhaps he really couldn't make it then . . .'

'Stop it. We gave him a choice of three evenings outside normal working hours. Nobody is so busy that they can't make one of those.'

And sure enough, he rang back to say that, at huge inconvenience to a lot of people, he had managed to shift one very important date and would be round the following Tuesday evening.

'I'm going to ring Sophie,' said Jess, once they'd put the phone down on a very irritated Bill. 'She's worried about you.' She took the phone into the sitting room and told Sophie what she had found.

'Jess! I cannot believe that you are buying into this ridiculous

242

story,' shouted Sophie. 'Dad told me that this Ruth woman was incredibly damaging and now I find out that you're behaving irresponsibly too. Dad may have a bit of a short temper – and I'm not justifying his actions – but to call it domestic abuse, as if they lived in a council house and he got drunk every night – is absolutely wrong. I should have known you'd screw this up, I should never have allowed you to—'

'You didn't *allow* me,' said Jess. 'I make my own decisions. And he *does* get drunk every night. What sort of house you live in has nothing to do with it.'

'He's just stressed. He works too hard. And Mum benefits from that. She has a life most women would envy, she has to make *some* sacrifices. Putting up with a bit of bad temper from time to time isn't going to kill her.'

'It might. And it doesn't matter if he's "just drunk" or "just stressed", or even "just a murderer",' Jess shouted down the phone. 'Mum has the right to live her life without being told she's stupid or mad every moment of the day, and she's certainly got the right to live without being terrified that he's going to hurt her. I've heard the threats Dad made, which were recorded on the bug he placed in the kitchen.'

'Bug?' demanded Sophie. 'Bug? Now I really have heard it all. Thousands of people have those recorders, they use them for interviews and making notes on the train. I've seen them and you must have, too.'

'Until I met Jake, who obviously needs one because he's a journalist, I'd never met anyone with a recorder. Do you have one? Does Harry?'

'Don't go off at a tangent. Try to keep that butterfly brain of yours on the right track. It's perfectly clear that someone left their recorder in the kitchen, it got tidied away, and it accidentally picked up a very bad argument between Mum and Dad. You are so fucking incompetent. You *know* you shouldn't be encouraging these stupid fantasies of Mum's.'

'They're not fantasies. Go on the Refuge website. Read the

questions that define abuse. Does he verbally abuse her? Does he blame *her* for it? Does he constantly criticise her? Does he control her life? Her money? Who she sees? What she wears? . . . Yes, yes, yes, yes, yes and yes. Sophie, wake up and smell the coffee.'

'It isn't abuse, he just loses his temper . . .'

'He doesn't *just* lose his temper, he makes her dance round it every moment of the day and night,' said Jess. 'She lives in fear of the next outbreak. Like we did when we were kids. That's unacceptable. I left home because of that. She stayed because she thought it was better for us to have two parents when we were kids, and after twenty years of it she thought she *was* incompetent. Listen, Sophie, she's afraid. Afraid to be on her own with him in case he hurts her or even . . . kills her.'

'It's quite absurd to accuse him of something like that. This is all about that therapist, isn't it? That woman who doesn't have a man of her own so has to wreck other people's marriages. She's clearly a man-hater. She should be struck off, and I've a good mind to . . . oh, but she's probably not even properly qualified anyway, is she?'

'I've heard the threats, Sophie. I would be afraid if I was Mum.'

'If that was really true, don't you think she would have got out years ago? This is completely unfair to Dad, and it's going to add a layer of bitterness and victimhood to the whole divorce and make it slower and harder – and more expensive – than it need be. That's why it's so irresponsible to encourage her. Jess, I'm coming down to try to sort out this fuck-up. You obviously can't be trusted to bring any sanity to it all, and are as hopeless as she is. *Why* do I have to do everything in this family? Why?' And she slammed down the phone.

Jess looked up to see Paige standing at the door. 'Not good?'

'Not good,' agreed Jess. She was surprised by how shaken she felt.

Paige knelt down in front of Jess and took both of her hands.

'Ruth warned me that one or both of my daughters might not be ready, might deny that there's a problem or try to minimise it: you know, "it was only stress" or "but only if he's drunk". It's a completely normal reaction. You know, "It was just a push, she shouldn't take things so seriously . . ." Was that the sort of thing she was saying?'

Jess nodded. 'She's always been bossy. But she was horrible. Really nasty.'

'Don't blame Soph. It's very scary for her. She's frightened. She doesn't want to have everything she's been told all her life turned upside down.'

'Well, I believe in you, Mum. And we're going to get through this together, aren't we?' Jess forced herself to smile.

Paige squeezed Jess's hands and looked into her eyes. 'And Ruth said that another response might be "phoney but positive".'

'That's me,' said Jess, trying to smile. 'Phoney but positive. Definitely. You can count on me for positive phoniness. Whenever you need some.'

'Just as long as you know you don't have to pretend to me.'

'I need to get back now.' Jess withdrew her hands and got up. 'Jake's home at six and I'd like to be there.' She packed up her laptop, hitched on her backpack and picked up her helmet. 'Don't let Sophie bully you.'

'I won't.' Paige opened her arms and Jess let herself be hugged.

For the first time in as long as she could remember, Paige felt like a mother. Someone whose arms were safe.

Chapter 41

Anthea helped Bill put together his Form E, a document she liked to think of as his 'For Me'. It was supposed to be a full disclosure of his personal finances and a list of the expenditure he needed, so that the division of the family finances would be fair to both sides.

Well, that was the theory. Anthea knew that, in practice, men got taken for a ride. Most women were manipulative bitches. Every week there was something in the press about some gold-digging female, some court case about a man who had given his ex-wife more than he himself had been left with, some greedy wife fighting for an absurd sum like thirty-four million pounds. Anthea hated these women, these glittering blondes – for they all seemed to be golden-haired, and were photographed full length either in evening gown, or striding out of courtrooms in a smart suit with immaculate hair, occasionally looking stressed because they 'only' had twenty-seven thousand pounds a month to live on. She, Anthea, worked for a living. She didn't expect handouts, and neither should they. Nor should Paige.

By the time she'd finished with the Form E, no judge would be awarding Paige half of anything.

'We'll start by offering her a hundred grand,' said Bill. 'If she's got any sense, she'll take it. Who wouldn't like to be given a hundred grand? For nothing? And if she doesn't . . . well, she'll only have herself to blame for what happens next. We'll take her to court. She'll never find the money to defend herself and she won't get legal aid, not with how much we've got between us.'

Anthea cooked a light supper and they both worked late into the night, facing each other across her kitchen table, working in harmony. She had a sense of rightness. She knew Paige had never worked like this, at a table with Bill. Paige, obsessed with paint charts and fabric swatches, and the progress of her children, had buried her head in the sand when it came to the business.

But this was what a partnership should be. They had a rhythm now. Bill ate with her every evening, parking his car a few blocks away and bringing his laundry over each day because he didn't have a washing machine. 'I don't know how to work them even if I did have one,' he said cheerfully. Occasionally he slept at his flat, or got up at six to go back there to shower and change. They were still being careful not to be seen in public together, and Anthea was sporadically anxious when well-meaning villagers such as Andrew and Rose invited him to supper because they felt sorry for him or wanted to line him up with someone.

'I can't refuse the invitations,' said Bill. 'I need to hear what that bitch is getting up to. And we need to make sure we counter any lies she puts about.'

He never used Paige's name, Anthea noticed. It was always That Bitch, the ex-wife or just She. Even Jenny had started referring to Paige as TB, code for That Bitch.

Chapter 42

The returning traffic was heavier than Jess had expected and it was slow going, even on the bike. As she put her key in the door Jake opened it. 'Where have you been?'

She kissed him and hung her helmet up. 'Mercy dash to Mum. Who seems to be somehow more herself than I've ever known. Which is great, considering.' She realised that Jake's face had darkened. 'What is it?'

'Do you know what it was like for me, waiting here, thinking you'd been hit by a car? You know what I feel about that bike.'

'It's OK. I'm a good driver. I've had a bike for ten years.' Jess walked through to the kitchen and opened the fridge.

Jake followed her. 'Jess. Look at me. It's not your ability that I'm worried about. It's the other guys. Do you know how vulnerable you are? There's a reason why they call bikers organ donors, you know.'

'Yeah, I've heard that one before.' She grinned and began to pull out ingredients for supper.

'Jess, stop that and let's talk properly. We need to get a few things straight.'

Jess heard a new tone in his voice. One she had never heard before. 'Yes?' she replied cautiously.

'Jess, how can we plan our lives together if you take these

absurd risks all the time? Would you use the bike if you were pregnant? Would you endanger our child?'

Our child. It took Jess's breath away, but she tried to keep calm. 'I'm not pregnant. I do know that. And no, I wouldn't use the bike if I was.'

'Well, then, you're as valuable to me as any child. If it's not safe for a baby, it's not safe for you.'

'I suppose so.'

'You take the Tube to work, and when we're together we use my car, so you hardly need the bike anyway.'

'It's useful if I have to see Mum. She can't do this without me. I'm the only one on her side, Dad's being a monster and Sophie . . .'

'Yes, well, Sophie's called about that.'

'Sophie called you? Why?' Jess felt threatened. Sophie was certainly trying to line all the guns up against Mum.

'Because she was worried about you. She's got a lot of sense. Jess, we are at the beginning of our lives together. Sophie seems to think you're encouraging your mother in some dangerous fantasies, but that's not what concerns me. I need you. We need each other. If you get drawn into your parents' divorce, that will impact on our relationship. I know it will, I've seen it happen. Cassie . . .'

Jess felt her heartbeat speed up. They still hadn't talked about Cassie. Not properly. 'Yes?'

'Come on.' He shrugged his coat on and handed her hers. 'We're going out.'

'Now?' He often did this. He would find some special little place, just opened, or get a booking somewhere where people waited for months to get in. 'Where are we going?'

'Secret.' He gave her that sideways glance: amused, quizzical, tender.

With a backward look at the vegetables she'd taken from the fridge Jess left the flat and got into his car.

Jake parked outside an alleyway between two warehouses and said, 'Follow me.'

For a moment Jess was afraid. It all seemed very dark and quiet. Then Jake pushed open a door into a cavernous space, where tables were set for dinner. An empty restaurant.

A solid chunk of a man in a chef's apron came out, wiping his hands, his hair pasted to his forehead by the steam of the kitchens. 'Jake.'

'Marco.' They shook hands.

'You see.' Marco spread his hands towards the vast restaurant. 'Choose a table.'

'Marco's opening up this as the new hot place to be tomorrow night. Marco Three. You'll have heard of Marcos One and Two. Tonight it's just us,' said Jake. 'Marco's an old friend.'

Jess settled nervously at a gleaming table crowded with glasses and cutlery. Bread and olive oil appeared immediately.

'First we order,' said Jake. 'Then we talk about Cassie. The seafood is Marco's speciality, by the way. I can recommend any scallops he's had a hand in.'

They both ordered scallops and steak. Jess didn't care about the food, she just copied Jake. All she wanted was to know about Cassie.

'So,' he said when the menus had been taken away and Jake had exchanged an agonisingly long gossip with Marco – presumably if the man was opening his new restaurant just for Jake then the least they could do was talk to him. 'Cassie.'

'Yes.' Jess was dreading the conversation but she couldn't live without it. She'd seen a picture of Cassie once, crumpled and dog-eared in Jake's wallet, right at the back where he'd probably forgotten about it. She was beautiful, with long, straight blonde hair and a cute face like a kitten.

'A lot of things went wrong with me and Cassie. She was always wanting to do her own thing, have her own way, and it got so that she never listened to me. It was as if I didn't exist in terms of arrangements. She'd just agree to something and expect me to go along with it.

'And her family came between us. So often. She has this

250

damaged sister, Camilla, who probably has some borderline personality disorder, and she was always ringing at odd hours of the day and night. She's a rather strange girl, always having problems with her love life or getting sacked from work. I think she might also have had a crush on me, because she occasionally used to . . .' He looked embarrassed. 'Well, you know. Make a bit of a pass at me. In the end I asked Cassie to restrict her calls to her sister – and to the rest of her family *about* her sister – because we had no free, uninterrupted time together as a couple at all. She agreed, but went behind my back. Over and over again. Then lied about it. That hurt me. It hurt me so much.'

Jake took Jess's hand, turned it over and kissed her palm. 'That's why I don't want you to get too involved with your mother and her problems.'

'But . . .' said Jess.

He held his hand up. 'Of course you must support her. I know that. I want us to do what's right. You and I will support her together. If . . . well, that's if you want to stay with me when you've heard the full Cassie story.'

'Of course I will.' Jess felt frightened at the thought of being given information so terrible that it would split her up from Jake. The scallops arrived, with a flourish of pepper and a list of unlikely ingredients delivered in an Italian accent. They tasted of wool to Jess, because her mouth was so dry with nerves.

'Her family problems weren't the only thing. There were a lot of things wrong between us by the end,' continued Jake, when the waiters had finally returned to the kitchen. 'And they came to a head one day when I discovered she was having an affair. When I accused her of it she began to throw things at me. Mainly our wedding presents, of course. She threw a vase and a jug. I caught the vase, but the jug broke, and then there wasn't anything else to hand so she went for me, trying to scratch my face. I raised my arms in front of my face to defend myself, but I must have pushed her away with the action – I think we'd both had a bit too much to drink – and she went flying backwards.'

He took a sip of wine. His face was sombre. 'Unfortunately,' he continued, 'we had a glass coffee table and she landed on it, flat on her back, breaking the plate glass. She had to have one hundred and twenty-two stitches.' His voice almost broke with emotion, and he clutched Jess's hand. 'I called the ambulance immediately and told them everything, and they got her to hospital before she could bleed to death. There was blood everywhere. Most of the cuts were across her shoulder and down her left arm, but she also hit the back of her head.' He closed his eyes. 'It was the most terrible sight I have ever seen. And, of course, the police had to be involved. They interviewed me, asking the same questions over and over again. She wasn't conscious, so she hadn't said anything, and they let me go, but made it clear that I was in the frame for assault and grievous bodily harm. They even mentioned . . .' – he cleared his throat – '. . . attempted murder.'

'No! But it was an argument. How could they even think that?'

'I don't think they could ever have made it stick, but I knew that if she came round and did accuse me, it would be my word against hers. And I knew she'd told me lies, so I didn't think she'd have too much trouble telling them to the police. If she hated me enough. Which I think she did by that stage.'

'What happened?'

'Her father offered me a deal. Give up all rights to the flat we'd bought together, plus make a lump sum over to her, and she'd keep quiet. She'd agree that it was her fault, that she'd just fallen, and that would be an end to it. It would spare her the court case, they said.'

'So you agreed?'

Jake spread his hands out over the table. 'I had no option. It was that or up to ten years in jail for GBH. And, even though it was her fault, I did feel very sorry for her. She's partially lost

252

the use of her left hand, and the scars on her arm mean she won't be modelling bikinis any time soon. You see, she was a model, so it was the end of her career.'

Jess hadn't realised that. 'I'm so sorry.'

'I suppose that's the price of getting involved with that sort of woman. Beautiful, selfish, amoral.' He squeezed her hand. 'I've learned my lesson now. Can you . . . forgive me?'

'Forgive you?' For a moment Jess wondered if he was asking forgiveness for implying that she wasn't a beautiful woman but, on the other hand, she wasn't and it didn't worry her. Then she realised. 'What for? Getting involved in a fight that wasn't your fault?'

He gave a tiny shrug. 'Not everyone would see it that way.'

'Well, that's how I see it. I'm on your side.'

He took her hand. 'But can you understand why we have to be completely honest with each other? Why we can't let our family or friends and their problems come between us?'

Jess nodded. The steak came and tasted delicious. Marco came out of the kitchen, wiping his hands on his apron, and he and Jake talked about the opening night and the coverage Jake's paper would give.

'I didn't know you had an influence on the restaurant pages,' said Jess after Marco had gone back to the kitchen.

Jake winked. 'The restaurant reviewer's an old friend. Besides, there's something else I have to tell you. I've been promoted. Deputy editor.'

'Wow.' Jess was pleased. 'That's amazing. You are clever.'

The steaks were taken away and two small sorbets and a finger bowl appeared. 'Try the sorbet,' said Jake. 'It's one of Marco's signature dishes.' He watched her dip her spoon into the narrow glass flute.

'Mmm, delicious.' Jess delved in for another spoonful of what tasted like apricot and aniseed. 'What's this? There's something in here.'

'Dip it in the fingerbowl,' said Jake. 'See what it is.'

It was a diamond ring. There was one chunky diamond at its centre, encircled by eight smaller ones. 'Jake? What's this?'

Jake got up from his seat and went down on one knee. 'Jess, will you marry me?'

She looked at the ring.

'Try it on,' he urged. 'It belonged to my mother. And to hers. It's a family treasure. But I secretly borrowed one of your rings and had it altered. Does it fit?'

It fit perfectly. Of course. 'Jake, this is . . .'

He looked at her steadily, his dark eyes intense and focused.

'. . . wonderful.' She held her left hand out, stretching out the fingers. It was someone else's hand, someone who belonged, who was in love and who would have children, someone who would matter the way Sophie mattered, who would no longer be Jess, the difficult single sister everyone had to feel sorry for, but would be 'Jess and Jake' . . . 'Yes, Jake, of course, a thousand, thousand yeses.'

As Jake stood up he raised a hand and suddenly there was music and laughter, and kisses and congratulations from all the waiters, and Marco out of the kitchen again, beaming, and Jake very, very close to her, whispering that this was for ever, that he'd never loved anyone as he loved her, that they must be first and only with each other. 'No lies,' he said. 'No family arguments. No bike. I love you so much I couldn't bear to lose you. All we need is honesty and each other.'

'You'll always come first,' agreed Jess, watching the diamonds twinkle in the light over his shoulder as she linked her arms round his neck.

'Always?' He held her tight, as if she might slip away from him.

'First and only,' she said. 'For ever.'

Marco brought out the champagne and poured it into two glasses.

Chapter 43

Sophie was furious. Her anger burned steadily over the next six weeks. Her first instinct was to pile the girls into the car and drive straight down to The Rowans, to insist her mother saw sense, but there was school and two photography commissions, and then there was Harry.

'I think you should let your Mum get on with it,' he said as they were clearing up one evening. 'She's had enough of people telling her what to do and how to think.'

'What?' screeched Sophie. 'Stand by while she makes one appalling mistake after another? She'll get all Dad's money and she'll waste it. She's so extravagant, you know she is.'

'I've no idea how she spends her money. But all the conspicuous expenditure – the personalised number plate and converting the stables – seems to have been directed by your father as much as by your mother. And you don't see her with designer clothes or anything.'

'You wouldn't know designer clothes if they rugby-tackled you.' Sophie found a stray doll's shoe and put it away in the toy box. 'Anyway, Dad keeps a close eye on the money and stops it getting out of hand, but without him she'd go mad.'

Harry put a tablet in the dishwasher and turned it on. 'She seems perfectly sane to me. And there's another takeover coming up, so I'll need to work late, overnight sometimes, so it's not a great time for you to be away. Unless we move Patrizia into the spare room or something, but that'll mean paying her more.'

Sophie decided that he was being like her father, retreating behind work whenever it came to emotional issues.

She also wasn't quite sure why, but there was something irritating about the story of Jess's engagement. Although it had completely taken Jess's mind off Paige and Bill. Jake agreed with Harry, apparently, that they should provide support when and if asked, but that otherwise it wasn't their business. 'Jake says that divorce is catching: you just find yourselves taking sides, and then before you know where you are it's not about their relationship, it's about yours,' said Jess in the irritatingly breathy tones of someone imparting the holy words of a guru.

'Hmm, well, the trouble with husbands is that they don't like the attention off them, that's why they don't want us to get involved,' said Sophie to Jess. 'You'll learn. But Jake has a point.'

Jess was too dizzy with happiness to care. 'I hope we'll get married at The Rowans, but it depends on whether Mum and Dad are talking.'

Sophie's friends were riveted by the story of Marco Three being opened especially for Jess and Jake the day before its glitzy official launch. 'It's been reviewed everywhere,' said Bev, one of her mother-and-toddler group friends. 'Simon tried to get a booking but there's a three-month waiting list.'

Sophie had a seaside shoot – buckets and spades mixed with brightly coloured china and glass – which took place on a beach in a howling gale. Being March, it was for the magazine's August issue, so they dodged hail while trying to create some kind of sunlight with a wholly inadequate studio light. Sophie told the story of Jess's engagement when a thunderstorm sent them scurrying for cover in the van, where they cowered with Danish pastries and a Thermos of coffee. Caroline was amazed.

'Not Jess the biker sister who never keeps a job for more than half an hour?'

'Not Jake Wild?' asked her new assistant, Mark. 'Not *the* Jake Wild, surely? The business journalist? My father says that, if I wanted to be in the media, why couldn't I be like him? Instead of being here in Margate, out of season, taking photographs of spotty china mugs.'

Sophie was surprised. 'He's deputy editor now. You wouldn't think he was a business correspondent, he's always advising Jess what to wear and rather girly things like that. He's actually got quite good taste, as she's looking fantastic these days.'

'Ooh, there ought to be more men like that,' said Caroline. 'I've always thought they should send stylists into battle to instruct the Army which buildings to keep and which to blow up.'

Harry was amused to hear that Jake had even been heard of in the world of photography.

'Well,' said Sophie. 'He certainly doesn't boast about his fame. My respect for him has risen.'

Harry raised an eyebrow. 'Well, it wasn't exactly rock bottom, was it?'

'What's that supposed to mean?' demanded Sophie. 'What are you accusing me of?'

'I'm not accusing you of anything. Just that you liked Jake anyway. There's nothing wrong with that.'

But Sophie had heard her father berate her mother about her flirting too often to let it drop. She wasn't going to let Harry treat her in that way. 'My mother only had to be slightly pleasant to a man and Dad would call her a slut.'

'That's why she's leaving him now. And I didn't call you a slut.'

But they argued about it all the same, and Sophie was wearily beginning to think that Jake was right, that getting too involved in other people's lives put too much of a strain on your own relationships.

She wondered if Harry was perhaps a bit abusive himself. Presumably this was a problem – if it was a problem, of course, and not just a fashionable way of turning women into victims yet again – that started small and grew. She remembered her parents being happy, she was sure she did, so whatever it was that was wrong must have grown worse after the early years. Maybe she should check out those websites and find out what her mother could have done to make her father so much worse. So she could avoid falling into the same trap.

But first she decided to ring Bill and find out how he was.

He was miserable, living in a rented flat on a half-built housing project. 'It's pretty dismal. Staring your own failure in your face when you step out of your door in the morning. But I suppose that's what you have to expect when your wife chucks you out.'

'Has she started talking to you yet?' Sophie didn't like to ask about Anthea. It clearly wasn't all that serious. 'Have you been back?'

'She let me back to The Rowans once, and insisted that Rose and Andrew were there. Rose and Andrew can't understand her attitude – she's just not prepared to be reasonable, or even to answer my calls. I managed to pick up a few things I needed, but I didn't want to strip The Rowans. Otherwise we're talking through solicitors. I'm paying the running costs of the house and shelling out for her to live there while I'm camping among bull-dozers and mud. Oh well, I suppose that's what people call fair.'

'That's very good of you Dad,' Sophie soothed him. 'Although . . . I heard . . . well, Jess said . . . that she was short of money and was selling a couple of paintings.'

'Is she? Well, thanks for letting me know. I can't think what she wants more money for, she's taken all mine already. Maybe to hire hotshot London lawyers.'

Sophie decided that her father needed to know the truth. It might help. 'Dad, Jess also says Mum's physically frightened of you at the moment, that's why she's not returning calls.'

'But that's mad. I told you she was mad. Sophie, I ask you. I know I haven't been Mr Perfect, but what man is? But surely, if I was violent I would have hit her by now? There would be some record of violence, some time when she called the police? You or Jess would have seen something? There would have been bruises?'

'That's what I thought,' said Sophie. 'That's why I thought you ought to know.'

'And is Jess buying into all this?'

'Jess can think of nothing but her wedding.' Sophie evaded the question.

Her father snorted. He wasn't fooled.

'Would you like me to nip down at some point and make sure she's not getting rid of anything really valuable? I've heard that people often try to hide their assets in a divorce, selling stuff and hiding the money.'

Her father sounded like a broken man. 'That's so sweet of you. I just want everything to be fair, that's all. For her as well as for myself.'

'Oh, she and Jess found some recorder thing behind a jar in the kitchen. It had been taping everything anyone said.'

'I wondered where that had gone. I bought it so that I could make notes on site without having to pull out paper and pencil, then it went missing around Christmas. I suppose someone must have tidied it away, probably your mother. She doesn't understand technology. I'm always finding the remote controls in some absurd place.'

So that was a perfectly sensible explanation for that.

Sophie idly checked out the Refuge and Women's Aid websites after she'd put the phone down, but they made her even crosser than ever. If her mother had really been treated badly, and if she'd had any sense, she'd have left. The Rowans was a little isolated but it was hardly a prison, and her mother had enjoyed a very nice lifestyle until she'd got these ridiculous ideas into her head.

Sophie stomped downstairs and snapped at Harry when he asked what was wrong. 'Nothing. Mind your own business.'

'You are my business,' he said.

'Oh piss off. Don't be such a . . .'

'Such a what?' He folded his arms.

Sophie backed off. 'Nothing. I'm tired, and I've had a long day.'

But she suddenly knew why she was so angry, though, as he retreated upstairs, his shoulders blocking the light, stiff with resentment.

She had fallen out of love with him. She did not love him at all. Not one tiny bit. It was a cold, hard, empty feeling, like death. She wanted him never to have existed. Or to have a traffic accident so she could be a grieving widow. She was tied to him, trapped by the girls, who were dearer to her than anything else in the universe.

And she didn't know what to do about it. The thought was even more frightening than the idea of her father being violent to her mother.

Chapter 44

Paige was still afraid to answer the phone at home. And she could hardly bear to listen to her answering machine messages, often eight or ten a day, almost all from Bill, each one declaring that he was sorry, that he had changed and that he still loved her. He also bombarded her with texts, including one that said 'I'll pay the running expenses of the house, and also the mortgage, until we get everything settled.'

Feeling guilty, and grateful, she texted back. 'Thank you.' Perhaps she was wrong. Perhaps she was mad, after all. Perhaps he was a nice man who was occasionally bad tempered, who loved her. Perhaps that's what marriage was like.

And she still didn't have the money to eat, or to run the car. Or to pay for a solicitor. It was all so tiring. She often fell asleep in the middle of the day, in the middle of what she was doing, her head bent over her book. She even fell asleep weeding the rose border one day, when there was a little thin sunshine, and woke up on the cold earth, feeling stiff.

Then she found another message on the answering machine.

'I don't know why you've done this, Paige, it was quite unnecessary to throw me out. Do you want to use The Rowans as a whorehouse, is that it? We brought our children up there. Think about that while you're fucking some bloke.'

Paige put her hands over her ears and pulled the answering

machine's plug out of its socket. It came in waves: the hurt, the bewilderment, the fear that she really was mad. She couldn't understand what he was up to. Why should he blow hot and cold in this way? Had he wanted her to leave or had he misunderstood something? Why did he say he wanted her back when he was the one who'd decided it should end? Ruth said it wasn't her fault, that it was his choice to act in this way, but she must have done something.

Even Rose thought so. Getting Andrew and Rose to help Bill move out had been torture. Andrew had avoided her eyes, his movements stiff with resentment. He only spoke if he had to, and then it was gruff and directed at the carpet. Rose's eyes had been bright with curiosity.

Bill had looked shambolic, with flyaway hair and a smattering of stubble around his chin. His clothes weren't quite clean and hung off him. His shoes needed re-heeling. One was clumsily tied up with a broken lace. Anthea was clearly not looking after him.

'Sorry Paige,' he said several times, looking abstracted. 'Sorry. I just can't quite concentrate. What did you say?'

'I thought you'd want your golf clubs.'

'Golf clubs.' He blinked, puzzled. 'I don't think I'll be playing golf. I can't afford it any more.'

'All the same,' said Paige, heaving them up and giving them to Andrew. 'You might.'

Andrew quickly looked from Paige to Bill. 'Shall I put them in the car?'

Bill sighed. 'I suppose you might as well. It'll get them out of Paige's hair anyway. I don't want to have to bother her again.'

'I didn't . . .' Paige began, but Andrew hoiked them onto his shoulder with a palpable air of resentment. Rose's face signalled 'Sorry.'

Eventually Bill and Andrew went to the pub and Paige offered Rose a glass of wine.

'Paige, he's in a terrible state,' Rose curled up on the sofa next to Paige. 'We've seen where he's living. He's sleeping on a mattress on the floor. In a tiny little flat with no furniture.' She waved a hand around to indicate Paige's pea-green drawing room, as if in comparison.

'Can't you see how much weight he's lost? His clothes look two sizes too big now. And he's so sorry. He's broken it off with Anthea. He says he'll never risk his marriage again if you only give him a second chance. I feel so guilty, I should never have told you about her.'

'But Rose, it wasn't me who ended it. He rang Sophie and told her that I'd asked him to leave. And I hadn't. We were in the middle of couples counselling, we had an appointment that night. I thought I was still trying to make my marriage work.' Paige had the usual sensation of dizziness when dealing with Bill – that she had imagined things. Maybe she really was too stupid to understand.

Rose smiled and placed her hand on her chest to signify her sincerity. 'I'm not blaming you, Paige, not at all, please don't get that idea. But he says that you told him you wanted a divorce at Christmas, then you both went to counselling but it didn't work.'

'Well, strictly speaking, that's true, but then . . .'

'In that case, it sounds as if there's been a terrible misunderstanding. Paige, he's been *so* honest with us. *So* straight. He's told us about the interior designer and Anthea, and he is so, so sorry about them both. He's even asked if we thought he should sack Anthea and find another accountant, but we thought that that would perhaps be not quite fair. And he's said that if you want to divorce him for adultery, citing Anthea, he'll understand. Isn't that sweet of him? When he doesn't even really want a divorce? He says he knows how embarrassed you feel about George Boxer.'

'But I didn't . . .' Paige was confused. Did Bill want her to divorce him now? Why the turnaround? He always seemed to send his message via other people. 'Why hasn't he said that to me?'

'Presumably because you're not speaking to him.' Rose held up her hand. 'I'm sorry, I need to finish this because it's hard for me. The reason why Andrew is being so stuffy this evening is the tit-for-tat thing with George. He takes that sort of thing awfully seriously. I'm really sorry, I have tried to say that what's sauce for the goose is sauce for the gander, and that Bill has given you more than enough reason to play away, but Andrew's rather old-fashioned about it all. He says two wrongs don't make a right, and revenge is never the way forward.'

'I didn't have an affair with George Boxer. And Bill knows I didn't.'

The expression on Rose's face was wise and discreet, as if she'd expected Paige to say that. 'Look, Bill's not perfect and he knows that, but you are good together as a couple, you've been married for thirty years, and if *he's* prepared to give it another try, then don't you think you owe it to yourself? And to him?'

'He threatened me with a knife,' blurted Paige. 'Twice.'

Rose looked astonished. 'Whatever did you say to make him do that? Paige, I know that some people in Martyr's Forstal are saying some dreadful things about you, but I want you to know that we're not among them. We're your friends.'

Chapter 45

Jess wasn't used to happiness. She woke up tingling with excitement. Jake's love – the kisses on the back of the neck as he took his toast, the phone calls he made to tell her he'd got to work or was coming back, the tiny intimacies of knowing that he liked expensive soap and strong coffee – carried her through the day on a cloud of warmth and security. She sold the bike and put the money aside for her wedding dress. She wanted to get married at The Rowans. It had been a secret childhood dream, a result of a lifetime of games in Sparrow Palace, to be the princess at last, and Jake agreed. With his new job, some courses he was going on and the need to sell both their flats and buy something together, it would be at least next March before they'd be ready. 'My wedding to Cassie was a hole-and-corner affair, and I don't want to make that mistake again.'

With a flutter of fear – quickly suppressed – that he had agreed to putting it off because he wasn't really sure, Jess smiled. And dreamed. A spring bride. Surreptitiously, she bought bridal magazines and wavered between chic fitted satin and floaty asymmetric chiffon. Retro glamour or fashion-forward? Or whether she'd be Jess and go for something like green snakeskin or even black. Jake suggested helping her choose, but she knew it was unlucky for the bridegroom to see the wedding dress before the ceremony.

Meanwhile she flashed her engagement ring at the Dizzy Donkey and cut down her shifts so that she mainly worked weekdays. Jake thought it was better for them to have similar working hours 'or we'd never see each other. Don't worry about the money, I've had a raise.'

It was lovely not to have to worry about the money. To have someone who would do that for her. Jess felt protected and privileged. If she worked an evening shift Jake was always outside in his car to pick her up so that she didn't have to risk the Tube. She no longer had to count out whether she had enough money for a pizza or hesitate over whether she should buy value fruit juice. After Jake left in the morning she idled with a coffee, reading the paper.

But she couldn't forget Paige. Now that her mother had told her about how Bill pointed out news stories of women who'd been killed by their partners, the stories leapt off the page at her too. Relentlessly. Here was a woman and her four year old, shot in a small house in Aylesbury. Nobody knew how the man, who had a history of being aggressive to women, had got hold of a gun. Three days later a woman was found strangled and wrapped in loft insulation. Then, a few days after that, a thirty-two-year-old found dead of head injuries. She had obviously fought back because 'a man living at the same address, with serious wounds' was being interviewed by the police. Jess ran her hands through her hair. It was carnage. Relentless. And if you read down the story you always found a few similar details – that there'd been a dispute over custody, that the woman was trying to leave the man, that the couple had recently married or recently become engaged.

Jess sighed. Surely her mother wasn't going to end up like that. Her father was only disagreeable, not violent. But it niggled. Should she be doing something?

It was easier to think about redecorating her flat to make it more saleable, but she phoned Paige every day.

Until Jake got the phone bills for the mobile he'd bought

her. 'What are these long calls? Half an hour, maybe three quarters? Almost every day?'

'I'm sorry. I'll pay for them, I hadn't realised they were so long. I was calling Mum. She needs support. She's sold a few things and found a lawyer, but quite a lot of people think she's treated Dad very badly, and . . .'

Jake sat down heavily, looking bleak. 'I'm not worried about the money,' he said. 'I'm worried about it starting again. The stuff that went on with Cassie.'

'No, I promise it isn't. I never phone her when you're here . . .'

'That's what Cassie said. At first. And then there was a crisis. And another crisis.' He sighed. 'I don't know what to do. I'm getting trapped in the same relationship mistakes over and over again. It must be something I'm doing wrong.'

'No, you're not!' she cried. 'You're perfect. And there's nothing wrong with our relationship. I always put you first.'

'First and only,' he said heavily. 'That's what you said.'

'You are my first and only. But I do worry about Mum. Look, if we could go down together and really help her with some paperwork, we always said we would but we haven't had time . . . oh, Jake, please, please. This isn't about me putting you second, putting us second . . . it's . . .'

Jake got up. 'It's OK.' He ran his hands through his hair. 'It's OK. Don't worry.' His eyes were blank and his voice was distant.

'Jake, I'm sorry. I said I was sorry.' Jess was frightened.

He gave her a small, withdrawn smile. 'I'm not angry. But it'll just take me some time to get over it, that's all. To come to terms with it. I think it's better if I go for a walk, if that's OK with you.'

'Yes, of course it is. And Jake, you know I put you first. I really do.'

That slight, sad smile again, and he nodded. 'It's just that with Cassie I almost ended up in jail and she almost ended up dead. And I don't want to go there again. It was . . . hell . . . I don't think you can have understood how much hell it was. This is just a few phone calls to you. To me, it's the beginning of a nightmare I thought I'd escaped from. I know I'm over-reacting, but I can't help it.'

'I do understand, I do.' Jess was frantic. 'What if I agree only to call Mum once a week?'

He shook his head sadly. 'I can't impose those sorts of rules on you, and you can't impose them on yourself. If ringing your mother is what matters to you most, you must do it.'

'It doesn't. It doesn't. I didn't think. I'm sorry.'

He touched her lightly on the arm. 'Nothing to be sorry for. You did what you thought was right at the time. But just give me some time to absorb it all. To work out what it means. I need to be on my own.' He repeated, 'On my own to think it through.' And the door closed on him, leaving Jess chilled to the bone, frightened that he would never come back.

She lay awake until four in the morning, wondering if he'd had an accident or been mugged. Nine hours. No one could walk for nine hours, could they? He must have gone some-where else.

But when she heard a key in the lock at half-past four, she jumped up. 'Jake! I was worried.'

'It's all right,' he said. 'I was just walking.' He looked exhausted. 'Can you ring work at nine and say I'm not coming in today? I'm going to sleep.'

Jess went to the Dizzy Donkey frightened and tired, won-dering if she would ever be happy again, whether she would get home to find Jake saying it had all been a terrible mistake and that he didn't want to marry her after all. If they came through this she would be more considerate. She would. But she was also worried about Mum. 'Mel, you have a pay-as-you-go phone, don't you? If I gave you some vouchers to cover the cost could I use it? Mine . . .' She tried to think of an excuse. '. . . needs repairing.'

Mel nodded. 'Sure thing.'

Paige seemed cheerful. 'I've just heard from the auction rooms. That picture I inherited from my parents was worth something after all. So I can pay some of my legal bills, for a bit anyway, and I've got something to live on. Are you all right, darling? You sound a bit low.'

Jess didn't want to say anything about her argument with Jake. 'Nothing, Mum, but I'll be a bit busy for the next few weeks, I might not be able to call so often.'

'Don't worry about me,' said Paige. 'By the way, your father is insisting that if I want a divorce, *I* have to divorce *him* for adultery with Anthea. Otherwise I have to wait five years because he'll contest it. It seems very odd, don't you think?'

'It's his pride. He can't bear everyone to know that you've kicked him out.'

'But he's *telling* everyone I've thrown him out because I'm having an affair with George Boxer,' exclaimed Paige. 'I'm so confused, I don't know what to think.'

'Don't think anything. Just divorce him for adultery if that's what he wants. Unless you want to go the unreasonable behaviour route.'

Paige shuddered. 'I couldn't. Half of Martyr's Forstal isn't speaking to me as it is. I went to a residents' association meeting the other day and when I arrived there were only about six people in the room. They all looked away from me as I came in. Fortunately Rose, and then that nice woman we don't know very well . . . Sandra . . . came in and both of them started talking to me.'

'Why is it any of anyone else's business? Are we still living in the fifties, when divorce was a disgrace?'

'No, it's that I'm considered to have thrown him out just when he's lost all his money. Everyone thinks it's disloyal.'

'Tell them what he did to you. How you had to live.'

'Well, I have tried, a bit, but they don't believe me, and I don't want to destroy his reputation. It might be bad for the

269

business. It's easier to stay quiet, and hope people work it out for themselves.'

'So you're letting him destroy *your* reputation instead? Hmm, I wouldn't say you've progressed a lot down the healing path. I must go.'

Jess got home to find Jake in the shower, singing.

He turned round to look at her, his eyes alight again. 'Hi babe. Good day?' He kissed her, wetting her face.

'So-so.' Jess wasn't sure how to proceed. 'Um, you know, I'm sorry.'

She shrieked as he pulled her into the shower. 'How sorry?' He was laughing as he deftly unzipped the short black skirt she wore for waitressing. It clung to her thighs briefly, then dropped around her feet. He kicked the sodden heap away. 'Very sorry?'

'Very, very sorry,' she whispered as his hands pushed under her bra and found her nipples, sending sparks of electricity shooting through her body. He tugged the soaking shirt halfway over her head as the shower pounded down on them, and for a moment she panicked as she breathed in, and her wet T-shirt clung to her nostrils. She tried to pull the T-shirt off so that she could breathe, but he held her hands behind her back. He was powerful, far stronger than she was.

The shower pounded down her face and now she really couldn't breathe and began to struggle in earnest. Panic over-whelmed her. She had never been so frightened in her life, then suddenly the shower was off and the T-shirt was off her face.

'Jess! Jess!' Jake was bundling her out the shower. 'What hap-pened there? I was trying to take your T-shirt off and you began fighting me. What was that about? Luckily I was able to break free and turn the shower off, or you could have drowned.'

Jess was coughing and gasping. Jake wrapped her in a towel, picked her up and laid her on the bed. 'You have to trust me, Jess. Or accidents could happen.' He dried her tenderly, each finger and toe separately while she lay, exhausted.

He rubbed her face tenderly. 'Now say after me: I . . . trust . . . you . . . Jake.'

'I trust you, Jake.' She felt weak and foolish.

'And I won't do anything silly like that again.'

'I won't,' she promised. 'I won't.'

He smiled down at her.

Jess began to cry with relief and exhaustion. 'You don't know how sorry I am.'

'Why not show me?' he whispered, struggling to get her tights off.

In the end they couldn't wait. Jess was desperate to feel him inside her, to see the tenderness in his face and to know that the last twenty-four hours had just been a tiff, the kind of argument lovers have when they're working things out between them. She left the tights round her ankles, twisted in a curious semblance of bondage, and realised as he plunged into her that she found it exciting. That was Jake, unexpected and exciting.

Afterwards he lay beside her thoughtfully, tracing one finger down her body. 'You know, if you want to help your Mum we could go down together,' he said. 'Why not get the diary now and we'll put a date in?' He kissed her shoulder.

She finally untangled herself and raced off to get it. They fixed a date five weeks ahead, which was the first weekend they both had clear. Then she changed the duvet cover because it was soaking wet.

'These romantic adventures are all very well,' she laughed, 'but a wet bed isn't much fun.'

He tapped her naked bottom playfully. 'It's your penance,' he said. 'For making me suffer.'

She would be more careful with his feelings from now on, she thought. It was probably a case of post-traumatic stress over the accident with Cassie and the interrogation at the police station. And Mum was doing much better. If necessary, she could always call her on Mel's phone.

But above all, she felt ashamed of having found the scene in the shower, for that one moment when he pinned her hands behind her back and the water was pouring over her mouth and nose, so terrifying yet so . . .

She tried to shut her mind to it, but the thought burst through her defences.

So exciting.

No, Jess, no. You're not that kind of girl. Submission is not your thing. You've always said you'd never give in. To anyone. She resolved to forget the whole episode.

'Jess!' His voice, from the other room, was stern. 'What's this?'

'It's my laptop, recharging.'

'You've left it on the sofa. That's the way fires start. I had some friends who left their laptop charging overnight on their kitchen cushions and the fire wiped out their whole kitchen. They were lucky to get out alive.'

Jess unplugged it and set it up again, on a table. 'Satisfied?'

He took some juice out of the fridge and drank it from the carton. 'Jess, Jess, Jess, I don't know. What with the bike and the shower, and now the laptop, it looks as if I've taken on a full-time job of just keeping you alive.'

Chapter 46

The Prince of India curry house was roughly halfway between Jess's flat in Peckham, and Sophie and Harry's tiny terraced house in Clapham, so Sophie arranged to meet Jess and Jake there to talk about the wedding. And what to do about Bill and Paige. Sophie hadn't managed to get down to The Rowans to 'sort her mother out', as she considered it, but getting Jess on side first was almost more important. There was no point in persuading Paige to be sensible if Jess simply undermined her with the next phone call.

Sophie and Harry arrived first. Harry, lumbering to the table, looked like an ox. Sophie wondered how she could ever have found him attractive.

Then Jess and Jake burst through the door, Jess's eyes shining as she shook a few drops of rainwater off her hair. Jake handed their coats to the waiter. Two women eating together turned to look at him.

He hugged Sophie, shook hands with Harry and commandeered the bench seating, wrapping one of Jess's hands in his and anchoring it on her knee. Harry and Sophie sat down opposite the happy couple and she could feel the space between her shoulder and his, each slightly turned away from the other like outward-facing bookends.

'We've been choosing fonts,' said Jake. 'For the invitations. And the order of service. And the escort cards.'

'What's an escort card?' asked Harry.

'Dunno,' said Jake, 'but apparently if you want to be a bit different you can hang them from the ceiling. Getting married is like learning a new language.'

'Oh,' said Harry. 'Sophie showed me a whole lot of things and I said yes. I don't think you asked me, did you? Anyway surely Jess is the graphic designer, wouldn't choosing fonts be her area of expertise?'

'I don't think you can call six months at a design company where everyone criticised everything you did "being a graphic designer",' joked Jake.

'Jake's turned into Groomzilla,' teased Jess. 'Fanatic about whether we're having sugared almond favours or sparkling table gems. Obsessive about New World wines versus classic French. Traditional wedding cake or *croquembouche*.' Jake squeezed her knee and they kissed.

Sophie looked away. 'Never mind the font,' she said. 'How are you going to word the invitations? Mum and Dad are separated so you can't call them Mr and Mrs. And will you be inviting Anthea? Or George Boxer?' She knew she was being churlish, but Jess was being so unrealistic. Not understanding the seriousness of it all.

'We'll make a decision on that when it comes to it,' said Jake.

'So,' added Jess, breaking a poppadum. 'Bridesmaids.' She handed the menu to Jake. 'I'll have whatever you have, order for me.' She kissed him again, and he kissed her back, a lingering kiss on the lips. Sophie's stomach clenched. Couldn't they do that sort of thing in their own flat?

Jake conferred with Harry, then briskly ordered a selection of curries, two beers and two mineral waters.

'We'd like Lottie and Bella to be bridesmaids, and Summer too if you think she's old enough,' Jake said, looking intensely at Sophie. 'How would you feel about that?'

'They'd love it. I saw some gorgeous little satin and organza frocks with rosebuds the other day in . . .'

'I've decided on rose silk dupion that I saw in Monsoon, with tulle underskirts,' interrupted Jess.

Sophie had thought Jess would consult her on the choice of bridesmaids' dresses, but suppressed her annoyance.

'And matching silk dupion for the page's waistcoat,' said Jess. 'Jake's nephew. Unless Jake's sister vetos it, she's such a nightmare.'

Jake and Harry talked in undertones – about the Grand National, or possibly the Six Nations, Sophie thought, catching snatches – while Jess rabbited on about perhaps having a very simple theme for the wedding, say everything in white or pale pink, or going for broke with red-carpet glamour. She was looking so pretty, gamine and sparkly with curly hair. So much more flattering than the sullen look she'd always favoured. Sophie allowed the thought to curdle for a few moments, then decided to change the subject. 'Let's talk about Mum. Is she seeing sense yet?'

'I think she's always been sensible,' said Jess. 'Apparently Dad's insisting that if there's to be a divorce she's got to divorce him for adultery. She's still trying to work out why. I mean, what does he have to gain by it? Unless he's frightened that she'll divorce him for unreasonable behaviour, which she could.'

'I meant *sense*,' said Sophie. 'Not nonsense. Dad is miserable. He's living in a rented flat and he doesn't need these ridiculous allegations making life even more difficult than it is already.'

'He should have thought of that before he started bugging her or throwing knives.'

'He didn't. Mum has exaggerated the whole thing about the knife. In fact, Dad says *she* threw the knife at him and she's been trying to shift the blame ever since. The recorder was his, bought for work, and it got lost in the kitchen. And the things she's said to him have been pretty unforgivable. I was shocked . . .'

'It might be better not to go into detail,' said Harry, placing a hand on her arm. 'I think . . .'

275

Sophie shook him off. 'Look, Jess, you know the sort of thing women do when they get divorced. They turn the man into a monster in order to justify a whacking great settlement. There was that TV presenter the other day, Marilyn . . .' She clicked her fingers to remind herself '. . . or was it Marnie . . . or maybe it didn't begin with an M . . . Anyway, you know who I mean. Let's face it, women are grasping bitches when it comes to divorce. Even women we love, like Mum.'

'So if you divorced Harry you'd be a grasping bitch?' asked Jess.

'No, of course not.' Sophie's heart lurched. She didn't want the words said out loud.

'But you said that women are grasping bitches, and you're a woman, so the logic is that you must be a grasping bitch.'

'I meant . . . *older* women. The iron butterfly generation who think men are their meal tickets. Women of Mum's age. I'm not blaming them, they were brought up to think that.'

'And *we* were brought up, by Dad, to hate other women. He always said that women weren't logical, that they couldn't drive, that they were bitches to each other, that they were underhand and greedy. Materialistic and lazy. We were told, over and over again, that we couldn't trust our own sex. That an office full of women would be ineffective, gossipy and bitchy. And you've swallowed it, lock stock and two smoking barrels.'

'That's ridiculous! Jess, read the papers. Take your head out of your own little cloud for half a minute. Look at the way women take men for a ride. Claim enormous fortunes that they haven't worked for in unfair dismissal claims and divorce cases. Everyone knows that . . .'

'Jake?' Jess switched her attention to him. 'Tell me. Are newspapers still mainly run by middle-aged men, many of whom have been through a divorce?'

Jake nodded. 'I'd think maybe six out of seven senior staff are probably men. At least half divorced. In my office anyway. They love a story about a woman getting an unfair share of the loot.

They give it extra space, especially if the wife's tasty.' There was a gleam in his eye, as if he enjoyed lobbing this grenade into the sisterly argument. 'No stories about men getting away with a larger share though. I can't remember when I last read one of those.'

'You see,' said Sophie. 'That proves it. Men behave better.'

'In that case,' countered Jess, 'why are nine out of ten women below the poverty line single mothers who have been abandoned or cheated by the fathers of their children?'

'Because,' Sophie's nostrils flared, 'quite a few of them are silly little sluts who got pregnant to get benefits.'

'Sophie! You have bought Dad's line. You have *so* bought it. It's one of the ways controlling men exert power is by depriving women of their female friends. Isolating them by telling them how unpleasant women really are. How untrustworthy. How unworthy full stop. Mum doesn't have close friends because Dad's stopped her trusting any of them.'

'Jess, stop spouting feminist theory. This is *life*. When you're young you have lots of girl friends. When you grow up, you have a partner and you don't see so much of them. How often have you seen your gang since you and Jake got together? Are you still doing your regular Thursdays?'

'When I can,' said Jess, hesitating for a moment. 'Although I do miss a few. But if you really think most women are greedy, stupid or sluts, what does that make you feel about yourself? Have you been trying all your life to be better than the rest of us? More moral? Less stupid? Because, if so, all you've managed is to conceal exactly how much you must hate and despise yourself. For being a woman.'

'Um, Jess, er . . .' Harry looked worried. 'This isn't quite cricket, I don't think . . .'

'Jess, if you expect some feminist rant to make me believe that Dad has been "abusing" Mum, you can forget it. They have both made mistakes and, at the moment, Dad is the one who is suffering for them while Mum lives her comfortable life in the family home.' Sophie had been determined to make Jess understand that this wasn't a simple, black-and-white case, but Jess was being so wilfully obtuse. She'd clearly made her mind up and no amount of presenting her with the facts was going to change that.

'Look, Sophie,' said Jess. 'Does Harry treat you the way Dad treats Mum? Does he call you names? Or tell the children not to take any notice of you? Or tell the girls that women are stupid?'

'I wouldn't dare,' joked Harry. 'I'd be toast. Anyway, as the father of three daughters, my girls will grow up to know they're as good as any man.'

'Well, you need to watch out then,' said Jess, 'because it's Sophie who doesn't like other women. She's even proud of it.'

'I do, I have friends. I have Bev, and . . .'

'But you're always saying how bitchy the women at the school gate are.'

'They are,' insisted Sophie. 'They can't bear women like me who work.'

Jess rolled her eyes. 'You are incorrigible. I bet you've never tried to get to know them, just flounced by in your ten-inch heels. Anyway, back to what Mum's had to go through. I mean, do you see Jake telling me I'm silly?'

'Only when you leave laptops charging on flammable sofa cushions,' interjected Jake, still looking amused. 'She nearly set us on fire a few weeks ago.'

'Um . . . do you think we should change the subject?' suggested Harry. 'Did you see Chelsea play Liverpool last night, Jake?'

'I am not going to talk about fucking football,' said Sophie, 'while Jess sits there smugly, thinking she's got the meaning of life in her hand. We've got a responsibility, Jess, to broker peace between Mum and Dad so that, at the very least, they reach a fair agreement between them that doesn't completely bankrupt Dad. And Mum is so . . .'

'Are you worried about your allowance?' asked Jess. 'Or your inheritance?'

Sophie stood up and flung her napkin down on the table. 'I don't think I've got much more to say to you on the subject. As you clearly aren't prepared to listen.'

As Sophie pulled open the door of the restaurant, hooking her coat over her shoulder, she heard Harry's chair scrape as he got up. 'Er . . . I think I'd better . . . er . . . see how she is. Recently, she's been . . . er . . . rather . . . um . . .'

'A bitch?' enquired Jess sweetly, her tones carrying across the half-empty restaurant. 'According to her all women are bitches anyway, so maybe she's just living up to her own beliefs.'

Chapter 47

When the telephone rang in the kitchen at The Rowans, Paige hesitated to answer it. Bill still phoned once or twice a day – a mix of messages calling her 'a fucking slut' and 'a whore' along with ones, usually left late at night, where he sobbed down the phone, told her she was destroying him and begging her to come back. She couldn't understand what he was trying to achieve because there was no real sign that he truly wanted her back. But he rarely called in the morning and she'd left her number with several job agencies. There wasn't much around for an unqualified middle-aged housewife.

So she answered it tentatively. It was an agency on the line, and it was a job she could do.

'It's an old lady who lives near Ashford. She needs round-the-clock care and although she's got a live-in girl we need someone to give her a break three or four mornings a week. There's no nursing, just helping to lift her, doing some house-work and gardening, playing games of snap with her, that sort of thing.' A tinge of desperation seeped down the line. 'It's very easy work and quite well paid, considering you don't need qualifications.'

Paige didn't have a choice. 'OK. But it's about forty minutes' drive away, I'd need petrol money.' She crossed her fingers. Perhaps they wouldn't want someone who made demands.

'Oh, I don't think that should be a problem.' There was no mistaking the relief at the other end of the phone. 'By the way, Mrs Grey is . . . well, she's bedridden with arthritis and in some pain a lot of the time, so she can be a little snappish sometimes. She's ninety-two, but her mind is completely clear. She's as sharp as a tack. But she can . . . er . . . be difficult.'

'I know difficult,' said Paige. 'I think I can cope.'

'When can you start? Tomorrow?'

Mrs Grey lived in one half of a semi-detached Edwardian cottage with a neat semi-circle of lawn in front, ringed with pale pink peonies. The door was opened by a Chinese girl who ushered Paige through to a room with drawn curtains, fusty and crowded with photographs and knick-knacks. Invalid apparatus – a bed tray on wheels and a commode – cluttered the room.

'Come in, come in.' Mrs Grey beckoned with a claw-like hand. 'This is Joy. She is about as joyous as a funeral. Are you the new girl?'

'I'm Mrs Raven,' said Paige.

Mrs Grey looked at her sharply. 'Are you now? Most people use Christian names these days.'

'You don't, so I thought you'd prefer to call me Mrs Raven.' Paige hoped she wasn't going to lose her only job before she'd started it. But it was her new resolve to stand up to people. She tried to change the subject. 'I like your garden. The peonies at the front are wonderful.'

'Don't butter me up, Mrs Raven. I won't fall for it.'

As Paige cleaned the floors, polished the silver, re-organised the photographs, aired the small, stuffy room, picked flowers, made little meals and ran errands while Mrs Grey rarely praised her and often snapped, she decided it was like being married to Bill again. Except that she had money in her pocket at the end of every week, to spend how she liked. And she could close the door on it all at the end of her shift.

Best of all, neither Mrs Grey nor Joy knew anybody in

Martyr's Forstal and they didn't care about Paige's private life. They appeared not even to be interested.

However, when Paige had an injunction served on her by Bill to prevent her from selling any more things from the house Mrs Grey quickly picked up on it.

'You've got a face as long as a horse's this morning. What's wrong with you?' she demanded as Paige brought her morning coffee.

'My husband has served an injuction on me. Stopping me selling anything from the house.'

Mrs Grey wasn't interested. She picked up the paper and started to do the crossword. 'What's . . .'

Joy rarely volunteered a remark but she handed Paige a cup of coffee and a biscuit when she came into the kitchen. 'Men no good,' she said.

'Yes, Joy, I'm beginning to think you're right. Men no good. But surely some men are good? They can't all be bastards?'

Joy giggled, as if Paige had cracked a very funny joke.

One day Paige received a letter from Bill's solicitors. And another from the tax office. Her shift was starting at eleven so she only had time to glance at the envelopes before stuffing the papers into her bag and setting out.

She let herself into Hazel Cottage and lit the fire for Mrs Grey. 'I'll just get your coffee.' While the kettle boiled she slit the letters open, her heart thumping.

What she saw numbed her. She made the coffee with shaking hands and, halfway across Mrs Grey's bedroom, she dropped the cup.

'I'm so sorry. So sorry.' The patch on the carpet blurred in front of her eyes. 'So sorry. I'll get you another.' Paige hurried to find a sponge, terrified of losing the only job she was qualified for. 'I'm sorry. Sorry. I don't think it'll stain.'

'I'm bored today,' snapped Mrs Grey. 'Stop all that irritating cleaning. Sit and talk to me.'

'I don't want to leave it for Joy, she'll . . .'

'She won't mind at all. Now, Mrs Raven, I want to hear why you look so terrible. You're shaking like a leaf. You always look like a frightened rabbit but you're worse than usual today.'

'My husband has . . .' Paige's eyes filled with tears. She swallowed. 'He's . . . his solicitors . . . they've offered me a hundred thousand pounds. For the end of my marriage. It won't even buy a tiny flat. I haven't worked for twenty-two years. I don't have a pension and it's too late for a career, I'm useless. I can't even make a cup of coffee, he always said . . .'

'Don't be ridiculous. You make an excellent cup of coffee. Has he run off with someone else?'

'Yes. No. I don't know.'

'It's beginning to sound interesting. Why don't you start at the beginning, as my father always used to say, then go on through the middle, then get to the end and stop?' Mrs Grey lifted her cup and took a sip. 'Yes, excellent coffee.'

'He left me. No, I threw him out. But before I threw him out he told people I'd left him. I don't know . . .' Paige was finding it increasingly difficult to talk about her divorce. So often people tried to persuade her that she must have misunderstood, that Bill was a sweet man and that no one was perfect. Everyone loses their temper occasionally. Everyone knew how down he was. Some clearly wanted detail to pass on as gossip, and others said that they didn't want to take sides and refused to listen to anything she said.

Mrs Grey waved a gnarled hand. 'Don't worry about how long it takes. I'm not going anywhere.'

In the shadowy room she talked about Bill's explosions of temper, of the way he often didn't bother to reply when she spoke to him or didn't even listen, how he'd discouraged her from working and often created some kind of diversion whenever she tried to do something on her own. 'I feel so stupid for putting up with it.'

Each time she told the story it became a little clearer, and there seemed to be more of a pattern. Episodes she'd buried in her memory emerged, no longer so easily dismissed as coincidences or because 'Bill was so stressed'.

'When the girls were little I wanted to do a French cookery course,' she said, 'but as soon as I started he came home late on Tuesday nights. Only Tuesday nights. There was no one else to look after the children, so I'd never get to class on time. He always said it was unavoidable, that I didn't understand business, that I'd no idea what it was like to go out to work. I went to just one of the ten sessions in the end, and he was furious because he said I'd wasted money by paying for the whole course. So I didn't really feel able to take another evening class.'

And there was the drinking. 'He goes to the pub regularly, then drinks a bottle or more of wine a day. He comes in and opens a bottle, and keeps it beside him for the rest of the evening.'

'What about the children?' asked Mrs Grey. 'How did he behave with them?'

'Sometimes he was a wonderful father. But he always refused to take care of them in any practical way – he just wanted the fun side of it – because he said I didn't work, so all that was my business. Well, in the early days I did some part-time work as a secretary at a health club when we needed the money, but he called it a little hobby-job. Two nights a week he was supposed to care for them while I worked, but I'd come back to find the house in a mess and that they hadn't been fed or put to bed. But he always said it was my fault, that the children were my responsibility and if they weren't looked after properly Social Services might take them away. In the end I lost the job because he often didn't come home on time and I was late because I couldn't leave them. The manager said I was unreliable.'

'Friends?' asked Mrs Grey succinctly.

'It was difficult. We had a social life as a couple, but I don't think he liked me doing too much on my own. I had a lunch once and invited six women I met through the girls' school, and he came home unexpectedly. He was absolutely charming, and went round kissing everyone, but then kept popping his head round the door and, very politely, asking us to keep the noise down because he had an important telephone call. Several times. There didn't seem to be any reason why he wasn't at his office, where he usually takes phone calls. You could see that everyone felt uneasy about having to whisper, so they all left early. It got so that it was easier not to have people round. And he didn't like me suggesting that I share school runs or offering to pick other people's children up from parties. He said it would be inconvenient.'

'Physical violence?'

Paige shook her head. 'Only the newspaper items that he used to show me. They still jump out at me whenever I read the paper, even though he's no longer around, pointing to them. All the different ways men kill women. The other day I saw a piece about a man who killed his wife by throwing a remote control at her in the middle of an argument. He didn't get a very long prison sentence. Bill said that men don't, the courts think it's OK, they understand that sometimes a man is driven beyond sanity by the way some women behave. If you're having an argument, or if the woman's unfaithful, it isn't considered murder.'

'It most certainly is,' said Mrs Grey. 'I used to be a magistrate and the law is quite clear. It is perfectly legal to have an affair or an argument or to leave your marriage. It is not legal to kill anyone.'

'The trouble is,' Paige sighed, 'that each of these episodes are so tiny, and so easily explained away on their own, that it seems so silly of me to make a fuss about any of it, but I never knew when the next one was coming along. Because of the jealousy I barely dared say hello to most of my friends' husbands. But he plays golf or sails with them all, and is on lots of committees, so everyone knows him and likes him. They don't want to hear anything bad about him. People tell me that they don't want to take sides, but I think they already have. They've heard his side of the story and made up their minds. They don't want to hear mine. Or am I being silly?'

'People don't like women who are divorcing,' said Mrs Grey. 'They never have. Too threatening. Rocks too many boats. Much more comfortable to paint them as scheming hussies.'

'They blame me for leaving him but I didn't think I had. I thought we were still trying to save our marriage when he told our daughter that it was over. But I'm so confused. He keeps ringing and asking me to have him back, then the next message calls me a slut and accuses me of running a whorehouse. Then he wants me to divorce him, then he asks to get back together. I'm so tired. And now I've had all this . . .' Paige opened her bag and pulled out the letter from the solicitor and the brown envelope from the tax office and held it out to Mrs Grey, trembling with panic.

'This is the worst. According to the taxman I owe about eleven thousand pounds in income tax. But I've never had any income. How can that be? I haven't got eleven thousand pounds. It's something to do with dividends I've been paid for my shares in his company, apparently, but I've never had any dividends.' Paige felt sick with fear. The tax office wanted the money within the month and it would strip Paige of everything she'd managed to get together. And more. She would be thousands of pounds in debt.

'You will have to go to a lawyer,' pronounced Mrs Grey. 'And an accountant.'

'I can't afford them,' whispered Paige. 'Not if I owe eleven thousand pounds. I can't afford anything.'

'Mine is coming this afternoon. Dear Pratik. He will understand it all. Your case is much more interesting than my boring affairs so I will ask him to look at it. I'll pay.' She sipped the last drop of coffee and waved the cup towards Paige for her to take. 'Just this once, mind you. You needn't expect anything else.'

'Thank you,' said Paige humbly. 'I wouldn't expect anything

else. That is very generous. But I don't know what he can do – my husband says he's virtually destitute.'

Mrs Grey held her hand out for the letters, took them and patted Paige's hand.

'Divorcing men are always virtually destitute, my dear.'

Chapter 48

Sophie refused to talk to Harry. There was no point, he was too stupid and she couldn't bear the sight of him, his reproachful face like that of a kicked puppy. Why couldn't he . . .

He flagged down a taxi and she plumped down on the back seat, her arms folded.

'Soph . . .' He put an arm out but she shook him off. Once they got home he paid Patrizia and, on hearing one of the girls cry, went upstairs, while Sophie poured herself a glass of wine.

I hate him. I hate him. I hate him. And I hate Jess and Jake, with their smugness and the way they're always touching each other, and the way Jake's eyes burn into you when he talks, and the way he smiles. I hate the spark of electricity that arcs between us when he lays a hand on my sleeve.

And most of all I hate what they're doing to Dad. All he's ever done is try to provide for his family and give us a better life than he had. Nobody wants to hear his side of the story. They listen to all the poison that seeps from Mum's psychiatrist – or whatever the stupid woman is – and . . . Sophie took another slug of wine and dialled her father's mobile.

He picked up immediately. There was an empty echo to his voice, as if he was in a room without furniture. 'Dad?'

'Sophie?'

Sophie began to sob. 'Dad, it isn't fair, they're all against you.

Mum thinks you're going to try to kill her so you don't have to pay her off. They don't realise that you're just stressed and tired, and that you'd never hurt anyone and . . .'

His voice came down the line, soothing her as it had always done. 'Sophie, darling, don't listen to what Jess and Mum and her malicious therapist say. When a whole load of women get together they always talk nonsense. You and I know better.'

'But Dad . . . do you think Mum is really going a bit mad? Do you think she's paranoid? Medically speaking, that is?'

'Sophie, darling, I'm afraid I think that's quite likely. She's in the hands of this man-hater, who is frightening the life out of her, but I don't know what to do, short of trying to get her sectioned. But then, she can be very convincing, you know, so I'm not sure I could find two doctors to back me up. All I care about is your mother's wellbeing, and I don't think anyone else is putting that first. The therapist just wants her fees, and Jess has always turned against me on principle.'

Sophie blew her nose and agreed. 'I think the way through is to get Jake on side. Jess agrees with every word he utters. She just sits there and looks at him adoringly and it makes me sick.'

'You used to be like that with Harry.'

'No,' said Sophie. 'I never did. Harry and I discussed things and then we agreed. Jake lays down the law and Jess follows it. It's quite sickening to see, to be honest. Luckily I get the impression that he's not too keen on her getting over-involved with Mum, so perhaps I should have a quiet word with him? What do you think?'

Bill laughed. 'I think that's a very good idea.'

'Let me come down and see you, and then go on to Mum's. Let's see if we can sort all this out amicably without getting involved in huge lawyers' fees.'

'That's what I've wanted all along. But it's very difficult when your mother won't even talk to me face to face.'

'It's so bleak,' exclaimed Sophie as her father opened the door to her three days later, at nine o'clock in the morning. 'It's just a building site.' Dismayed, she looked at the sweep of earth in front of the four cottages, set in a semi-circle, and another swathe of dark mud, churned up by the diggers in front of the squat block of flats. She tried to imagine there would be gardens here one day.

Bill hugged her. 'It's so good to see you. I don't like to have people here, it's not exactly set up for entertaining.'

She followed him up a narrow stairwell, its breeze block walls and concrete floors exposed, with the occasional structural iron girders or metal re-inforcing rods emerging from the soup of construction. He pushed open a door to a small hallway. A bare lightbulb dangled overhead and a few pots and pans sat in the sink in a galley kitchen. 'I'm no good at looking after myself,' Bill admitted sheepishly.

'Dad!' Sophie sighed, but after looking round to find a bedroom with a single mattress on the floor, with a lamp and an open suitcase beside it, then a box room piled high with suitcases and his golf clubs, she felt so sorry for him that the least she could do was tidy up a bit. And it was so cold. Even on a May morning it had the chill of a building that had never been heated, almost as if there were still windows and doors missing. 'Is this block actually finished?' she asked.

'Not quite. We've still got the penthouse windows to be slotted in,' he said. 'That's why it's so cold. Also, the heating isn't properly installed yet. Technically, I suppose I'm probably not really allowed to live here yet, but I won't go into that because the company I sold it to isn't charging me too much rent. They quite like having someone on site to keep an eye out for vandalism, and I've got The Rowans to maintain while your mother and I sort things out so I couldn't afford anything better.'

He made several phone calls, pacing around the small flat like a lion while discussing materials for another site and an estimate that was late. Sophie washed up the dishes. 'Where's your study?' she asked. 'When you come home you always used to go straight to your study.'

Bill looked regretful. 'Well, there's no room here so I stay late at work. Live on takeaways or baked beans, all that kind of thing. I know I've got to . . . well, learn to take care of myself, but it's so hard at my age.'

Sophie looked up from the pans. 'What about Anthea?' Her heart beat faster. In all of this, all this sympathy she instinctively felt for her father, she couldn't forget what she'd seen on the day of her thirtieth birthday.

The galley kitchen opened on to a small living room where there was a table and two chairs. He sank down on to one of them. 'Sophie. Come here.'

Sophie dried her hands and sat down.

Bill looked into her eyes. 'Anthea is a good friend. I'm not denying that. She has been – and still is – fantastically support-ive over all this, and I'll always be grateful to her. I've tried to support her in return, as you saw at your birthday party. But these reports of an affair between her and me have been . . .' He sighed. 'Well, shall we say "greatly exaggerated"? You know what gossip is like round here, and even Rose and Andrew, who have been loyal, loyal friends to both of us – which, as you can imagine, isn't easy – are reading a bit too much into my relationship with Anthea. Your mother and I have been very unhappy recently – ever since she started seeing this dreadful therapist – and I'm ashamed to say that . . .' He cleared his throat and looked out of the window.

'I'm sorry,' he said, his voice breaking, 'I'm so sorry . . .' He hid his hands in his face. 'I leant on Anthea too much after I found out about your mother and George Boxer. I allowed her to comfort me and, yes, it did turn into an affair. Very, very briefly. But I never meant for all this to happen . . .' He indi-cated the bare, cold flat and the view outside, where a digger had just started reversing over the lumpy earth, beeping in warning. 'I never meant it to come to this,' he repeated in despair.

'Dad, Dad.' Sophie got up and put her arms round his heaving shoulders. 'Dad, please. I'm sure Mum never meant it to come to this either. Let me talk to her.'

'It's too late,' said Bill heavily. 'We've gone too far down the road. She's making these terrible accusations against me and I . . . well, I don't think I can trust her any more. Not since the business with George.'

Sophie sighed. 'I do find all that absolutely incredible. The man looks like Humpty Dumpty.'

'A woman like your mother, naive, lacking in confidence, not all that bright . . . she can so easily be misled by someone who seems rich and powerful,' murmured Bill. 'I know how vulnerable she is, and I could punch that man in the face for what he's done to her.'

'That won't be necessary,' soothed Sophie. 'Mum says she doesn't see him any more. In fact, she denies ever having had more than a single lunch with him.'

'Your mother doesn't always tell the truth.' He held a hand up to forestall Sophie's objections. 'Don't get me wrong, I'm not blaming her, it's just that I used to catch her out in little lies and I think she tells them because she feels she has to. It's part of her paranoia.'

Sophie had also seen her mother tell little lies. 'Don't tell Daddy,' was one of the commonest refrains she remembered from their childhood. She frowned and rested her chin on her hands. 'But Dad . . .' She mulled it over. 'I thought Mum only started to see that therapist later, after I saw you with Anthea. When Jess insisted . . .'

His eyes widened. 'Is that what she's been telling you?' He shook his head in bewilderment. 'I give up. I really have no idea what's she been up to or how long she's been doing it. All I know is that that therapist has completely destroyed our marriage. And I bitterly regret finding comfort with Anthea, but she is a good friend, a very good friend, and sometimes there is only so much any man can be expected to endure.'

Sophie kissed the top of his head. 'Daddy, I *will* do everything

I can to sort this out.' She finished wiping down the kitchen surfaces and dried the pans, leaving them in a neat pile. There were no cupboards to put them away in.

When Sophie arrived at The Rowans the first thing she discovered was that her mother had changed the entry code at the gate. She couldn't get in.

Paige was apologetic, once she had been located. 'Sorry, sorry. Sorry, I forgot to tell you.'

Sophie kissed her, irritated as usual by the fulsome apologies. Paige made fresh coffee and its aroma filled the kitchen with a warm welcome. The cluttered walls and scrubbed pine table seemed unchanged, and Sophie couldn't believe that her father was shivering, surrounded by bare breeze blocks while Paige had her collection of china, her range cooker and three freezers.

'Mum, this isn't fair, you know. I've just come from Dad's flat. It's horrible, and here you are in this lovely house, with everything paid for by him.' She hadn't meant to get stuck in quite so soon, but it made her angry to see the comfort that Paige was enjoying.

'Not quite everything,' said Paige. 'He pays the household bills, just until we decide what we're going to do. I have to earn money if I want to eat or buy clothes.'

'Yes, Mum, welcome to the real world. We all have to earn money if we want to eat.'

She expected Paige to apologise again, but she nodded. 'Of course, darling. And I've always wanted to work, at least part-time, to contribute so that your father didn't have to do it all, but he said I was needed here. So I'm actually glad to be working again.'

'You can't blame him for everything that's gone wrong with your life,' said Sophie. 'You have to take responsibility for yourself.'

'Yes,' said Paige. 'I do.'

'So why won't you talk to him directly about how to go ahead?'

Paige's face collapsed at last. 'Sorry, darling. I'm sorry. I know I ought, but . . .'

'Please, please do not tell me you are afraid he's going to kill you.' Sophie looked her mother straight in the eye. 'You know that that is ridiculous, that it's unfair and that it's the sort of thing that spreads rumours and could damage his company.'

Paige looked at the table, and her fingers went white where she clutched her coffee cup. 'I *haven't* said I think he's going to kill me, I don't think, even now, that he really could . . . maybe if he was angry enough . . . but that's not it. Sophie, he ties me in knots. I don't know what to think, and . . . I don't know what to believe. I can't think when he's shouting at me, and I have to think, I know I have to *think*, if I'm to survive.'

Sophie sighed. 'It doesn't have to be this complicated. All you have to do is to be fair. Sell The Rowans. Split the money between you.'

'There's hardly any money left,' whispered Paige. 'Not enough for either of us to buy somewhere new. At least that's what he says.'

'Mum, don't be ridiculous. You've lived here for twenty-two years. It's a five bedroom house with two acres of garden and a holiday cottage. I know you've spent a lot of money on it, but at least some of that will be reflected in the value.'

'Your father gave me a budget and I stuck to it,' flashed Paige. 'Then every single purchase was always checked with him before I made it. I know he likes to say how extravagant I am, and how I waste money, but I spent what he allowed me to spend. He made me account for every penny.'

'Well, perhaps it's just gone on your lifestyle generally.' Sophie shrugged. 'Or into the business.'

'But Jess looked up the company accounts for the last few years and they were very profitable. That's what I don't understand. And we never went on holidays or to restaurants, I drive an old banger and Dad's car is on the company – what is extravagant about our lifestyle?'

'Well, yes, you probably don't understand,' said Sophie. 'You've never got involved with the business, have you? It's probably the losses from Orchard Park, that's what's done for him.'

Paige took a deep breath. 'Sophie, I don't want more than my fair share, and I accept that I must earn, but I have spent over thirty years married to your father, looking after him and you two, and I must have somewhere to live. That's all I ask for.'

'Well, it's all Dad wants too, and he's renting a freezing, half-finished flat in the middle of a field, so unless you talk to him I don't see how you can come to any agreement.'

'I handed over everything I had, including your father's letter and a tax demand I received, to an accountant,' said Paige.

Sophie maintained steady eye contact. 'So you're going to fight it, are you? You're going to take Dad to court rather than talk to him and get it settled in a civilised way?'

Paige's shoulders sagged and she leant back, closing her eyes. 'I can't afford to fight it. I've had a tax demand for eleven thousand pounds. For dividends I received from the company last year.'

'Well? Didn't you put money aside for tax? It just shows, without Dad you're . . .'

'Sophie, I never had any money. Just the usual housekeeping, which was paid into our joint account, and which I used for food and other living expenses. But, apparently, that was my dividend, so I've got to pay tax on it. I don't know what your father did with his dividend, or what he's ever done with it. All the money he gave me for housekeeping was my dividend, over the years, because I have shares in the company that I inherited from my father. In the past, Anthea's done my tax return, apparently, and your father signed it for me without ever telling me anything about it. But now I've got to do it myself, and I've got to pay tax on last year's housekeeping money.'

Sophie frowned. 'It doesn't sound right. But isn't that another reason why you need to get in touch with Dad? So you can sort all of that out?'

'I know,' said Paige, suddenly looking old. 'But all these so-called dividends, plus my half share of the house – it all means I'm much too rich for legal aid. And meanwhile that little lump sum I got from selling my parents' pictures all has to go to the tax man. In thirty days.'

'Oh, they were your parents' pictures?' Sophie remembered Jess saying that Paige was selling pictures from the house, and that she'd passed the information on to Bill. Now she wished she'd reassured him that Paige was only selling stuff she'd inherited from her family. If only Jess was clearer about things.

'I can't sell anything else because your father's placed an injunction on me,' added Paige, reading her mind.

Sophie felt shaky. As Bill had said, Paige could be very convincing. If you didn't know better you'd think she'd have a case. 'Can I see the letter he sent?' she asked. Perhaps Paige wasn't being realistic. Perhaps she was expecting to buy another property like The Rowans.

Paige scrabbled in her handbag and pulled out a dog-eared document. 'Here,' she said. 'Read it.'

Sophie read it, then folded it up. 'I don't understand. There must be some mistake. There should be more money than this, unless the company that bought Orchard Park really ripped him off.'

She read the letter again. None of it made any sense, and she didn't know who to turn to.

Jake. Jake was a business journalist – or had been – and he might be able to help them find out. Perhaps Anthea was embezzling money.

That must be it. Bill had become very dependent on Anthea and obviously trusted her completely. He'd always been very good at what he did, building and decorating houses, but had himself admitted that he got taken for a ride sometimes. Anthea was obviously a sharp – possibly criminally sharp – cookie.

'I'm going to ask Jake about this,' said Sophie.

'What shall I do?' asked Paige, her voice almost breaking. 'I'll be homeless if I accept this. I literally won't have anywhere to live. I wouldn't be a priority on any council list.'

The buzzer sounded at the garden gate. Sophie got up to answer it. 'Yes? Who is it?'

'George Boxer,' said a scratchy voice. 'To see Paige.'

'Mum,' said Sophie, her heart suddenly hardening. 'It's your boyfriend.'

Paige looked guilty and flustered. 'But he isn't ... I didn't ... we haven't ...'

'Oh, save it for your counsellor or the divorce court,' said Sophie, losing patience, as she went to the back door to take her coat off the peg. 'I'm not in the market for any more lies myself.'

That evening Sophie repeated herself. 'I'm going to ask Jake about this.'

Harry contemplated her over the sausage and mash he'd cooked. 'Do you want me to look at it?'

'You're in insurance, you wouldn't understand.'

'Actually,' he said, 'we have to understand the businesses we insure.'

'Whatever.' She didn't want Harry poking his nose into it.

'Sophie, would you like to talk to me? Properly? I know it hurts that your father and your mother are splitting, but you've been like a bear with a sore head ever since it happened, and it's not fair on the girls.'

'On the girls?' queried Sophie. 'Or on you?'

'Well,' he nodded his head. 'It's not great for me, but it's the girls I'm worried about.'

Sophie didn't bother to answer. He might dress his attitude up as concern about the girls, but all that really mattered to him was that his comfortable existence was a little less cushioned. Well, Harry would have to learn that life didn't have the offside rule. Whatever that meant. She screened out his sport. There was no point in her getting interested.

Chapter 49

Jess and Jake had been mildly amused by Sophie storming out of the restaurant.

'She's like that,' said Jess, secure in the cocoon of Jake's love. 'When she doesn't get any attention. She's furious about us getting engaged.'

'Is she?' Jake's eyes gleamed.

'She's always had to be the princess. She doesn't like me bagging the role,' said Jess with a sudden glimpse of awareness, 'not even for a short time.'

He studied her. 'You don't sound as if you liked your sister very much.'

'I love her, but that's not the same as liking. You can love people and know their faults. Also, if I was in trouble she'd be the first to help.' She grinned at him. 'I could *so* rely on her. It's things being good for me that she can't quite handle.' She lifted her glass in acknowledgement of the sudden insight and tried to smile. 'She's incredibly kind but she likes to be in charge. And with you around she isn't. Hey ho.'

They finished their meal and discovered that Harry had phoned the restaurant to pay for the whole thing. 'The gentleman called with his apologies,' said the waiter. 'The bill is taken care of.'

'Harry must be doing well,' said Jake.

'No,' replied Jess, 'I think he's just nice and a bit embarrassed about Sophie.'

'He's not really up to a firecracker like our Soph, is he? She needs a real man.'

Jess didn't like the way he said 'our Soph'. 'Harry *is* a real man. And nice.'

'Real men,' said Jake with a wolfish grin, 'aren't nice. Nice guys finish last.'

A few days later, after a tearful phone call from Sophie, they decided to visit Bill themselves. 'Sophie wants me to look into it,' reported Jake over supper, putting his mobile back in his pocket.

'Did she apologise for her behaviour in the curry house?' Jess was mildly irritated by the fact that Sophie had rung Jake rather than speaking to her first.

'What? That? No, that's water under the bridge. But she thinks I need to talk to the accountant, Anthea, the one you thought was having an affair with your father, to see if she's embezzling money.'

'I didn't *think*. She *was* having an affair with Dad. And how are you going to get to talk to her?'

'I'm not sure,' said Jake thoughtfully. 'But we journalists usually manage to talk to anyone.'

They visited Orchard Park on a Saturday, so the diggers were parked, their mechanical arms in the air. Churned-up mud had settled into hard curves. The houses perched against the blue sky like toys arranged by a careful child, but the air was still and quiet.

'I always associate May with birdsong but Dad's dug up all the trees and hedges, so there aren't any birds,' said Jess, stretching her limbs after the car journey. Jake drove fast, straining even Jess's love of danger. Perhaps, she thought, she hadn't really cared before, but now she had something to lose. A life she loved. A love that was her life.

'They'll be back. Sooner than you think.' Jake locked the car and strode towards the block. 'It's a bit Stalinist in design. Didn't your father invest in a decent architect?'

Even Jess couldn't help feeling affected by the bare concrete corridor and bleak emptiness of the flat.

'Welcome to my humble abode.' Bill stretched out his arms and nearly touched both walls.

'We're taking you out to lunch, Dad. To celebrate our engagement.'

Bill advised that the Black Prince was doing good food and at the pub made his way through the Saturday throng, acknowledging the landlord and several other drinkers.

'Do you come here a lot, Dad?'

He looked regretful. 'Can't afford it now, of course, but it used to be one of our haunts. Hello Carol.'

'Hello Mr Raven,' chirped the waitress, her pen poised over a notebook. 'Your usual?'

He slapped the menu shut. 'Got it in one, Carol.'

'Presumably now that Mum's not cooking for you, you're having to go out more?' questioned Jess.

His face looked serious. 'I live on takeaways, toast and the odd pub meal, but I can't afford to go out often. Your mother has pretty much taken all I've got.'

'But you haven't done the financial agreement yet?' Jess was puzzled.

'No, but I'm maintaining everything at The Rowans and having to fund myself as well, so it's all a lot more expensive than it was. Still,' he sighed. 'That's not what you young want to hear.'

'It was clever of you to get Orchard Park sold,' said Jake. 'Jess said that you found a Lithuanian buyer.'

'Jess doesn't understand business,' said Bill, 'and it was a company based in Bucharest.'

'Bucharest!' exclaimed Jess. 'Was it nice?'

'Nice? What do you mean?'

'You must have gone there, I thought, to meet the buyer.'

Bill rolled his eyes at Jake. 'She doesn't even realise that business these days is transacted online or by phone. Meet the buyer! I took advertisements, dimwit, in the trade papers. They answered one. That's how you sell a company.' He laughed. 'Getting engaged to a journalist hasn't sharpened your intellect, I see. Well, I don't suppose you can expect anything much from a waitress.'

'So you sold the company to someone you haven't even met?' blurted Jess, and was rewarded by her father's glare, over folded arms.

Jake touched her knee almost imperceptibly and leaned forward. 'These emerging markets are fascinating, don't you think? We might be doing a piece on investment from emerging markets coming back in to the UK, and I'd be interested in your impressions on it all.'

'I don't have impressions,' said Bill. 'I'm just a businessman.'

'Obviously a very good one,' said Jake, and Jess flicked a glance at her father to see if he might have overdone the flattery.

'I've had debts,' said Bill heavily. 'In my field a bad debt can wipe you out. This year, for example . . .' He tutted through his back teeth and took another swig of beer.

Jess had heard the words 'bad debt' throughout her life. As a child, she'd thought a bad debt was a monster lurking in a cave, waiting to eat them all up. She could still feel the flicker of fear the words had engendered, and her food turned dry in her mouth.

But Jake had engaged her father in questions and was laughing. Bill was smiling back, man to man. They mirrored each other, Jake leaning forward and deferring to the older man.

'So,' said Jake, 'what did you get in the end for Orchard Park. Three, three-and-a-half mill?'

Something flickered in Bill's eyes. The look was gone almost before Jess registered it, but Bill picked up on her attention. 'So why all these questions, Missy? Are you after some money for your wedding?'

Jess opened her mouth to say that it wasn't her asking, but closed it just in time.

'I was wondering if I could help,' said Jake. 'Have a look at the way your business is structured and see if there are any savings that could be made?'

'That'd be very good of you,' Bill replied, equable again. 'So, the wedding. Where are you going to hold it?'

'We thought perhaps The Rowans?' Jess was on the edge of her seat, waiting for her father's bonhomie to switch off.

'Well, I'm not sure that your mother's health is up to that sort of thing. All the organising would be a terrible strain for her and she's fragile enough as it is. And, of course, it's on the market.'

'On the market? Already?' Jess was shocked at the flip of terror she felt inside. She didn't want to say goodbye to The Rowans. Not yet. She'd visualised walking hand in hand with Jake along the path through the field that ran from the church to the front of the house. She would be wearing bohemian crepe and net, with a twenties net veil, or perhaps a glamorous silk tube sewn with tiny beads, and roses in her hair. They would be smiling at each other, and everyone would be walking behind them smiling too.

But her father had dashed that image. The waitress brought three plates of food and fluttered around with napkins, pepper, salt and bread. When Carol left them Jess repeated her question, hoping she'd misheard in some way.

'I've instructed an estate agent,' said Bill. 'Of course, your mother is being obstructive as usual and isn't letting them in, but I rather hoped you might have a word with her about that. I simply can't afford to go on maintaining the place any longer, and the sooner it's sold the sooner we can all get on with our lives. But I'm afraid your mother is clinging to some idea that she'll be able to go on living there the way she always has.'

'I'm sure she isn't,' said Jess. 'Whenever I speak to her she seems quite clear that it will have to be sold.'

Bill shrugged. 'She says different things to different people. She likes to say what she thinks you'll want to hear.'

And who taught her that, thought Jess, but she kept her eyes on her plate.

'Anyway,' said Bill cheerfully. 'The Rowans is out. We don't want to lose a good buyer who wants to complete quickly just because we've got a family wedding planned. So where else will you go?'

Jess darted a look at Jake. His parents were dead and he didn't get on with his sister.

'London, I suppose,' said Jake. 'It's where we live and work. But it's an expensive place to throw a party.'

'I'm afraid you can't look to the bride's father for any help,' chortled Bill. 'I'm being been stripped to the bone by my wife. But see if you can get her to part with some readies. She's got it all.'

'But you'll be there? You'll give me away?' asked Jess, digging her nails into her palms. It shouldn't matter to her. She hated her father. But somehow it did.

'That depends on your mother. She doesn't want me around at the moment, so it could be rather difficult.' Bill winked at Jake. 'Women, eh?'

On the way home rage ran through Jess's veins. When Sophie got married, life at The Rowans seemed to have been put on hold for months and months. Bill had got involved in every aspect of the decision-making process, from testing the canapés with the caterer to supervising the erection of the marquee, getting in everyone's way and insisting on everything being done his way. When it had all been acknowledged as a huge success everyone had commented on Bill's involvement and how valuable it had been.

But for Jess's wedding, all he would do is say that he couldn't help. He wouldn't even commit to being there. Tears stung behind her eyes. But she wouldn't care. She was determined not to. She had Jake now.

'Oh, I think we should show your father we can do it without him. I'm getting a bonus,' said Jake. 'Take out some credit cards. You do it, I haven't got time, but I'll pay them off if you pass them over to me every month. We'll do it that way.'

Jess thought for a while. 'OK. If you're sure that'll be all right.'

Jake flashed her a smile. 'I'm sure.'

'He got about what you thought for Orchard Park, didn't he?' said Jess. 'I saw his face. He didn't want to tell us.'

'There's something funny about it all.' Jake frowned. 'Bucharest is interesting, though.'

'Would a Romanian company really buy a British development?'

'Well, they might. Property in the UK has always been a sound investment. But it's unusual.'

A few miles later, Jess identified another niggle. 'Where do you think Anthea is in all this? I mean, do you think she's in the background pulling the strings, or is she waiting for Dad to get divorced and marry her?'

'Well, she's a fool if she is,' said Jake. 'Do you want me to try and find out about her?'

Jess hesitated, then nodded.

Chapter 50

Paige was horrified to see George Boxer.

'I really haven't seen him since that lunch,' she had pleaded to Sophie as she stormed out. But Sophie's eyes were shuttered away.

'All I ask,' she said as she picked up her bag, 'is that you're fair to Dad. He should not be living in that flat while you are living here. And you deserve something, but not everything. Please, please, don't be greedy.' She left without kissing Paige goodbye. 'And, by the way,' she shouted at the door, 'it would be good if you could be honest. For a change.'

George saw Sophie shoot out of the drive, her wheels scattering the gravel. 'Oh dear,' he said. 'My timing is appalling. Again.'

'It doesn't matter.' Paige wanted to get him out of there before anyone else came round. Not that people did.

'I've come to apologise,' he said.

'There's nothing to apologise for.' She folded her arms, to protect herself.

'May I come in?' He indicated the door and offered her a bunch of stiff, garage roses. It was sweet of him but she didn't want them.

'I've come to apologise because Rose and Andrew have finally confronted me over the affair that you and I have allegedly had. A few people in the village were giving me the cold shoulder, and I asked Rose if I'd offended anyone without realising it. I was horrified to hear the rumours that were circulating, and that I was supposed to be the cause of your marriage breaking up.'

'You weren't,' said Paige, mortified. 'Things had been bad . . . for years.'

'I thought they must have been. Normal men might be slightly surprised to find their wives lunching with a man, and they'd certainly ask questions. Just as normal women might raise eyebrows if they found their husbands lunching somewhere smart with their female accountant. But to go straight from that into accusing – and telling everyone – that we were lovers is . . .' He searched for the words. 'Frankly, it's lying,' he said. 'There's just one good old-fashioned word for it. It's a lie.'

'I don't think Bill saw it as lying,' said Paige, her heart easing slightly at the word 'lie'. 'I think he really did believe, in his heart of hearts, it was a betrayal, and, to him, a betrayal's a betrayal. Having lunch with you was as bad as a full-blown affair. It hurt him. It humiliated him. It embarrassed him in public.'

George looked at her steadily. 'I don't accept any of that. We're all intelligent human beings, and you're not his possession.'

'Really,' said Paige, 'it's my fault. I haven't handled things properly. I should have . . .'

'I don't care what you should or shouldn't have done. He has no right to treat either of us like this. There is no justification for it.'

'I am so, *so* sorry.' Paige felt as if she'd spent her life apologising for Bill.

'It's hardly your fault,' insisted George. 'And I've been hearing other rumours, about the money.'

Paige froze. 'What, that I've taken it all?'

'So some people say. Others say that you've barely enough

money to eat. That you've had to sell some pictures you inherited from your father.'

'I have,' said Paige. 'But no one believes me. They see me in this great big house and him in the Orchard Park flat . . .'

'And in restaurants. And driving round in a top-of-the-range car. And someone saw him coming out of Anthea's place.' George placed his big hands flat on the table. 'Look. Everybody thinks we've had an affair. I've said we haven't, you've presumably denied it too . . .'

'Of course!'

'But we can't *prove* we haven't. And I presume he's spreading lies about the money, too?'

'Yes,' said Paige, numbly. 'I don't know what to do about it. Some people don't even want to talk to me.'

'Well, I won't be treated like that. And I don't think *you* should be treated like that.'

Paige felt her eyes fill with tears. She couldn't reply.

'Paige, look at me,' he said. 'I've come here to say that if you don't have the money to pay a lawyer, so that you can get a fair deal, I'll lend it to you.'

She shook her head. 'I couldn't ever pay you back. It could run to tens of thousands of pounds.'

'He bid for the renovation of my house, so I got references from his business bank manager. They were glowing. His company is sound and it has a good reputation. The only reason why I didn't engage him was that I wanted a company with more experience with listed buildings. That's a relatively small part of the Raven portfolio and Thomas's specialise in conservation work, so they were the obvious choice. I explained that and Bill seemed to understand.'

'He told me you were embarrassed about the rumours of the affair. That it was my fault he didn't win the contract. He told all his staff that, saying it was why they didn't get a bonus last year. They all think I was being incredibly selfish in getting involved with a potential customer. He told me that too.'

George raised an eyebrow. 'That's ridiculous. I've only just heard about the rumours. So I'm betting that these claims of poverty are yet another lie. And that's something we *can* prove. He's a successful man and you should have a fair share of that success. So you will be able to pay me back. And, if not, I'll take that risk. I'm angry, Paige, and you should be too.'

Paige was usually afraid to be angry, but the word 'lie' was a like a stone. Solid and distinct, but with smooth edges, something she could turn over in her hand and that felt cold to touch, but which would warm up the longer she held it. It would never change, whichever way you looked at it. Yes, Bill had lied. Not been misunderstood or misled. A liar. And George, who was almost a stranger, believed her. He believed Paige. He said Bill was the liar, not her.

And she thought about how or where she could live, and how she would ever pay the tax bill, and she knew. She was trapped in an impossible situation and could only go forward. 'Thank you, George,' she said. 'I'd be glad to accept your kind offer.'

'It's hardly kindness,' he said. 'Bill has placed us both in a position that leaves us no other option. We have to fight. I'm not prepared to have someone accuse me of having an affair with a married woman.'

Paige hoped she wouldn't end up even more in debt, with even less to live off. That could happen, she'd heard: that the cost of the fight meant that no one was left with anything in the end. She smiled at George. 'Joy – someone I work with – says men are no good. But I think some men are good.'

'Well, I'd hardly describe myself as a saint,' said George, smiling. 'But not all men are liars and cheats, and I'm determined to prove that.'

Chapter 51

Sophie phoned Jake at work. 'Hi, it's Sophie.'

His voice was warm and welcoming. 'Hi. How are things?'

She felt like bursting into tears at his concern. 'Fine. I've got a commission to photograph the head honchos of various businesses. To illustrate some article on the Top Twenty Most Influential or some such. One of them is practically next door to you.' This was a slight exaggeration, but several of the Most Influential worked within a few streets of Jake's office. 'And, um, well I wanted to talk to you about Mum and Dad and the financial settlement. I think you're probably the only person who can see it without getting too emotionally involved.'

'Sure thing. Are you working all day or can I take you out to lunch? Or a drink after work?'

Sophie said that she would only need an hour or so for each photograph, so once she had the dates, and that would be soon, she would let him know.

'I'll look forward to it,' he agreed.

'Oh, and . . . er . . . Jake . . . I'm not telling anyone else in the family about seeing you.' The tears were breaking through in earnest now. 'I'm so muddled I don't know who to believe, and Jess is so against Dad . . .' Sophie blew her nose. 'I mean, I know she had a tough childhood and I feel so guilty I wasn't there for her more, but I had to survive too, you know. She thinks everything's so easy for me, but it isn't.'

'Sophie,' his voice was very gentle. 'I know it isn't easy. Listen, we'll have that drink and you can bring me any detail you have on your father's financial situation, and we'll go through it all, bit by bit, and try to see if we can get everything a little clearer.'

'Thanks.' She tried not to snuffle down the phone.

'And, Soph, it'll be our secret. Just for the time being. You don't need to worry about that.'

Chapter 52

A week later Paige sat in the pastel-decorated reception area of George Boxer's lawyer, waiting for Judy Wright and her assistant Tricia Lawson.

They both seemed very young. About the ages of Jess and Sophie. Judy wore a grey suit and no make-up, and Tricia looked like she was doing work experience. Paige hoped that George's confidence in them wasn't misplaced.

Judy led the way into a conference room and they placed themselves at one end of a long, imposing table. Tricia made them all coffee and put some biscuits on the table.

Paige started by explaining that she owed eleven thousand pounds in tax. She hadn't wanted to ask George to lend her money for that too as she still didn't believe she really owed it.

'Ah,' said Judy. 'The old tax-return trick. That often happens when the wife has shares in the husband's company. She leaves and he stings her with a tax bill for money she didn't know she had. I'm afraid it's quite often followed by a visit from the bailiffs as the husband usually hangs on to the tax return until it's very seriously overdue. Did you do your own tax return during the marriage, or did he do it?'

'He . . . he must have done it,' stammered Paige. 'I . . . er . . . didn't think I had to do one, as I didn't earn anything. But that must mean he's faked my signature all these years – he never told me anything about tax returns. Isn't that illegal?' She hoped that if Bill had committed a crime, then perhaps he could be persuaded that it would be better for him if he just paid the bill.

Neither Judy nor Tricia seemed very interested. 'Husbands and wives forge each other's signatures the whole time, especially if they're in a family business,' said Judy. 'You'll probably find there are lots of documents to do with the business that you've "signed".'

Paige hoped that none of them would get her into trouble. 'In that case, surely the Inland Revenue will understand?'

'It's not their concern. All they care about is that the money has been earned and so tax must be paid on it. But we can add the eleven thousand to the amount we ask for in the final settlement.'

'So I've just got to find some way of paying it in the meantime?' Paige could feel a lump in her throat. 'I can't sell anything in the house, there's an injunction on it.'

'We might be able to lift the injunction,' said Judy. 'But I doubt it. You may be able to work out some kind of deferred payment, though. You need to consult an accountant on that.'

Paige then told the story of her marriage yet again. Tricia took notes and Judy regarded Paige with a steady, careful gaze as she listened.

'So he was very controlling throughout your marriage?'

Paige nodded. 'Almost the only area he let me make a decision about on my own was the garden, but even there he'd sometimes insist on something, often something quite trivial. That's why I've refused to meet him face to face so far – I've been too frightened that he'll muddle me or persuade me into something I know isn't right.'

'Is he violent?' Judy tapped her pen on her teeth, watching Paige.

Paige hesitated. 'Not normally. But he has made threats. Subtle ones that he can deny, like showing me stories about

313

women who are killed by their partners. Over and over again. It makes me think that maybe he wants to see me so we can have an argument and then he'll have an excuse to . . .' Her voice trailed off. 'Today there was a piece in the paper about an estate agent who killed his girlfriend when she refused to make their relationship permanent. He strangled her with a dressing-gown cord. He was provoked, he said, because she argued all the time. He says he got fed up with it. I think . . . if anything happened to me Bill would say that he had never been violent before, but that he had been provoked beyond reason.'

'Well, in that case I think you're probably right not to agree to a face to face meeting,' reassured Judy, making a note. 'I think you should trust your instincts.'

It was like hearing George say the word 'lie' and feeling a numb limb come to life, an uncomfortable prickling sensation. The idea that she should trust her own instincts after years of being told how stupid she was, was both frightening and exhilarating.

Judy read the letter from Bill explaining his financial position and offering her a one-off lump sum. Then she looked up. 'This certainly wouldn't normally be considered a fair offer after thirty years of marriage. Not from someone who runs a successful business and has a large home.'

'I don't know how successful it really is. Are there ways of finding out?'

'There are forensic accountants, but they are very, very expensive. Possibly up to hundreds of thousands of pounds.' Judy took a deep breath. 'Listen, there are a few things we can predict about a contested divorce. And the first is that all the men are either about to be made redundant or bankrupt. Or that the women have some difficult-to-diagnose illness that means they can't work. Then, when you ask for the evidence to back it up, such as the consultative procedures companies now have to go through if they're expecting to make redundancies . . . well, let's just say that, in ten years of being a divorce

314

lawyer, that paperwork has only been produced in a satisfactory way once.' Judy smiled at Paige.

'But surely that means that the judge would know that and . . .'

Judy and Tricia exchanged glances. 'One would hope that the judge would see through it.' She didn't sound too sure. 'Shall I explain the next stage?'

Paige nodded. 'At least, I don't have any difficult-to-diagnose illness.' She tried to smile.

'You'll both fill in a form listing your assets, attaching copies of your bank statements, valuations of your home and any other assets, and a list of what you need to live. Those will be exchanged simultaneously . . .'

'Does he have to tell the truth? Can he fake the documents?'

Judy shook her head. 'He'd be in contempt of court and could face jail. Although . . .'

Paige didn't want to think about 'although'. 'What happens next?'

'There'll be three hearings: an initial hearing, where the judge will agree further questions you can ask each other, the second is a Financial Dispute Resolution, where we all hope you come to an agreement, and finally, if you can't agree, there's a fully contested court case, presided over by a different judge, who will make a final decision. Of course, you can agree on a settlement at any time in between.'

'He will never agree to give me anything more than what he's already offered,' whispered Paige. 'He would rather die. Or . . .' The alternative, too frightening to consider, hung in the air between them.

Judy looked worried. 'I'd like to say we could get an injunction preventing him from coming anywhere near you, but without actual physical violence I think it's unlikely we'd get anywhere. Wives don't usually go for injunctions unless they are absolutely terrified. Your best bet is the police, because all those messages on your mobile phone could count as harassment under the Harassment Act and the police usually take these things quite seriously.'

Paige reached home three-quarters of an hour later and, as she opened the kitchen door, she saw something that stopped her heart. A note on the kitchen table, anchored by a newly delivered bottle of milk.

Mail, and notes, were left in the mailbox beside the gates to save the postman having to press the buzzer for the gates. Nobody else had the key to the house.

Paige unfolded the piece of paper, her heat beating fast. There were just nine words written on it, but no one would ever understand how much they frightened her. With blunt fingers she crammed the note into her pocket and stumbled back into the car, nearly hitting the gatepost as she drove out in a blind panic.

Chapter 53

After ten months of working at the Dizzy Donkey Jess had slowly got to know the silent, introverted Dan. He'd had a breakdown after living a high-octane lifestyle, according to Mel, and was inching his way back to normality. He had let his hair grow longer and he now tied it back in a ponytail. He worked intensely, always arrived on time, never hung about around the back, smoking, or took too long a break, and often cleared Jess's tables as well as his own.

He told her that his parents were disappointed in his working in a restaurant. 'They say it's not the reason they paid for me to have an expensive education.'

'Mine too. At least, my father can't resist digs about how stupid waitresses are,' said Jess. 'But he says all women are stupid anyway. Except for my sister Sophie. She can do no wrong.'

They cleared the last glasses and plates away and wiped down the tables, then upturned the chairs on top. While Dan mopped the floor Jess tidied the bar and prepared it for the following day. Dan leant on his mop and said something, and Jess leant across to hear better. 'What?'

The door opened. 'Jess,' said Jake. 'I've been waiting outside.'

'Sorry.' She hastily straightened the last of the glasses and took off her apron.

'Don't worry,' said Dan. 'I'll finish up here.'

Jess didn't like the way Jake stood at the door. He seemed angry.

'What's up?' she asked as she put her seatbelt on.

Jake didn't reply while he steered the car out into the traffic. When they stopped at a red light he turned to her. 'You seem very friendly with that guy.'

'Dan? He's a colleague. He used to work in the City but had a nervous breakdown and has downshifted.'

'Stupid cunt,' said Jake. 'I know that kind of man. They try to make women feel sorry for them.'

'I don't think Dan's like that.' Jess defended him. 'He seems—'

'Oh, so you've fallen for him, have you? Been back to his place yet?'

'No, of course not. He hasn't asked me.'

'But you would if he did?'

'I don't know. Why would he ask me?'

'To get into your knickers, you idiot. Really. Why does any man ever talk to any girl? There's only one reason and you know it.'

'I don't think so. I've got lots of friends who are men, and they don't . . .'

'These male friends,' said Jake. 'How many of them have you slept with?'

'Jake, are you drunk?' There was something erratic about his driving, she thought.

He accelerated through a red light and she let out a cry. 'Jake, don't! We only just missed that van.'

'It was your fault,' he said. 'You wouldn't answer my question. It distracted me. How many of your men friends have you slept with?'

'None, that's the point of men who are just friends.'

'I don't believe you. You must have slept with some of them, and I am simply asking how many.'

He was right, of course. There had been a few weeks when

318

it looked as if she and Callum might be an item, but that had petered out, and two one-night stands with Nigel and . . . Jess made a quick calculation. Of her group of friends there were probably about six men with whom who she had had some kind of sexual encounter over the last ten years. But she couldn't say six. It sounded so slutty.

'Well?' he asked, turning to look at her.

'Two!' cried Jess. 'Two!'

He didn't reply and parked the car outside the flat in silence. As soon as they got inside he slammed the door shut and turned to her. 'Suppose I said I knew of three?'

Jess wondered how. But he could have talked to her friends, and she hadn't kept anything secret. 'Oh. Well, maybe three then.'

'Or four?' he raised an eyebrow.

'Not four,' she said hastily, but she was no good at lying.

'All I want is the truth. We have to build our marriage on being absolutely honest with each other. Don't we?'

She nodded.

'So,' he said. 'How many? I will know if you lie.'

'Six,' she whispered.

'Six! You have slept with *six* of the men I see when I go out with your friends? Why don't you just throw yourself open to the public while you're about it? Do you know how this humiliates me?'

'It doesn't,' said Jess. 'It was all over long before I met you. Everything. With anyone. It was over ten years. I bet you've slept with more women than six in ten years.'

'I saw how you were looking at that Dan guy.'

'Yes,' shouted Jess. 'I looked at him. Because he's a poor sod who's struggling to stay alive, and actually it doesn't cost me anything to be nice to him. He works hard, he's very fragile and I don't fancy him, I don't love him. I love you.'

Jake glared at her and then sagged back, walking into the flat and sitting down suddenly on the sofa, his head in his arms.

'Sorry,' he mumbled. 'Sorry. I saw you laughing with him and it seemed more intimate than it was. I had such a bad time with my ex, she must have slept with a dozen other men while we were together. I never knew where the next one was coming from. Everybody seemed like a threat. I swear, if our postie hadn't been a middle-aged woman, she'd have done it while the post was being delivered.'

Jess sat next to him and put her arm round him. 'Jake, I would never be unfaithful to you. I just wouldn't. I couldn't. And, as you said, you'd know if I was lying.'

He felt for her hand and squeezed it. 'Yes. I know. I know. It's just that, after my ex, I find it very difficult to trust another woman.'

'I understand,' soothed Jess. 'But you can trust me.'

He looked at her, the humour back in his face. 'But six,' he said. 'Six men is an awful lot. I think I'm going to have to punish you.'

With a tingle of anticipation, Jess wondered if he was being serious. 'Haven't you slept with six women since you ended it with Cassie?'

'My darling Jess,' he said, pulling her towards him. 'That is absolutely none of your business. You don't know them, and you never will. You, on the other hand, have introduced me to these men, and so you deserve a smacked bottom.'

'No I don't.' Jess laughed and jumped up but, laughing too, Jake got up to pull her down. She slipped from his grasp and, shrieking, ran away from him.

He was too strong for her. He picked her up at the door of the bedroom and threw her down on the bed.

'Now then, Missy, let's a have a proper talk about saying sorry for all these men you've slept with.' He pinned her wrists down and leaned over her.

'They didn't mean anything.' Jess found it hard to breathe. His dark eyes were very close to hers, dancing with humour. And something else . . .

Excitement. She struggled away, but he pulled her down again. They wrestled, but he was too strong for her and she found herself over his knee.

'One smack for each man,' he whispered, pulling her skirt up.

'No.' Jess wriggled, but the palm of his hand landed on her backside, stinging surprisingly hard, and setting off sparks of fear and anticipation.

'One!' he said. 'I read somewhere' – his voice grew hoarse – 'that this stimulates the flow of blood.' He raised his hand over her. 'Now take your punishment and say sorry.'

'Sorry,' she gasped.

'Two! And then you can show me how really sorry you are.' She felt another stinging slap. 'Three!'

Later they lay entwined in each other's arms, Jake asleep immediately and Jess still breathing hard. It had been a game in which she had more than played her part. She had been sucked in, like sand being drawn out by the tide. Nobody else had ever found that part of her, the dark part, deep down, where she was ashamed of herself. But should she be? All she knew was that she and Jake connected at a level she had never dreamed existed.

But that was what made it so right and special. She would be careful how friendly she got with Dan, though. Jake wasn't exactly the jealous type but he was more sensitive than the men she was used to, and when she thought about how she would feel if he was too friendly with another woman . . . well, she'd like to spare him that kind of pain. Especially after Cassie and what she did to him.

Chapter 54

Paige phoned Judy and told her about the note she'd found.

'What did it say?'

'It's not what it said,' said Paige. 'It's *worse* than a threat. He's making it clear he can get in, any time, no matter how many locks I've put on the door.'

'Nevertheless,' insisted Judy, 'we need to know what it said, because it could help us with that injunction.'

'He's been too clever for that. I can hardly bring myself to tell you what it said. And no judge would take it seriously.'

She could hear the tiniest of frustrated sighs at the other end of the line. 'We can't help you unless you tell us everything.'

'I don't think anyone can ever help me anyway,' cried Paige. 'He will always get me. Always. I'm stuck like this for ever. He will always control everything I do. I'll never, ever get away from him. I should accept the hundred thousand and go and live somewhere abroad. As far away as I can get.'

'You wouldn't get very far. There are various residency rules and you probably wouldn't be able to earn if you didn't speak the language,' said Judy. 'The note. Please. Unless it's embarrassing and you'd rather hand it to me.'

'What's embarrassing about it is its . . . sorry. I'll read it out to you.' Paige was overwhelmed with despair. No one would believe how frightening she found these words. Everyone would think she was silly. 'All it says . . .' She tried to control her voice. 'All it says is "We must meet to talk about Jess's wedding." It was on the kitchen table. He knows it would frighten me. No one else could understand.'

'I do understand,' said Judy evenly. 'It's the breaking in to leave such a mundane message.'

'But if I was . . . found dead . . . then it could never be used as evidence that he'd threatened me, could it? The prosecutor would be laughed at.'

'We won't let it get that far,' said Judy. 'Now think. How could he have got in? A side window? An unlocked door?'

'I would never, ever leave a window or a door unlocked,' said Paige desperately. 'He would have been furious if I had. But maybe he's right, I'm going mad and didn't check properly.' She thought of the way she left the house now, double and triple-checking everything, often going back a second or third time. Had she left one window unchecked somehow? She must have done.

'I'm sure you're not.' But Judy's answers were sounding more and more automatic. 'Has anyone else got a key? Your daughters? A neighbour?'

'No, I didn't give any keys to anyone. I didn't know who I could trust. He must be able to walk through solid walls or something. Or maybe a co-operative locksmith's in his Masonic lodge, or he sails with a former burglar. There seems to be no end of favours he can call in from people. They all think he's a good bloke.'

'Listen to me, Paige. What he is doing to you is called gaslighting. After the film *Gaslight*, where the husband decides to make his wife, and everyone else, believe she's mad so he can get his hands on the loot. It's about manipulating people so they don't trust the truth. It happens much more often than anyone realises. We've seen it before. All lawyers have.'

'Does that mean the court would understand? If it came to it?'

Judy hesitated. 'It would depend on the judge. We would hope so.'

But she clearly wasn't sure. Fear ticked away in Paige's throat.

'And he *can't* walk through solid walls or locked doors,' added Judy. 'He got in somehow, and you'll be able to find out how if you concentrate. Meanwhile, go to a safe place. Until you know how he got in you won't feel safe at home. I still think your best bet is the police.'

Paige agreed another date to see the solicitors, and then rang Jess.

'You don't have a spare set of my keys, do you?' She was sure she hadn't given keys to either Jess or Sophie, but perhaps she had. Maybe she was vague, mad . . . senile . . .

Jess sounded surprised. 'No, why?'

Paige explained. 'I can't ask Sophie, she's furious with me.'

'I'll do it,' said Jess, ringing back a few minutes later. 'She says she knows nothing about any keys. She's in a terrible mood though; she was vile. She's always vile at the moment. Do you think Harry's up to something? It's the only explanation I can think of.'

Paige decided that she must have left a door unlocked or a window open. She would be brave and go back, and do a fingertip search of the house, first checking that Bill's car wasn't parked anywhere nearby.

Chapter 55

Anthea frowned at the pile of clothes in the laundry basket. Bill had been out shopping and had brought back the most dreadful shirts. Two sizes too big by the looks of them, and made of nasty, cheap fabric. Plus an oversized pair of jeans. She sighed as she picked them out of the basket to check the cycle they should be washed on.

'Bill, what are these?'

He shrugged. 'Casual clothes. You know, things you wear whenever.'

'You need to check the sizes more carefully. These must hang off you.'

Bill grinned at her. 'Paige always used to buy everything. How am I supposed to know what to get?'

'Well, don't wear these anywhere near me. They must look totally unsexy.'

A flash of irritation shot across his face. 'I can't afford smart clothes.' He suddenly changed the subject. 'I heard from that bitch's lawyers, though. She wants more. She wants the lot, basically.'

Anthea was stung with fury. Paige had no right to 'the lot'. 'How can she afford lawyers?' she asked. 'I know she sold a few things before you managed to stop her, but I thought the tax return would take care of that.'

'Christ knows. Never mind, if she's taking out a loan she'll only find that whatever she wins in court has to go to pay off legal fees and interest.' But he looked worried.

That night he reached for her after they turned the light off, but after a few minutes of furious jiggling up and down she felt him soften. Eventually he pushed her away, turned his back to her and sighed.

'It's not your fault, darling,' said Anthea. 'Every man has the odd problem from time to time, especially when he's worried. It's all Paige's fault.'

There was a short silence. 'Have you ever thought about surgery?' he asked. 'I mean, with a vagina as sloppy as yours there's no grip. It's hard to keep a hard-on.' He gave a short laugh. 'No pun intended.'

Anthea was shaken, flushed with embarrassment. 'What do you mean?'

Bill sat up in bed and put the light on. 'Well, usually women only get baggy once they've had children – not that the wife had that problem because she had caesareans – but maybe in your case it's to do with age. Hormone levels dropping and all that sort of thing.'

Anthea was too horrified to answer. She had never thought she could ever have a problem 'down there', as she preferred to think of it. As Bill said, she thought it was something you had to worry about after giving birth. 'I do Pilates,' she said weakly.

'Never mind,' he said, giving her shoulder a squeeze. 'I still love you, even if doing it is rather like throwing a sausage up the Finchley Road.'

She lay awake all night, terrified. She had been wondering about whether she should have her eyes lifted a bit, just to make her look a bit more awake, but now she realised there were more important priorities.

Perhaps, she thought, chilled to the marrow, that was why none of her relationships had ever worked out. Maybe it was only Bill, now that they'd got so much closer, who'd ever cared for her enough to tell her the truth.

Chapter 56

Jess was happy. Now that a spring wedding at The Rowans was definitely out, they'd decided to go for a winter wedding in London, bringing the date forward to the middle of December, at a pretty old church just fifteen minutes from Jess's flat. They discussed the order of service, readings and music with the minister and hired the church hall for the reception. It would be swathed in tenting and entwined in flowers, with a chic green and white theme. They were talking about wrapping candelabra in white roses, and maybe having topiary flamingos.

They had no more arguments. Jess was careful not to be too friendly to Dan, although Jake seemed to have forgotten about it all. She no longer had to worry about money. She applied for the credit cards as agreed, and paid deposits for flowers, the groom's suit, her dress and the caterer. Jake simply took the envelopes from her and paid the bills. Eventually he took one of the cards himself in order to pay for the honeymoon ('I want it to be a surprise, just give me the pin number and forget about it,' he instructed her with a kiss. 'And do not open the statements or you'll spoil the secret.') She'd been a little concerned that there might be a repeat of the mobile phone row, where he would look at what she spent, but he never seemed to mind. Not that she spent a lot – Bill had schooled them all never to have credit cards and to count every penny carefully. 'Never a borrower or a lender be,' he'd pontificate. Another of his favourite sayings was 'Income twenty shillings a year, expenditure nineteen-and-six, happiness. Income twenty shillings a year, expenditure twenty shillings and sixpence a year, misery.'

Which made it all rather odd, she suddenly thought, that Mum thought he was so heavily in debt. So, after musing intermittently on it over the day, she decided to risk a quick call to Paige.

Paige had just had a letter from the bailiffs, to do with the tax bill. 'I've paid half of it, and worked out an agreement about the rest, but apparently not soon enough and they might come tomorrow. So I've got to be out. I mustn't answer the door, apparently, I've got that right. Once they're in, they can take anything. I'm going to try to stay longer at work or something.'

'Mum, you're living under siege. You must fight back.'

'Well, I'll be getting your father's Financial Statement soon, showing his income and expenses, and debts and that sort of thing. We have to exchange them simultaneously and I've done mine . . .'

'Shall I come down and help you?' Jess was burning with curiosity. Her father had never let her know anything about his affairs, and now it would be all spread out in front of them.

'If you could manage it.'

Jess calculated quickly. Jake was on a course towards the end of the following week, so she could nip down without having to mention it. Not that he'd be cross, of course, but nevertheless . . . She made the arrangement with Paige, and asked her not to tell anyone. 'I wouldn't want it getting back to Dad.'

'I try not to tell anyone anything,' said Paige, but with a laugh in her voice. 'Your father seems to have ears and eyes everywhere. How are the wedding plans going? Do you want to have it here?'

Jess was puzzled. 'But Dad says the house is on the market. He told us weeks ago. That the estate agents have been trying to get in touch with you, but you won't let them in.'

Paige's voice conveyed the usual bewilderment when the earth shifted beneath her. 'Well, I don't often answer the home phone, but your father knows that. I open letters and I haven't heard from any estate agents. Though I suppose this will all go to show how uncooperative I am.'

Jess could tell the news had frightened Paige, although even Jess wondered, in a tiny corner of her brain, whether her mother was telling the truth. Maybe she was turning estate agents away. Perhaps Bill wasn't lying. But she pushed the thought away. 'We're having the wedding in London anyway, Mum, as it's where our friends are, so don't worry. Dad says that you might lose a good purchaser if you had to stick to a particular date because of the wedding.'

'Is he . . . contributing at all?' Jess could hear the hope in Paige's voice and knew she should protect her. She should just say, 'Don't worry, Dad's being fine about it all', and Paige would let it rest.

But the cry of 'it's not fair' was too close to the surface. 'I don't know if he's even planning to be there,' said Jess, trying to conceal the pain. 'He seems to think that it's all up to you. He says he doesn't think you'll want him around.' She still hoped that Paige and Bill could at least be civilised for the day itself. And it hurt that he would spend such a lot on Sophie's wedding yet completely disconnect himself from hers. But the circumstances were different, she reminded herself. 'Don't worry,' she reassured her mother. 'We'll pay for it all.'

'That's not fair. Maybe that's why he wants to talk to me about it,' said Paige. 'Of course he must be there. It's your day and you need your father present. I wouldn't dream of doing or saying anything that would prevent that. And with all the money we spent on Sophie we must at least contribute to yours, even if things are . . . I'm so sorry, darling, Oh, why is he so difficult? I'll have to see him.'

'Be careful, though,' said Jess with foreboding. 'Look after yourself.' As she put the phone down she wished she hadn't said anything.

Chapter 57

As Paige worried about Jess and her wedding she realised that she was growing more, not less, frightened of Bill. Shadows lurked in every corner of The Rowans, and the creaks of the older part of the house sounded like someone tiptoeing to come and get her. She kept her mobile phone with her all the time, and often locked herself in a room to eat.

Paige rang Judy. 'The more of a victim Bill seems – because I'm refusing to see him – the more dangerous it is for me. Because when we do meet he could claim he was provoked or that he was defending himself, or that there was some tragic accident caused by me or both of us.'

'I think you should trust your instincts on this,' said Judy again. 'If you feel he's dangerous, then he almost certainly is. Don't meet him without someone else present. Meet him at our offices.'

'I can't do that. Even you would come out thinking that I was exaggerating, or perhaps a little bit unbalanced. That this is a situation of my making, not his. Suppose he did . . . well . . . hurt me . . . or – well, I know this sounds silly, but even . . . kill me, there'd be any number of people to testify at his trial, who'd say that he was a great bloke and that he'd never been violent . . . people think Bill is a decent man under stress, who just loses his temper occasionally. And every time someone thinks that, my life is a little less secure.'

'Well, I can understand you might believe that, but I have seen manipulative people before, you know. I don't think I would necessarily be fooled.'

'I can't take that risk,' said Paige. 'But I don't think he'll do anything unless he has something to gain, and unless he is sure that he will get a short or a deferred sentence. He'll want to look like the victim. He *seems* like a very angry man, but I think he's quite in control. If anyone ever turned up in the middle of an argument at home he could switch immediately into charm mode. But I think it's all about the money – once we're divorced and there's a final settlement he'll have nothing to gain from hurting me.'

'So what do you propose to do?' Judy sounded cautious.

Paige told her.

'OK,' said Judy. 'But be careful. Be very, very careful.'

'You'll remember we had this conversation, won't you?'

'As you know,' said Judy, 'all of our telephone conversations are recorded.'

Chapter 58

Anthea was astonished to get a phone call from Jake. 'Hi,' he said, his voice easy and confiding. 'I hope you don't mind me calling, but I was impressed with the way you talked when we met, and I wondered if you'd consider being my accountant?'

'Well, yes, but . . .' Anthea was surprised.

'You're probably wondering why I don't go for a London firm. To be honest, my affairs are pretty simple and the London charge-out rate is so high. And I like the idea of someone I know, although of course I'd quite understand if you felt there was a conflict of interest.'

'No, I don't see why there should be.' Anthea wondered if Bill would mind. There didn't seem to be any reason why he should. He had never enquired about other clients. She made an appointment to meet Jake.

'Evenings are best for me,' he said. 'It's pretty full-on during the day on the paper.'

They agreed to meet in one of the brick-and-glass wine bars in St Pancras station. He got up from the table as she came in and kissed her on both cheeks. He had a deep cleft in his slightly unshaven chin, she noticed, and very definite eyebrows. She liked men with strong faces and wiry, hard bodies.

'So.' Jake poured her a glass of wine. 'Tell me about yourself.'

She did. Her struggle to emerge from a sink school – although she described it merely as 'not very good' – through her mathematical ability, the degree from Liverpool (although she omitted the fact that, unlike most other students, she'd had to spend almost every evening waitressing in order to fund herself), her accountancy exams, her time with a big-name firm and the realisation that she'd do better as an independent. She omitted to add that this latter decision had been made urgent by an affair she'd had with a senior partner and the discovery of it by his wife. Occasionally she looked back and wondered where she'd be now if Janet hadn't kicked up such an appalling fuss. Maybe she'd have finally got that senior partnership.

'I get the feeling you're putting a very brave face on what must have been quite a difficult life,' murmured Jake, as if he was reading her mind.

'Well, I thought it would be good to move out of London. Less stress, you know.'

'So why Kent?' asked Jake, leaning forward.

It had been because of Bill. She and Bill had met six years earlier, when she was deciding to move out of London so that she could buy somewhere big enough for her to have an office too. She explained that, omitting the mention of Bill.

'Smart move,' Jake acknowledged. 'Just the sort of woman who should be handling my accounts. No wonder Bill does so well.'

'He's very good at what he does,' acknowledged Anthea. 'People rate him. Very highly.'

'And he's got an excellent accountant.' Jake touched his glass to hers.

For a moment the memory of Bill telling her that it was 'like throwing a sausage up the Finchley Road' flashed into her mind and she blushed. 'Oh well, you know, I do what I can.'

'Presumably you were involved with the purchase of Orchard Park?'

She smiled at him. 'Client confidentiality.'

'Of course.' He filled up her glass. 'Tell you what. Let's go out for dinner. I know a delightful little family restaurant just nearby.'

After hesitating, she nodded. It seemed harmless enough.

'You know,' Jake continued, 'it's great to talk to a woman of my own age. In their thirties. I love Jess to bits, but she is very young.'

'Well . . . I'm a bit more than my thirties.'

'Me, too' he said with a wink, as he helped her with her coat. 'But that's our little secret, isn't it?'

Chapter 59

Paige prepared carefully for her meeting with Bill. He rang the doorbell and she let him in, walking through to the kitchen ahead of him, the back of her neck prickling with fear. 'Can I offer you anything?'

He looked round at the room, as if reminding himself what it looked like. 'A drink.'

'I don't have one,' she said, switching the kettle on. If he got drunk he could say he hadn't known what he was doing. She'd seen the excuses over the years, in the endless newspaper stories.

'Have you gone through the cellar then? Drunk the lot? Or sold it?'

She shook her head. 'No, but I've lost the key to it. Silly me. You know how stupid I am.'

He looked at her sharply and began to range round the kitchen pulling out books and feeling behind jars.

'If you're looking for the voice-activated recorder,' said Paige, 'I've given it to my solicitor. It's got a record of the last few times you were here.'

'Well that won't help you. I was angry. Anyone would be.'

Paige tried to keep her hands steady as she handed him a cup of tea.

He picked up a cookery book from a row of six and felt

behind them, then swept them all to the floor. Paige jumped out of her skin.

'What are you looking for?'

'The key to the cellar. Helping you find it. You said you'd lost it.'

'You wanted to talk about Jess's wedding,' she reminded him.

'Ah yes. That. I'm bankrupt. Almost. I can't pay for any wedding. Not while you're sitting on my only asset, refusing to give it up.'

She reminded herself not to argue with him. 'What would you like me to do?' she asked. 'I'm happy to put it on the market now, if that would help.'

He ignored her again. She was used to that and waited, her heart pounding, as he opened a cupboard and looked inside it. Then he ran his hand along the main worktop, sweeping everything off it. Her blender and five storage jars smashed into pieces on the floor.

Paige instinctively cringed. He ranged across all the cupboards, faster and faster, wrenching their doors open and pulling out the contents as he felt inside: tins of food, plates, glass jars of instant coffee, roasted peppers and jam . . . Crash, crash, crash.

Paige edged under the table, too frightened to speak, but she knew she had to. 'Don't break the china Bill, please. The key isn't there. I've looked thoroughly.' She had hidden the knives and even the pans, but she hadn't been able to take every potential weapon out of the kitchen.

'I'll do what I fucking like.' As Paige crouched under the kitchen table in a self-protective ball, fumbling in her pocket for her mobile phone, he pulled open each cupboard in turn, breathing heavily. 'It's *my* house – *crash* – and my fucking china – *crash* – and I'll break what I fucking like.' When the entire contents of the cupboards lay in a mound of broken glass and china and spilt food around their feet he stopped and took one last careful look round the kitchen, still breathing hard.

'Listen, you bitch,' he said, poking his head under the table. The veins stood out on his forehead. 'I'm only going to say this once. If you take me to court over the money I will kill you before you even get there. And it will look as if you provoked me beyond anything a man can take. People see me as the victim round here, not you. Is that clear?'

Bill began kicking the mess on the floor, stepping on the broken glass so it crunched into tinier and tinier fragments. 'You little bitch,' he said. 'Look what you've made me do.'

It seemed an age before a police car swung into the drive, its blue lights flashing. Bill picked up a broken jam jar, quickly cut the corner of his forehead with the edge, then smeared some jam on his sweater and repeated the action with the mayonnaise, before running to open the door, covered in blood and food. 'Thank God you're here, my wife has gone quite mad. I had to tell her I didn't have any money left to fund our daughter's wedding and she has thrown almost everything in the kitchen at me.' He put a hand up to his head. 'I think I'm bleeding . . . she went wild . . . said she was going to kill me.'

Two police officers looked from Paige to Bill as they stepped into the kitchen and surveyed the chaos. Paige clambered out from under the kitchen table and lifted her handbag, making sure the police were between her and Bill. She held up a small silver item.

'I think this is what he was looking for, officers. He tore the kitchen apart trying to make sure that I wasn't recording him. But I was.'

Bill let out a roar of rage as he threw himself at her.

As Paige explained to Judy the following day, she had a text ready to go on her mobile phone, alerting George, and he had called the police. Now Bill had been arrested trying to assault her in front of two police officers. There was also a record of him threatening her life, which Judy would keep a copy of. It didn't completely guarantee that Paige was now safe from him, but he knew he had a good chance of being found guilty of murder if she died.

'And he won't go that far,' said Paige, hoping she was right. 'It wouldn't be worth it.'

Chapter 60

Anthea lay awake almost all night waiting for Bill to come back. He'd said he would. At midnight she tried his mobile. It was switched off. Eventually, risking his rage, she drove to the flat but no one was there.

She was afraid he might have agreed to go back to Paige. Anthea had been dumped too many times not to see it coming. Other women – privileged, fragile, needy – fluttered their eyelashes at men and they caved in. They always told Anthea that she was 'so strong' and that they knew she could look after herself.

But I can't, she cried inside. I'm not strong at all. I need you, Bill. Just as much as silly little Paige does. Perhaps Paige had persuaded him. She might have apologised, and promised to be a better wife in future, talked about their lovely home, their grandchildren . . . Anthea thought there was a chance that Bill might give in. When they'd been keeping their affair secret everything he said about Paige had been critical, but now he'd occasionally let something positive slip, such as, 'Say what you like about that woman, but she certainly knew how to iron a shirt.'

Anthea knew that ironing shirts wasn't her strong point and suggested they send Bill's shirts to be professionally laundered. He'd exploded with wrath. 'Do you think I'm made of money?'

Anthea was hurt, but also frightened by the signs that Bill might be beginning to realise that she, Anthea, wasn't perfect. An affair was one thing. A life together quite another. She had to work at it because she knew how furiously he was pedalling underneath it all to keep everything going. Superficially, Raven Restore & Build was a well established company with a good reputation. An excellent reputation, even. People often said Bill was the best builder around and she knew they meant it.

But, as she'd explained to Jake over dinner, each contract had to be bid for, and Raven Restore & Build had to compete with three or four other strong companies. He had to emanate a confidence she now knew he didn't really feel. Then, once a contract was signed and sealed he had to find another. It was relentless. He always felt he was one contract away from collapse. Clients often paid late and occasionally didn't pay at all. They beat him down on price. Expected extra. Were reluctant to pay more when a problem was uncovered. Sometimes they went bankrupt, leaving Bill unpaid and low on the Official Receiver's list of priorities.

The actual art of quoting was difficult in itself, because even if you'd been in the business for thirty years it sometimes wasn't absolutely clear how long a job might take. Quote too high and you lost the work. Quote too low and you lost money. By the end of the year, overall, Bill had usually got it right and Anthea was able to show him that he had. But for the rest of the time he was on a financial knife-edge, with the payments going out every month not always balancing with the irregular way they often came in. 'Everybody thinks he's rich,' she'd said as Jake topped up her glass. 'And by your standards or mine, I suppose he is. But . . .'

Jake traced his finger down her arm. 'Has anyone ever told you that you have beautiful eyes?'

Bill's words about . . . well . . . she could only think of it as 'the Finchley Road' came flooding back to her, shattering her confidence. Until she'd had the operation she couldn't even flirt with a man. 'I must go,' she said, getting up hastily. 'I'm so sorry. I'll miss the last train.'

'Of course.' Jake called for the bill.

As she leaned her flushed face against the glass of the railway-carriage window Anthea wondered if she'd been mad to accept Jake's offer of dinner. She belonged to Bill. Jake belonged to Jess. How could she have, even for a moment, allowed herself to enjoy his company?

How could she do it to Bill? His public face was smiling and confident. The private face – the one Anthea was finally getting to see – was, she thought, fractured by insecurity and fear. Real fear. Unlike Paige, Anthea understood how tough it all was on him, and that's why she was prepared to put up with a bit of bad temper. And why she realised he needed complete loyalty.

But she needed to get on with that operation before her self-confidence collapsed any further. Priding herself on her pragmatic approach, she had researched vaginal surgery and had spoken to a number of women at the gym about cosmetic surgery in general. She'd identified several surgeons, had checked their qualifications, made sure they belonged to the right professional organisations and that their clinics were well established. She knew to avoid fly-by-night set-ups, and had eventually booked an appointment with a Mr Cooper, just off Harley Street, who was generally considered to be the best of the best, if a little more expensive than the rest. She'd even put several thousand pounds on notice in her high-interest account. It was for emergencies like this that she saved.

Back in her flat, waiting for Bill to return from The Rowans, she lay tossing and turning, occasionally dozing off as the night crept past. She visualised Bill in bed with Paige. Or could Paige have hurt Bill in some way? Even killed him? As three o'clock turned into four, and then five, Anthea had fantasies of Paige getting a shotgun and somehow lugging Bill's body into the boot of her car, or digging a grave in the garden.

But Bill was six foot three and Paige was only five foot five.

It was difficult to see how she might manage it. When the sun came up, Anthea was able to dismiss such ideas as fantasy.

But where was he? Had he had an accident? There were only two hospitals he could have been taken to, but they both confirmed that they had no record of him. With her head aching and her eyes feeling dry and sore, Anthea went to the office, but could hardly tell Jenny that he hadn't come back all night.

'Do you know when Bill's coming in?' she asked, trying to sound casual.

They both tried his mobile phone, but it was off.

Anthea could barely concentrate. 'Perhaps you should phone Paige?' she suggested. 'Maybe they've had a reconciliation?' The words stuck in her throat. Perhaps Bill had wanted sex with a woman whose caesareans meant that . . . She couldn't even complete the sentence in her head.

'I don't want to speak to Paige,' said Jenny. 'Not after the way she's behaved. I don't think I could be civil. Someone saw her the other day, looking very smart and happy. When you *think* how Bill's looking at the moment. His clothes are hanging off him, he's lost so much weight.'

Anthea thought about this, slightly puzzled. She didn't think Bill necessarily looked much thinner when he was in the shower. It was probably her fault for not ironing things properly.

At ten-thirty Bill strode in, and they both gasped.

Anthea jumped up. 'What *has* happened to you?'

There was a plaster across his forehead and another on his cheek. He was unshaven and his clothes were rumpled. They smelt. He looked as if he'd been in a fight, then slept on a park bench all night. He sank down on to a chair, his head in his hands.

'The ex-wife went demented,' he said. 'I told her I couldn't afford to pay for Jess's wedding, that I was almost bankrupt, and she threw every single plate, glass and jar in the kitchen at me.

343

I managed to call the police, whereupon she told them that it was me who'd thrown the stuff at her. I ask you! There isn't a scratch on her. Not one drop of food or blood. And look at me . . .' He opened his arms to reveal a trail of jam, mayonnaise and other stains down the front of his sweater. 'The police arrested me, and I've spent the night in jail.'

'No!' gasped Jenny. Anthea could see her reaching for the phone, then remembering to hold back until he'd gone.

'You should have called me,' said Anthea. 'I'd have come and got you out.'

Bill glared at her under his eyebrows.

'I mean, either of us,' amended Anthea hastily. 'We wouldn't have minded being woken up, would we, Jenny?'

'Andrew picked me up. I didn't want to wake anyone so I called him at nine. Andrew and Rose gave me a bit of breakfast and he's going to take me back to The Rowans to pick up the car, then I'll go home and clean up. But I just wanted to pop in and reassure you that I was all right.'

Anthea followed him out, whispering that she'd been worried. 'I'd have come and got you much earlier. At four in the morning, if necessary. I wasn't asleep anyway – I was worried.'

He turned and pressed close to her in the narrow corridor. She could smell the old food and his stale breath and sweat. 'Listen,' he whispered. 'We do not and cannot tell anyone about us. I cannot be seen to be picked up from the police station at four in the morning by my *mistress*. Have you any idea how that would look? How it would undermine everything we're trying to do?'

'It's all right for us to have an affair, though,' said Anthea. 'You're separated, I'm not married, and it's not as if it's taken into consideration in any way in court.'

He rolled his eyes and pushed her away. 'Have you taken leave of your senses? Earth to Planet Anthea? Wakey-wakey!' He tapped her forehead and sighed. 'I don't know,' he said. 'You used to be quite an intelligent woman. Perhaps it's the menopause or something.'

344

Exhausted and hurt, Anthea wanted to crawl away into a hole. It was true, it was difficult to think straight when she was so tired and worried. 'It's too early for the menopause,' she said weakly. 'I'm only . . .' – she deducted a few years for luck – '. . . forty-one.'

'Look at her Financial Statement for me, will you? See what the bitch is spending the money on. And, more importantly, what she isn't spending it on. Find some questions we can ask for the first hearing, will you? Focus on the lovers. I've had a quick look and it's clear that someone else is footing the bills.'

He left without saying goodbye, and Anthea went wearily back into the office to find Jenny on the phone: 'Don't you think it's terrible? That Paige threw so much stuff at him that he's got cuts all over, but he was the one who was arrested?'

Anthea hands were shaking as she took out Paige's Financial Statement to the Court and began to go through it. Her spending did seem to be surprisingly modest. Bill might have a point. Paige's luxuries were obviously being paid for by someone else. But it was difficult to concentrate after no sleep and Bill's fury. He was falling out of love with her, she could see that. Was she, Anthea, so very unlovable that any man who got to know her always walked away?

As she worked her way through Paige's figures she felt a prickling of interest. You could tell so much about a person from their bank statements, and Anthea had never seen Paige and Bill's – and now Paige's own – personal account before. She took her copy of Bill's bank statement out of her files again, then returned to Paige.

Hmm. Now, at last, she had the sense of a door opening and a ray of sunlight beyond. Think, Anthea, she told herself, think. You have to look after yourself.

Chapter 61

Once Sophie heard that Jess was going to help her mother to go through the divorce paperwork and Bill's bank statements, she shifted all her childcare and photo shoot arrangements round. There was no way she was going to let those two loose in fantasyland together. Sophie had visions of some kind of Magical Accounting whereby they decided that Bill had far more than he really had. She drove down to Kent, picking Jess up on the way.

'By the way,' said Jess. 'I didn't mention my going to see Mum to Jake. He still thinks we shouldn't get involved and he knows what my shifts are. We tape them to the fridge door so he knows where I am.'

'Jake has a lot of common sense,' said Sophie grimly. 'And you shouldn't be fibbing to someone you're about to marry.'

'It's not really a fib,' protested Jess. 'I just haven't mentioned that the shifts have changed.'

'Or that you changed them.' Sophie glanced at her sister and saw the shaft had hit home. 'What are you going to say if he phones?'

'Well I won't say anything much. It's just because of his bitch of an ex-wife . . .' She told Sophie the story of Cassie.

Paige opened the door looking grey. 'It's awful,' she said. 'I got your father's Financial Statement yesterday. It's worse than I thought. Raven Restore & Build is worthless, your father's loaded up with credit-card debts, he's living off a loan from the company and our only asset is The Rowans, which is heavily mortgaged.'

Paige thumped a daunting pile of papers down on the kitchen table. Sophie and Jess leafed through it, uncomprehending at first. Bill's salary, apparently, was less than Paige earned three mornings a week as a carer. And there was a letter from his accountant – Anthea, of course – saying that, in view of the current debts of the company, its value was just Bill's own reputation. 'If a sale was forced tomorrow, it is unlikely that a buyer would be found and therefore the company's value should be seen as nil.' Then there was the mortgage statement for The Rowans, for a little over half its value.

'If you split it that's still more than his original offer, Mum,' commented Sophie. But she had no idea what to look for. She flicked through the bank statements, curious to see what Bill was spending his money on.

'He's taking out an awful lot of cash,' Jess remarked. 'Look, two hundred pounds from one cash point and then another two hundred from another near by on the same day. And he did it again the following week and twice the week after. What is he doing with it?'

'Grocery bills? Train fares? Clothing? He needs to live.' Sophie ran her finger down the statement, frowning. It was more cash than she drew out, and she had three small children and a raft of babysitters to pay. 'No, he buys most necessities on his debit cards. Coffee? Maybe he has to buy coffees from those expensive coffee bars when he's travelling.'

'Perhaps we should just count up everything,' suggested Paige, 'and then maybe we can work out what he's doing with it.'

After two hours of patient counting they worked out that Bill had taken out twenty-five thousand pounds in cash over the year. By running company names on the credit and debit

347

card statements through Google, they also established what else he was spending money on. Some were easy. Supermarkets, train fares, a barber. A dentist. Shoes.

'Quite a few payments for the Black Prince, and the White Horse. And this is a restaurant too,' said Sophie, feeling anxious. 'He told us he couldn't afford to eat out.'

'These statements start before we split,' said Paige. 'But he never took me.' Jess saw her close her eyes as if in pain. 'He told me he was working late. But he was out two or three times a week.'

Sophie ran her finger up and down the list of figures, her eyes catching a list of dates. 'Look, Mum, this is the week you came to babysit for us when Harry had that business trip to Prague and I went with him. He was eating out because he doesn't cook.'

'I pre-cooked him meals to heat up every night. Plus left him instructions. Presumably he threw them all out, as they weren't there when I got back.'

The sums danced in front of Sophie's eyes. She knew how much restaurants cost, and she knew the figures in front of her did not denote a man eating on his own. They were sums for two.

Anthea. It was Anthea spending their father's money. The cow. But it also meant that Bill had lied to Sophie about how long the affair had been going on. Sophie felt sick. She knew her father wasn't perfect, but she hadn't thought he would lie to her.

'Dad says he's too broke to eat out now,' said Jess. 'But look, there are quite a few restaurant bills for the later months, after he'd left.' As the figures rolled on, the spending on restaurants, pubs, off-licences and even hotels continued. 'I can't believe that someone who was about to go bankrupt would actually spend so much.'

'It's that woman,' said Sophie. 'Anthea. I'm sure he wouldn't be going out like that if it wasn't for her. She's clearly as hard as nails and only out for what she can get.'

Jess tapped more company names from the credit card statements into her computer. 'A roof tile supplier. A plumber's merchant. A brick company. Someone who lives in a rented flat does not need ten thousand pounds' worth of roof tiles or eight grand of plumbing equipment. He's running the business on these cards.'

Sophie had the company accounts in front of her. There were just a few lines. 'Dad owes his company – i.e. himself – about seventy thousand pounds. Surely you can't be in debt to yourself? And Raven Restore & Build itself owes a huge debt – about nine hundred thousand pounds – to Anjo, the company that bought Orchard Park. It wipes out all the possible profit for the year. But wouldn't Anjo be paying Dad, not lending him money?'

Paige pushed her hair off her face and sighed. 'So I own forty-nine per cent of absolutely nothing.'

'Forty-nine per cent?'

'Yes. The shares my father left me. But if the company's worth nothing, then so are the shares.'

'Well, they must still have some value,' said Jess. 'The company has traded profitably for so many years. One bad year can't wipe it out.'

Paige looked at the accounts again. 'I'd just like to know why it's got so bad suddenly.'

Sophie resolved to ask her father herself. At the very least he deserved a right of reply.

At four, Sophie took Jess to the station so that she could get home before Jake.

'Those figures show what he's been up to, don't they?' said Jess. 'He's trying to make out that he's much poorer than he really is so that Mum doesn't get a fair share.'

'I'm sure everyone does that,' said Sophie, her heart heavy. 'But Dad isn't bad, he really isn't. It must be Anthea's doing.'

'Everyone likes to blame women for everything. I think Dad has to take some responsibility.'

After dropping Jess off, Sophie pulled into a lay-by and tried to remember what Bill had said about his affair with Anthea. He'd said that it was short. That he had allowed a friendship to go too far after Paige had the affair with George Boxer. George had moved in last summer, hadn't he? He hadn't been living in Martyr's Forstal when Sophie had her birthday party in the spring, and her parents had met him in the autumn.

But the trip to Prague that Harry and Sophie had taken – when Paige had babysat – had been *before* her birthday. So the Anthea thing had been going on for longer than her father said. He hadn't just been 'comforting her' when Sophie disturbed them at the party.

Sophie dialled her father's phone. 'Soph!' he said, sounding pleased.

'Hi Dad. I'm just going through a few figures with Mum, and wondered if you could clarify a few things for us.'

'I'll try.' He sounded jovial. And confident, as if he had nothing to hide.

The two main problems seem to be that, instead of having a salary or dividends, you've taken a loan from the company.'

'That's true. There was no other way of doing it without the company going under. Your mother simply doesn't understand the knife-edge I'm on.'

'Even so, you're still taking a loan from *yourself*. And charging yourself interest by the looks of it. And the reason why Raven Restore & Build has so little money is a huge loan it's taken from Anjo?'

'That's right.' He sighed heavily.

'Why did you need such a big loan if they were paying you to buy Orchard Park anyway?'

'Sophie this whole thing is far, far too complicated. I couldn't even begin to explain it to you in terms you'd understand. It's all about cash flow.'

'But if there's been nothing wrong with the cash flow for the past few years, and the accounts lodged at Companies House show that everything has been going well, why have you got problems in a year when you actually sold Orchard Park and should have had money coming in? Anyway, you seem to be running the company on credit cards, so surely they're your cash flow?'

'Sophie,' he said, sharply. 'Don't try to punch above your weight. You don't understand anything about business. You'll just have to take my word for it. I've been doing this since before you were born.'

'And if you were in such financial trouble, why did you go to so many restaurants, and even to hotels? And who did you go with? Was it Anthea?'

'Your mother is lying about that,' he said. 'She sees one entry for a restaurant and suddenly it's "Bill's going to restaurants all the time."' He mimicked a whine, then returned to his normal voice. 'I *occasionally* eat in a pub if I haven't got anything at home.'

'I saw the entries, Dad. With my own eyes. What about the week when Mum was looking after the girls? She left you meals to heat up but you spent over six hundred pounds in restaurants. Just in one week.'

'Sophie, how dare you?' he roared. 'You have no right to question me in this way, and no idea of the pressures I am under. I have behaved entirely honourably throughout this sorry affair your mother has got us into, and I do *not* deserve to have my actions questioned by an ignorant little girl. Do I make myself clear?'

'Yes,' said Sophie, her heart fracturing. 'Absolutely. Even to me.'

She drove back to The Rowans. 'Mum?' she said, sitting down at the kitchen table.

Paige looked wary.

'Mum, I'm sorry. I don't think Dad has . . .' – Sophie swallowed – '. . . behaved very well. I think those figures . . .' – she pointed to the bank statements – '. . . do show that he lied and is

351

still lying.' She tried to keep her voice steady. 'And I'm sorry, it was me who gave him the house keys. Last time I was here.' She felt the tears well up and her throat begin to tighten. She didn't know who her father was any more.

Paige stretched her hands across the table to take Sophie's hands in hers. 'Sh, sh, Sophie, no. I worked it out quite quickly and I knew why you did it. You mustn't cry . . . it isn't your fault. It really isn't. Your father is very, very clever about how he manipulates people and . . . I should have protected you from that. I should have left earlier.'

Sophie took a hand away to blow her nose and brush tears away. 'Why does he do it, Mum? Why? It's so unfair. So horrible.'

'I've asked myself that. And I've read up about it. People who do it – and there are women as well as men behaving like this, remember – are probably using it as an addictive behaviour, something that keeps the fear deep inside from taking over, because if they can control the people in their immediate circle they can kid themselves that their lives are under control.'

'What, you mean like an anorexic thinking that everything will be fine as long as they don't eat?' asked Sophie, who had had a brief struggle with anorexia when she was fifteen. She could remember the haunted sense of desperately measuring life out in calories and ounces, and the belief that if only she could eat less all her other problems would go away.

Paige nodded. 'People like Dad don't believe anyone can really love them, so they keep them close by force and manipulation, and by pitching them against each other. And addictive behaviours always escalate over time.'

'But we'd love Dad so much more if he *didn't* behave like this.'

'I don't think he really knows about love,' said Paige sadly. 'He only knows about getting his own way, and he knows he's right, which means everything he says and does is therefore justified.'

The telephone rang. It was Judy, about a date for the first

court hearing. Paige switched on speakerphone and told her about their findings.

'I'm afraid taking a lot of cash out of your account as a way of hiding it from a divorcing spouse is a very common trick,' said Judy, unsurprised. 'The reason why most take it out in relatively small instalments is to stay under the radar.'

'But surely the courts would see through it, then?' asked Paige.

Judy was non-committal. 'In theory, they should. But it can all be quite difficult to prove. Anyway, you can put that question to the judge at the first hearing and he will decide if Bill has to answer it.'

Sophie said she would help her mother sort out what questions her mother wanted to ask. Although it hurt. It hurt to realise that her father had lied to her all his life.

'Not all his life, darling,' said Paige, after they'd ended the call. 'Only over money, really.'

'He said you were stupid. And useless. And I believed it. Now I'm a mother myself I should have realised how much you do. And how well you do it.'

'I always felt I *was* a useless mother. And you're so good with Lottie, Bella and Summer. They're such lovely children and so happy . . . you have a much better relationship than I had with you and Jess.'

'Well, with Dad setting us all against each other, I'm not surprised.' Sophie felt weary and heartsick. 'I feel such a fool. I can't tell Harry, he'll say he told me so. Can I stay tonight?'

'Of course.' As Paige bustled around cooking supper and making up a bed, Sophie felt safe and looked-after. Just before she went to sleep, in the bedroom she'd had as a child, she got a text from Jake. 'Jess says thanks for the lift. Hope everything OK.'

She was relieved that Jess had, in the end, told Jake what she was doing, and texted back: 'Dad a complete liar, just like you said. Feel v stupid. xxx'

Her phone rang. 'Hi. Your text sounded down.'

Sophie tried not to cry. 'Well, discovering that everyone was right when they said your father is a liar and a cheat, and realising he's determined to leave your mother in absolute poverty, is not a nice experience. I daren't tell Harry, he'll only say "I told you so."'

'Well, that would be arrogant of him,' said Jake. 'Your father's so affable a lot of the time, it's hard to believe what he really gets up to. You have to see the figures to believe it. I think you've done really well today.'

'Has Jess told you about it?'

'Yes. She's gone to bed early and I'm just out walking clearing my head. It's nice to have someone to talk to. I thought I'd walk up to Regent's Park.'

'From Peckham?' asked Sophie, 'but that's miles.'

'I like long walks,' he replied, and she could hear his confident footsteps striding along the pavement. They carried on talking for half an hour, Jake teasing her gently until he said: 'Oh, I've been meaning to ask you. I'm doing a feature on hip London hotels for the travel department and I need a photographer — are you for hire? The first one is The English.'

'The English? I don't believe it! It's the hottest place in town.'

'Well, you know you either have to be a member to use their bar, or to have a room — well, they've given me a room and membership for a night. Do you fancy the gig?'

'Do I fancy it? I'd have to be mad not to.' Sophie felt better immediately. Work always smoothed out the edges of life.

'I'll text you the details. The deadline is quite soon, is that OK?'

Sophie smiled as she flipped her phone shut. Jake could always cheer you up.

She ought to contact Harry. He would think she was so stupid. Sophie's faith in herself and her own judgement was rocked. Suppose Harry turned out to be like her father? She'd been fooled once. And didn't they always say that you married people who were like your parents? She texted him 'Night night, xxxx' and switched her phone off.

When she fell asleep the comfort of The Rowans wrapped itself around her and her old bedroom seemed exactly the same as it had always been. But Sophie knew she'd changed for ever.

Chapter 62

Jess was careful not to mention her trip to Kent when Jake arrived back that evening, pretending that she'd spent the whole day reading bridal magazines and trying to tidy the flat.

'I talked to Anthea,' said Jake casually, as they were about to go to bed that evening.

'How?' Jess was jolted out of an article on 'Five Kinds of Bride.' Her heart dropped in a sudden, painful swoop.

He grinned at her. 'I took her out to dinner a few nights ago. Flattered her.'

'You never told me.'

'I'm telling you now. She's a very sexy woman. I can see why your father—'

'Did she tell you anything interesting?' Jess felt terrified. Jake and Anthea were quite close in age. Perhaps he . . .

His eyes danced in amusement. 'Your father's not going bankrupt. Reading between the lines.'

'Oh. OK.'

He pulled her to him. 'Do I detect a note of jealousy?'

Jess bit her lip nervously. 'Well . . .'

He smiled at her, and kissed her on the lips. 'I had to do what I had to do,' he murmured, 'to get the information I needed.'

Jess kissed him back, tasting red wine. 'It was worth it,' she whispered back, hoping that it was. 'Anything to contradict that monstrous pile of paperwork. It pretty much covered the kitchen table.'

He drew back. 'You sound as if you'd seen it?'

Jess was no good at lying. 'Mum, well, she described it.'

'Described it?' he said. 'Do people describe piles of paper?'

Jess bit her lip.

'Jess,' he said, holding her by the shoulders. 'Look at me. Are you lying to me?'

'No, not really. But Mum was in a state, so I did nip down and I must have forgotten to tell you.'

He let her go so suddenly she fell against the sofa. 'I don't believe this,' he said in a low tone. 'I ask you one simple request, which is that you and I deal with your family together, when we're both there, that we tell the truth to each other, and you go behind my back and—'

'It wasn't behind your back. I was going to tell you.'

'When? We've been together all evening and you haven't mentioned it.'

Jess didn't dare look at him.

Jake picked up his coat. 'I don't think I can take much more of this. I'm going for a walk.' The door slammed behind him.

He stayed out two nights that time, as Jess waited, her eyes sore from crying, not daring to confront the ever-growing pile of bridal preparations that cluttered the flat: confetti-like paper-work, the first wedding presents, recently unwrapped, and her wedding shoes, of very high-heeled satin, which she was trying to break in without getting them dirty. She shoved them under the sofa so that they couldn't reproach her with their air of pristine perfection. She might have lost it all. She knew she shouldn't have lied. She'd promised not to get too involved.

Would he forgive her?

Sophie called, and said that Jake had called her during a long walk to Regent's Park, but he didn't seem to have said anything to her about any argument, and Jess's pride prevented her from saying anything either.

When he walked back through the door he smiled down at her. 'Jess, I've been thinking.'

'Yes?'

'You have one more chance. Complete honesty between us or it's off. Is that fair enough?'

She nodded. 'Yes, of course. I understand.'

'When you speak to your mother on the phone I must be in the room. Is that clear?'

She nodded.

'And we go down to The Rowans together, all right?'

'But . . . what if you're busy? If I asked you . . .?'

'We go down together. We are either a team or we are not. If I am too busy we cannot go. I believe a marriage can only survive on complete openness and honesty.'

'Of course, we're a team,' she agreed.

'Good.' He looked down at her. 'Now then . . .' His eyes danced. 'Your punishment.' He leant down and kissed her on the lips. 'Because we're all agreed that you need to say sorry, aren't we?'

Jess felt her breath tighten and her legs turn to liquid, as she dared not look him in the eye. 'I am sorry,' she whispered. 'Really . . . very . . . sorry.'

He slid his hands down her body and slowly lifted her T-shirt, as every nerve end tingled in fear-tinged anticipation. 'I don't think you quite understand what sorry means,' he murmured as he unclipped her bra and pulled it off her shoulders. It fell to the ground. Her skin prickled in the cool air.

Chapter 63

The first court appearance went well for Bill. He came back to Anthea's flat in a good mood.

'Got a man as a judge,' he said as Anthea put a ready meal in the microwave. 'Makes a difference not to have a silly woman with PMT on the case, don't you think?'

'I'm sure a woman judge would be just as good,' said Anthea, deciding not to point out that the age of the average judge would probably rule out PMT in any case.

Bill snorted derisively. Anthea wished she could be like Paige, who would have had no trouble in cooking Bill a proper meal no matter how busy she'd been. As Bill often reminded her. But Paige didn't work. Anthea suppressed resentment and put two M&S cod mornay down in front of them. 'Tell me everything.'

'Paige submitted a whole list of stupid questions, and at one point the judge had to tell her that this wasn't a companies court, it was the family court. She sat there, looking crushed – you know, her "poor little me" act – but the judge wasn't having any of it. I could tell he sympathised with me.' Bill chortled and poured himself a glass of wine. 'The fact of the matter is that Paige hasn't got a leg to stand on. No court in the land is going to award her a fat settlement now.'

'But she still hasn't accepted your original offer?' Anthea couldn't see why, or how, Paige was managing to fight, and she had to suppress another twinge of unease. 'It is going to the next stage?'

'It'll go to the next stage unless she runs out of money. Some of the questions the judge allowed through are for you to answer, by the way.'

When Anthea looked at the list of questions that the court had authorised Paige to ask, she didn't feel quite as confident as Bill did. How much was Orchard Park sold for? Why was a further loan needed from the company on top of the sale price? Please supply a copy of the application form for the mortgage taken out on The Rowans ('We'll just tell them the bank has lost it,' said Bill). What was the mortgage needed for? ('Ridiculous,' spluttered Bill. 'I have bad debts, people who don't pay their bills. Of course I need money.')

Anthea frowned as she read down the list. 'These questions imply that you're not presenting your financial situation honestly,' she said. 'Whatever answers we give.'

'Not presenting it honestly?' Bill thumped his fist down on the table. 'Why am I always surrounded by idiots?'

Anthea flinched. 'I just thought I ought to point out that if we answer all these questions we'll destroy your case, although I suppose we could always "forget" to include documentation or say that financial institutions haven't got back to us. I mean, we can't lie on these statements, it's perjury.'

'Of course we can lie. The court isn't going to check. Don't be ridiculous.' Bill leant over so she could see his red eyes. 'Don't tell me you've gone over to The Bitch's side!'

'Of course, I haven't, I—'

'Well, then! Here are the answers. What do I need the money for? Because I'm in debt and fear personal bankruptcy! What do I need the mortgage for? Because my company has been awarded contracts and I need money to fulfil them! What do I need a two-thirds share of The Rowans for? Because people are dependent on me for employment and without sufficient capital my company will collapse!'

'Don't shout,' said Anthea softly. 'I was just thinking that they might want details of the debts and contracts, and exactly how much money you'd need . . .'

'Well, they can't fucking have details, can they? It's not a companies court, it's a family court. As the judge said. We'll just tell them it's far too complicated. And don't tell me not to shout, you're *making* me shout. With your daft questions.'

Anthea was worried, though. Presenting a case that was true as far as it went was one thing. Lying to make that case stand up was another. Her professional reputation was at stake. What would happen to her livelihood then? She told herself that Bill's behaviour was the result of stress, and that once the divorce was through he would go back to his normal loving self. As he poured himself another drink, she also wondered if perhaps she should suggest – once the case was over, of course – that perhaps he was drinking a bit too much.

Meanwhile, she needed to address her side of the problem.

Two months later Anthea sat in a Harley Street waiting room, reading an old copy of *Country Life* and wishing it was all over. She found it difficult to function with the thought of a surgeon snipping away at her, and the idea of changing dressings terrified her, along with everything she would have to do to avoid infection and prevent scarring.

She sighed. But she and Bill hadn't had sex since *that* conversation, and when she'd told him, very diffidently, that she thought she might 'do something' about 'that problem down there, you know, the, er, Finchley Road problem', he nodded and smiled, and said he thought she was very wise. She was rather relieved – but also slightly hurt – that he hadn't offered to come with her, but then the date of the Financial Dispute Resolution, the second court hearing, came through and it was scheduled for the following day. Bill seemed cheerful and confident about it all, but she knew how quickly that slipped into depression and anger. Perhaps it was just as well she was away for the day. He wished her good luck very tenderly and had risked a lingering kiss on the lips in the office, even though Jenny could have come in at any moment. The gesture warmed her, and gave her courage.

Mr Cooper had a chiselled face, a lock of greying hair only just ruining the symmetry of a boyish cut, and he wore a pin-striped suit. She told him, stammering with humiliation, what she wanted. He looked at her as if musing over an unusual specimen in the British Museum, put on a pair of reading glasses, got out a form and began to fire questions at her.

'Hmm,' he said to most of her replies. 'Hmm. Hmm. Weight? Smoker? Hmm. Hmm. Alcohol consumption? Mmm. Right.' He slapped the folder shut and leant back. 'Why do you want this operation?'

'Well,' Anthea forced the words out. 'My um, boyfriend and I were, um . . . trying to . . . um . . .'

'Have sex?' he suggested briskly.

Anthea nodded. 'And he couldn't. He said it was because my . . . er . . .' She was surprised that she was finding this so difficult. She wasn't usually so lacking in confidence.

'Vagina?'

She nodded again. 'Was too, you know, er . . . well, flabby, he couldn't really . . . Well, he said it was a bit like throwing a sausage up the Finchley Road.'

Mr Cooper put his pen down. 'Just pop up on the couch so I can examine you. Would you like a chaperone?' He swished the curtain shut around her. She could hear him washing his hands and the rustle of surgical gloves.

'No.' Anthea wanted as few people as necessary around. She wanted to pretend she was someone else completely as she stripped off her pants and tights.

'Just relax,' he told her. Anthea nearly laughed. As if.

'Hmm. Hmm. Hmm. Well, that's fine. You can get dressed now.'

When she drew the curtain aside he was sitting on the edge

362

of his desk, looking serious and confiding. He indicated she should sit on the chair beside him. 'I'm afraid I'm going to be completely honest with you,' he began and her heart plummeted. She was deformed. No one had told her. That was why all her long-term relationships had failed.

'Is your boyfriend's penis of a normal size?'

'Oh yes, absolutely.'

'And had you had any problems in your sex life before this incident?'

She shook her head. 'I mean, he does get worried, and it's been a bit stressful because his wife . . . his company . . . he's separated now so it's all all right, but we have . . . well, sex has never been the major thing about our relationship, but . . .'

'But you have managed it without difficulty?'

She nodded, feeling her cheeks go pink.

'Right. OK. Now, I'm going to show you something. Are you sure you don't want a chaperone?'

Anthea shook her head vigorously and let out a small shriek as she saw what had come up on the screen on the wall.

'These are twenty normal vaginas.' He pointed to them with a pencil. 'As you see, very different in many ways. But they are all fully functional sexually and, provided there's no erectile dysfunction, even the smallest normal penis would have no problem in giving or obtaining pleasure and a full sexual act.'

Anthea was beginning to wonder if he was a bit perverted, when he called up another set of slides. 'These are vaginas where there has been significant damage, often after a traumatic birth, or, sadly, rape. Or just where, as some people have longer earlobes than others, there are flaps of skin that make women feel very self-conscious. I never operate on the first category. I will operate on the second.'

He switched off the slides. 'Your vagina belongs in the first set of slides. There is nothing wrong or unusual about it, or any reason why your boyfriend should have any problem. And because the problem isn't physical the solution isn't surgical.'

Disappointment washed over Anthea. She had been hoping that Mr Cooper would sort it all out. 'Please help,' she said. 'Please.'

'Listen.' He put his glasses on again. 'Many men think their penises are too small and an increasing number of women are starting to worry about how their vaginas look or feel. But the vast majority of penises and vaginas get together very happily indeed – it's what goes on at the other end, in people's heads, that gets in the way. In my experience, an accusation of small penis or large vagina is never made in the context of a loving relationship and such remarks are often made to hurt or insult, rather than to identify a real problem.' He held up his hand. 'I can't say that's what's behind your boyfriend's statement. But I can say that this is something that can only be solved by talking openly and honestly. Maybe counselling. Not surgery. Surgery can only solve specific problems. It can't change your life. It can't make your relationship work. I'm sorry.'

He took his glasses off and leant back, signalling that the consultation was at an end. 'I really am sorry,' he said again. 'You probably hoped for some answers today, and all I've given you are more questions. But you're an attractive, intelligent woman and in theory you could still have a child, and I wouldn't want to see you mutilate yourself in a way that might cause problems further down the line, such as tightening your vagina so that you couldn't give birth safely.' He got up and handed her her coat. 'Good luck,' he said as her eyes filled with tears.

'Miss Jones?' he said as she opened the door. She turned back.

'There are other surgeons who will do the operation. But you deserve better.'

Chapter 64

Sophie met Jake in the English Bar, the ultra-chic members-only bar on the ground floor of The English hotel. She wasn't used to feeling dowdy, but compared to the wine-dark walls and deep red leather chairs, and the girls who fluttered around, kissing men in black and laughing confidently, Sophie suddenly saw herself as middle-aged. She climbed up on a leather stool and leaned her elbows on the bar. Was her skirt too short? Were black opaque tights too safe? But she could see herself in the mirrors behind the bar and there was a sparkle, the anticipation that tomorrow might be different from today, that she remembered from long ago.

Jake strode in, clearly at home, nodding at the guys on the door, smiling at the bartender and kissing Sophie on both cheeks. He perched on a stool beside her, his long legs tangled casually round the chrome.

'So, Sophie. You need a martini.'

'Do I?' Sophie had planned to order a spritzer.

'Yup. Doctor's orders. You need strong liquor to revive you.' He ordered two cocktails, chatted to the barman and then swung back to her with a smile. 'So how's life? Really?'

'Fine.'

He raised an eyebrow, clearly disbelieving. 'It hurts, doesn't it? Your father being such a fraud?'

In spite of everything Sophie's stomach flipped. Her father had been her rock. He might be bad-tempered, hard-drinking and difficult to please, but sometimes she still couldn't quite believe that he was no longer the Dad she turned to, the one that always had an answer to everything. And here was Jake stripping away his credentials as casually as someone tearing cling-film off a sandwich. 'I know,' she forced herself to say. 'He's an out-and-out liar. He always has been.' She tried to sound casual as she took a quick swig of her cocktail and felt the alcohol warm her inside. 'But I'm fine about it.'

'Sure you are.' Jake touched her on the shoulder in sympathy.

She felt like flinging herself into the muscularity of his arms and sobbing, so she didn't dare speak.

'Incidentally, I looked up that company that bought Orchard Park. I can't find any trace of it anywhere, so it hasn't been investing anywhere else in Britain. But if you're not a forensic accountant there's a limit to how far you can go.' He swigged his drink and looked at her. 'Sophie, I've never seen you look so miserable. You look gorgeous, of course, but your eyes are very sad.' He touched her cheek with tenderness. 'Is it just your Dad? How's Harry? He's not playing around, is he?' He ran the edge of his hand along her arm and her skin fizzed. 'Because if he is, I'll punch the living daylights out of him.' He smiled down at her.

'I wish he would, in a way. He's just being dull and ponderous and terribly responsible. And not really talking to me about anything.' She knew she wasn't being quite fair, because it was she who wasn't confiding in Harry. But she simply didn't want to. Harry was part of the past. He seemed a long way away, as blurred and unsteady as a black-and-white home movie. Sophie as a daughter, wife and mother was a Sophie she could hardly remember. That Sophie had disappeared when she discovered that her father was a liar.

She remembered what it was like before she felt so responsible for everyone. When any encounter had an endless sense of potential. How you felt special and touched with fairy dust. No longer weighted down with chores and responsibilities. To Jess and the girls . . . and now Mum and Dad. They never seemed to realise that sometimes Sophie felt invisible, unappreciated . . . hurt.

'Sophie, I get the feeling you give so much more than you get back,' murmured Jake. 'I know how you've tried to help Jess in the past. And now your parents.' Jake tangled his fingers gently in hers in a gesture of support. 'You need someone to take care of *you*. For a change.'

'Really, I'm fine.' She could feel his skin burning against hers. His hand felt dry and strong.

'Sophie. You run around rescuing everyone. You give all the time. No wonder you're angry – you're not being appreciated.'

Sophie wondered how he knew. 'I *have* to take care of everyone. They can't take care of themselves. There's only me, and I'm . . . well, I'm getting so tired of it all. Jess was hopeless until she met you, and I've tried to look after her all my life.' Sophie slid her hand away from Jake's.

'I know how you feel,' said Jake. 'Jess is so young and she does need looking after. Sometimes we have arguments because she doesn't realise that. I think you and I are very alike in many ways. Kindred spirits. But I think, underneath it all, my beautiful Sophie, that you have self-esteem problems. You really don't think anyone can love you unless you make yourself indispensable.'

Sophie was surprised. 'I don't think I've got low self-esteem. Jess tells me I think rather a lot of myself.'

Jake gently stroked a lock of hair off Sophie's face. 'Jess can't see through to the real Sophie. I can. A very beautiful, caring woman who will go the extra mile for anyone. Even if they don't ask her to.'

Sophie swallowed down the resentment that she often felt, especially towards Jess and Paige. The years of her father saying, 'We must look after them, mustn't we? They're typical women, they aren't clever. They don't think things through.' Maybe Jake was right. Maybe he could see the real Sophie.

'Look,' said Jake, 'why don't we treat ourselves? Let's have a bottle of champagne from the mini-bar in the room I've been lent. It's all on expenses. And you can decide how you want to photograph the place.'

'The decor here is legendary,' said Sophie, getting up eagerly. 'I've seen it in magazines, and I have always – always – longed to see what the rooms are actually like. Suede carpets, I gather.'

'That's only the half of it,' he said, steering her towards the lift.

'When's Jess arriving?'

'Late shift, so midnight, I suppose.'

They laughed over the lift, which had symbols instead of floor numbers, and mirrors all round. When they reached their floor it had suede floors and walls, and they were softly padded. Jake and Sophie burst out laughing. 'Do you think it's so that drunk guests have something to bounce off?' she asked.

'Sh,' Jake put his fingers to his lips. 'We have to tiptoe through the temple of modernity. Not disturb anyone by having a rational thought.'

They shut the hotel room door behind them, still giggling, and Jake looked down at her, his arm against the door. 'Champagne?'

'You bet.' Sophie sat on the enormous bed, bouncing slightly. 'This could take a family of six.'

He pushed the cork out of the champagne bottle and filled two glasses, handing one to her. 'Cheers.'

He ranged round the room, testing out gadgets 'When the doors are shut you can hardly see them. How mad is that? Presumably people go feeling around the walls with their fingertips until eventually the cupboard door springs open.' Eventually he topped up her glass and pulled up a chair opposite her, put his glass down on the bedside table and leant forward to unfasten the top button on her shirt.

Sophie was slightly embarrassed. But Jess always said that Jake had a very good eye for clothes, and the top button probably looked better undone. When he undid the second button she wasn't quite sure what to do. 'Jake? When will Jess be here?'

He smiled without answering and swiftly continued unbuttoning her shirt, taking the glass out of her hand and pushing the shirt off her shoulders before she realised what was happening. She tried to clutch the shirt back but he waved it in the air, just out of her reach, then flung it into the corner of the room.

'Jake!'

He ran his hands around the lines of her bra. 'Now this, Sophie, is much too pretty to be hidden. Isn't it? You wouldn't be putting something like this on without wanting to show it off? Would you?'

'Well, I . . .' Sophie wondered if this was all about the 'underwear as outerwear' trend. Some women – people who knew more about fashion than she did – probably thought it was quite normal to sit in hotel rooms with male friends in just their bra, and Jake was very knowledgeable about all that sort of thing.

His hand slid behind her back and suddenly the bra was unclasped. It fell forward with the weight of her breasts and he slipped it off almost before she noticed. Topless was fine, she told herself hastily, still seeking for the rational explanation that seemed further and further away. French women went around topless all the time. In public. On beaches. She would just make some polite conversation and retrieve her clothes as quickly as possible. 'Um . . . should we look at what I might photograph now?'

'What beautiful breasts,' he said dreamily, stroking first her left breast and then her right with one finger. 'I've always wondered. And these . . .' – he traced his fingers over a few silvery stretch marks – '. . . are just stripes of honour. Signs that you're not as perfect as you look.'

Sophie had never worried about her stretch marks before, and she tried to ignore the tingling sensation that trailed after his hand. 'Jake, I don't think . . . I mean we're friends, aren't we, and I wouldn't like to do anything that I couldn't tell Jess or Harry about.'

He circled both nipples and they obediently hardened as Sophie tried to ignore the liquid desire darting through her body.

'Ah, but you already have,' he murmured. 'Lots of times. Secret phone calls, texts, meetings . . . mmm?'

She tried to get up. 'Jake, we should think before we do anything we can't take back. We owe it to . . .'

He lifted her up and threw her on the bed, kissing her. 'Trust me, Sophie. This is the right thing to do.' His weight pinned her down and her body couldn't help stirring in response, although she was beginning to feel slightly frightened. 'Jake,' she said, when he raised his head. 'Let's talk about this.'

'I believe in talking,' he said. 'How about you starting off with saying how much we've wanted to do this ever since we met.'

'Well, I have, quite, but . . .'

'Sophie, this is a little bit of time that no one will know about. A secret that no one will ever find out about. You and I. We deserve each other. You know we do.'

'But Jess and . . .'

'Sophie, Sophie. I think you and I have something special and different that stands outside time . . .' – his hands cupped her breasts and she tried not to gasp – '. . . and convention and the rules.' He leant down again so that his lips were close to hers. 'I think we could heal each other in a way that no one else could understand,' he murmured. 'You know what I thought when I first saw you?' He stopped, just inches away from her lips.

Sophie didn't dare answer. She remembered the way he'd looked at her, how they'd connected at that Sunday lunch back at The Rowans.

'I thought . . . I chose the wrong sister.'

'Don't say that,' begged Sophie, the last few tendrils of desire disappearing at the thought of the pain she would cause Jess. And Harry. She twisted away from him but he caught her. 'Jake, please. I am so fond of you.' She tried to wriggle off the huge bed. 'But you're marrying Jess, and I love Harry.'

He moved on top of her, pinning her hands down on either side of her head. 'No you don't. You're bored stiff of Harry. I can see it every time you look at him.'

'Jake, this is wrong . . .' But he silenced her by kissing her. She tried to struggle, but he was far too strong and heavy. She tried to push his tongue out of her mouth with hers, but it only seemed to encourage him.

He lifted his head again. 'I love the show of reluctance. If you can look me in the eyes and tell me, honestly, that you haven't fantasised about this moment, that you haven't had erotic dreams of me, that you haven't thought of me when that ox Harry was grinding up and down on top of you . . .' His eyes gleamed. 'I'll let you go.'

Sophie looked into his dark eyes and tried to force herself to lie. She opened her mouth but couldn't make the words come out. A tear slid down her cheek at the sound of Harry's name. If Harry was here she would be safe. But she hadn't told him where she was going. She'd said she was meeting Caroline about *Shore Style* and would be back late.

He grinned. 'Honest little Sophie. Far too honest for your own good. Sweet, really. And now you will get what you have always dreamed of.'

'Dreams are one thing,' Sophie tried to free herself again. 'But the reality is that I love Harry. I do . . .' She could hear pleading in her voice, as Jake turned her over and began unzipping her skirt. 'No!' she tried to shout, but he pressed her face into the pillow.

'Harry's like your father. Only interested in himself. You'll see. When you're fifty you'll be rifling through his bank statements for the divorce court, while he takes a younger mistress. Face it.'

She couldn't say that Harry wasn't like that because her face was in the pillow. And he might be right. She'd misjudged Bill and Jake. Why not Harry? A terrible bleakness overwhelmed her.

Afraid of suffocating, she stopped struggling, resolving not to try to fight until his guard was down. It was her only hope because he was far, far too strong for her. She lay still as he pinned her hands behind her back with one hand, and pulled down her skirt and tights with the other. 'Good girl,' he murmured in her ear, then flipped her over on her back. 'You know you want it really. This way you don't have to feel guilty. It isn't your fault.' He grinned. 'Guilt-free adultery. What could be better?'

'Consensual love,' spat Sophie as he held her hands down again while he unbuckled his belt.

'Any more of that . . .' She saw his penis spring from his trousers as he knelt between her legs, one hand still pinning hers down. '. . . and I'm really going to have to hurt you.' He looked at her naked body. 'Mmm. Quite nice. A few more stretch marks over the tummy, and not quite perhaps the tautest . . .'

'Jake, don't do this,' she begged. 'We've got a lifetime of being almost brother and sister ahead of us. This will affect our relationship for ever.'

'Oh quite,' he replied. 'You won't be confiding much in your sister in future, will you? You won't be seeing any more of us than strictly necessary, will you? Because that would mean admitting to all those flirtatious texts and secret assignations. You don't think she'd ever forgive you those, do you? Mmm?'

The weight of his body landed on her as she desperately tried to escape. But it was too late. 'Help!' she shouted. 'Help!'

'Shout all you like. One of the selling points about this hotel is the padded walls. So that guests won't be disturbed by each other's nights of passion or television at high volume.' He sounded as if he was quoting the brochure.

'No, Jake, this is wrong.'

His eyes were close to hers. 'Tell me you don't want it.'

'I don't,' she cried. 'I don't. Stop. Jake. I'm sorry we got this far, but please stop. I don't want it.'

'You're a liar,' he said, plunging into her. 'You're a filthy, dirty liar. And you know it.'

She cried out in pain and detached her mind to pretend she was someone else or somewhere else, counting up to twenty, fifty, two hundred and fifty, until he slumped on top of her, and then rolled off. Feeling bruised and tainted, she slid off the bed, collected her clothes and showered, turning on the hot water and furiously scrubbing herself over and over again to eradicate the shock of being marked by him, deep inside. For ever.

He leant across the door to the shower. 'Trying to wash me off? Well, I'm glad to see you're not planning on making any silly rape allegations to the police. Once we'd had testimony from the bartenders that you willingly came upstairs, and once I'd said that you'd admitted you fantasised about me – which, being a rather transparent little Sophie, I think you might have trouble denying – I'm not sure the case would stand up. Not to mention all those flirtatious emails between us. I don't think your husband or your sister would ever forgive you.' He looked her up and down, and she tried to cover herself with her hands. 'In fact, seeing you like that makes me want you again.'

'Jake, please don't. I won't tell the police. I don't want trouble any more than you do.'

He laughed. 'I'm sure you don't. Because if you do tell anyone you'll destroy them. And dear little Sophie doesn't like to hurt people, am I right? And as for tearing apart Jess's life, your own life, your children's lives, and then having neither Harry nor Jess ever forgive you . . . Harry's not the sort of man who'd want you when you've been had by another man. And I don't blame him.'

Sophie felt too sick to reply.

She turned away, her heart ticking furiously. He urinated noisily and then left the shower room. She sighed with relief.

373

Her hands seemed like fingers and thumbs as she dressed, trying to pull her tights over not-quite-dry legs and the zip of her skirt sticking as she hurriedly tried to pull it up. He watched her and she half expected him to pull her back and make her do something else. Hurry, she begged her wooden fingers. Hurry.

Once the door was open and she was halfway through it she turned back. 'This is what happened with Cassie and her sister, isn't it? You seduced or raped Camilla, and she had a nervous breakdown because she couldn't tell anyone about it. When Cassie finally found out she went for you and you punched her from here to hell and back?'

He laughed. 'You've got it. Sisters always betray each other. Think of all those little betrayals, all down the years. The day you gave her favourite doll to Oxfam behind her back. The time you told your father that it was Jess who'd taken his best pen . . .' He laughed. 'She'll see this as just one more in a long line.' He took a sip of champagne. 'And as for Harry . . .' He laughed. 'No, really, Sophie, if you want to keep your life intact you'll keep quiet. And if you don't . . . I've got quite enough evidence to show how much you colluded in creating this situation.'

She made it to the ladies' room in the foyer before she vomited into a smart steel sink, watched by an impassive attendant who silently handed her a towel.

Chapter 65

Anthea left the clinic in a daze. Mr Cooper had said . . . she carefully spelt it out in her own mind . . . that Bill had been trying to hurt her with his comments. That he had invented the whole 'Finchley Road' problem. And Mr Cooper had no reason to lie. Indeed, he had every reason to garner another customer. He was a stranger. He didn't care about either Anthea or Bill.

He was just telling her what he saw.

And if Bill hadn't been telling the truth about this, then . . .? Anthea's eyes began to blur with tears. Perhaps Bill was sexually insecure and had invented the problem to take the pressure off his own performance. Surely he hadn't meant to lie? Not as such. But, on the other hand, there were Paige's financial statements, that indicated she was far from the extravagant spender that Bill always described. She was beginning to wonder what or who to believe.

She saw George Boxer on the train on her way back from London. She was walking through a carriage looking for somewhere to sit. He lifted his head and looked directly at her. And through her, as if she didn't exist.

Anthea flushed. There was no need for him to be like that. She turned her head away and passed him without acknowledgement.

But the train was crowded. There was barely even standing room, but in the end Anthea found a spot at the other end of George's carriage. Her feet were aching and she swayed with the train's movement. She had to think. Ever since Bill moved in she had been so very tired. He came to bed around one, always switching on the light and making little effort to undress quietly. His sleep was restless, probably the result of too much alcohol. She was worried about how much he drank. Perhaps he was an alcoholic, perhaps that was why he was so angry and difficult. The divorce was also a terrible strain on him. She must be understanding.

She felt a presence at her shoulder. It was George. 'Take my seat,' he said, quite kindly. 'You look done in. I'd be glad to stand.'

'That's fine,' she said stiffly. 'I'm quite capable of standing myself. Thank you for the offer.'

'No, you're not,' he said. 'You look terrible.' He took her elbow and propelled her back to his seat, recapturing it just as someone else was about to take it. 'There.'

She was too tired to fight. 'Thanks. I'll just rest for a short time and then you can have the seat back.' She put her head on her arms and slept.

When she woke up the fat couple opposite had gone and George was in their place, reading a newspaper. 'Hi,' he said. 'I'm sorry I cut you dead earlier. I just don't like lies being spread about me.'

'I didn't lie. I saw you.'

'You saw me having lunch with Paige, and putting my hand on hers because she was worried about Jess. On reflection I think perhaps that was an unwise thing to do, but it was not evidence of an affair.'

Wasn't it? Bill's sureness had been so convincing. Ever since then he had spoken confidently of 'Paige's lover' and 'Paige's affair'. She met George's steady gaze with an enquiring look.

'I'm not having an affair with her,' he said. 'I never have and it's unlikely I ever will. Paige is a friend. I am lending her the money to pay her legal fees because I don't like being lied about. Does that make everything clear, or am I going to hear more rumours next week, about me funding my lover's divorce?'

'Not from me,' murmured Anthea, blushing.

'Of course, no one can prove they haven't had an affair.'

The same thought had occurred to Anthea. She looked at him again, and remembered the 'Finchley Road'. She made a judgement. 'In fact, I do believe you.'

George smiled. 'Good. Thank you.' He went back to his paper. When they reached Canterbury he folded it and got up. They got off the train together. 'Will you tell Bill? About the legal fees?'

Anthea hesitated, then shook her head. It was the first time she'd acknowledged something about Bill that had been trying to push itself up from her subconscious for several months. He couldn't be trusted. He twisted facts.

'Look after yourself,' he added. 'That lovely spark has gone out of you.'

Lovely spark? What was he talking about? Anthea still felt as if she was in a dream. When she got back Bill had left her a note. 'Staying in the flat until after the case. We don't want anyone to get the wrong idea.' More pretence, thought Anthea. Her life seemed to be based upon pretence, fraud and deception. It was so far from what she'd intended. She didn't think she could even recognise the truth any longer.

Anthea fell asleep at eight, woke up briefly to get undressed around eleven, then slept until eight the following morning. When she got up she went to Bill's wardrobe and found one of the two new pairs of trousers he'd bought and compared them with a pair of his old ones. Waist 44 inches, compared with waist 38 inches. Could he really have made such a mistake? And a XXL shirt. She could hear Jenny's voice in her head. 'His clothes are hanging off him. Poor Bill.'

Anthea made herself a cup of coffee as she thought it through. She went to her desk and wrote a letter, then made three photocopies of it.

Chapter 66

Sophie had to make things right. She felt grubby, stained and overwhelmed with guilt. She could barely look Harry in the eye. She buried herself in her work, and in looking after the girls, spending extra time reading stories and playing games. She finished *Shore Style* and the publishers declared it 'brilliant'. She cleaned Harry's rugby boots for him when she found them hidden in a smelly carrier bag, in secret penance, and cried over their stolid, muddy innocence. She avoided calling Jess.

But she couldn't let her marry Jake. She had to do something.

All her old confidence had gone, though. Once she'd been so sure as to what was right and wrong. She wouldn't have hesitated. The important thing was to stop her sister marrying an abusive, manipulative and possibly violent man. However, Jake was right when he said that if she simply told Jess what had happened, Jess would blame her and was likely to swallow any explanation of Jake's, particularly when accompanied by the revelation of flirtatious texts and secret assignations. And Harry – well, how could she tell him? Harry was a stranger to her these days. Maybe she'd pushed him away. Maybe he suspected she was having an affair with Jake.

Maybe he didn't love her any more. Perhaps Jake was right. Sophie screamed as Harry's hand landed on her shoulder, then

379

recovered herself. 'Sorry,' she said. 'Sorry. You gave me a fright.'
She tried to stop her hands shaking.

'You're always doing that these days,' said Harry. 'And you're
not sleeping either. What on earth is wrong? Is it your father?'

She wondered if she could tell him, and watch his love for
her drain away. 'Trust me,' said Harry. 'Tell me.'

She heard Jake's voice in the hotel room, saying 'trust me',
and the nausea engulfed her again. 'Sorry, Harry.' She suddenly
broke away and threw up into the sink.

Harry held her hair back from her face, then handed her a
glass of water. 'Rinse. Perhaps you ought to go away for a bit.
Have a change of scene? You might come back feeling better.'
He sounded as if he wanted the problem out of the way. Go
away and come back better. Don't bother me with it.

As she stared at him over the glass of water he added, 'Try
not to feel too bad about your father. He fools a lot of the
people a lot of the time. And you were a child when he first
started to manipulate you.'

She seized at the excuse as she spat the water out. 'Yes. But
I feel so . . . stupid. Such a fool, and . . . and I think Jess is
making the same mistake.' She tried to think about what she'd
read about the early warning signs of abuse. 'Jake's another
completely selfish man. All that stuff about controlling what she
wears. And those romantic gestures that made her cancel
evenings with her friends.'

'I thought all the makeover stuff was pretty spooky,' said Harry,
standing back with his arms folded, a slight frown on his face. 'But
you can't go telling her not to marry him just because of that.
Why don't you go down and stay with your mother for a bit?'

Sophie thought of the comfort and warmth of The Rowans.
And her mother. Bill had denigrated her so often that it had
never occurred to her that Paige was the only person in the
world she could confide in. 'Good idea,' she said, trying to look
as normal as possible, picking up the potato peeler again and
focussing on supper. 'Thanks. I can help her with the divorce.'

Harry continued to look puzzled. 'You would tell me if it was something more than just your father, wouldn't you?'

'Yes, of course, Harry,' she said wearily. One day, she added mentally.

As he turned to go back upstairs to his study she called him back. 'Harry, if I did something really wrong, would you forgive me?'

He looked hunted. 'Well, er . . . wouldn't that depend what it was? I mean, um, I can't really answer that, not unless I knew what . . . um . . .'

Right. So much for unconditional love.

'I mean, if you murdered a child or something . . .' He sounded hopeless.

'Well I haven't,' she said crisply. 'So don't worry about it.'

Sophie slept in the spare room that night, so that she wouldn't disturb Harry with her nightmares. 'You have to work in the morning.'

'I don't mind,' said Harry, but she could see that he looked relieved.

The following day Paige buzzed open the gates of The Rowans, as Lottie, Bella and Summer ran screaming off down the garden. 'Sophie.' She wrapped her arms around her when she saw the expression on her daughter's face.

'We can't let Jake marry her,' sobbed Sophie. 'We can't. We have to save her somehow.'

Paige drew her into the kitchen. 'I don't think you can ever save anyone from the wrong man, Sophie. My friends tried when I was marrying your father and I just cut them out of my life.'

Sophie sank down on to a kitchen chair and blew her nose. 'Do I look as if I've been crying? I don't want the girls to see.'

'They're in Sparrow Palace. I can hear them. They'll play for hours. Tell me everything.'

And Sophie did.

Paige hugged her. 'I'm so sorry. That terrible man. How is Harry about it all? I hope he's supporting you.'

'I haven't told him. Although he clearly minds that I'm no longer happy, smiling Sophie. I don't think he'd want me if he thought I'd had an affair, or if I'd been raped. It's like a burglar crapping on your duvet. You'd throw it out afterwards.'

'Except that you're not a duvet. And until you talk to him about it you don't know that's what he thinks.'

'It's what any man thinks,' said Sophie bitterly. 'Dad, Jake, Harry . . . they're all the same. That's why Jake did it. To destroy me. To destroy us. Me and Harry.'

'That's handing him quite a lot of power without a fight.'

'Oh, I fought,' replied Sophie, the anger rising to the surface again. 'Is that what you think? That I caved in?'

'I'm just saying that the fighting isn't over. Talk to Harry.'

'And if that's the end between us?'

Paige squeezed Sophie's hand, and Sophie could feel the strength in it. 'Then you'll rebuild your life without him,' murmured Paige. 'I know you will. You're very competent and clever, and a wonderful mother. But until you have that conversation – until you face your worst fears – you'll be running scared.'

'And we need to tell Jess,' Sophie pointed out. 'She can't marry him. She can't. But I'm afraid she'll never forgive me. Mum, he's evil.' Sophie was shaking.

'I don't know how we can stop her. She may not believe us, and she'll be furious with us. She'll think you did it deliberately. And then she'll be even more isolated and we won't be able to reach out to her at all.'

Sophie blew her nose again. 'I have to take some responsibility for the situation. Which is why I didn't go to the police. But even having agreed to go to a hotel room with him, I had a right to say no. I'm very clear about that. What's done is done, but I'm pretty strong, I think. I'm not going to let him win by having a breakdown like that other girl did. But it's Jess's future I'm worried about. I love her, Mum, I can't bear to see him destroy her.'

'I love her too,' said Paige, 'but remember, ultimately your father didn't destroy me.'

'Speaking of which . . .' Sophie looked at her watch. 'It's your court case in an hour.'

Paige drove off shortly afterwards, and the girls came racing in from Sparrow Palace demanding fruit juice. Now doing colouring-in in the snug kitchen at The Rowans, showing Summer how to hold a big fat wax crayon, she felt, just for one moment, safe again.

But The Rowans would be sold. And Jess would be married and she would have to face the growing distance between herself and Harry. Her family would be scattered. Sophie felt bereft. Shamed, contaminated and bereft.

Chapter 67

The courthouse was a huge modern red-brick building with a
bland interior and toweringly high ceilings. Paige, Judy and
Tricia queued to be allowed through the scanner just inside the
revolving doors. A cheerful woman in stout shoes waved a
wand around Paige's head, then all the way around her body.
'Fine,' she pronounced, gesturing them on, up a flight of echo-
ing stairs. Court officials clacked up and down the corridors,
doors opened and shut quietly. Paige was introduced to her
barrister, Gillian something-or-other, a middle-aged woman
with short dark hair and a fierce smile.

They were shown to an anonymous room, with a table and
cream louvred blinds over a view of the car park. Tricia
dumped a huge pile of documents on the table in front of
Gillian.

'Glad to see you don't earn much,' she said, briskly, flicking
through documents. 'That's a help. Although wives who don't
earn anything at all are my favourite.'

'I don't think I *can* earn much. I would if I could.' Paige tried
to tell herself that, whatever happened, she would make something of her life. This didn't need to be the end. It would be the
beginning. At least she'd fought.

Judy passed Paige the letter Bill had written for the court
outlining their marriage and its collapse. Paige had written one,

a short factual document with dates and addresses. She had decided against providing any detail.

Now she regretted it. She read Bill's letter giving his version of what had happened.

I, William Raven, of Flat 3, Orchard Park, Martyr's Forstal, near Canterbury, Kent, make this statement in these proceedings in response to the order that statements are to be filed pertaining to issues relating to contributions and to the financial agreement between myself and my wife, the applicant. To the best of my knowledge the contents of this statement are true.

1) In July last year I discovered the applicant lunching and holding hands with her lover in the Fishing Smack, a well-known gastropub. Later that evening she became hysterical when we discussed the matter, saying that she wanted to leave me for him and even holding a knife to my face, telling me that she would cut me if I didn't agree. Over the next few weeks her behaviour became increasingly aggressive and incoherent, and I was concerned that she might be having a breakdown so I suggested that we go to a counsellor. Instead of going to our GP or friends for a recommendation, she found a therapist off the internet and we visited her together. During the appointment the therapist made it clear to us that the problem in the marriage lay with my wife, and not with any behaviour of mine, so she suggested that she have sessions on her own with her. Foolishly, I agreed to this, and from then on the therapist poisoned my wife's mind against me, making her think that I was going to hurt her, although I have never been violent at any point during our marriage.

2) Over Christmas my wife stormed into my office while I was getting ready to dress up as Father Christmas to entertain our grandchildren, and said she was going to leave me. I asked

385

her to wait to discuss it at a more suitable time, at which I suggested another therapist as I wanted to save our marriage. At the first session with the new therapist she was jumpy and said little, and I got the impression that her mind was made up and that she'd given up trying. She refused to come to any further sessions. A week later she walked out on me, following an argument when she threw a knife at our kitchen table. She returned later that evening with police officers, having alleged, completely untruthfully, that it had been me who threw the knife at her. The following day she changed the locks and put my suitcases outside the door, telling me that she was determined to 'take everything'. She has since refused to see or speak to me except by occasional prior arrangement, in spite of my leaving a series of messages begging her to reconsider her decision. In this time she has made several allegations that I have threatened her with violence, although she does concede that I have never struck her.

3) She knows my company, Raven Restore & Build, has been through an exceptionally difficult year, but has declared that she intends to bankrupt me by applying for a settlement that I could not possibly afford. I have suggested that we sell the house, our only asset, and split the money between us after paying off the mortgage, but she has rejected this because she is determined to take her revenge by leaving me destitute. She has told me this on more than one occasion, and appears to be obsessed with destroying my reputation. She has been telling our friends and family that she fears for her life.

4) The applicant has deliberately chosen low-paid part-time work to make it seem as if she is unable to earn a living. Throughout our marriage I encouraged her to improve her skills and to seek work, but she always said that she preferred to be in the garden or entertaining friends, and that a job would get in the way of her social life. However, she did complete part of a degree and is now working in the highly

profitable sector of elder care where she could certainly find a better paid job.

5) The applicant is claiming large sums because she said that she ran the house for me while I worked. However, I had to get involved with almost every detail as the applicant was careless, incompetent, selfish and lazy. When our children were small I often had to come home from work early because she wanted to go out, and she even left our youngest daughter alone in a playground one afternoon because she said she 'wanted some peace'. I frequently had to cook my children's supper or put them to bed so that she could go out to an evening class or to meet friends. She has never even been able to engage a window cleaner, plumber or electrician without having to consult me, and I frequently had to shop for her or accompany her shopping as she could not – or would not – manage on her own. My levels of stress due to both running the household and doing everything for the family along with also running my company have been very high at times and the applicant often complained that I was short-tempered as a result.

'These are lies,' said Paige to Judy in despair, after she'd finished reading another five paragraphs about their financial situation and how little Paige had contributed. 'He never let me do anything without consulting him. But all this makes me sound mad. Evil. Selfish.'

'No,' reassured Judy. 'It makes *him* sound mad and selfish. Really. You don't need to worry too much about it. If anything, a rant like this will count against him.'

'Are you sure? What if the judge believes him?'

'He won't,' said Judy. 'He won't.'

But Paige wasn't sure. Bill was very convincing. 'Now we know exactly what he's been telling everyone, and why they all think I'm such a bitch.'

She went through the case with Gillian, but no one knew

what the judge might think of it or how seriously he would take Bill's claim of 'fear of bankruptcy'.

'Even if he agrees to pay me something,' asked Paige, 'what guarantee do we have that he will ever do it?'

'He'd end up in court again if he didn't pay.'

'I don't think that would worry him,' said Paige wearily, as they were eventually ushered into the courtroom to sit on one side of a long table. 'It would give him another chance to say more horrible things about me.'

Bill and his team followed, Bill striding confidently, his body taking up almost the whole width of the doorway. They sat on the opposite side of the table. He smiled up at the judge with the half-weary, complicit smile of someone forced to go through a ridiculous charade to satisfy a toddler with a tantrum.

The judge, seated at a separate table at the end, put a tape in his recorder. Gillian got up to put Paige's case as a hard-working and supportive wife and mother who was seeking only enough to make a new life for herself. She sketched out their assessment of Bill's finances, making the case that his business was fundamentally sound and that he could look forward to a comfortable lifestyle, while Paige was necessarily limited as to what she could earn in the future. Bill's barrister, an older man with a flushed face, then put Bill's case, his fear of bankruptcy, the debts and the difficult times his company was going through.

There was a tap at the door and a court usher slid into the room, acknowledging the judge then handing Bill's lawyer an envelope. He opened it and handed it to Bill. Paige knew his body language. For one second he froze. Then the confident smile was back and he exchanged murmured whispers with his team.

The judge asked a few questions of them both, after which he began his summing-up. He spoke in a musing voice, almost as if talking to himself. Paige noticed, with interest, that he took a very broad brush approach, speaking of Raven Restore & Build's excellent reputation and that it had survived difficult times. He was sure that Bill would go on to continue to make a success of it. He said that both parties had contributed to the marriage. He went on to say that Bill had a substantial pension that Paige might have expected to enjoy had they remained married, and to say that after a marriage of thirty years a non-working wife would normally expect both a lump sum and maintenance.

Bill surveyed Paige's team with scorn on his face. Both his lawyers were men, and one she recognised from the golf club. The other was very young and pimply. Each side of the table had three water glasses and a carafe of water in front of them. Bill's team finished their water before the judge ended his summing-up. Without asking permission, Bill reached out and helped himself to Paige's carafe, filling up his glass with all the remaining water.

That's how much he despises us, and how confident he feels, thought Paige, her own confidence trickling away. The judge concluded by saying that he hoped the two parties could now reach an agreement, and that they would be spared the expense of a fully contested court case. Both parties went back to their respective rooms.

'We're doing well. The judge clearly considers you should have a decent share. He hasn't swallowed the bankrupt argument. He's talking about maintenance and a share of the pension. Let them make an offer first,' urged Gillian.

'Something happened in there,' said Judy. 'Didn't it, Paige?'

'There was something in the letter,' agreed Paige, not believing that they were doing well.

After twenty minutes Bill's barrister knocked on the door and Gillian went outside. She came back. 'They're on the run. He's offered the whole of The Rowans, with the mortgage paid off, in return for your shares in the company. That's it. Nothing more.'

'I'll take it,' said Paige. 'Plus just enough cash to pay the tax bill and pay George back. If you can get it.'

'Oh, we can get it all right. What about his pension?'

'I don't care about his pension. I can sell The Rowans, buy something much cheaper and live on the difference and what I earn.'

'They're on the run,' insisted Gillian, 'and I could get you more.'

'I don't want more, I want out.'

Chapter 68

The day after Paige returned to The Rowans, her face lighter and younger with the relief of the settlement, Sophie went home. She knew Harry would be working late so she put the girls to bed, telling them that they'd see Daddy in the morning. Once their rosy faces were slumbering peacefully she kissed each forehead in turn. They didn't know what an awful mother they had. It would be better for them not to know.

She slipped off her shoes and got into bed, still dressed. She was so cold. It was as if her entire system had shut down. There was a world outside – a car hooting, a door opening and some people shouting farewell, a plane overhead – but it all felt very far away. Sophie knew she would never be a good person again. If only she could sleep.

She closed her eyes – briefly, it seemed – but was awoken by the sound of familiar footsteps in the hall: three steps to hang up his coat, pause as he passed the hall table to check the post, a door pushed open and her name called, softly. She pulled the duvet over her ears and closed her eyes tightly as the footsteps came upstairs, two at a time. She heard the girls' doors open and shut softly. Perhaps they would wake and there'd be a distraction.

But their doors shut quietly and he came in to their bedroom, pausing for a moment. Then she heard him padding across the room. A soft swish, swish as each shoe came off. He laid each one down and she felt the bed rocking as he sat down beside her, putting a hand on her shoulder.

She was too tired to twitch it off, and stayed still, pretending to be asleep. 'What's up?' Harry asked, seeing through the pretence.

'Some virus,' she muttered. 'I'll be all right in the morning.'

He stayed beside her and she tensed up as she listened to his breathing. His hand moved to her hair, stroking it.

Please, please, she thought, don't want sex. It would make me feel sick.

'Is this virus . . .' he asked gently, 'called Jake Wild?'

Sophie really didn't want to have this conversation now. They would say things they didn't mean. The girls' sleeping faces suddenly seemed so dear to her, and their rooms – Lottie and Bella's with ballerina wallpaper and Summer's little box room a bright summery yellow with a frieze of animals round it – seemed so safe and happy. Everything they said now endangered those rooms, and the happiness of those beloved faces.

Harry didn't press the point, and continued to stroke her hair.

'How did you know?' she eventually mumbled into the pillow.

'Because I know you. You're not naturally duplicitous. I could see what was happening.'

Sophie sat up, pulling the duvet up to her chest. 'Why didn't you stop me, then?'

'How could I? Ask you to account for every moment of your actions? Monitor your phone calls? You're responsible for your own life, Sophie, I couldn't stop you. I just had to trust you.'

Sophie rested her head on her knees.

'And I did trust you,' he added.

Did, she thought. Did. She waited for him to call her a liar or a slut. She deserved it.

'I'm a terrible person,' she said.

She heard him sigh softly. 'Of course you're not a terrible person. You're still Sophie, with all your faults. I know you, you see, and Jake didn't. He thought your flirting was for real, and I know it's just the way you make life more . . . fun.'

'Fun?' Sophie was puzzled.

'Yes,' said Harry. 'You're actually a very serious person, who runs round in circles trying to look after her children, her husband, her mother, her father, her sister and her friends, and sometimes you need fun. Everyone needs fun. So you sparkle and laugh and it cheers everyone up, and makes the day a little bit brighter, and then you come home with me at the end.' He took his hand away. 'But this time you didn't.'

Sophie's heart twisted. 'I wanted to,' she said.

Harry's hand was back on her shoulder, forcefully this time, shaking her and turning her towards him. 'Sophie, *talk* to me. Tell me what happened.'

'Harry,' Sophie sat up. 'I don't know whether to trust you. I don't know if you're the sort of man who thinks of his wife as a possession, who believes he has a right to demand what he wants of her . . . and when you try to force the truth out of me, that makes me trust you less? Do you understand?'

'Very well,' he said, getting up. 'If you don't know me by now I don't think you ever will.'

'Probably not,' she said, hurting. She imagined telling him the story, then him shouting at her the way her father shouted at her mother as they went on down the years, him getting angrier and angrier and her feeling guiltier and guiltier. He would never let the 'Jake thing' go, and she would bear the burden of it for ever. It would be easier to end it now, to accept responsibility and go through all the painful business of untangling their lives.

'We don't have to decide now,' said Harry, getting up. 'I'll sleep in the spare room if you like.'

'Why should you? You haven't done anything wrong.'

'I don't know. Working too late. Spending too much time watching sport . . .'

'I liked you watching sport,' said Sophie sadly. 'I wanted you to be happy.'

'And I wanted you to be happy.' He took off his shirt. 'I just don't seem to have done such a great job of managing it.'

'No! It's all my fault, I . . . we all have to take responsibility for our actions, don't we? Isn't that what you're always telling the girls?'

His face softened at the mention of the girls. 'Yes, but that's not quite the same as wallowing in guilt.' His face crinkled in a crooked, sad smile that cut Sophie to the core. 'I'm not sure where the line is, though. Between taking responsibility and guilt.'

'The most important thing at the moment, though,' said Sophie. 'Is what we tell Jess. She can't marry that man.'

'Whatever happened between you, Jess needs to make her own judgements.'

'That's easy to say when it's not your sister,' flashed Sophie. 'I think we have a responsibility to stop her making the biggest mistake of her life.'

'Sometimes it takes more strength to stand back and do nothing. And what matters here and now is us. Sophie,' he said, touching her, 'if he's the sort of man I think he is, he would have done this anyway, whatever it was he did. With someone else. It's part of his power play.'

'You think?' She turned her face up to him. 'Do you really think so?'

'Yes. And I *don't* think we can tell Jess about it. Sometimes you have to step back.'

'Not from your own sister.'

'You can't control people. We must all make our own decisions.'

'Caring about someone's well-being isn't controlling them.' She and Harry stared at each other for a minute, then he opened the door. 'Maybe I will sleep in the spare room, if that's all right by you.'

'Of course,' said Sophie, politely. 'I quite understand.' A terrible emptiness overwhelmed her.

Over the next few weeks, Sophie and Harry were like strangers sharing a train compartment. They moved aside politely for each other and made stilted conversation. They hid their private thoughts behind strained smiles and buried themselves in looking after the girls. Sophie researched everything she could find about abusive men, the websites, the books, the chatrooms, looking for ways to warn Jess, or anything that might remind her of Harry. She would not be fooled again. She would not finish up where her mother had, in the divorce court at fifty without a career, afraid for her life. Her head ached with the lists of ways people could abuse others, the men who raped their wives while they were asleep, the ones who trained their dogs to keep women in certain parts of the house . . . Sophie rested her head on her hands. How do you tell? How, when you have been fooled twice, do ever know what is right?

Sophie woke up on the morning of Jess's wedding and knew she had to warn her. 'Harry,' she shook him awake. 'I've got to tell Jess.'

He sat up. 'Sophie, tell me what happened first.'

'OK,' she said. 'I arranged to meet Jake at The English. He told me it was a possible photography assignment, but I knew I was flirting. He showed me the bedroom, and then he raped me. I tried to stop him, but I didn't see the danger signs early enough. I thought he was a friend – we'd been texting and emailing, mainly over my father. But I shouldn't have done it. I shouldn't have gone behind your back and Jess's, not even to talk about Dad.' She stared at him, willing him to forgive her.

Harry's face turned the colour of putty. 'Sophie,' he said. 'This is even worse than I thought. I thought . . . you'd just had an affair with him . . . that you were upset because he was still marrying Jess . . .'

'Well,' she said briskly. No sympathy there, she noted. 'Now you see why I couldn't live with myself if I didn't do everything I could to stop her. Can you get the girls ready and bring them on afterwards? They're all changing at Jess's, Mum and Dad, the girls, that's where the flowers are being delivered . . .'

'I know,' he said, still looking stunned. 'I can get the girls there on my own, you know. But I still don't think you'll achieve anything by telling Jess. Except to alienate her from the only people that can help her when things turn bad.'

'I've got to do it,' insisted Sophie. 'Even if she never speaks to me again.'

He put a hand out as if to hold her, and then dropped it. 'In that case . . .' he said with a shrug. 'Good luck.'

Sophie expected more argument. Good luck. Dismissing her. She stepped under the shower, resolving not to listen to anything more he said, and by the time she got out he was in Lottie and Bella's room, getting them up. She could hear the low rumble of his voice and their light, delighted squeals.

As she left the house he called her name but she pretended not to hear.

Jess was already up and showered, her hair in rollers, when Sophie arrived. 'You're early.'

'Yes,' said Sophie. 'I wanted to talk to you.'

Chapter 69

Jess didn't want to hear what Sophie had to say. On the back of the door her dress, in fitted white satin with a fifties skirt, its pinched-in waist emphasised by a diamanté belt, was waiting for her. The florist had just arrived with a huge box of white rosebuds and lime-green Guelder roses wired with silver taffeta bows. And Milly, the hair stylist, was hovering with a hairdryer to complete her task of turning Jess into a cross between Audrey Hepburn and Jackie Onassis. 'Hi Soph,' she said. 'Help yourself to coffee. I'll be out in a minute.' And she shut the bedroom door in Sophie's face.

As far as Jess could make out, through the whirring of the hairdryer, Sophie seemed to spend the next two hours answering the doorbell, to Jake's disapproving sister and her son, to Paige in a grey silk suit and a sweeping hat ('Charity shop buy, do you think it's OK?' Jess heard. 'Yes, Mum, it looks great. Really.'), two of Jess's girlfriends, chattering like birds, and then Mary, the make-up artist, who poked her head into the bedroom to suggest she should do Sophie's make-up, too.

'No, really,' said Sophie, coming in behind her. 'I don't need it, I just . . .'

Jess felt like screaming at her. 'I know you want to stop me marrying Jake. Get out of my life.' It was typical of Sophie, to try to spoil everything under the guise of wanting to help.

Then Harry and the girls arrived. The one-bedroom flat was so full of people that everyone had to stand back every time anyone wanted to walk across a room.

Jess and Milly fixed a tiny ivory-and-crystal cap at an angle on her head. It had a minimalist net veil that ballooned out and barely covered her eyebrows. Checking it in the mirror, Jess suddenly lost all her confidence. 'Do think I should have asked Jake what he thought? Do I look silly? Jake has such good taste.'

Sophie met her eyes in the mirror. 'So have you. You look adorable, like a mixture of Audrey Hepburn and a very pretty pixie. Very chic, and perfect for a London wedding.'

Paige, standing behind Sophie, echoed her. 'Sweetheart, you look so pretty. He'll love it.'

The anxiety that he might not ticked away behind Jess's excitement, especially as she saw Sophie in the mirror, shutting the door on the hovering make-up artist, hairdresser, her future sister-in-law, two friends, Harry and the three bridesmaids and page, leaving the three of them alone together.

'Jess . . .'

'Sophie, I hope this is wise advice from a married woman to a soon-to-be-married woman.' Jess kept her tone light as she put on pearl and crystal earrings. She didn't want a fuss, she didn't want a fight.

'Jess, every bride needs someone to say "are you sure?" before they leave the house,' said Sophie, 'and that's usually the father's job, but we know that Dad . . . Well, let's not go there. But that's all I want to ask you: are you quite, quite sure that you absolutely trust and love this man beyond anything? Because if you're not, you can turn back. Now or at any time.'

Jess had been expecting something less theoretical. She'd expected Sophie to issue an order or to try to persuade her to do something.

'Oh yes,' she said. 'Jake is everything I've ever wanted. So,' she turned round to her mother, 'what advice do I get from you?'

Paige looked flustered. 'Well, I'm hardly . . .' She straightened up and looked Jess in the eye. 'In fact, maybe I am the right person to say something. Trust your instincts. And you should never call each other stupid. Even if you are. That's it. That's my advice for a happy marriage.'

'And I'd like to say one more thing . . .' said Sophie.

'I don't think we have time. We should be going.' Jess spoke in a throwaway tone, and picked up her bouquet, as if in a hurry.

Sophie hesitated. 'It's important . . .' – she took a deep breath and began counting on her fingers – 'to recognise what you've got. If that's a man who listens to you, is cheerful, shares responsibility for everything . . . let me see . . . welcomes your friends and family, encourages you to be the best you can be, tells you you're terrific, and who really cares about whether *you're* happy or not . . . well, if that's the kind of man you've got, the kind who makes you feel good about yourself, then *never* let him go.'

'Sounds like Harry.' Jess tried to divert her. 'But you got there first, so I'll have to settle for Jake.'

'Joke,' she added, before anyone could wade in and talk about it any more.

Sophie kept looking at her intently. 'I'm sorry if I haven't been the best sister, but . . . Oh, Jess, don't listen to any of us. If you know what you want, go for it.'

'You're a wonderful sister.' Jess hugged her, suddenly meaning it, holding on for slightly longer than she'd intended. 'And you and Harry are, well, you know. The best.' She pulled back and looked at her watch. 'Dad should be here by now. Why don't you all set off, so I know that at least my bridesmaids are at the church?'

Sophie texted Bill and got a text back to say he was five minutes away. 'Dad'll be here soon.' She called the bridesmaids. 'Lottie, Bella. You look so pretty, darlings. So very pretty.' She knelt down to hold her daughters. 'I'll take the floral headdresses, Harry, if you can take Summer.'

He hoisted Summer up and Jess saw him look down at Sophie.

Still crouching on the floor, she looked up at him. 'Thanks, Harry.'

He looked puzzled. 'What for?'

'Just for being you,' said Sophie. She reached out a hand to him.

His face widened in a tender smile as he helped her up, and Sophie kissed him on the lips.

They did seem to love each other in spite of Sophie being a bit of a bully, thought Jess. She was surprised by the stab of loneliness that shot through her.

By the time everyone had got in and out of two black taxis several times, and Sophie had counted out the flowers, then nearly forgotten her handbag, and they'd all driven off, leaving Jess one blissful moment alone in her flat, ten minutes had passed and there was no sign of Bill.

Jess knew better than to try to hurry him.

In the silence of the empty flat, with its wedding detritus, she was transported back to her childhood. They would all be ready and dressed up, sitting in the car, waiting to go, but he would be reading the papers or making a phone call and would refuse to come until he'd got, in a very leisurely way, to the end of whatever it was. Sophie and Jess would become hysterical about missing the film, the train or the party, and Paige would be tensely trying to calm everyone down, but he carried on as if they didn't exist. If you even politely asked him to hurry he deliberately slowed down. Then, on the journey to wherever it was, he would be jolly and cheerful, or blaming Paige, telling her that her 'moods' always made family outings such a strain or criticising Jess for crying.

Jess rested her face against the front door, closing her eyes for a second. Why had she thought this might be the moment she and her father connected? She should have known she couldn't trust him.

She dithered over phoning him. It would be better just to give him another few minutes, then to set off without him. 'Come on, Dad,' she muttered, looking at her watch again, then getting carefully into the back of the big white Bentley Jake had ordered, smoothing her satin skirt out so it wouldn't crease, and adjusting her diamanté belt.

'You look very nice, miss,' said the driver. 'I think we'd best be off, though.'

'Yes, of course. My father must have been delayed.' It was lonely, travelling to your wedding on your own. If she'd known she'd have asked Sophie. Or Mum.

Looking very smart in a grey morning coat Bill tapped on the window. 'Oh, Dad! You made it, get in, get in.'

'I've got to take a piss first,' he said, leaning into the car. She thought he was going to kiss her, but he hissed. 'Don't you *dare* go without me. Or you'll be sorry, young lady.'

Perhaps she should. There was nothing he could do to her now, was there?

But Jess was used to being frightened of him. She edged herself out of the car and unlocked the flat again, anxiety tightening her chest as he disappeared inside. The wedding should be starting now. But they were only ten minutes away.

'It won't take long to get there, will it?' she asked the driver.

'As long as there are no hold-ups, no more than fifteen.'

'Fifteen?' Jess didn't know whether to scream at her father to hurry up, thus guaranteeing that he would slow down, or simply to jump in the car without him. She got into the car. 'One more minute and we go. And please drive fast. If you can, of course, I wouldn't want you to get points on your licence,' she added politely.

Bill strolled out of the flat, doing up his flies. 'Don't you want to lock up?'

She tried to keep her voice calm. 'It'll be fine. As long as you shut the door behind you, I think we can take that risk.'

Jess had imagined that when her father took her to the

church to get married they might communicate at last. She could tell him she forgave him everything. He might say sorry. Maybe they would even say they loved each other. Jess's heart craved just one encounter with Bill that didn't leave her furious, helpless and hating herself.

But Bill droned on about 'that fucking bitch, your mother, she took everything, you know. She's got The Rowans, no splitting it down the middle for *her*. Her lover paid her legal bills, did you know that? She actually told me. Her fucking lover. And meanwhile my business is on its knees. That's why I was late. I had to come by bus. I can't afford taxis, not since the divorce. I've been left destitute, you know, absolutely destitute.'

There was no point in replying. Jess stared out of the window as the London streets crept past far too slowly and prayed that Jake would understand. That the vicar would understand. That Sophie – who she'd texted with 'on our way' – would explain to everyone that their father was like an improvised explosive device, likely to go off under anyone at any time. That no one could hurry him up. Twenty-nine minutes late. It was too late, even for the latest bride. Jess closed her eyes tightly and prayed.

Sophie and the bridesmaids were on the wide stone steps of the church with the vicar, all eyes straining down the street. Jess almost tripped as she got out of the car but the vicar took her hand. 'Don't worry,' he said. 'Everything is fine.'

Bill kissed Sophie. 'The lovely Soph. Outshining the bride as usual, I see.'

Sophie put her father's arm into Jess's. 'Jess looks gorgeous. And just get up that aisle, Dad.' She gave him a little push.

For a moment Jess thought that Bill was going to create a scene, but she realised that, with the vicar present, he would play the role of the perfect father of the bride. They walked calmly up the aisle, to the sound of 'The Arrival of the Queen of Sheba', Jess smiling at a bobbing sea of faces turned towards her, then steadying herself by focusing on the worn flagstones on the floor ahead and occasionally looking up to see Jake's back, in a tailored grey suit that showed off his powerful shoulders and long greyhound legs. Little bouquets of white roses and ivy were tied to the end of every other pew, and the sunlight burst through the stained glass window, lifting Jess's heart.

She'd done it. She'd finally done it. She was safe. Bill let go of her arm to allow her to step up beside Jake. She looked up to him for reassurance and saw the dark eyes, the cleft chin, that dark shadow he could never quite shave away and his face coming towards hers. She felt his lips on her ear.

'You stupid bitch,' he hissed, his breath warm against her skin, 'Don't ever, *ever* dare to do this to me again. Do you understand?'

'It was Dad,' she tried to whisper back, but Jake had turned to face the vicar, his face composed. Jess stood between two handsome, smiling men – Bill and Jake – as the vicar opened the service. 'We are here today . . .'

As his words drifted over her head, she thought about Paige. 'Trust your instincts.' And Sophie, obviously so unhappy, yet very clear about who Harry was. A man who made her feel good about herself.

She remembered what Jake had told her about Sophie only last week. 'Sophie,' he'd said, 'asked to meet me at The English last week. She'd booked a room for us.'

Jess had crumbled with fear. 'Did you go?'

Jake sunk his head into his hands, opening a bottle of wine and pouring himself a glass. 'I'm sorry, Jess, I am so sorry. I didn't know what I was doing. After Cassie, well, it's pretty scary to think of making a commitment like this again, and I suddenly panicked. I was drunk. I was flattered. It's very hard for a man to say no when it's laid out on a plate for him.'

Jess gazed at him in horror.

He groaned. 'Oh God, Jess, I was afraid I might doing the wrong thing marrying you.' He took her hand. 'But it made me realise how special you are. How you're the only one I love. I feel sickened by myself. Can you ever forgive me, darling? I promise to stay well away from her in future. I just felt we should be honest with each other. Always honest, don't you agree?'

Jess's first instinct was to ring Sophie, screaming with fury, to tell her that no way could her daughters be bridesmaids, not if that was the way she behaved.

But then she thought about Lottie and Bella. They were so excited and it wasn't their fault. She resolved to think about it after the wedding and buried the pain as deeply as she could. When Sophie arrived that morning Jess thought she'd come to confess. Even to try to stop her marrying Jake. Jess had resolved that if she did, that would be it. No more sisterly meetings. Ever.

But she hadn't. Jess turned round and caught her eye. Sophie's face was serious, and her gaze was steady. Sophie was straight. She would flirt with Jake. She'd flirt with anyone. But suddenly Jess didn't believe that she'd actually booked a hotel room herself.

'Will you, Jake Oliver Wild, take Jessica Mary Raven to be your lawful wedded wife . . .'

'I will.' Jake's voice was strong and clear.

'And will you, Jessica Mary Raven take Jake Oliver Wild to be your lawful wedded husband, to have and to hold, in sickness and in health, till death do you part?'

Jess's heart tightened and hardened. 'No,' she said, her voice singing out over the high stone arches. 'I'm very sorry, but I won't.'

The crowd rustled in shock, and Jess heard the sound of high heels against stone, as someone got up and walked towards her. Then she felt Sophie's hand in hers, clutching it tightly. 'It's your decision, Jess,' she whispered. 'No one else matters.'

'Was he lying? About you and him?'

Sophie went white. 'No,' she whispered. 'He told me he'd

got a room because he was doing an article. And that the paper wanted me to photograph it. But in the end I said I didn't want to and he . . . I *said* I didn't want to, Jess, but he called me a . . . filthy, dirty liar.' Her voice shook. 'I'm so sorry, so terribly sorry.'

Behind them the low murmuring of the congregation mounted almost to a hubbub, as everyone asked each what was happening.

'No,' said Jess to the vicar, still clutching Sophie's hand for support. 'There's been a mistake. I'm very, very sorry, but this can't go ahead.'

The vicar raised his hand and the church fell silent. 'I must ask you again, do you take this man to be your lawful, wedded husband?'

'No.' Jess's voice rang out clear and strong. The church remained completely silent to the sound of Jake's footsteps as he strode out of the church, followed by his best man.

'Well done,' murmured Sophie.

Jess tried to smile. 'It was such a lonely walk up that aisle.' She said softly, to Sophie. 'I kept seeing faces I hadn't seen for months and realised I was beginning to distrust everyone: you and Mum, and of course Dad. And then Dad in the car on the way over calling everyone a stupid bitch and banging on about the money, always the money, nothing about me or Jake, but I thought that didn't matter, I had Jake instead of him. And then I got to the altar and it was like hearing Dad all over again. So maybe he did do me a favour in taking me to the church after all.'

She turned to the congregation, still silent and shocked. 'There's a party, everyone, just in the church hall behind us,' she shouted, in a shaky voice. 'It's all there and waiting, so we might as well enjoy it. See you there.' She took off her veil, shook her hair out, removed her shoes and walked down the aisle in stockinged feet, kissing and hugging people on the way out.

Chapter 70

Sophie, Harry and the girls went home to Clapham before the party finished, taking Paige with them. Jess insisted that she would go back to her flat when the party was properly over. 'You go,' she said, kissing Sophie. 'Get the girls into bed and give that hunky hubby of yours a really good hug. He's proof that nice men exist and next time round I'll know what to look for.'

Harry put an arm round her and Sophie stretched up to kiss him.

'What's that for?' He kissed her back.

'You backed my judgement about telling Jess. Even though you didn't agree,' she whispered as they headed for the car. They strapped the girls in, and Harry, who hadn't been drinking, took the wheel.

'I've been thinking a lot over the last few weeks,' continued Sophie, 'and poring over books and websites for signs and symptoms of abuse. There never seemed to anything that sounded like you, but I couldn't trust my own judgement. Then, at Jess's today, I suddenly realised I'd been reading about myself. That in lots of ways I handle things the way Dad does – when things get difficult I get frightened, blame other people, get angry and try to control them.'

'You're not that bad,' grinned Harry. 'Believe me. I would not have married a female version of your father.'

'I'm not as bad as he is *yet*,' corrected Sophie. 'But, unless I try, I could go that way. And I realised that telling Jess would have been trying to control her. And you *weren't* trying to control me. You told me what you thought but left it up to me. So thank you.'

'Well, I reckoned yours was the final call. You're her sister, you'd know best.'

'And in the end, I thought the same thing. She needed to make that decision on her own. You had faith in me, then I had faith in her, and now I have somehow have more faith in myself. I think I could face your setting up your own business, for example.'

He laughed. 'Let's go one step at a time, shall we? Some of your concerns are valid.'

'And some are just about trying to maintain control.'

They let themselves in, tripping over the newspapers that had been posted through the letterbox. After getting the girls to bed they rifled the fridge, made cheese on toast and, turning on the television, fell asleep in each other's arms. 'Upstairs,' murmured Harry, shaking her awake. 'It's nearly two in the morning.'

Sophie, rubbing her eyes, picked up the papers they'd left on the floor, about to throw them away. She saw a story, a small one in the corner of the front page about a man who had pushed his wife over a balcony on holiday and thrown his young daughter after her. Both had died.

Sophie suddenly remembered all the other women in the papers left open at a particular page on the kitchen table at home. All those women over the years: Rebecca and Susan and Miriam and Shamila, Betty and Elizabeth, Ann and Annabelle, Pauline and Doreen, Kylie, Asha, Shawna and Siobhan, Esther and Gwyneth, Laila and Lakshmi, Caroline and Karen, and all the others whose names she couldn't remember, the endless procession of names and faces, of mothers and sisters and daughters who were killed – day after day, week after week –

because they'd tried to leave a man who believed they had no right to go. Some of the men had been violent before, others hadn't. Some men only used violence when they thought other tactics were failing. They could usually control without it.

As a young child, then a teenager, she'd read these stories, knowing these women weren't her. Weren't Jess. Weren't people she would ever have been friends with. That they were women who should have or could have done something to save themselves. Now she knew that they were just unlucky.

'Harry,' she said, cold with apprehension. 'Leaving someone like Jake is dangerous. Look what happened to his first wife. And Jess is on her own. At home.'

Harry's face reflected her own. 'Your mother's here to look after the girls,' he said. 'We'll drive to Jess's together.'

As Harry drove Sophie frantically dialled Jess. No answer.

Red light after red light stopped them. Sophie dialled again. And again. 'She's either not there,' she said. 'Or she's . . .'

There were no lights on in Jess's basement. Sophie banged the door and pressed the buzzer repeatedly. She knelt down and pushed the letter box open, and then she smelt it. Smoke. And felt the heat. She could see a glow at the end of the corridor.

'Is she OK?' Harry was behind her.

'It's a fire. She's in there, I know she is.' Sophie began shoving her shoulder against the immovable door.

'I'll batter down the door. You phone the fire brigade.' Harry picked up his foot and crashed it against the door, which barely gave way, as Sophie, her voice shaking, called 999.

'What's up?' It was a neighbour, leaning out of a window at the noise.

'There's a fire. We've got to get in. Jess is in there.'

The neighbour appeared, pulling on a coat and boots as he ran.

'One, two, three.' Harry and the neighbour coordinated their kicks and door gave way on one side.

'One, two, three,' shouted Harry again. With a splintering

noise, it partially collapsed and Harry fought his way in through a thick cloud of black smoke. Sophie could see a powerful glow and a crackling noise coming from the sitting room at the end. The heat baked her face.

'Harry, come back,' screamed Sophie. 'Come back.'

The neighbour continued to kick the door again, splintering it further. Sophie could hear a choking noise from inside. Sometimes you only have two or three breaths before you're unconscious. She'd read that somewhere.

'Come out of there mate,' shouted the neighbour.

'He's gone, he's unconscious, we must get him,' screamed Sophie, trying to clamber in. Hands pulled her back.

Harry, coughing and choking, appeared in the smoke with Jess over his shoulder, manoeuvring her limp body upstairs to the pavement just as the fire brigade arrived. Sophie could hear shouts, doors slamming and windows being wrenched up. Blue lights flashed and footsteps hurried towards them.

Sophie bent over the lifeless Jess, holding her hand until she heard footsteps and urgent calls around her, and a paramedic gently but firmly moved her aside. She watched them work over her and saw the oxygen mask go on. She saw Harry being helped into the ambulance, too, and given an oxygen mask.

'Is she alive?' asked Sophie, touching a paramedic on the arm.

She hesitated but nodded as they rolled Jess on to a stretcher and inserted a drip.

'It will be arson,' said Sophie to a firefighter. 'Even if it looks like an accident, it will be arson. Remember that.'

Three weeks later it was confirmed that the fire had been started by a laptop being left recharging on some cushions. Jess, only just released from hospital with concerns that she'd have permanent damage to her lungs, was resting at home. She had admitted that she often left the laptop charging, but she didn't accept that she had spilt lighter fuel on the cushions underneath it.

'Why would I be doing anything with lighter fuel near the cushions? I only use lighter fuel outside, for barbecues. Although I know I'm not supposed to,' she added. 'By the way, have you met Dan? We used to work together and he's starting up his own restaurant now. He's offered me a job when I'm well enough to work.'

Sophie shook hands with a quiet looking man with a goatee beard and a ponytail.

'Hi,' he said softly. 'Jess is so good with people, better than me. She's wasted as a waitress. She's going to be my manager.'

'That's more words than I've ever heard Dan speak to a person he's just met,' joked Jess. 'I see another man has fallen under the Sophie spell. By the way, guess what? A few of Jake's friends have dropped by to see me – probably to find out more gory detail – and, one way or another, I've picked up quite a bit about what he's saying about it all. He seems to have been banging a girl from the office all along, and he told her that, up at the altar, he realised that *she* was the one he really loved, so *he* got me to turn him down.'

'No!' exclaimed Sophie. 'But that would have meant quite an argument, surely? How can they think that? They were there.'

Jess shrugged. 'Nobody quite knows what they saw. And Jake took her on our honeymoon. Where . . .' – she paused for effect – '. . . he *married* her. On the beach. Everyone thinks it's the most romantic thing ever. I'm getting lots of pitying looks.'

'She must be mad,' said Sophie. 'Do you think we ought to warn her in some way?'

'She wouldn't believe us. And he got me to pay for that honeymoon on my credit card, and is refusing to pay me back. Along with a lot of stuff he got on it. So I've now got a major credit-card debt. God, I was stupid.'

'No you weren't,' said Dan. 'He was just convincing. I gotta go now, my shift's starting.'

410

'And guess what?' added Jess. 'We took out wedding insurance but it doesn't cover the bride and groom deciding not to get married.' She began to laugh. 'That's like taking out house insurance and finding out it doesn't cover burglary.'

They kissed briefly, on the lips, and Sophie's eyebrows went up after Dan closed the door of the flat behind him.

'I think I know the early warning signs now,' said Jess, looking slightly shame-faced. 'There's no love-bombing, no romantic gestures or suggestions about how I should dress. He's encouraging me to have a career, seems perfectly happy to meet my friends . . . Anyway I've worked side by side with him for over a year, and I've got a checklist now. I'll keep a close eye on it.' She smiled, still looking pale.

A few days later Paige and Sophie waited for Jake outside his office.

'What do you want?' His nose was in a splint and he had two black eyes.

'What happened to you?' asked Sophie.

'Oh don't give me that,' he snarled. 'You know perfectly well how I acquired three broken ribs and a bust nose. Count yourself lucky I'm not pressing charges.'

He turned round and tried to head in the opposite direction but Paige and Sophie outflanked him. 'Well, I don't suppose you want to go that close to a courtroom,' said Sophie, having to walk very fast to keep up with him. 'We just thought you should have a copy of the statement Jess made to the police, saying that she believed you started the fire because she ended your relationship.' She shoved it in his hands.

He dropped it on the pavement and speeded up. Awkwardly, Sophie noticed.

'It's very, very difficult to get enough evidence to prosecute a man in these situations,' he said. 'When there's enough doubt and it's just my word against hers.'

'You're right,' said Sophie, 'but after Cassie and Jess, I doubt you could pull it off a third time. Particularly as people gossip.'

He turned again and limped across the road to get away from them. This time they let him go.

'What on earth do you think happened to him?' asked Paige.

'I can't help feeling it has something to do with Harry,' said Sophie, trying not to smile. 'And his rugby friends. Not, of course, that I approve of violence in any way . . .'

Epilogue

Anthea slid out of her chauffeur-driven limousine – just an upmarket taxi, really, but it made her feel good – as the door of the smartest restaurant in Kent was opened by a young man in uniform. 'Your guest is already here,' he said, bowing slightly and indicating the drawing room on her left.

Bill was indeed there, looking hot and large on a plumped-up floral sofa, holding a menu at arm's length, as if he wanted nothing to do with it. Too vain to wear his reading glasses, thought Anthea.

'Bill, darling.' She kissed him ostentatiously on both cheeks. 'We'll have two glasses of champagne,' she ordered and the deferential young man withdrew.

'This lunch is on the company – Anjo, I mean,' she said.

Bill's eyes widened slightly, but she placed a manicured finger on his lips, admiring the dark nail varnish at its tip. There was a waiting list for that colour of nail varnish, apparently, but when you could afford to pull strings . . .

'Now don't say a word, Bill, dear. I'll explain. When I sent that note into the court, saying that I would be giving you back the money from the Orchard Park development provided that you offered Paige a fair settlement, I was, of course, painting a broad-brush picture.' She smiled at him. 'But the devil is in the detail, as you know. Let's order first.'

The waiter took their order and offered them two glasses of champagne on a silver tray. Anthea touched the rim of Bill's glass with hers. '*Salut!* First . . . I think we should re-cap the situation, just so we all know where we are.' She counted on her fingers. 'I started Anjo – short for Anthea Jones, of course – based in Bucharest. Anjo bought the Orchard Park development for a great deal less than it was really worth, thus stripping away your major asset. OK, so far?'

Bill nodded, helping himself to a handful of peanuts.

'So,' continued Anthea, moving to the third finger, 'Anjo also then loaned Raven Restore & Build – theoretically, of course – a large sum of notional money so you now have a big hole in your profits for the year. With two side agreements that say you never have to pay that money back and that I will make Anjo over to you after your divorce. Both actions might constitute fraud, of course, if the wrong people were to find out. Never mind, let's get back to the bigger picture. Assets down, profits down . . . well, poor Bill. That's what Jenny always says. Poor Bill. Poor, poor Bill.'

Bill's eyebrows bristled at her like a lobster's antennae.

'Jenny, by the way, seems to have the impression that Paige has stripped you of everything. I went into the office and she was very upset that Paige has The Rowans while you, apparently, have nothing.'

'I can't help what Jenny thinks,' grumbled Bill. 'You know what women are like.'

'Well, I do now, thanks to you. I've always thought of women – i.e. myself – as somehow second-best. I've twisted myself in every possible way to prove that I wasn't one of these awful women that men despise but, of course, I am. The more I ran away from that the more I denied who I really was. So now I've decided it'll be no more "men are . . ." and "women are . . ." Some men are shits . . .' She lifted her glass to Bill's and smiled. 'And some are great. Some women are lazy or greedy, others are unselfish and hard-working. While I'm judging everyone based on what sex they are, I can't see what they're really like.'

Bill rolled his eyes and let out a sigh.

'And, do you know? It works. I'm meeting new people and making friends. But Bill – it's most unwise to hand all your money over to someone and then to abuse them. As soon as you moved out of The Rowans I started to feel even more worthless than ever. You criticised my housework, told me how stupid I was over and over again, refused to acknowledge our relationship openly, never said anything nice to me, never even bothered to be quiet when you came to bed late so I was always exhausted and, finally, sent me off for a completely unnecessary and humiliating operation. Which, by the way, I didn't have.'

Bill opened his mouth to say something but Anthea raised the immaculately manicured hand again. 'I presume you believe you're fully entitled to behave like that. I mean, you'd hardly do anything that you didn't consider justified, because it might endanger the money. Am I right?'

'Of course, I've done nothing wrong!' he exploded. 'I was only trying to *help* you get better at housework and to point out what was wrong with you, and if you can't take a bit of constructive criticism, well ... no wonder no man's ever wanted to marry you. And you don't seem to have taken into account how stressed I was by the antics of that bitch, not to mention the problems with the business . . .'

'I am your accountant,' said Anthea. 'And the business is profitable. As you know.'

A waiter arrived to tell them, in a hushed voice, that their table was ready. Anthea smiled her thanks and got up, followed by Bill, who was breathing heavily and had turned very red. 'Have you thought of beta blockers, Bill?' she enquired as she allowed the waiter to pull back her chair for her to sit down, flashing her napkin over her lap. 'That high colour might indicate a blood-pressure problem.' She looked down at the exquisitely arranged confection of quail's eggs, smoked salmon

415

and salad on her plate, and then at his. 'Your pigeon-breast salad looks lovely. They really earn their Michelin star here, you know.'

She took a mouthful. 'Mmm, delicious, don't you think?' She raised her voice slightly. 'Anyway, I'm sure you'll agree that a post-mortem isn't very helpful. I mean, *you* don't want *me*, with my baggy vagina . . .' Out of the corner of her eye she saw the couple at the next table stop talking and look at her, startled.

'And I expect you feel I've turned into one of those mad feminist lesbians that you simply can't bear, so I can't visualise that Happy Ending we were planning ever happening . . . mmm?' She shook her head at Bill. 'Isn't that right?' She shook her head from side to side until he started mirroring her, as if hypnotised.

'It's *so* lovely when everyone agrees,' said Anthea. 'Don't you think? So now the good news. The whole "poor Bill" thing . . .' She waved a hand vaguely. 'You know, I've begun to feel that it *is* a bit worrying just to give you back the money and see you lose it to one of those bad debts you're always talking about.' She leant forward. 'So I will be keeping it safe for you. I'm going to continue to manage Anjo. You'll get dividends, of course, and if you need funds to make capital investments, such as to buy a little flat to live in, you can present a case to me and Anjo will consider it. I'll insist on your paying interest, *naturally*, but much less than you'd expect to pay elsewhere.'

Bill's eyes bulged at her but his mouth was full of frisée and pigeon breast.

'It seems the perfect solution to me: you get the access to investment without being exposed to risk, and I get management fees for handling it,' she added, before he could swallow his food and protest. 'We both share the profits . . .'

Bill's colour rose. 'But . . .'

'Lettuce in teeth, Bill,' she said, pointing. 'Just a little frond stuck there. Left a bit, there! Now I can see a little issue with the loss of control. After all . . .' Anthea put a sympathetic hand on his forearm. 'You're a man who controlled his wife by preventing her from earning then making her account for every penny, and controlled his daughters by divide-and-conquer, making one the favourite and one the fall-guy. And controlled your mistress by belittling your wife and then manipulated us all by lying to us. You've raged and threatened and played favourites . . . and guess what? It hasn't worked.'

She leaned close to him and spoke in a whisper. 'Your wife has left you and is happily enjoying her freedom. Your daughters are closer to each other and to her than they are to you, and your mistress . . . well, let's just say that you're over fifty and nobody really loves you, Bill, do they? All those friends and neighbours who think you're such a great guy. You know they'd change their minds if they found out what you were really like.' She sat back again, smiling, and took another sip of champagne. 'That's why I'm proposing you do it differently next time round. You tell people the truth – about money, about love, about how vulnerable you feel – because, Bill, I know you are a frightened little boy underneath all that bullying, and you learn to trust them . . . and see what you get back. Look at this, Bill, not as a financial setback but as a huge opportunity for personal growth.'

'You fucking bitch,' he whispered.

'Oh, and Anjo will be running a company swear box. Every time someone swears, then that's a hundred pounds out of this year's profits to a battered women's refuge.'

She saw his fist clench.

'Might I just add,' she hissed, 'that if you assault me in a Michelin-starred restaurant it will go right round the county, and the "poor Bill who is such a nice man" image may be severely dented.'

'How is your meal?' enquired a waiter, hovering.

Bill smiled at him. 'It's fine, thank you,' he said dismissively.

'Interesting,' murmured Anthea. 'I used to think you were angry because life had dealt you a raw deal. Now I've come to realise that anger is something you can switch on and off at will.' She took another mouthful. 'There's one other issue, of course. What happens to Anjo if anything happened to me. You wouldn't want to be left high and dry, would you?'

Bill put his knife and fork together without finishing his food and stared at her.

'I went to see Paige,' said Anthea. 'She's setting up The Rowans as a bed-and-breakfast and, by the way, as I don't think the payoff was perhaps *quite* fair enough – giving her about a quarter of the pot isn't the same as fifty-fifty – I've arranged a generous lump sum for her to equip the place and get her through her first year. And I talked to her, as women do . . .' – she treated him to a particularly glittering smile – '. . . you know, little frilly girly confidences about the issues that came up in our relationships with you. She gave me some very interesting literature, and I've looked at the topic in that forensic way we accountants approach things.' She put her knife and fork down and leant forward. 'One thing that I have to consider is this business of it being so dangerous to leave an abusive partner. Now, of course, I could be talking about men or women here, because, of course, you get abusers of both sexes, but *five* times as many women are killed by men every year as the other way around, a statistic that worries my very accountanty brain. So even though we are having this delightful conversation in a very pleasant environment . . .' She fixed Bill with a steely gaze, and let her words hang.

'So, Bill,' she concluded, 'if anything happens to me, Anjo will be wound up and sold, and the money will be inherited by your daughters. And Paige. In three equal parts.' She nodded to the waiter to fill her glass with vintage Pouilly-Fumé, and then nodded her thanks. 'So that's all clear, is it?'

'Pretty fucking clear,' said Bill.

'Another hundred into the swear box.'

He glared at her so furiously that even though she was surrounded by diners and waiters she still felt a tremor of fear.

418

'You know, Bill,' she said after a few minutes, 'even after all the insults, the lack of support, the lies, the fact that Paige quite clearly wasn't the big spender you made her out to be, and even the Finchley Road issue . . . I might still have gone on believing in you if it hadn't been for one thing. Do you want to know what it was?'

'I think you're fucking going to tell me,' snarled Bill.

Anthea sighed. 'Three hundred. Still, it's a good cause. And it comes out of the dividend of the one who swears, by the way. What was I saying? Ah yes. It was your trousers.'

'My *trousers*?'

'The trousers and jacket that are two sizes too big. Specially bought so that everyone would think your clothes were hanging off you because you had lost so much weight going through the divorce.'

'That was your fault,' said Bill. 'The wife always used to buy my clothes, so of course I'd no idea what size I was.'

Anthea took a sip of wine. 'Call her Paige, it's her name. And Bill? You're a control freak. You know exactly what size trousers you take.' She sighed. 'If you didn't despise women so much you would probably have seen this coming. But then, of course, if you didn't despise women so much, a lot of this might not have happened in the first place.'

Bill got up, kicked his chair back and strode out of the room.

'Is everything all right, madam?' The maître d' stepped forward, looking anxious.

'Oh yes,' she smiled. 'Everything is quite perfect. The gentleman had to leave. An unexpected crisis. But I am fine. Thank you.'

Acknowledgements

This book is fiction, and the characters are not based on real people. However the psychological bullying – financial, emotional, sexual and social – used to control Paige and Jess is commonly experienced by real cases of domestic abuse everywhere.

Over a hundred women a year are killed by their partners in the UK, usually when they have left or are trying to leave the relationship. Not all of these men will have been physically violent before, as some only resort to violence when their usual methods of control and manipulation have failed. I consulted various experts, books and websites while researching this book, and *Living with the Dominator* by Pat Craven (Freedom Publishing) is a must-read for anyone who needs to define the difference between a supportive, loving partner and a manipulative, controlling one. Also useful are: *Power and Control* by Sandra Horley (Vermilion), *Why Does He Do That?* by Lundy Bancroft (Berkeley) and *Men Who Hate Women & The Women Who Love Them* by Susan Forward (Bantam). Two good websites are www.refuge.org.uk and www.womensaid.org.uk. They jointly run a free helpline: 0808 2000 247. If you think you could be monitored, use a friend's phone or computer.

A special thanks to the following for sharing their professional expertise and answering lots of questions: Penelope Williams, Posy Gentles, Emma Daniell, Anthony Gordon, Liz Bauwens, Simon

Brown, Jenny Beeston, Jacqui Eggar, Graham and Jane Campbell, and Nicole Hackett of Family Law in Partnership (www.flip.co.uk). Thank you so much, too, to my editors Joanne Dickinson, Caroline Hogg and Zoe Gullen, to Anthony Goff, and finally to David, Freddie and Rosie.